NANCY WAKE
WWII WOMEN SPIES

KIT SERGEANT

CONTENTS

Also by Kit Sergeant — v
Glossary of Terms — ix
Character List — xi

Prologue — 1
1. Chapter 1 — 9
2. Chapter 2 — 18
3. Chapter 3 — 26
4. Chapter 4 — 30
5. Chapter 5 — 35
6. Chapter 6 — 46
7. Chapter 7 — 50
8. Chapter 8 — 54
9. Chapter 9 — 63
10. Chapter 10 — 67
11. Chapter 11 — 73
12. Chapter 12 — 86
13. Chapter 13 — 95
14. Chapter 14 — 101
15. Chapter 15 — 106
16. Chapter 16 — 112
17. Chapter 17 — 122
18. Chapter 18 — 131
19. Chapter 19 — 137
20. Chapter 20 — 143
21. Chapter 21 — 151
22. Chapter 22 — 162
23. Chapter 23 — 172
24. Chapter 24 — 177
25. Chapter 25 — 184
26. Chapter 26 — 193
27. Chapter 27 — 199
28. Chapter 28 — 204
29. Chapter 29 — 210

30. Chapter 30	216
31. Chapter 31	221
32. Chapter 32	231
33. Chapter 33	237
34. Chapter 34	250
35. Chapter 35	260
36. Chapter 36	272
37. Chapter 37	284
38. Chapter 38	291
39. Chapter 39	298
40. Chapter 40	305
Epilogue	316
The Spark of Resistance Prologue	321
41. The Spark of Resistance Chapter 1	325
42. The Spark of Resistance Chapter 2	332
43. The Spark of Resistance Chapter 3	336
44. L'Agent Double Prologue	342
45. L'Agent Double Chapter 1	346
46. L'Agent Double Chapter 2	358
47. L'Agent Double Chapter 3	373
Selected Bibliography	387
Acknowledgments	389

ALSO BY KIT SERGEANT

Historical Fiction: The Women Spies Series

355: The Women of Washington's Spy Ring

Underground: Traitors and Spies in the Civil War

L'Agent Double: Spies and Martyrs in the Great War

The Women Spies in WWII Series

The Spark of Resistance

The Flames of Resistance

The Embers of Resistance

The WWII Women Spies Series

Marie-Madeleine

Nancy Wake

Virginia Hall (Coming soon!)

Be sure to join my mailing list at www.kitsergeant.com to be the first to know when my newest Women Spies book is available!

Copyright © 2024 by Kit Sergeant

All rights reserved.

No part of this book may be reproduced in any form or by any electronic or mechanical means, including information storage and retrieval systems, without written permission from the author, except for the use of brief quotations in a book review.

Although this book is based on real events and features historical figures, it is a work of fiction.

This book is dedicated to all of the women who lived during the Second World War and whose talents and sacrifices are known or unknown, but especially to the real-life Nancy Wake

And for Belle

GLOSSARY OF TERMS

Boches: a derogatory term for Germans

Doodlebug: German V-1 flying bomb named for the sound it made when in air

Gestapo: Nazi Secret Police

Gendarme: a member of the French military police force

Luftwaffe: the aerial branch of the German armed forces

Lysander: a British bomber plane, typically used for reconnaissance and agent pick-ups

Milice: a political paramilitary organization created by the Vichy régime to suppress the French Resistance

Mufti: civilian clothes worn by someone who normally wears a uniform, especially by military personnel when off duty

Picon: a French aperitif made with bitter orange-flavored liqueur, often mixed with beer or sparkling water

Puttee: a long piece of leg cloth worn by French soldiers for warmth and protection

RAF: the Royal Air Force, the aerial warfare service branch of the British Armed Forces.

Sked: slang for the schedule kept by wireless operators when contacting Britain

Stuka: a German dive bomber aircraft used during World War II

Wehrmacht: the German armed forces

CHARACTER LIST

Below is a record of the real-life people featured in the novel, in order of appearance. They are listed by their code name (or name used in the novel), their legal name, occupation, and, when possible, age at the start of the novel (September 1939).

Henri Fiocca (40)
Wealthy Marseille businessman and Nancy's husband

Ian Garrow (31)
A British army officer who founded the PAO line

Albert Guérisse (28)
AKA Pat O'Leary
Born in Belgium, but was a British Navy POW before joining the PAO line, which is named after his code name

Madame René Sainson
A member of the PAO line with a safehouse in Montpellier

CHARACTER LIST

Mary-Louise Dissard (57)
AKA Françoise
A member of the PAO line with a safehouse in Toulouse; later became founder of the Françoise Line

Maurice Buckmaster (37)
The leader of SOE's F (French) Section

Vera Atkins (31)
Secretary to Major Buckmaster of F Section

Denis Rake (37)
AKA Justin
An openly gay F Section wireless operator

Violette Szabo (18)
F Section courier

René Dussaq (28)
AKA Bazooka
Former Hollywood stuntman who became an SOE weapons instructor.

John Farmer
AKA Hubert
F Section agent and leader of the Freelance circuit

Jean Antoine Llorca Villechenon
AKA Laurent
A Maquis member who worked with Gaspard

Henry Fournier

A Maquis leader in Auvergne

Gaspard (32)
AKA Émile Coulaudon
One of the main leaders of the French Resistance in Auvergne

Reeve Schley (31)
An American Office of Strategic Services (OSS) agent and former cavalryman

John Alsop (24)
Also an American and OSS agent

Henri Tardivat
A French Resistance leader

PROLOGUE

SEPTEMBER 1937

Nancy's stomach flipped as they turned the corner onto Wilhelmstraße and she caught sight of more of the spider-like swastikas, the blood red fabric sounding like faint gunshots as they flapped in the wind. The National Socialist German Workers' Party ideology was everywhere, hanging over Berlin as heavily as the gathering rain clouds. A part of her longed to turn back and hide in her hotel room for the rest of the day, but witnessing the Nazis' influence firsthand was the exact reason that she, Louis, and Gervais had decided to come to the city.

And there it was, mostly taking the form of massive buildings with imposing façades meant to intimidate visitors. Even more formidable were the men in brown shirts—the *Sturmabteilung* paramilitary army, better known as the Storm Troopers—who marched through the streets in their sturdy leather boots, striking out at any pedestrian who dared get in their way.

As the trio walked down the edges of the Tiergarten, Nancy's gaze fell upon a vacant park bench sitting directly in the open sun, marked with the words *'Nur für Juden'* in bold black paint. She'd heard about the recently passed Nuremberg Laws—which stripped anyone of Jewish descent of their rights and reduced them from citizens to subjects of the Reich—but hadn't yet seen the evidence for herself.

Now it was hard to ignore, especially after they ventured onto the Kurfürstendamm, a fashionable boulevard in the western part of the city, where many shops and restaurants had posted signs declaring that Jews were unwelcome in their facilities.

On the next block, a man clad in a brown shirt stretched too tightly across his immense stomach stood over a young boy painting the word *'Juden'* on the door of a stationery store. When the obviously exhausted boy dropped his brush, the fat man struck him hard on the back with his baton.

Louis put a restraining hand on Nancy's arm, as if he could sense how badly she wanted to seize the pistol tucked into the man's wide brown pants and turn it on its owner. The poor boy, who had now resumed his degrading task, was only a child, a child who had done nothing wrong but be born to a race the Nazis deemed inferior.

Nancy glared back at the man as Louis dragged her down the street. She had never been to Berlin before, but surely there had to be scraps of humanity somewhere in the city—its citizens couldn't all be soulless Nazis in ill-fitting brown shirts. She was so wrapped up in her thoughts she barely heard Gervais ask if she fancied getting something to eat.

She stopped walking as Louis finally loosened his grip on her arm. "I'm not hungry." After a moment, she added, "I just want to go back to the hotel," though what she really wanted was to return to France as soon as possible.

It had almost been a lark when she agreed to accompany Louis, her immediate boss, and Gervais, a colleague, to Berlin. She'd only been working at the paper for a short while and figured she could get some scoop on the New Germany. She'd heard stories from the refugees who'd managed to make it out, but, like everyone else in Paris, had chalked them up to gross exaggeration. Now it was clear that the Nazi party was even more cruel than she could have imagined.

Louis checked his watch. "We're going to have to catch the next train if we're going to make it to the Deutschlandhalle on time."

Suddenly overcome with a vulnerability she hadn't felt in a long time, Nancy pulled on a piece of dark hair that had fallen free from her updo. "I don't know if I can handle that right now."

Gervais's voice took on a pleading tone. "C'mon, Nancy, this is what we came for."

Knowing she didn't have a strong argument, she muttered, "You're right."

Trailing after the two men toward the station, Nancy let her mind wander. Growing up in Australia, she had never been into politics. After a few unsuccessful attempts at nursing and a couple of sojourns in Vancouver and New York, she'd enrolled in a London business college. Deciding to become a journalist hadn't been so much about fulfilling a lifelong dream—it was more about satisfying her insatiable craving for adventure.

She had hardly believed her luck when, days after graduation, she stumbled across an ad seeking a newspaper correspondent with an extensive knowledge of Egypt. Nancy didn't know the first thing about the country, but she wasn't about to let such a minor detail get in her way. She even told her interviewer that she could write Egyptian.

In order to gauge her skills, he'd grabbed a book off the desk. As he dictated to her, Nancy, taking the chance that he didn't know any better, started writing his words in the Pitman's shorthand she'd learned at school, but with backward strokes to make it look more like hieroglyphics.

When the interviewer finished, he gazed wondrously at the symbols she'd jotted down. "Can you read that?"

"Of course," Nancy replied before repeating what he'd recited, word for word.

"Well," the man had said, obviously impressed. "There's still the question of whether you have a knack for news, but that can work itself out. Though my boss, William Randolph Hearst…" The man paused briefly but after seeing the name had no effect on Nancy, continued, "isn't so much a fan of the British, so you'd be moving to Paris, which serves as our news base for Continental Europe."

Nancy resisted the urge to cover the interviewer's face with kisses. Paris had been next on her docket, and here he was, offering her the chance to relocate there on the dime of this Hearst person, whoever he was.

"Nancy, hurry up!" Louis shouted, already a block ahead of her.

She'd been so occupied in her remembrances that she'd forgotten where she was. A quick glance upward at the ubiquitous swastika flags quickly brought her back to reality.

Still, she couldn't help stopping in front of a half-timbered building adorned with a double-headed eagle door knocker. On either side of the main door were flower boxes bursting with brightly-colored geraniums, as if the owner was trying to cover up the stink of their obedience to the Nazi party.

Without warning, the gray sky opened up. As it began to pour, Nancy left the house behind as she raced toward the train station.

Hours later, Nancy found herself in a different kind of gathering storm. This one was located inside the largest event arena in the world. Originally built to house sporting events for the 1936 Olympics, the Deutschlandhalle was now filled to the brim with Nazi supporters and patrons of the *Winterhilfswerk Des Deutschen Volkes*, a public charity institution purportedly established to assist less fortunate Germans during the harsh winter season. Its slogan claimed, "None shall starve nor freeze," though after what she'd witnessed that afternoon, Nancy could hardly imagine their so-called generosity extended to everyone, especially Jews. At any rate, it appeared the gathering was more about invoking a sense of pride among the German people rather than providing charity.

A couple of men bearing prominent Nazi insignia—and whose names Nancy would never remember—spoke for a few minutes before it was Chancellor Hitler's turn.

The crowd roared for what seemed like an eternity as Hitler marched toward the podium and then grasped it with both hands. He began to speak, shouting his words even after the crowd had hushed. Nancy, who only knew a little German, couldn't tell exactly what he was saying, but she was close enough to see his beady eyes flash and the spittle fly out of his mouth.

This ugly man with the toothbrush mustache, who would

otherwise be insignificant if it weren't for the fact that he'd gotten himself elected Chancellor, held the audience in rapture. A natural orator, he pumped his clenched fists to emphasize his words. Every now and then he would pause, to great audience applause, taking a moment to breathe and smooth his oily hair back against his head.

After working himself into a fury, he ended the speech by grabbing his paper off the podium. Stepping back, he stood with his arms crossed in front of him as the crowd erupted into an ecstatic frenzy. Nancy watched, open-mouthed, as a sea of mostly men extended their arms at an unnatural angle, not as if to say *Stop*, but to encourage the brutality of this man, this Adolf Hitler.

Nancy's own voice felt hoarse as she asked Gervais, who was standing beside her, "What are they saying?"

"*Sieg Heil*. It means hail victory."

"Victory? Victory over what?"

"I don't know," Gervais replied, his tone glum. "But it seems a bit ominous."

Nancy had heard the name Adolf Hitler many times before, in the safety of a Parisian café or at someone's apartment over a late night glass of brandy, but to her knowledge, Germany had remained the 'beast that slept on the opposite side of the Rhine.' Yet here she was, watching it rouse itself and rear its ugly head, with these people, Hitler's followers—whom he'd clearly brainwashed—ready to march down whatever dark path he would lead them down. "Hitler's a lunatic," she murmured, mostly to herself.

Louis, on the other side of her, caught it anyway. "And that makes him more dangerous than anything else."

As the military band struck up the German anthem, Nancy felt like she might be sick. She didn't know if she wanted to vomit, run from the Deutschlandhalle as fast as she could, or crawl under a blanket and hide away from the world. One thing was for sure—her desire to see everything the Nazi party stood for be obliterated from the world, forever.

She grabbed for her companions' hands. "Let's get out of here."

CHAPTER 1

SEPTEMBER 1939

*A*s the train screeched to a stop at Waterloo Station, Nancy rubbed the grimy window to get a better look at the figures racing around the station, which was far more packed than it should have been in the early afternoon.

An unfamiliar uneasiness washed over her as she passed several British soldiers in khaki uniforms while making a beeline for the nearest newspaper boy. "What's happening?" she demanded before tossing him a pence.

He shoved the top paper at her. "Chamberlain's just declared war on Germany."

War. For the past year, as Germany annexed Austria, then Czechoslovakia, and now Poland, she'd had an inkling that some sort of conflict was on the horizon. But now, confronted with the actual reality of it, Nancy was in such a state of shock that she wasn't even sure if she'd replied.

. . .

As she raced across the River Thames to her room at the Strand Palace Hotel, Nancy couldn't help noticing the stark change in atmosphere—gone were the bustling crowds and racing double-decker buses. Now there was hardly any traffic and dozens of people stood in silent queues outside of the local banks and grocery stores. The day, which had started off so innocently with a visit to one of her old friends, had turned into a nightmare, the pleasant breeze replaced by an undercurrent of fear.

When she reached her hotel room, Nancy sank down onto the couch and closed her eyes against the art deco chandelier, which was now spinning. "War's been declared," she said aloud. She knew without even glancing at the paper that Chancellor Hitler had refused Chamberlain's ultimatum to pull out of Poland. In a small way, she was glad that someone in power had finally stood up to Hitler.

Her eyes snapped open as she recalled what Berlin had been like in 1937—a city of contradictions, blending its grandeur and modernity with oppression and hatred. That nasty little man, who insisted his people call him Führer, was a monster who had undoubtedly been plotting years for this very day.

"Well, I suppose that's that." She picked up the phone and cancelled her appointment at the Champneys Tring, the famous health spa which had been her reason for coming to England in the first place. It was no matter—she supposed she'd easily lose the weight now that she, and the rest of France and England, would be put on the sort of drastic diet that only wartime deprivation could offer. Not to mention she might be stuck in London for a while, away from Henri, and would need to save all the money she could.

Henri. With all the fuss, she'd momentarily forgotten about her fiancé. She reached for the receiver again, but hesitated before dialing the operator. Chances were that Henri would probably not be home in the middle of the afternoon—it would be surprising if she were able to reach him at all. Besides, international calls were expensive and she had a sneaking suspicion she'd be cut off from receiving Henri's generous funds for at least the near future.

As she hung up the phone, she could practically hear his booming voice telling her, "Nannie, it's time to come home."

Though France isn't really my home. For a brief while, England had been, and then of course, there was New Zealand, where she'd been born, and Australia, where she'd spent her formative years. But she'd left Sydney for Canada at eighteen and hadn't looked back. If France wasn't technically her home now, she supposed she didn't have one. It didn't matter anyway, so long as they were all going to war against Hitler.

Her eyes landed on the discarded newspaper and the photo of Adolf Hitler wearing a military uniform and swastika armband, his mustache resembling a blot of ink. Ever since that day in Berlin, Hitler's rhetoric and the accompanying chorus of *Sieg Heils* had haunted her. The threat that Hitler and his followers posed was not just to her and her loved ones—it was to the entire free world.

She stood as it occurred to her that, though she was no soldier, the war would need more than just those who fought on the battlefields. Grabbing her purse, Nancy rushed out the door.

Figuring Henri would understand if she were slightly delayed in her return, she hurried to the first recruitment office she could find. She wasn't sure if she wanted to join up with the women's branch of the navy, army, or air force, but ultimately decided to go with whichever uniform was the most becoming, and said as much to the goggle-eyed man seated behind the recruitment desk.

Clearly the hue of the uniforms was his least concern. His prominent Adam's apple bobbed up and down as he cleared his throat. "Perhaps the armed forces aren't the most suitable for a lady with your…" He cast his eyes up and down her chic dress disdainfully. "Particular style. If you want to serve, I think the canteen would be more appropriate."

"Canteen? You want me to stand behind a counter and hand out cookies?"

When the man didn't reply, Nancy threw her fur wrap back around her throat and let herself out of the recruitment office. She knew she could contribute something more to the war effort than just being a pretty face. And if England didn't want to take advantage of her offer, then she'd simply go back to France… and Henri. Most of the battles were sure to be fought on the Continent anyway.

When she returned to the hotel, the concierge informed her that she had a message.

It was from Henri.

I'm sure you know by now that war is imminent. Please come home, my darling. I've made the arrangements for our wedding date to be moved forward. Let me know if you need me to cable you any money to help you on your journey.

She answered him that she was on her way.

After a week of begging the French Consulate for a permit to return, Nancy finally seemed to get somewhere.

"There's talk of Hitler invading France," the clerk informed her as he looked over her passport. "Are you quite sure you want to return there, miss?"

She shifted her weight, but not because she was nervous. She'd been standing in a queue for days on end and her feet hurt. "I'm sure."

"Well, if you go now, you'll probably never return to England." As if to emphasize his point, he stamped her passport with far more force than necessary.

The boat crossing was pitch black, as England, in its fear of being bombed by the Luftwaffe, had implemented a blackout beginning at dusk. The captain, clearly as equally terrified of being torpedoed as his passengers, insisted that everyone on board stay silent for the whole journey across the Channel. He'd also banned smoking, which, in Nancy's opinion, might have been taking it a bit too far. After all, it wasn't as if the dimly lit embers could betray their location to any U-boats lurking beneath the water's surface.

She spent the first few minutes of the crossing with her hands grasped tightly on the railing, staring into the inky black water for any telltale signs of an enemy submarine below. As a siren began to wail, Nancy briefly wondered if the French Consulate had been right. Was her desire to return to France, the next-door neighbor to the menace, pure madness after all?

Thankfully, after a few ear-splitting minutes, the alarm stopped and she stepped away from the railing to take a seat on a nearby bench. In order to distract herself, she fiddled with the flawless three-carat diamond on her engagement ring. She had never envisioned herself as someone who would get married. Or move to Marseille, for that matter. From her first steps down the Champs Elysées to moving into her practically barren apartment on the Rue Sainte-Anne, she'd loved everything about her life in Paris.

The apartment had been a studio, which meant no bathroom, but Nancy had used the last of the money her aunt had left her to purchase a bathtub, which she'd put in the kitchen. She barely spoke a word of French but she'd had no trouble making friends with her fellow journalists. As most of them were male, they taught her the dirty words, which she used to say with relish during smoking and drinking sessions at the café around the corner from her flat. Though females were rare in the Hearst offices, unless they were secretaries, there were always a few hanging about their circle and Nancy did her best to copy their effortless sophistication.

There had been many men who'd tried to pursue her, but Nancy was content with being alone and trying to devour as much of the *joie de vivre* as she could. Every so often, she'd grow bored and take up one of the more handsome men on their offers. In fact, she'd been traveling with an American, Frank, in the south of France when she'd first met Henri.

Frank was a fabulous dancer and she had been having a grand time waltzing cheek to cheek with him when she'd noticed a man lingering in the shadows, staring at them.

The American had obviously noticed him too. "That's Henri Fiocca. I'm surprised you've never met him, actually. The Fioccas are one of the richest families in Marseille."

Nancy watched as the man picked up a purse from a nearby table and handed it to an exquisite blonde in a low cut red dress. "Let me guess—he's also a bit of a playboy."

"You've got it," Frank said with a knowing smile.

For the next few days, it seemed that every time Nancy turned around, she spotted Henri Fiocca with a different woman, sometimes up to four in one day. Though with his slick-backed hair and robust frame, he wasn't exactly unattractive, Nancy found herself admiring his energy the most—even though he appeared significantly older than herself, he was the only one besides her who never seemed to tire from the endless parties.

After Frank had gone back to Paris, Nancy found herself alone at one of the nightclubs.

"Care to dance?" someone asked, and Nancy wasn't overly surprised to see Henri Fiocca standing in front of her.

"Where's your blonde?"

Smiles lines appeared on his tanned face. "Where's your American?"

"He's not here."

Henri held out his hand. "The same can be said about the blonde."

Nancy gave him her hand and he pulled her to the dance floor. He was nowhere near as good a dancer as Frank, but what Henri lacked in technique, he made up for in confidence, the kind of self-assuredness that, Nancy assumed, could only come from being raised in the elite circle of an affluent family.

"How do you do it?" she managed to gasp out in between the tango steps.

"Do what?" Henri asked, his breath more labored than hers.

"Date so many beautiful girls at once."

"Ah that." He guided her into a spin. "Because they call me."

"They call *you?"*

"Yes." He spun her again. "Every girl in the French Riviera calls me except the girl I want to."

Nancy, feeling suddenly dizzy, stopped dancing. This man

was obviously a true playboy, and though she herself wasn't a stranger to dating multiple men, he was operating on a much different level than her. "I will never ring up a man. If they don't call me, they'll get nowhere." With that, she left the dance floor.

When the phone jolted her out of her slumber the next morning, Nancy wasn't overly surprised to hear Henri Fiocca's voice on the other end. "What are you doing today?"

"The same thing everyone around here is doing—beach, café, and then a party. What about you?"

"Ditto," he stated casually. "But I seem to have run out of dates."

Despite herself, Nancy let out a small chuckle. "I hardly doubt that's true."

"It's not," Henri admitted. "I cancelled on all of them. What do you say? Would you be my only companion for the day?"

"Henri, I don't think—"

"Don't think. It's just for a bit of fun. We both know you and I are not the get-serious type. What do you say?"

He really was persuasive, she'd thought. And probably perfectly harmless—after all, Nancy had been around long enough to know not to fall for a skirt-chaser. What harm could come of spending time with a handsome, charming man? Not to mention one with a large wallet?

Henri was indeed older than her, by fourteen years in fact, but moved with the stamina of someone much younger. Despite being the heir to a vast fortune, he was the perfect blend of a gentle soul and a gentleman. On Henri's arm, the doors to even more social settings opened to Nancy, and when he'd asked her to marry him after a few years of a long-distance relationship, she, of course, had said yes.

. . .

When the boat finally approached the harbor at Boulogne-Sur-Mer, Nancy blinked hard as the deck was suddenly bathed in light. In contrast to darkened England, France was aglow with streetlamps and the headlights of vehicles still whizzing along the highway.

"And now I know I'm back in France," Nancy said to herself, relief washing over her as she joined the queue next to the gangway.

CHAPTER 2

NOVEMBER 1939

*D*espite the declaration of war, not much action was seen during the waning months of 1939. The citizens of France—especially the older ones who remembered the trauma of the Great War all too well—seemed content with the relative calm and began to refer to the lack of action on the Western Front as 'The Phony War.'

Nancy, for her part, would normally have been chafing for France to do something about Hitler, but she had a wedding to plan. Phony war or not, the occasion was set to be the social event of the year and would be attended by everyone who was anyone in Marseille.

She spent hours planning the wedding breakfast with the Hôtel du Louvre's receptionist, Madame Richard, who in turn promised that their head chef Marius would be able to provide a gourmet meal, even in the face of wartime constraints.

Nancy had balked at the tradition that the bride's family pay for the wedding dress and reception. After all, her father had left when she was three, and things with her mother, while better than when Nancy ran away from home when she was sixteen, were still strained. When Nancy had reminded Henri that she had no money, he told her, "Never mind, Nannie, I'll pay for it. But don't tell Papa."

Not that she would. Henri's father had made no secret of the fact that he considered Nancy to be an opportunistic Australian who only cared about the size of his son's wallet. She was also learning the hard way that Monsieur Fiocca, with his air of condescending superiority, would never be impressed by anything she came up with, not Marius's meals nor her wedding dress of pure black silk, embroidered with tiny pink orchids, which she had purchased at one of Marseille's most exclusive shops.

That day she'd also bought something purely for herself, which turned out to be far more meaningful. She'd been strolling past a pet shop when she felt a pair of eyes staring at her. She put a finger up to the glass, and the owner of the eyes, a wire-haired terrier puppy, came over and licked at the window.

In Australia, dogs were viewed more as workers, used to herd sheep across the vast landscapes, than as pets. Yet, Nancy was captivated by the French approach, where a dog peeking out from a handbag was a chic accessory. She'd often thought about getting her own puppy, but her lifestyle in Paris had certainly not lent itself to taking care of another living creature. But now that she was about to get married and would have a household full of staff... Without thinking twice, Nancy marched into the store and pointed toward the little terrier in the window.

Nancy named him Picon, after one of her favorite French apéritifs, and she brought him everywhere, even to her wedding, much to the chagrin of her future father-in-law. But even Monsieur Fiocca, with his dour looks and surly attitude, couldn't ruin Nancy's wedding day. Though none of Nancy's family made it to the wedding—her mother and most of her six siblings were still in Australia—Henri had arranged for her Paris friends to attend.

The rest of the guest list included the richest and most notable figures in Marseille. Many of them, especially the younger husbands and sons, seemed determined to celebrate Nancy and Henri's wedding day as if it would be their last. Under French conscription regulations, males between the ages of 20 and 48 were mandated to serve, and Nancy knew that even Henri, with all his money, wouldn't be exempt should the war necessitate a draft.

A similar thought was clearly on Henri's mind too. As he slipped the gold ring over Nancy's knuckle, he whispered to her that their love would be able to endure any challenge, even the most difficult ones.

"Together forever, my love," she whispered in return, her voice wobbling as the tears that had been threatening finally made their way down her face.

Marius, the chef, delivered as promised. The guests were so impressed by his delicate sea urchin mousseline—covering fried fish filets as light as a soufflé—and lamb loin that they gave him a standing ovation each time he and his team revealed what was underneath their silver platters. As Henri squeezed her hand, Nancy hadn't realized how much she'd wanted to impress the guests until that moment. Henri fit into that crowd simply because the Fioccas were the crème de la crème of Marseille. Her place among them was not because they liked her for who she was, but because she was Henri's wife.

She fingered the tulle of her ostentatious dress. Everything she'd done, every franc she'd spent in the middle of a war—phony or not, it was still war—was to impress these people and convince them she wasn't just a simpleton Australian.

Henri, sensing her change in mood, stood up and reached out his arm. "They always love everything and anything when they're drunk enough." He helped her up—her dress made every movement more difficult—and then led her over to the bar.

After ordering her a drink, Henri leaned in to have a conference with the bartender. Although he tried to keep his normally booming voice low, Nancy heard every word her new husband said as he told the bartender to be rather generous with the vodka whenever he was pouring Henri's father—or any of their more conservative guests, for that matter—a drink. She couldn't help smiling at the way Henri took charge, and the fact that he was willing to do whatever it took to make her feel more comfortable.

The alcohol seemed to loosen them up a bit, and soon Monsieur Fiocca was bragging about the details of the reception, none of which he had paid for himself, of course.

He did not extend any of this drunken goodwill toward his new daughter-in-law, but Nancy, who'd had quite a few glasses of champagne herself, couldn't have cared less. She had just married the best man in the world and was about to start the rest of her life with him. Consequently, as the guests started to leave, she suggested to Henri that they go out partying with her journalist friends. Henri, as always, was game, and they stayed up until the early morning, Picon sleeping most of the night away in Nancy's enormous purse.

After they'd returned from their honeymoon on the Côte d'Azur—where there was no sign of war, only sunbathers lounging next to a sparkling cerulean sea—they purchased an apartment on the top floor of an opulent building on the Canebière, Marseille's most famous boulevard.

Nancy spent the next few days shopping for the new flat, but she found that becoming a homemaker was a striking departure from the exhilarating lifestyle she had enjoyed in Paris. She had never been particularly great at reporting, but a part of her wished she was back at the Hearst office in Paris on the front lines—at least as far as the news of war was concerned, anyway.

As on the Côte d'Azur, the war had little presence in Marseille, except for those households whose male members had been enlisted. On the surface, everything seemed normal, but shortages of food and essential items were starting to show, and the prices were beyond the reach of those with modest incomes. Which didn't include Henri and Nancy, of course. Like most people in their social circle, they could afford to turn a blind eye to the grim reality of war.

Henri would leave for work in the early morning, after Claire, their maid, had served them tea. Nancy would then enjoy the luxury of staying in bed until noon, perusing the newspapers while Picon lazed at her feet. Henri often came back home for a leisurely lunch, and afterward, Nancy ventured into town to meet up with friends and embark on a series of visits to dressmakers, beauty salons, and tearooms.

In the evening, they would dine out in town with various friends, the women dressed in the latest couture, their hair freshly done. One night, the dinner, which was supposed to be a holiday celebration, turned into a bittersweet farewell to

Claude Ficetole, an old friend of Henri's who was departing for the Maginot Line.

"Cheer up, laddies," Henri commanded in his most posh British accent. "It can't be all that bad."

"So says you," Claude's wife, Nicole, shot back. "I have two children at home. What will become of them, if he…" she nodded toward her husband, "doesn't come back?"

Even Henri didn't have a reply to that.

Claude patted his now sobbing wife. "It's just as well that they are finally mobilizing the troops. The news from Germany is not good—the first anniversary of Kristallnacht has just passed, and from what I hear, they're making it worse now for Jews."

Nancy's paper had reported about Kristallnacht, or, The Night of Broken Glass, when thousands of Jewish businesses and synagogues were burned. Ordinary civilians—Nancy assumed they had been jeered on by those horrid storm troopers in brown shirts—were allowed to loot Jewish schools, homes, and even hospitals and cemeteries by smashing in windows, hence the pogrom's name. The paper also had reported that the police and fire services had been commanded not to intervene unless the fires threatened to spread to non-Jewish-owned properties. "How could it possibly be worse?" Nancy demanded. "They've basically taken away every human right they had."

Claude shook his head. "Hitler has his ways of finding fates worse than death for his enemies."

At that, Nicole burst into a fresh round of tears.

Claude handed her his handkerchief. "But we in France have nothing to worry about: the Maginot Line will protect us."

Nancy, remembering her time in Berlin and the vengeance Hitler was determined to sow among his followers, wasn't convinced the Maginot Line—the system of defenses that the French government had constructed along its German border after The Great War—was as impenetrable as they claimed.

As she opened her mouth to voice her opinion, Henri shook his head, his meaning clear: *now wasn't the time.* "More wine?" he asked Claude, who nodded. Henri emptied the bottle and then signaled the waiter.

After years of living paycheck to paycheck and weighing every expense, Nancy took a small pleasure in watching Henri reach for the check without blinking an eye, knowing that even the largest of bar bills wouldn't make a dent in his substantial bank account.

"Thank you, old pal," Claude said, clapping Henri on the shoulder. "That might be the last great meal I have for a while."

This time when Nicole started sobbing, Nancy felt her pleasure disappear. Someday Henri too might be deployed. Were they all just living on borrowed time?

In those first few months of marriage, Nancy's love for Henri strengthened even more. He was always up for a long drive around Marseille or an all-night party; his energy, much like his generosity, was apparently boundless. Nancy mused that it couldn't have been easy for him to go from so many women down to only one for the rest of his life, but if he found fidelity a struggle, he never let on. While they never explicitly discussed starting a family, neither one of them made a deliberate effort to prevent it. Nancy and Henri's marriage might have seemed unconventional to some, but to them, it worked—even on the brink of war, they continued to enjoy their extraordinary life together. And of course, drank a lot of alcohol.

However, their newlywed bliss was shattered a week before

Christmas when the letter Nancy had been dreading finally came: Henri had received his summons to serve in the French army.

Henri, seemingly nonplussed, refolded the letter and stuck it in his jacket pocket. "Perhaps now Prime Minister Daladier plans on fighting back instead of ignoring Hitler's growing power. He's already taken over Czechoslovakia and Poland. If we're not careful, France will be next."

A million sentiments flowed through Nancy's head—worry that Hitler would invade France combined with her trepidation of life without Henri, but in the end what won out was anger at him for leaving her. "What am I supposed to do without you?" she demanded.

A bemused look played on Henri's face. "You'll do what you always do, only now, instead of meeting me for lunch, I suppose you can spend the afternoon in the bathtub, reading and drinking champagne."

She put her hands on her hips. "I'm not just going to sit around pining away for you. I was a nurse, you know."

"You can't be a nurse at the front. It's too dangerous."

"Well, then, maybe you can use your contacts to find me an ambulance." One of her coworkers at the Hearst paper had been an ambulance driver in 1917 and had often regaled her with stories of saving the walking wounded.

"You hate driving, Nannie. Not to mention you don't have a license."

Her voice took on a whiny tone. "Please, Henri? Let me at least do something for the war effort."

He sipped on his brandy as he thought. "I'll see what I can do." It was clearly meant to be an empty promise, but Nancy planned on holding him to it anyway.

CHAPTER 3

JANUARY 1940

A few days after the New Year, Henri was requested to go into town and get fitted for his uniform. Nancy knew that the military was short of armored vehicles and weaponry but it had not occurred to her that they would also lack proper uniforms until Henri returned. Even though it was the middle of winter, he was wearing a pair of white summer trousers that ended well above his ankles and a greatcoat that was much too large.

"What is all that?" Nancy sputtered. She pointed at the puttees around his legs which were so frayed they might well have been battlefield souvenirs from the Great War.

Henri took off his dirty, misshapen cap. "They said I could trade them in for the right sizes when I got to camp."

For the first time in a few weeks, Nancy smiled. "Hold on, I can help you complete the outfit." She retrieved a pair of fur-lined gloves and a silk scarf, which Henri put on. They laughed so hard, the neighbors came over to see what was happening, and they ended up having an impromptu dinner party.

. . .

The following morning, Henri brought all his items to his tailor for a custom fitting. Such a process was no big deal for someone like Henri, but what did that mean for the rest of the men who didn't have as deep of pockets? It didn't give Nancy much confidence that France was ready to challenge the power that Hitler wielded, which made her all the more determined to do something herself.

When Henri returned from the tailor, Nancy greeted him with a glass of brandy before reminding him about the ambulance.

"If France can't afford uniforms, what makes you think they have extra ambulances lying around for a woman to drive?"

"That's why it's even more important," Nancy insisted. "Convert one of the firm's trucks into an ambulance."

"Nannie—"

"What else am I going to do while you are gone? You've got to at least let me try and help."

He drained his glass. Luckily for Nancy, it hadn't taken him long to realize that it was futile to argue with his new wife when she wanted something. "All right."

~

Even Nancy, persistent as she was, had nearly forgotten about the ambulance by the time morning dawned on the day Henri was to leave for camp. Clad in his uniform, which now hugged his frame, Henri presented a striking figure, and, as Nancy watched him pack his things, she was swept up by a wave of admiration. This was soon replaced by sorrow when she thought about how empty the flat would be once he was gone.

"Chin up, Nannie. I've told you many times that I won the last war for France, and I am about to win it for her again."

"You served in the Great War for a few months. I would hardly agree that you managed to win the whole thing." She managed a tiny smile. "Besides, maybe this time, *I* will win it for France, and England, too."

"You really just might." He took her hand in his. "Come see what I got you." She expected yet another piece of jewelry, but Henri led her out of the room. After telling her to put on her coat, he pulled her out to the porch and pointed at a weather-beaten utility van parked on the street.

Nancy squealed in delight. "Is that for me?"

He laughed his deep, hearty laugh, causing another pang of sadness to swell in Nancy's chest. "I don't think any wife has been more pleased at the sight of a rusty jalopy." He stopped laughing as his eyes flashed. "But Nannie, you have to promise me you'll be careful. I won't be able to help you if you get into any scrapes."

She wanted to reassure him that she would be fine on her own—she'd managed the first 25 years of her life without him, hadn't she? But that was before she had known the comfort of his mere presence and the warmth of his embrace, things she was sure she couldn't live without. As she didn't want to lie to Henri, she simply promised to be careful.

Picon, as if sensing her inner turmoil, sat back on his haunches and emitted a plaintive whine.

Henri reached down to pat Picon. "You take care of your mamma, now, do you hear?" He turned back to Nancy and caressed her wet cheek. "I love you Nannie, and you'll see, I'll be back soon."

"I love you too."

She'd always been terrible with goodbyes. And, as beautiful as the French language was, *au revoir* didn't sound any better. "I'll be seeing you."

And with that, Henri was gone.

CHAPTER 4

MAY 1940

Nancy inhaled sharply as she caught sight of an oncoming vehicle. She wasn't used to driving on the right side of the road and instinct caused her to turn the steering wheel to the left. Her dilapidated van, loaded with medical equipment, responded too slowly, forcing the other car off the road.

She shouted an apology into the rearview mirror instead of stopping. She was on her way north, to France's border with Belgium, where it had been rumored that the Germans had penetrated France via the Ardennes Forest. Due to its rugged terrain and dense foliage, the forest had been believed to be impassable and had been left relatively unprotected compared to the extensively fortified Maginot Line. It hadn't been the first time the government had been wrong regarding Germany's ruthless ambitions and Nancy had a sneaking suspicion it wouldn't be the last.

Unfortunately, it appeared she'd been right about the Maginot Line. And, equally as unfortunate, her newfound driving skills didn't seem to be holding up in the face of so much danger. Occasionally she'd spot planes marked with swastikas traveling overhead, which made her press down harder on the van's accelerator, causing her to swerve even more.

She yanked the handbrake after spotting the body of a child sprawled in the middle of the road. Grabbing the makeshift first aid kit she'd fashioned together by emptying the shelves of Marseilles' most expensive pharmacy, she rushed to the child.

Bile bubbled up from the back of her throat as it became clear that both her somewhat limited nursing experience and her first aid kit would prove to be completely inadequate in the harsh reality of war. As Nancy began to clean the lifeless child's wounds, she saw that his body was riddled with gaping holes that could only have been made by the guns of a German plane. His arm was at an odd angle and tire prints showed that he'd been run over.

Her eyes clouded over and all she could see was Henri wounded, Henri lying in the street, abandoned. She continued her futile task even as she heard another car pull to a stop.

"Madame Fiocca, what are you doing?"

She looked up, her vision still blurred. She hadn't realized she'd been crying, but now she tasted the salty tears. "Trying to help."

"I don't think you can do much more." Her colleague, Charles, nodded at the child, who had obviously been dead for hours. "And besides, the Germans are coming this way and the French Army has been ordered to evacuate. We've been called back to Marseille."

"Called back? But what about..." Helplessly, she gestured toward the north.

"Forget about it. There's nothing we can do to stop the advance."

Nancy wasn't sure why France had given up so easily, but that was a question for another day. "Surely the evacuated refugees will need assistance."

Charles scratched his gray beard. "Do what you want, but know that you'd be disobeying orders."

"Got it." Nancy kissed her finger and then put it on the child's forehead before getting up from her perch on the ground and climbing back into the ambulance. Instead of turning her van around to follow Charles, she continued heading north.

It wasn't long until she encountered a procession of people walking slowly along the roadway.

She reminded herself to pull over to the right side of the road. Rolling down the window, she asked if anyone needed medical attention.

"He could use a ride," one woman called, pointing to an elderly man who was lagging several steps behind. "His heart isn't right."

Nancy soon filled her ambulance with the elderly, the very young, and the walking wounded. When there was absolutely no room left for anyone else to sit, she turned the van around. Those passengers who felt like talking spoke about the horrors they'd experienced: the separation of families, the general panic brought on by the advancing German troops, and, worst of all, the Stuka aerial attacks.

"Boches." Nancy gritted her teeth as a million worse descriptions passed through her head, words that she'd never utter out loud, at least not in mixed company.

As they approached Nîmes, they overcame a French tank

heading south. "Why aren't they at the front?" Nancy demanded.

"They too probably realize the situation is hopeless," Francis, the elderly man with the heart condition, returned.

No one they encountered on the road seemed to have any news, except that the Germans were coming. The confusion persisted throughout the entire journey, even after Nancy deposited her passengers in Nîmes.

Exhausted, Nancy thought about pulling in for just a short nap, but she turned the car back north. This time she didn't have to travel far before the van was once again filled, the condition of the weary passengers worse in both morale and health. She continued this way for several trips, despite her passengers' warnings that the Germans were now on the same road. She longed for a hot bath and a warm bed, but, as she reminded herself, the people lying wounded by the side of the road superseded her own needs.

On what she resolved would be her last trip to pick up passengers, she hadn't even made it twenty kilometers past Nîmes when the van began smoking. She pulled over and tried opening the hood, which was burning hot. When she finally got it up, she gazed at the blackened insides, realizing there was no use—the intricacies of smoking vehicle engines were completely beyond her scope of expertise. She'd have to abandon the van where it lay. With a sigh, she gathered as many medical supplies as she could load into her pack and started walking.

She spent a few days traveling south, sometimes catching a ride, sometimes walking. Exhausted, she fell into a bed at a cheap hotel in a small town. She was awakened in the middle of the night by someone screaming in the hallway.

Without opening the door, Nancy pounded on it. "Could you please keep it down? I'm trying to sleep."

"How can you sleep at a time like this?" the voice shrieked back. "The Nazis have invaded Paris."

Dumbfounded, Nancy opened the door. A woman in a nightgown was pacing the hallway, wringing her hands and muttering about how the Maginot Line was supposed to have kept them all safe.

"Never mind that," Nancy called. "The Germans are here. What do we do now?"

The woman stopped, her eyes focusing somewhere above Nancy's head. "I don't know."

CHAPTER 5

JUNE 1940

By the end of June, France had literally been broken into pieces, divided between Nazi-occupied territories in the north and the so-called Free Zone in the south, its new capital in Vichy.

In Nancy's opinion, the whole of France—what remained of it, anyway—had become a puppet state after signing the Armistice with Germany. While the ceasefire was designed to last until a formal peace treaty was reached, Nancy found it difficult to believe that there would ever be peace again, not with Britain now the last line of defense against the leviathan that was the Wehrmacht.

On her return to Marseille, Nancy was met with the unsettling sight of a city that had suffered bombings at the hands of Mussolini's troops. The once vibrant streets were now lined with ruined buildings and the air was filled with the dust of destruction.

Nancy's heart felt heavy as she navigated through the

remnants of what had been her familiar world, the silence broken only by the sound of her footsteps on the broken cobblestones. Without thinking, she turned off the Canebière toward the 7th arrondissement, which the bombings had left unscathed, as if even Mussolini knew better than to mess with Marseille's most prestigious neighborhood. She paused in front of one of the largest mansions, its ironwork balconies and shutters making it look more like a prison than a home, and knocked on the door.

A uniformed maid answered as soon as Nancy finished knocking.

"Is Monsieur Fiocca here?" Nancy inquired.

"May I tell him who is asking?"

She sighed. "Nancy Fiocca, his daughter-in-law."

The maid narrowed her eyes.

"Never mind," Nancy stated, deciding she was in no mood to deal with her father-in-law after all. "Do you know anything about his son, Henri? Did he receive news from the front?"

The maid's stony face softened. "No, madame, there has been no news."

"*Merci*," Nancy replied before stepping off the porch.

Once she got back to her nearly empty apartment, Nancy took to her bed for the next several days. Picon, who'd been looked after by the maid, Claire, once again occupied his customary spot at the foot of Nancy's bed. The humiliation of her newly adopted nation capitulating to Hitler—not to mention the terrible waste of the lives of so many soldiers and civilians, one of them possibly being her husband—proved too much for even her to bear.

She was lying in bed one day, watching the movement of the meager sunrays that were able to get through the blackout curtains, when someone burst through the door.

She sat up, blinking against the sudden light from the hallway. "Henri, is that you?"

He dumped his bag on the floor as Picon raced around at his feet. "I've been demobilized," he said grimly. "France's forces have been reduced under the Armistice. It was Pétain's doing."

"Pétain?"

"Marshal Philippe Pétain is a great hero to many Frenchmen for his leadership during the Great War." Henri shook his head. "I have to admit—it was very clever of the Nazis to put him in charge of Vichy. The citizens trust him implicitly, but now it seems he's just another Nazi sympathizer. Under the agreement Pétain signed, Hitler limited us to a force of only 100,000 troops, mainly for border protection."

Nancy tilted her head, the sudden movement causing a wave of dizziness. "Isn't Pétain the one who declared, 'They shall not pass,' as in the Germans?"

"At Verdun, yes. Apparently he's fine with them passing now, as well as invading most of Europe."

"So Pétain's not going to do anything to rid France of the Nazis." She decided to pose the same question she'd asked the woman at the hotel. "What do we do now?" Surely Henri, who always had an answer for everything, would tell her what she longed for—how to get back at the Germans.

Henri loosened the collar of his uniform. "There's nothing we can do—Pétain has handed France over to Hitler. So I'm going back to work."

She pulled back the cover of the bed and patted the space beside her. "But first come to bed."

. . .

As Marseille was part of the Free Zone, life took on a somewhat semblance of normalcy with Henri's return, although the new routine now included more food rationing and supply shortages. Nancy, vowing to make the most out of the challenging times, decided to try her hand at the black market. With Henri back to work making money, his fortune was as vast as ever, so Nancy just needed a way to spend it.

Of course, it wasn't easy to find people that you could trust. There were collaborators everywhere, ones who were willing to report their fellow neighbors to the French police, most of whom were also in league with the traitorous Vichy government. Nancy's approach to assessing loyalty involved inquiring about an individual's connections to the Great War, as she assumed those whose relatives had fought against the Boches would still hold anti-German sentiments. The local butcher, Monsieur Brisbois, was one such example—after mentioning that his father had been killed at Verdun, he looked at Nancy, one eyebrow raised. "And what about your father?"

At 44, she assumed Charles Wake had been too old to serve, not that he'd ever discussed it. "My father was a journalist, and a Brit. We moved to Australia when I was very young."

Now both of Monsieur Brisbois's eyebrows shot up. "You are not French? I would have never known."

Nancy, whose French was still far from perfect, beamed from the compliment.

He wiped his hands on his already blood-stained apron. "What can I get you? I'll give it to you at price."

"No, no." Nancy set her pocketbook on the counter and took out her bulging wallet. "I have plenty of money, but I'm out of ration coupons. Tell me what you'd charge a stranger."

When he named the outrageously inflated black-market

price of a hundred francs, Nancy did her best to hide her shock. Channeling Henri, she handed over the money and even included a small tip. In wartime, it was always helpful to have allies in unexpected places.

Thanks to Monsieur Brisbois and others, Nancy had soon filled both her pantry and her wine cellar and every night they invited guests to share in their good fortune. They still occasionally dined out, but only at places they were sure were still loyal to France.

One night she promised to meet Henri at the Hôtel du Louvre. She hadn't been there since her wedding reception, but hoped Marius would be able to provide the same quality meals.

As she passed by the main entrance off the Canebière, she was shocked to see several men in German uniforms crowding the doorway. The Hôtel du Louvre had become her second home in Marseille, and now it had been invaded. She stopped near the back door, wondering if she was better off going home. But then Henri might grow worried if she didn't show. Entering through the back, she flagged down Antoine, the brawny Corsican who was head waiter.

"What's all this?" she whispered, gesturing toward the Germans.

Antoine fidgeted with the gold bracelet on his wrist. "Times are hard, Madame Fiocca, and they are paying customers. But don't worry, I'll scat you away from them."

The small bar nestled inconspicuously within the foyer was nearly empty, save for one man at the far end who was dressed in mufti, a book sprawled open in front of him.

When Antoine returned with her drink a few minutes later,

Nancy gestured for him to lean closer. She lifted a finger toward the other man and whispered, "German?" into Antoine's ear.

"I don't think so," he murmured. "That book he's reading is written in English."

"Then of course he's a Boche," Nancy said in a louder voice. "No *Anglais* would be foolish enough to sit here, surrounded by German soldiers, and read an English book."

The man, immersed in his reading, clearly didn't hear Nancy and seemed immune to their curiosity. Antoine nodded toward the man's empty glass. "And unlike the soldiers in the main room, he still hasn't paid for his drink."

"Do you think he's biding his time in the hopes of eavesdropping once it becomes more crowded?"

"Possibly, but if that was the case, he'd at least buy another brandy."

Nancy narrowed her eyes. She'd never known a German to be that interested in a book and there was something about his mannerisms that made her think he wasn't pretending. "Well, let's see, shall we? Bring him another drink and put it on my tab."

When Antoine dropped off the order, the man raised his glass to Nancy before taking a sip. Straight on, Nancy could see that he had an angular jaw to go with his intense gaze. After meeting her eyes, he immediately went back to his book.

"Buying a good-looking blond drinks, my love?" Henri asked as he took the seat next to her. "And a Boche, no less."

"Antoine says he's not German," Nancy hissed. Her voice grew louder as an idea suddenly occurred to her. "What if he's a British soldier? What if he needs help?"

Henri shot her an amused smile. "A stranded British soldier, stopping by an expensive restaurant filled with German officers to read a book." He shook his head. "I highly doubt it." He signaled for Antoine and ordered before turning back to his wife. "Let me go ask him." He stood and sauntered over to the soldier before she could protest.

The stranger actually shut his book and spoke for a few minutes before Henri returned to Nancy to whisper, "He is indeed a British soldier, who has been interned in the fortress. He's now on parole and decided to come here for a drink."

Nancy perked up at that. "A Brit? Why is he being held hostage?"

"One of the provisions of the Armistice is that any Allied troops found on French soil must be detained for the duration of the war." Henri swung his arm out. "Why don't you go get more of his story for yourself?"

She rose. "Don't mind if I do."

Up close, the man's features seemed more worn, as if he'd spent many days in the sun. The skin around his blue eyes crinkled as Nancy sat beside him and offered, "G'day, mate."

The crinkles grew deeper. "An Aussie, eh? Nice to meet another member of the Commonwealth. Whereabouts are you from?"

"Mostly Sydney. What about you?"

"Newcastle-on-Tyne, England."

She wasted no time in getting to the point. "What brings you to France?"

He frowned. "I'm stuck here. I was a soldier, a captain, actually. Arthur Wilson. After the horrors of Dunkirk, some of my unit managed to flee to France, but then they interned us in Fort Saint-Jean."

Fort Saint-Jean stood at the entrance to the Vieux Port and

was once used for coastal defense. Now apparently it had been converted to a prison. Nancy tried to swallow back her mounting anger at the Vichy government before asking in a low voice, "Are there many soldiers being held there?"

"Around 200 or so."

"And the conditions?"

"Not horrible. It's no POW camp, so the guards can be more lenient. They sometimes let us go out, probably because there's not much food and the fortress is literally overflowing."

At last Nancy felt useful. "I have some food, and know exactly where to get more. And an extra radio, so you can listen to the BBC. Oh, and cigarettes, I bet you men could use those."

The crinkles disappeared. "Why are you offering all of this?"

She shrugged. "I can get things, and I want to help."

When he still didn't look convinced, she pursed her lips. "As I told you, I'm an Aussie. You don't think I'm a collaborator, do you?"

He met her eyes. "No, I don't suppose I do." He glanced over at Henri, who seemed unperturbed by his wife talking in a low voice to a strange man. "Shall I meet you somewhere tomorrow? They let me out for walks around noon."

Nancy knew just the place—another bar, but one the Germans would never deign to enter. "At Basso's on the Vieux Port."

With that, Captain Wilson left and Nancy returned to Henri and filled him in on what she had promised the man.

"Nannie, you do realize that he could still be a German, don't you?"

She paused, her brandy halfway to her mouth. It hadn't occurred to her that it could be a trap—after all, it was she who suggested aiding the man and convinced him she wasn't a collaborator. Not to mention, by telling him she was Australian, she practically declared herself to be aligned with the British. "I think he was who he said he was."

"Still, you'd better be careful. Let me come with you tomorrow."

She waved him off with more confidence than she felt. "You have work. Besides, I know the barman, Albert, at Basso's. He'll step in if I need him to."

Henri muttered something about Albert not being able to do much stepping in if the Boche had a gun, but Nancy ignored him.

The next morning, shortly before noon, Nancy walked slowly toward the Vieux Port, which was still a gathering place for locals and fishermen. The satchel over her shoulder felt as though it were filled with bricks and not just sandwiches and cigarettes. Despite what she had told Henri, she'd woken up that morning a little disconcerted that she might actually be meeting a group of Nazis at the bar instead of the soldiers she'd wanted to help. For that reason, she left the radio in her apartment.

"*Bonjour,* Madame Fiocca." Albert peered at her from behind the bar. The sleeves of his worn but clean shirt were rolled up to his elbows, revealing heavy forearms marked with faint scars. "You are here early today. We've just opened."

"I know. I'm meeting some people."

"Oh?" There was a discerning look in Albert's gaze, as if he could sense her nervousness. "Are these people you know?"

"Sort of." She lifted the satchel. "Can you put this behind the bar?"

"Do you want me to stow it in the back room?"

"Sure. And then, if you don't mind, I'd like you to stay out here."

"You got it, Madame Fiocca." He busied himself behind the bar and then delivered her favorite aperitif, a Picon. Nancy wrapped her fingers around the stem of the glass, trying to still her shaking hands.

The door creaked open precisely at noon and Captain Wilson stepped in, flanked by two others, one of them sporting an outlandish ginger mustache and the other a sort of half-beard with ample sideburns.

Albert folded his scarred arms across his chest, his eyes scanning the men for any sign of threat but Nancy's heartbeat had steadied. "Never mind, Albert. You can fetch the bag." She leaned in closer to tell him, "No German would ever sport such peculiar facial hair as these boys."

Albert handed over the satchel and then took their orders, his posture still tense.

The four of them sat down for lunch and Nancy handed each of them a pack of cigarettes. After Albert had served them, he stood protectively behind the bar, one eye on the door in case anyone unfamiliar came in.

"Tell me what it's like at the fort," Nancy commanded.

"It's fine enough," Ginger Mustache replied as he lit a cigarette. "A might overcrowded, for sure."

"And the food?" Nancy prompted, knowing what the answer would be, especially considering the scarcity of resources.

"Terrible," Sideburns answered.

"Then it's settled. You will come to dinner tonight, at my flat." She checked her watch, hoping that Monsieur Brisbois, the butcher, would still be open and would have something hearty to serve.

"That's very kind of you, but…"

She cut off Captain Wilson before he could finish. "Nonsense... I insist. And so does my husband." That last part wasn't strictly true, but Nancy didn't think Henri would mind. "Not to mention that the radio is at my flat."

Ginger Mustache set down his cigarette to pick up his drink. "Well, then, cheers to you, madame."

CHAPTER 6

AUGUST 1940

As the summer dragged on, Nancy and Henri welcomed an ever-shifting assortment of British internees into their home. Henri endured his wife's latest scheme without complaint, even as their once well-stocked wine cellar emptied. Occasionally he'd tell her in a wistful tone that he'd like to come home one day and be the only man in the house, but that was the extent of it.

Although sheltering and feeding prisoners of the Vichy government was a small act of defiance—and one that could get her and Henri into major trouble if anyone found out—Nancy longed to do something genuinely constructive against the enemy, and, frankly, something more engaging.

And then came the evening when a newcomer, tall and handsome with an athletic figure, joined them at their dinner table. His name was Ian Garrow and he was a Scottish officer. It was clear that he hadn't come over to dine so much as discuss business. The trio barely had time to exchange a bit of small talk before Garrow focused his green eyes on Nancy. "This disdain you have for the Vichy government—do you display it to everyone you meet or only to the men from the fort?"

She swallowed a gulp of wine before raising her eyebrows at Henri. He shrugged in return.

"I'm not ashamed of my disdain," she told Garrow. "I'm ashamed of Marshal Pétain's collaboration with Hitler."

"You've made that quite clear."

She laid her glass on the table with more force than necessary. "I suppose this is when you tell me I'll catch more flies with honey."

"Nazi flies?" Garrow shook his head. "Who needs them?" He leaned forward, the eager look in his eyes not unlike Picon's when he knew Nancy had a treat. "I don't blame you for your feelings toward Vichy. In fact, your hatred for them is the reason I'm here. But I *am* going to ask that you be more discreet in the future. Discretion being the nature of our work."

"What work are you referring to?" Henri asked, his voice uncharacteristically stern.

"I'm sure you know how desperate the other men are to get back home," Garrow replied, his gaze still on Nancy. "I'm organizing an escape route with the help of a Belgian named Albert Guérisse."

This sounded like it was exactly the kind of work Nancy was looking for. "We can certainly help, can't we Henri?"

He reached for his wallet. "I suppose you want money."

"Money is great but..." Garrow cleared his throat. "We're going to need safehouses, and people to escort the refugees along the Line." Once again he looked meaningfully at Nancy. "Women are probably the best suited for this role as the Germans don't tend to ask them as many questions. Not to mention I don't speak much French."

"I'll do it," Nancy replied.

From the other end of the table, Henri sighed heavily, but he knew better than to question his wife's resolve.

"Thank you, Nancy." Garrow's lips turned up into the semblance of a smile. "I'll have you meet Guérisse and the people running the nearest safehouse, but you shouldn't know more than that. That way if you are captured, and…" he cleared his throat, "tortured, you won't give up too much information."

Henri's fork dropped at the same time as his jaw.

Nancy waved away the concern with her hand. She knew Henri understood that even mingling with the British prisoners could lead to her arrest, but hearing someone actually say the words aloud probably made the risk feel more concrete. Reassurance would have to come later, after Garrow left. "Do you know who the first escapees will be?"

Garrow named Smythe and Evans, whom Nancy recognized as Ginger Mustache and Sideburns, men who had been over to their flat several times since she'd first met them with Captain Wilson at Basso's.

Nancy gaped. "But they made an oath that they wouldn't escape." That oath was the reason they were allowed to come and go from the Fort.

"They did, but it is the duty of every soldier to return to his own side if the opportunity arises. And it would appear that an opportunity has indeed presented itself." Garrow ran a hand through his thinning hair. "Would it help if they gave their guards a fair warning?"

She grinned. "I'm not too concerned about it myself. I just know that Smythe and Evans are gentlemen and don't like to go back on their promises."

"Well," Garrow said ominously. "War is war."

. . .

Her work for Garrow started off easy enough—as a woman of means, Nancy traveled around the Free Zone, specifically to Toulouse and Nice, carrying radio parts or messages to Garrow's operatives. Thanks to one of Henri's associates, she managed to procure new papers which, although they used her real name, conveniently excluded any mention of her being a British subject.

Garrow thought it best that he limit his contact with Nancy herself, so, at her suggestion, their go-between in Marseille was Monsieur Brisbois, the butcher. A few times a week, Nancy would stop by his shop to pick up meat and whatever messages or assignments Garrow had passed on.

In order to disguise her newfound secret operations, she maintained the patterns of her previous life by shopping with friends and spending hours at the beauty parlor. Nancy figured this was time well spent, as she considered her appeal to men to be her greatest weapon. If anyone stopped her on the street or asked to see her papers on the train, Nancy would hand them over with a flirtatious wink and then ask if they wanted to search her. Nine times out of ten, the young soldier would usually blush bright red, hand back her papers without looking at them, and move on. Occasionally they would bestow a lascivious smile in return, as if they were willing to take her up on the offer. This would be Nancy's cue to flash her own wedding ring, clear her throat and state firmly, "That's *Madame* Fiocca, monsieur." This was usually enough to get the soldier to continue on his way.

CHAPTER 7

DECEMBER 1940

Christmas 1940 in Marseille was a subdued affair, marked by the hardship of wartime rationing. Many families struggled to obtain even basic necessities, let alone festive luxuries. Henri was still doing well, however, and Nancy wanted to spread her wealth as much as possible, especially among the British officers imprisoned in Fort Saint-Jean. It might have seemed somewhat imprudent, but Nancy's motto had become, "Eat, drink, and be merry, for tomorrow we may die." *Or,* she often secretly added to herself, *get caught by the Gestapo.*

Nancy designed the meal for Claire to make, keeping it strictly French except for the plum pudding. The guest list included several officers, along with Antoine—the waiter from the Hôtel du Louvre—and Monsieur Brisbois, the butcher. In the past, they would have invited personal friends such as the Ficetoles, but nowadays it was hard to trust even those they had known for years.

Nancy bought scarves or ties for all the men, except Ian

Garrow. For him, Nancy purchased a homburg hat with a grosgrain ribbon, of the style that Winston Churchill wore.

"Don't you think that's a bit obvious?" Henri asked when she brought it home.

"I suppose." She attached a bright red bow to the top of it. "But it's not like Garrow doesn't already stand out." Towering over the average Frenchman with a markedly Scottish look, Garrow made for a conspicuous figure indeed. To make matters worse, his French, though improving, was still marred by a heavy accent.

"He definitely has the makings of someone who would be picked up immediately by the Gestapo," Henri agreed.

"Yet, somehow Garrow is still walking around the streets of Marseille." Nancy chalked his unlikely success to his hard work and dedication, though sometimes she wondered if it was because the Gestapo found the idea of him being in command of an established escape line too implausible to take seriously.

"Nannie, promise me you'll be careful. I don't know what I would do if something ever happened to you."

She put Garrow's hat down to give him a hug. "Same here."

"Hold that thought." He held up his finger. "I want to give you your Christmas present," he called from the hallway before returning with a small box.

"You definitely shouldn't have," she admonished. "I'm sure this money could have gone to the war effort."

He grinned. "I still have plenty for that as well. I just wanted to spoil my beautiful wife." She could smell the distilled alcohol he'd been using for aftershave as he helped her put the bracelet on.

"It's heavy."

His grin grew larger. "It's real gold."

"Henri—"

"You deserve it." He kissed her on the lips. "Besides, you can use it for leverage if you get in trouble. Or sell it on the black market."

She fingered the links as she held the bracelet up to the light. It really was beautiful.

Nancy had been looking forward to presenting Garrow with his new hat, but her plans were thwarted when he became ill and had to stay in the fort on the day of the dinner.

Still, the dinner was an outstanding success, as all the rest of the men seemed as determined to enjoy themselves as Nancy.

After dinner, they tuned in to *Ici Londres* on the BBC. Translated as "This is London," the broadcast, which often included coded messages for the French Resistance among the war news, had been quickly banned by the German authorities. Nancy and Henri always stuffed pillows in the door frames before turning on the radio and then afterward made sure they turned the dial back to a French station.

That night the BBC did not disappoint, and included a special Christmas broadcast aimed at boosting the morale of those living under occupation. Before he started the *messages personnels*, the announcer stated, "This is the French speaking to the French. We send our heartfelt greetings and wish that you know you are not forgotten. We stand with you in spirit this Christmas night."

He then began his diatribe of sometimes nonsensical phrases, such as *Jean has a hairy beard*, which most of the French knew were secret messages from Britain.

Henri reached over to turn the dial before shutting off the radio.

Monsieur Brisbois drained his glass of wine. "That was very

kind of them, to let us know they are thinking of us here in France while they go about their business, not worrying if they have enough food on the table or if some Gestapo man will arrest them on the street."

"I'm sure it's hard in London too," one of the soldiers stated.

"So hard that they can't come to France and rescue us from this hell," Antoine added.

"The Allies will be here someday," Nancy told them softly. She raised her own glass. "And until then, we'll do what we can to help them prepare."

Henri met her cheers. "To the end of the war."

"To freedom," Nancy said.

CHAPTER 8

MARCH 1941

After a few months, Garrow decided it was time for Nancy to meet Guérisse, the self-proclaimed leader of the escape line, which had now become known as the PAO Line.

"Why PAO?" Nancy asked Garrow.

"It's in reference to Guérisse's *nom de guerre,* Pat O'Leary."

"I thought you said Guérisse was Belgian."

"He is."

"Then why is he trying to pass for an Irishman?"

"I don't know," Garrow replied. "But I wouldn't suggest asking him yourself." He gave Nancy an odd look. "In fact, you might want to tamp down your usual inquiries altogether. Guérisse isn't the type to engage in casual conversation: he's all business."

Nancy decided not to question the relationship between Garrow and Guérisse or why the Line bore Guérisse's name and not that of Garrow, even though it had been his brainchild.

. . .

Guérisse strode into Nancy's apartment unhurriedly, as if he had all the time in the world, which Nancy found slightly odd, given that he must be under constant surveillance by the Gestapo. Like Henri, he seemed to ooze confidence from every pore, including from under his Brylcreemed hair. "Ahh, Madame Fiocca, I've heard about you," he said by way of introduction.

"Likewise." Recalling Garrow's warning, Nancy bit back a joke about his Irish code name and instead offered him a brandy.

Guérisse waved his hand. "I don't drink on the job."

"Neither do I," Nancy said before pouring herself some.

Guérisse watched her, his blue eyes unblinking even as she sat down on the sofa and gestured for him to do the same. Nancy suddenly felt as though she were back in grade school and Guérisse was a teacher who knew she was about to fail a test.

After a silence that seemed to drag on forever, Nancy set her glass down and cleared her throat. "I suppose Garrow has told you that I've already carried out several missions."

"Missions?"

"Trips back and forth from Toulouse and Nice."

"With messages only, I'm told, no passengers."

She quickly gathered that 'passengers' meant exiled soldiers. "That's right. But I'm assuming you wanted to meet me because you want me to do more, and I can tell you now that I'm ready."

Guérisse's eyes widened, making Nancy think that she had been completely off the mark. "You're clearly a wealthy woman, with, from what I've heard, a husband who's willing to give you whatever you want. Why do you want to work for the Resistance?"

She could have told him of her time in Berlin and witnessing the cruelty of the Nazis firsthand, but if this indeed was a test, Guérisse had probably heard it all before. She leaned forward. "What you are really saying is that the Resistance is not a club for rich, spoiled women." She patted her freshly coiffed hair. "And we both know the Gestapo would say the same—which is exactly why you need someone like me."

Guérisse crossed his arms over his chest as he once again stared at her intently. "All right then," he said finally. "Obviously you know that the RAF has been conducting bombing raids on the local area and there are many pilots whose planes have been shot down wandering helplessly around the South of France."

"And it's our job to help them return to England."

"Indeed, mainly out of a sense of duty to the Allies. Airmen are incredibly expensive to train and every one we return home is another way to stick it to Hitler."

Nancy nodded. "What do you need me to do?"

"We have a network of safehouses we use to pass the men on. You will escort the ones coming from the west—Nice or Cannes and the like—and take them to our Marseille safehouses. Once we've provided them with the proper papers and passes, they will move on to Toulouse or Perpignan, and then, eventually, cross the Pyrenees into Spain."

"And from there, back to England."

"Hopefully."

"You don't expect me to help them over the mountains do you?" Even Nancy, as adventurous as she happened to be, knew she would be no match for the treacherous terrain and unpredictable weather of the Pyrenees.

"No," Guérisse replied. "We have experienced men for that—former smugglers who are sympathetic to our cause." He gave her another searching look. "To be honest, I wasn't enthusiastic about you being an escort either, but Garrow convinced me to give you a try."

"Ah, of course. Garrow."

Guérisse cleared his throat. "The truth is that we need money—a lot of money—for food, clothing for the men, and payment for our mountain guides. That's really the reason I'm here, but Garrow knew you'd insist on helping with the Line yourself, so..."

"I see." She wasn't insulted, not really. Garrow himself often asked Henri for money, and if this was a way for her to get deeper into the Resistance, then so be it. It wouldn't be the first time that Henri's wealth had opened doors for her. She held out her hand. "Consider this a deal."

Nancy's first mission was a large one: she was to accompany twenty Allied airmen after they escaped from a fort on the outskirts of Nice. She didn't have the details of the jailbreak—that was all arranged by Guérisse and involved the men tunneling out of the prison—just the time and place where she was to meet them and then instructions to take them to the house of a certain Mademoiselle LeBreton to rest before she escorted them to Marseille.

The evening of the scheduled breakout was clear and unexpectedly warm for early spring. Nancy waited with a handful of other local agents in a thickly wooded area a few hundred meters away from the fortress. The escapees were supposed to arrive via a storm drain outlet.

Five minutes after nine, Nancy was relieved to see the first shadowy figure crawl out from the drain, his clothes drenched and his face streaked with dirt. After four more rather disheveled men emerged, she and one of the agents exchanged nods. Each member of the PAO Line would take five men to Mademoiselle LeBreton's, keeping the groups small so as not to draw further attention. The other agents would return to their homes while Nancy stayed with Mademoiselle LeBreton.

Nancy was the last agent to leave, and, after she counted off her five men, she was dismayed to see another figure emerge from the drainpipe. "What gives?" Nancy asked the man standing next to her as two more men shimmied out from the drain. "I thought there were only twenty of you."

"Twenty?" The man was obviously taken aback. "No madame, there are damn near forty of us."

"Forty?" Nancy's voice raised as high as she dared. "What am I supposed to do with twenty extra prison escapees?"

The man, probably knowing he couldn't give a satisfying answer, didn't reply.

When Nancy had confirmed that the last man was out of the pipe, she led her charges through the dark night to the safehouse.

Nancy estimated that Mademoiselle LeBreton, with her silver-streaked hair pulled back tightly, was in her late sixties, her heavily lined face punctuated by sharp, observant eyes that missed little. "Why so many men?"

Since it was her first mission, Nancy didn't want to get blamed for any mistakes. "There must have been some sort of communication error between Pat O'Leary and his contact at the prison."

"Errors like that cost lives," Mademoiselle LeBreton replied, but she waved the men into her home anyway.

The modest house of Mademoiselle LeBreton was soon transformed into a cramped sanctuary. Though the night was warm, the windows were kept shut, which only intensified the stifling atmosphere inside, the air thick with the cigarette smoke from many nervous men.

Sweat beaded on Nancy's forehead as she and Mademoiselle LeBreton navigated the overcrowded rooms with a tray of water glasses. The men, wet, weary, and bedraggled, curled up on any flat surface that could pass for a bed, including the dining room table. Since every available floor space was occupied, Mademoiselle LeBreton insisted that Nancy take her bedroom.

"I can sleep some other time," Nancy insisted.

"No. You will be taking some of these men—not all of them, of course—to the train station tomorrow. You will need to keep your wits about you, so be sure to get as much sleep as you can. We will leave some of the men here; I'll contact O'Leary to let him know he will need to make other arrangements."

"Thank you," Nancy told Mademoiselle LeBreton as she led her into the bedroom.

After settling into the narrow bed, Nancy found it difficult to sleep. Until then, everything she'd done had just been a playful attempt at doing something for the war effort, but now she was really in it: beyond the door frame was a house full of Allied soldiers. If any late-night German patrol decided to stop in and have a look inside, all of them would be arrested, Mademoiselle LeBreton and herself included. As the shadows danced in the moonlight filtering in through the ill-fitting blackout curtains, Nancy's eyes remained wide open, her mind going over tomorrow's plan to plot out every possible scenario.

. . .

Nancy awoke to the smell of eggs frying. As she entered the crowded dining room, she was informed that one of the agents from last night had dropped off as many eggs as they could gather from local farms. There were hardly enough to go around and she knew that even one egg wouldn't be enough to satisfy the airmen, who were probably used to eating three square meals a day in England.

One of the seated escapees stood and offered Nancy both his chair and his breakfast. But she was too nervous to even think about eating and waved him off.

"Who is in charge here?" she asked instead.

One of the men standing by the doorway stepped forward. "I suppose that would be me. I am Squadron Leader Davies."

"I will be taking twenty of you with me to Marseille, since that is all the paperwork I have." Nancy told him as she handed over the stack of false papers that O'Leary had given her. "Can you please round up these men?"

"Yes, madame."

"And remind them to follow my directions implicitly."

"Of course, madame."

Mademoiselle LeBreton did her best to outfit the men in French clothes that had been donated by members of the PAO Line. Right before they left, Nancy realized that they should not be caught smoking British cigarettes and asked for all of the men to give them up. Luckily Mademoiselle LeBreton had a few extra packs.

"These will have to last you until Marseille," Nancy told Davies.

Once again, Nancy thought it would be wise to have smaller

groups, so she, Davies, and another one of his men left for the train station first, and then the others filtered in behind them, accompanied by one of the other agents.

Nancy kept her conversations with the escapees to the necessities, understanding that the less they knew about each other, the safer it was for everyone involved. Among her few instructions was to not talk to anyone on the train as most of the men didn't speak French and all of them had very obvious British accents.

She could feel the men's nervousness as they stood in line to get their papers checked by the local gendarmes before boarding the train. Her own anxiety grew when one of the men from the other agent's group was pulled out of line. The gendarme clearly hadn't fallen for his false papers.

When it was her turn, the gendarme gave her papers a cursory glance before waving her forward. Her feet stumbled only a little as she walked toward the train car. Luckily the two men behind her were allowed to board as well.

After Nancy situated herself in an empty seat, she watched as some of the escapees entered her car. One of them was very tall and burly, and his pants ended several centimeters above his ankles. While it wasn't unusual for French citizens to be wearing ill-fitting clothes, the man clearly looked and felt out of place. As he bumbled down the aisle, he accidentally stepped on Nancy's foot. "I beg your pardon, miss," he said in English.

He caught the mistake as soon as the words came out of his mouth. His eyes wide, he looked from Nancy to the man beside her and then at the rest of the people on the train. Nancy's seat companion ducked his head while Nancy narrowed her own eyes, hoping her message was clear: *keep moving and shut your mouth.*

Once again, fortune was on Nancy's side—none of the other passengers commented on the man's obvious snafu, nor did they report the presence of a British man on the train to Marseille.

As the train pulled into the station, she felt a wave of relief wash over her. Her first mission was a success.

CHAPTER 9

MARCH 1941

In March 1941, the German military commander in France, Otto von Stülpnagel, issued warnings that anyone who provided assistance to downed airmen would be subject to severe punishments, including the possibility of death. This, of course, did not faze Nancy, but the worst of it was the Nazis offered significant sums of money for any information leading to the capture of those providing such help. Nancy found it hard to believe that any loyal French citizen would betray their own, but soon the PAO Line was filled with rumors about those who could no longer be trusted.

In spite of all this, Nancy continued leading the airmen through the ominous landmine of Occupied France. Most of her daily allowance went toward helping evaders through the PAO Line. Henri took all of this in stride, though he was somewhat miffed when Nancy gave away their bedspread and many of their blankets.

Her greatest reward for the risks she took—besides defying the Nazis—was the thanks given to her by the airmen. Most of them were incredibly brave—undoubtedly a prerequisite for their missions—but Nancy couldn't fathom what it would be like to parachute into enemy territory, watch your plane explode, and then be forced to rely on the goodwill of strangers to make it out alive.

As the Blitz dragged on in London, the RAF stepped up its aerial attacks. Consequently, there were increasingly more downed airmen coming through the PAO Line, which also meant that they needed more safehouses and agents. What began as a small, close-knit group quickly expanded into a vast network. Garrow and Guérisse soon found themselves forced to depend on new recruits, some of whom could be collaborators intent on destroying their operation or even German agents.

One of the new contacts in Montpellier, which was usually the airmen's next stop after Marseille, was a Madame Sainson. Though she had a rather cramped flat in a dilapidated building, her liquid brown eyes always warmed at the sight of more airmen.

Rookie though she might be, Madame Sainson was not oblivious to the threats that came with her role in the Line. She worked out signals that would let Nancy know it was safe to come in: if there were any threats, she would deliberately misalign the doormat, then bolt the door from the inside and ready the hand grenade she kept stashed in the entryway table drawer. In addition, she instructed Nancy to knock three times —the first time hard, and then the next two softer—to let her know the caller was a friendly one.

Madame Sainson never mentioned her husband. Considering how much she professed to hate Hitler and the Nazis, Nancy figured that Monsieur Sainson had either died for France or had been taken as a POW. At any rate, Madame

Sainson managed her husband's auto service station and took great pleasure in giving away the Germans' stockpiled fuel to local fishermen and diluting the remainder with water. She was closely allied with the town's clergyman, who told Nancy that "There was no more audacious foe of Hitler's Reich than Madame Sainson." Nancy had to agree, especially after she picked up a picture from its prominent place on the living room table.

"What's this?" Nancy asked, squinting at it. She recognized the subjects as some of the airmen she'd delivered to the apartment a few weeks ago.

"That's Aircraftmen Piper, Lowe, and Potts." Clearly Madame Sainson had no qualms about exchanging real names with the men.

"And who are these men in the background?"

"Italian soldiers. I like to show the men staying with me the Cathedral and the Jardin des Plantes, where I always take their picture. The Italians happened to be standing there, and I asked them if they wanted to be in the photo."

Nancy, after gazing at the self-satisfied grin the photographer had captured on Madame Sainson's face, set the photo down. "Don't you think it's a little dangerous to take the escapees on a sightseeing tour?"

Madame Sainson shrugged. "The airmen had never been to Montpellier, and, as we had to wait a few days for their papers to come in, I thought I'd show them around."

"You have to be more careful—there are people watching everywhere. And what if those Italian soldiers caught on to what you were doing?"

"Oh, I've already been picked up by the gendarmes," Madame Sainson replied loftily. "But those men, they hate tears, and I'm very good at crying on command. After somehow getting the wrong impression that I was a fake and merely bragging about an imaginary role in the Resistance, they let me go."

Nancy's eyes traveled over to the table by the door, where she knew the grenade was hidden. She could picture in her mind's eye the gendarme foolish enough to knock at Madame Sainson's door when the mat was askew, only to be greeted by the blast of a grenade. Working for the PAO Line demanded a blend of sharp wits and steely nerves, and Madame Sainson certainly had both.

The airmen, however, were sometimes another story—on the ground, they were like fish out of water, or more fittingly, pilots without their wings. Stuck on *terra firma*, they were visibly unnerved and often arrived in Marseille from Cannes disoriented, their PAO Line-provided false papers clutched in their fists. Nancy finally understood why Madame Sainson went out of her way to make them feel comfortable. Whenever they were out of earshot, Nancy would converse with her airmen in English, their voices often hoarse from not being used—other than a *oui* or *non* here and there—for weeks at a time. Remembering her own struggles in learning French, she appreciated the comfort of being able to speak one's own language while navigating a foreign world. Sometimes she would break her own rules and allow them to reminisce about their wives or girlfriends back home, but she would never offer any personal information in return. Considering the risks she was taking, it was the least she could do to protect Henri.

CHAPTER 10

JUNE 1941

*A*fter a few months, Nancy found herself helping more than just Allied soldiers and pilots trying to get back to England, and these were often the ones she stayed awake at night worrying about. They were referred to as *réfracteurs:* ordinary citizens who, for whatever reason, needed to leave France. Sometimes they were women who had been prosecuted for purchasing essentials from the black market to feed or clothe their needy family, and sometimes they were Resistance fighters or even members of the PAO Line. Increasingly though, they were Jews—occasionally whole families, including small children.

The Occupiers were clear in their hatred for Jews and persuaded Vichy to enact the same anti-Semitic laws in place in Germany and Poland. In late 1940, the French government had passed the *Statut des Juifs*, which excluded Jews from holding certain occupations, and had recently passed a second Jewish Statute which allowed French citizens to confiscate the businesses and even the homes of Jews.

Nancy's new passengers were usually refugees from the Occupied Zone, where conditions for them were even worse than in Vichy-governed France. As with the pilots, she usually refrained from engaging in extensive conversations with the refugees. Nevertheless, there were moments when she felt herself inexorably pulled in.

One of those moments occurred when Nancy picked up a mother and small child from the train station. The child, a boy who couldn't have been more than four, glowed with excitement as if this were a merry game they were all playing.

"He'd never been on a train before we left Paris," the mother told Nancy. She wore a pained expression, as though perpetually reliving what had occurred in the preceding months. The cut of her coat and its subtle details—a matted velvet collar and frayed silk lining—spoke of a time when fashion had mattered in her life. Her shoes were the same style as Nancy's own and, despite being scuffed and patched at the sides, still displayed evidence of expert craftsmanship.

Nancy, pretending to be a relative, gave the woman an enthusiastic hug, though the woman remained stiff beneath her embrace.

"I'm your Aunt Nancy," she told the boy.

"Aunt Nancy?" His little face wrinkled in confusion. "I thought she went to Drancy with Papa and Eliana."

Nancy cast a glance at the woman, but her expression remained unchanged. "Come Michel," Nancy said, clasping his hand in hers tightly.

"I'm sorry that there is no room at our usual safehouses," she said under her breath as they began to walk away from the train station. "Since it is a Sunday, there is no one at my husband's factory. You can stay the night there and tomorrow your next contact will bring you to Perpignan."

The woman merely nodded.

As Nancy was helping them get settled into the small corner of the factory that had been repurposed into a temporary sanctuary, she asked the woman what Drancy was.

The woman's lips tightened even more. "It's a suburb of Paris where they're detaining people. Foreign-born Jews, like my husband. They also took my stepdaughter Eliana, and my sister-in-law. Her name was—is—Nancy."

"Drancy is an internment camp?"

The woman sighed. "Supposedly, but I've heard from a friend who managed to get released that they were deporting people and sending them to Germany. God knows what happens to them there." She wiped a tear away. "I don't think my family is ever coming back."

"I'm so sorry." Even Nancy could hear how hollow her words sounded. What else could you say to someone whose entire life had been so thoroughly upended? "The PAO Line—the people I work with—will get you new papers in Perpignan and then help you over the border to Spain."

The woman looked at Michel, who was already snuggled into the threadbare blanket spread over a wooden shipping crate. "I know it won't be an easy journey. I'm doing this for him."

She was right—even in summer, the journey over the mountains would probably be downright treacherous, and Nancy wished she had more to offer the woman and her son. "Here," Nancy said, sliding off her shoes. "They're at least in a little better shape than yours."

The woman shook her head. "You've already done enough. I know what you are risking to do this job."

"I insist." After the woman didn't move, Nancy added, "Please. For Michel."

With another sigh, the woman removed her own shoes and then reached for Nancy's. "Thank you." After putting on the shoes, she picked up the other blanket, which she then layered over her sleeping son.

"Good luck." Once again, Nancy found her choice of words inadequate.

That night, Nancy couldn't sleep at all. She kept picturing tiny, helpless Michel, the wooden pallet the only separation between him and the freezing floor of the factory. And then there was the woman, with her once fine clothes serving as a stark reminder of what Nancy's fate could have been under different circumstances. Despite everything that had happened, Nancy had still managed to maintain a semblance of her old life, and she still had Henri by her side, while the woman had lost nearly everything, including her family.

Nancy nudged her sleeping husband as something occurred to her. "Henri, can you give me some more money?"

He rubbed his eyes sleepily. "What for now, Nannie?"

"Another flat."

He sat up, suddenly awake. "Are you planning on moving out?"

"Of course not. I need it for the PAO Line."

He held up his hand. They had both agreed that the less Henri knew of her activities, the better. "Here," he said, climbing out of bed and going over to the dresser. He tossed several hundred francs at her. "That should at least be good for a down payment."

. . .

A few days later, Nancy met with Henri's real estate agent, the same one who had helped them find their flat on the Canebière. He had a flat to show her on the Rue de l'Évêché, a street located in the older part of Marseille near the Vieux Port. The street itself was very narrow and labyrinth-like, with a high density of buildings. It was perfect for her purposes, as people would be able to come and go without drawing undue attention and there were plenty of escape routes if something were to go wrong.

"This apartment is much smaller than Henri's," Edouard commented as he showed her around. "You aren't planning on moving, are you? Has wartime deprivation gotten to you already?"

"No." Nancy felt her face grow hot. She'd never liked Edouard much and knew he couldn't be trusted with knowing what the apartment was really for. Struck by inspiration, she put both hands on her cheeks. "It's not for me or Henri." She looked down at the scuffed wood floors. "It's for... someone else."

"Ah." When she looked up again, Edouard winked at her, and she knew the deception had worked—he thought she needed the apartment for a lover.

The flat wouldn't be hers in time to help out Michel and his mother, but hopefully countless others would be able to sleep more comfortably on their way to freedom.

After Nancy signed the lease, she didn't venture to the flat often, but ordered milk and bread to be delivered once a week. A stream of airmen moved in and out and once again, Nancy kept contact with them to a minimum.

One day she was heading up the stairs to clean when she was intercepted by the woman who lived in the flat below.

"Madame Fiocca, is everything all right?"

Nancy's hand tightened on the railing. "Yes, why do you ask?"

The woman nodded at her stomach. "I imagine your colic must be very bad."

Her intimate tone heightened Nancy's suspicions. She was about to deny being sick, but thought better of it. "How did you know about my colic?"

The woman gave her a knowing look. "I can hear every time your toilet flushes, and it flushes so much at night, I can't help feeling sorry for what you're going through."

"What I'm going through," Nancy repeated as understanding dawned. "I'm actually feeling much better now, so hopefully you won't hear the toilet as much." She resumed her climb, trying to keep from running up the stairs.

As soon as she entered the apartment, she informed the latest guests that they needed to be more mindful of security, and warned them to not flush the toilet unless it was absolutely necessary.

CHAPTER 11

OCTOBER 1941

As autumn of 1941 arrived, it was evident that the spirits of Marseille's residents had markedly declined. Nancy could hardly blame them—fuel for household heating was already scarce and food rations often went unfulfilled. It was hard to remain optimistic while constantly shivering and suffering from severe hunger pangs.

Even though the war raged on, Henri had managed to expand his business and continued to fund many of Nancy's endeavors. But, as the PAO Line expanded even further, more money was needed. Luckily, the Line's reputation began to spread, helped in part by the many men who'd returned to England thanks to their efforts. One operative managed to get to the British Embassy in Switzerland and brought back toothpaste tubes stuffed full with tightly rolled francs, though it was not near enough.

Now that she was working mostly with Guérisse, Nancy barely ever saw Lieutenant Garrow, except for those few occasions when he needed help getting money or rationing cards.

One afternoon, as Nancy returned home from yet another excursion to Madame Sainson's in Montpellier, Claire told her that she had visitors.

"What kind of visitors?" Nancy asked warily. Claire knew even less than Henri about her mistress's new duties, but Nancy knew the maid could be trusted.

"Lieutenant Garrow and an associate. But," Claire leaned in closer to whisper, "I don't like the looks of this new man."

"I'm sure he's fine. Garrow would never bring anyone over who wasn't on the up and up."

But when Nancy entered the living room, she was shocked to see a man with slicked-back dark hair and a toothbrush mustache. For a moment, she thought it was Hitler himself who'd made himself comfortable in Picon's favorite chair. Picon, looking defeated, lay on the floor, his gaze locked on the strange man.

"Nancy," Garrow stood up from the couch. "This is Paul Cole, one of our associates."

Though the man didn't stand, on closer inspection, she could see he was taller than Hitler and his mustache extended further on both sides of his frowning mouth.

"I'd offer you something to drink, but I can see you've helped yourself." Nancy nodded at the glass in the man's hand before her eyes traveled to the open bottle on the bar. "Is that the whisky my husband was saving for when the Allies declare victory?"

"I don't know anything about that. But considering the circumstances, you might as well enjoy it while you can." Cole took a long sip. "And it's mighty fine whisky indeed."

Nancy's glare moved to Garrow, who cleared his throat. "Perhaps this isn't the best time. You look tired. Have you just come back from a mission?"

For some reason, she didn't feel comfortable discussing the matter in front of Cole, whose personality seemed as dark as his hair. "I *am* tired. Perhaps we could do this another time, just you and me." Her words left no room for argument.

Cole stood and drained his glass before leaving the room.

"You were a bit rude," Garrow admonished after the front door had slammed shut.

"I don't care. I don't like that man and hope to never see him again."

"That man, Paul, is the head of our operations in Occupied France and sticks his neck out in front of the worst of the villains to help us."

"I don't care," Nancy repeated.

"If that's how you feel, I won't bring him around again." Garrow put his hat on, the one Nancy had given him for Christmas. "I came here to ask you for something, but I can tell now is not the time."

"If it's money for his operations, then don't bother asking."

"Goodbye, Nancy," Garrow said before letting himself out.

When she recounted her afternoon to Henri, his face took on the look of amusement it usually did whenever he heard about his wife's antics.

"Do you think I was in the wrong?" she asked.

"Never. I trust your instincts. It's one of the reasons I'm letting you do what you do."

"Oh, you're *letting* me? I wasn't aware that you had a choice."

His grin grew larger. "I wasn't either, actually." He stretched his arms as he stood to check the bar. "Perhaps this Cole was right and this whisky should be drunk now."

"You don't want to wait for a victory anymore?"

He poured some of the whisky into two glasses. "It doesn't look like one is coming anytime soon, does it?" He passed her a glass. "Since it looks like you'll need to extend your efforts even further if we want that victory, you'd better drink up now."

∼

It turned out that Nancy had been right about Cole. The next time Garrow visited her flat, he didn't need to say anything—the dejected look on his face was enough admittance that he'd greatly misjudged the man.

"What happened?" Nancy asked, gesturing for him to sit down in the place of honor—Picon's leather chair.

He took his customary spot on the couch instead. "Cole was supposed to organize a prison escape in Lille, but he was seen around that time in Paris, with a woman. Apparently she is one of his many mistresses."

Nancy felt the need to placate her friend. "I suppose he thought he deserved to take some time off."

Garrow shook his head. "That's not the worst of it. The money meant for the escape in Lille also never made it there. And I don't think that's the first time something like that has happened."

She attempted a note of surprise. "Cole's been pilfering money from the PAO Line?"

"It certainly seems that way. I sent Guérisse to the Occupied Zone to find Cole and bring him back to Marseille to account for his actions."

"Is there anything I can do?"

Garrow shot her an odd sort of half-smile. "Not right now. I didn't even come to ask for money this time. I just wanted to let you know you were spot on about Cole and I should have listened to you."

For once, Nancy didn't gloat over being right. After fetching Garrow a drink, she let him pour his heart out about his guilt for the botched prison escape.

Nancy once again immersed herself in her work with the Line and nearly forgot about the Cole incident. Until the evening there was an abrupt pounding at the door.

She exchanged a look with Henri before rising from her chair.

"Are you expecting someone?" Henri's attempt at humor fell flat, and the smile he held was forced.

"No."

"Nannie, let me—" But by the time Henri had gotten up, Nancy had already opened the door.

The caller was Guérisse. "I have bad news," he declared as he strolled into the flat. "Lieutenant Garrow's been arrested."

Nancy's knees felt weak and she leaned on a table for support. "Arrested? Was it Cole?"

"Paul Cole? What do you know about him?"

With a shaking hand, she gestured toward the living room. Guérisse took Picon's chair while Henri sat on the couch, as close to his wife as possible.

Nancy wasted no time. "What happened?"

Guérisse shook his head. "I don't have many details—it's one of those things that sort of leaked its way through the Line. And he isn't the only one in prison; several other members of the network were taken into custody as well."

"Where is Garrow now?"

"Last I heard, he was in solitary confinement at Fort Saint-Nicolas."

"At least he's nearby." The fort stood at the entrance of the Vieux Port. "What are the plans for breaking him out?" As it was several centuries old, Nancy figured it wouldn't be too hard to rescue Garrow.

Henri had clearly had enough. "Break him out? Nannie, you have to stop this nonsense—if it wasn't clear before, this wave of arrests should convince you that this stuff is dangerous. You have to lie low, at least for a little while."

Nancy was about to voice her protest when Guérisse cut her off. "I agree with Henri. Just like you can't have freedom without sacrifice, *on ne saurait faire une omelette sans casser des œufs.* You need to break eggs to make an omelette. Consider the arrests to be our broken eggs."

"And Garrow is our lamb up for slaughter?" Nancy demanded.

"For now, at least," Guérisse replied in a grim tone. He leaned forward, his elbows on his knees. "You mentioned Paul Cole earlier. How do you know him?"

Nancy relayed the incident with the whiskey and then Garrow's later reaction.

Guérisse sat back. "I demanded that Cole explain the missing funds, but he denied everything. Then, when an agent arrived from Lille with proof that it was Cole stealing the money, we confronted him at a house belonging to a member of the PAO Line. Cole finally admitted to his thievery, and then we locked him into a bathroom while we decided what to do with him." The usually unflappable Guérisse faltered.

"Let me guess," Nancy prompted him. "Cole left out the window."

"It was a really small window—I didn't think it was possible he could fit through, but I clearly underestimated him."

"You wouldn't be the first one," Nancy told him wryly.

"This Cole character…" Henri rubbed the back of his head in thought. "Is it possible he's responsible for the arrests?"

Nancy and Guérisse exchanged glances. "It's definitely a possibility," Guérisse replied.

"And he knows where Nancy lives."

This time Guérisse was less hesitant. "Apparently."

Henri fidgeted in his seat, clearly agitated. And once again, it was all Nancy's fault. A double-agent in the Line jeopardized everyone, including Henri. "I guess it really is time to lie low," Nancy stated.

'Lying low' for Nancy did not translate into quitting her work altogether, it just meant, for the time being, she couldn't have any escaped airmen or members of the Line at her and Henri's flat. She still transferred men in and out of the rented apartment on the Rue de l'Évêché, however.

A week after Garrow's arrest, she met Guérisse in the back of a nearby café, only steps away from the Vieux Port and Fort Saint-Nicolas, where Garrow was being held.

"What's the latest on Lieutenant Garrow?" Nancy asked in a low voice.

Guérisse ran a hand over his neatly slicked-back hair. "I don't know what you mean."

"Surely there are now plans to get him out of prison."

"Not that I'm aware of. We're still working on trying to contain the Cole situation, warning his associates in Lille and such."

"But it was Garrow's idea to start this network in the first place."

Guérisse merely shrugged. As he rose to leave, Nancy added 'rescue Lieutenant Garrow' to her already extensive list of things to do.

As soon as she got back, Nancy wrote a letter to Garrow in which she 'reminded' him that she was the daughter of his mother's sister and that she will try her best to 'obtain permission to visit you.' Knowing that all letters to Garrow would be opened and read before they were delivered to him, she was sure the authorities would interpret the message in the way she intended—that the Scottish Ian Garrow and the 'Frenchwoman' Madame Fiocca were first cousins.

Henri arrived home for lunch to find Nancy seated at her desk, in the process of sealing the letter. He watched as she addressed it care of Fort Saint-Nicolas.

"What are you up to now, Nannie?"

"I'm going to try to visit Ian Garrow."

"Nannie, I have to draw the line somewhere." Henri put his hand over hers. "That's far too risky, even for you."

She hesitated. She was well aware that her every move put her husband in more danger, but still… there were some things that couldn't be compromised. "I have to do what I can to help. Imagine if it were me—or worse yet, you—in jail. Wouldn't you want our friends to try to do everything they could to get you out?"

"I thought you were talking about visiting him, not making plans for a jailbreak."

"For now, it's just a visit…"

"Although I still have my reservations, I know you won't

listen anyway." He reached out his arm to help her up. "Remember, you will always have my support for anything you need. Now, what's for lunch?"

After lunch, Nancy took the letter to the fort and demanded an audience with the military officer in charge. He refused to let her see Garrow, but, after much discussion, he consented to letting Nancy send food parcels to him three times a week via a government official whom Henri had known before the war.

Still, Nancy didn't give up on the possibility of seeing Garrow face to face and started a relentless letter campaign to the military officer, writing twice a day for nearly a week. Finally, probably because he was tired of seeing Nancy's handwritten address on the envelope, the officer finally gave his approval to let her visit.

As Nancy approached Fort Saint-Nicolas, the looming structure cast a formidable shadow over the harbor. Directly across the entrance to the Vieux Port on the north side was Fort Saint-Jean, where Ian Garrow had initially been held under less stricter circumstances. Both structures, which once served as guardians of the port, were now grim reminders of the Germans' occupation.

The entrance to Fort Saint-Nicolas was barricaded with barbed wire while armed soldiers stood at regular intervals.

Nancy's heartbeat quickened as she stopped at the first checkpoint where a stern-faced guard demanded her papers. She handed over her identity card and the letter from the military officer with as steady a hand as she could manage. "I have written permission from the commandant to visit my cousin."

The guard's gaze swept over her and then turned to the papers. He seemed to examine them for longer than necessary, and then asked, "What is the purpose of your visit?"

"Just a social one. We haven't seen each other in a long time."

He seemed ready to deny her, but that would be disobeying orders from a higher command, so he finally waved her on. She could feel his eyes on her back as she walked through the gate.

Once the outer world had faded behind the thick stone walls of the fortress, the air was much colder. Another guard who communicated solely in grunts led her down a series of dimly lit corridors. The only light coming from flickering bulbs that cast shadows against the damp stone. Another guard passed and behind him were two prisoners, their wrists shackled, their frail bodies appearing as if they would collapse under the weight of their chains.

The guard brought her to a small room, barren except for a plain table and two chairs. Arms crossed, he positioned himself at the doorway as Nancy took a seat in one of the chairs. After a few minutes of silence, the door opened and Garrow was brought into the room.

A wave of sorrow swept over Nancy as she watched the once-dignified man drag his chains along the floorboards. His once-athletic figure was gaunt and his cheeks were sunken, though his pallid skin looked freshly scrubbed, as if he wanted to make himself as presentable as possible.

"You're so thin!" Nancy couldn't help exclaiming out loud. "What happened to the food I had delivered?"

"Food?" Garrow's face twisted in confusion. "Clearly I haven't been given any food outside of the horrible stuff they give us here."

"Never mind that, we've got to get you out of here." She said this in a loud voice, not caring who overheard her.

The guard at the door grunted audibly as Garrow shook his head. "I've lost my appeal. They're transferring me to Mauzac in the Dordogne."

Nancy found it difficult to hold back tears. She reached out to touch Garrow's hand, carefully avoiding the shackles on his wrist.

The guard grunted again in protest over the contact, and then Garrow's guard came over to roughly grab his arm. Clearly their time was up.

As Nancy was escorted back through the corridors, her steps felt heavy. The prison in the Dordogne might just be a stopping point on the way to Germany. *If I don't save Garrow, he will end up in one of Hitler's internment camps.* Or maybe even suffer a worse fate.

Exiting the fortress, the daylight seemed blinding. Under the watchful gaze of the exterior guards, Nancy took a moment to compose herself.

Once her heartbeat had somewhat steadied, she headed back to the Canebière. Her steps were a bit lighter this time since Nancy had come up with a plan for what might be her most critical rescue operation yet.

Nancy met with Guérisse the next day at Monsieur's Brisbois's butcher shop. Since the day Garrow had warned that Guérisse was all business, she didn't usually bother with small talk. That day, however, he looked so worn down that she had to ask how he was.

"Not good," Guérisse replied grimly. "There have been dozens of arrests—no one you know or need to know about, of course. I blame Cole; I hear he's working with the Abwehr now."

The Abwehr was a German secret service organization, similar to the Gestapo, that was tasked with monitoring and suppressing Resistance activities. If Cole was indeed associated with them, then it wasn't a stretch to think that he was giving up names of people working the PAO Line.

Nancy rubbed her forehead. "Well, on that note, tell me what you know about a prison in Mauzac."

"It's probably one of the worst of the Vichy prison camps, if not *the* worst." Guérisse sighed heavily. "Does this have to do with Garrow?"

She nodded. "They're transferring him there soon."

"It's normally reserved for those French prisoners facing either life sentences or…" he hesitated before finishing, "execution."

She winced at the word. "We have to get Garrow out now then."

"Now is not the time…" he stopped short when he saw the look on Nancy's face. "I will look into Mauzac."

Monsieur Brisbois suddenly appeared beside them, wiping his hands on his apron. "I'm sorry, I couldn't help overhearing you speak about Mauzac. Is someone from the network in there?"

Nancy nodded.

"I think I can be of some help. A prisoner from there came through the Line a few weeks ago. They'd been sentenced to death and mentioned that the only way they'd been able to get out was by bribing a guard."

"Do you know who this guard is?" Nancy asked.

"No. I don't know too much about the prisoner, either." Monsieur Brisbois glanced at Guérisse. "I'm sorry for breaking the rules, but this escaped prisoner was rather chatty. I think he just wanted to tell his story to someone."

"Don't worry about it." Guérisse turned to Nancy. "If we could figure out who this guard is, we could offer a large sum of money for him to help Garrow as well."

"Would this money be supplied by Henri?"

"Some of it. But I've been in contact with men from London lately. I'm sure I could convince them to foot a portion of the bill, given all that Garrow has done for their countrymen, especially their airmen."

Nancy managed a small smile. "Sounds like a plan. I'll go to Mauzac and see if I can get an idea of who this guard might be."

CHAPTER 12

NOVEMBER 1941

*I*n mid-November, Nancy left for Mauzac, a charming village known for its picturesque landscape, which also happened to be home to the Vichy prison camp where Lieutenant Garrow had been transferred. It was not an easy journey—she had to get up at the crack of dawn to board the Bordeaux train bound for Agen, then switch to the Périgueux train, and finally connect to the Sarlat-Bergerac line. Henri, of course, had been against the idea of her visiting Mauzac from the beginning, but still made arrangements for her, including reserving her seats on the various different trains.

Her hotel was only a short walk from the 17th-century prison which once housed common criminals but had been repurposed to confine a different class of tenant. In stark contrast to the stone prison's ivy-covered façade, the newly installed barbed wire fences gleamed in the sunlight, while guard towers loomed above large metal searchlights.

As she drew closer, she could make out the gaunt figure of Garrow standing behind the barbed wire. His lips tightened as he recognized her. "Nancy, is that really you?"

"Of course it is, Cousin," she said in her loudest voice. She wasn't sure who the 'friendly' guard was, or if he was even in hearing range, but she figured it couldn't hurt to let any of them know of her supposed relationship with Garrow. She looked around, but the guards standing nearest to them kept their eyes straight ahead. Clearly they were not going to let her inside.

Garrow got as close to the fence as he could without touching it. "What are you doing here?"

She lowered her voice. "Trying to get you out. Do you know if there is anybody we can bribe to help us?"

His thin face seemed even more skull-like as his eyes widened. "No. They are all tools of Vichy. I doubt any of them would deign to help someone like me."

She sighed. It was growing dark, and she hadn't gotten very far in her mission, but at least she could see that Garrow was okay—still a stick with an even grayer pallor, but at least he was alive.

"Here." She slipped a small paper bag through the wire. It wasn't much, just a couple of crackers and some cheese, but at least it was something.

∽

The 1941 Christmas season in Marseille was a subdued affair. While the entry of America into the war was encouraging for those living under Hitler's jackboot, it also led to skyrocketing prices for the little food and fuel that hadn't yet been requisitioned by the Germans.

When Nancy called on the Ficetoles, she found that they too, once part of the elite of Marseille, had fallen into hardship.

"The only money to be made nowadays is on the black market," Nicole said bitterly as she served Nancy a cup of chicory coffee.

"That sounds like a decent idea." Nancy took a conciliatory sip, but the coffee, void of sugar and milk, was almost too bitter to swallow. "Why doesn't Claude get involved?"

Nicole shook her head. "Our car broke down, and besides, we can't afford petrol. Claude wanted to buy a horse and cart, but we don't have the money."

"I can see if Henri can help." Nancy set her nearly still-full cup down. "How are the children?"

"Not well." Nicole's eyes grew red. "These wartime rations are not enough for growing children."

"No." Nancy put a hand on Nicole's shoulder. "Let me see what I can do."

A few days later, Claude Ficetole became a member of the delivery service for the black market, complete with a cart and a horse that he named Picon II, in honor of Nancy's generosity.

Her pleasure at this was overshadowed by the fact that Ian Garrow was still in Mauzac. She couldn't help thinking about last Christmas, when she'd bought the homburg for him and mentioned this in her weekly letter.

Henri caught her posting it when he arrived home for lunch. "You don't love Garrow, do you?"

"Of course not," she replied, genuinely surprised at the question.

"Then why do you write to him so often?"

"You should have seen him—he's so skinny and sickly looking. If anyone I even remotely respected as much as him were in the same position, I would do something about it."

"You know that even writing to him puts you in danger."

And you, she silently filled in. Henri would never bring up endangering anyone else, but Nancy was well aware of how much he sacrificed just by being her husband. "I know."

He stared at her for a minute. "You know I'm not in favor of you going so far out of your way to help Garrow, but as always, I recognize that it's pointless to argue." He reached out to stroke her cheek. "Now, what does one have to do here to get an apéritif?"

In mid-December, Nancy had to visit their chalet in Névache. She had arranged with a farmer to sell her a black market pig for the holiday, which she figured would produce plenty of meat to share among the needy of Marseille, including the Ficetoles.

Dressed in a new ski suit, she arrived in Névache to find that the pig was even plumper than she had hoped.

The chalet was often used as a safehouse for the PAO Line, and soon enough, she was joined by four Frenchmen who had been ordered to work in a German munitions factory and were now on the run from the Vichy police. She arranged for them to accompany her on the bus from Névache to Briançon and help carry the suitcase into which she had packed nearly 45 kilograms of dead pig.

However, just before she was about to leave, the mayor of Névache, who was an old friend of the Fioccas, called on her to inform her that the Germans were going to form a roadblock on the road to Briançon.

The mayor tugged at his collar. "You should also know that

they had been asking around town about the young woman in the fancy outfit who rode the Névache bus alone."

"They're looking for me." It wasn't a question.

"Yes."

Nancy gestured toward the suitcase on the table. "It's because of my black-market pig, then." Neither the mayor nor the rest of the Névache villagers knew about her double life working the PAO Line.

"Yes, I suppose so."

"Well," she gave him a wide, fake smile. "I guess it wouldn't do to have them confiscate it, would it?"

Thankfully, the mayor agreed with her, and provided the four escapees with clothes so that they would appear as though they were farmers going to market. They took Nancy's pig suitcase and her regular bag with them while she made her way down the mountain with the mayor's skis. In this way, she was able to avoid the checkpoint altogether, not to mention make use of her new suit. The Germans were looking for a woman of her description, not four Frenchmen and a black market pig.

Nancy then hired a gasogene taxi to take them to Veynes. They coasted in on coal fumes just in time to board the Grenoble-Marseille express.

Understandably worn out after a day of skiing, traveling, and avoiding Germans, Nancy just about fell into her seat on the train. One of the men nodded as he deposited the suitcase in the luggage rack above her before moving on to another compartment.

As the ticket inspector passed by, he mentioned that Marseille had recently established a curfew.

"Curfew?" Nancy repeated. "Since when?"

"Yesterday, I guess," the inspector said over his shoulder as he moved down the line.

This definitely presented a problem: Henri wouldn't be able to meet her at the station, and as far as she was concerned, she and her four companions were now on separate journeys. She couldn't exactly go find them on the train and ask that they carry her bags back to her flat.

At the last stop before Marseille, a young man in civilian clothes sat beside her and tried to make conversation. His accent was perfect, but there was something about the way he eyed her up and down that made Nancy suspicious. As there was a Gestapo headquarters at Aix-en-Provence, it was highly likely that he was a German, or at least working for the Germans.

"Your outfit looks new," the man stated. "I didn't think the French cared much about their appearance nowadays."

Definitely not a Frenchman then. As she was on a train with four escapees and with nearly fifty kilograms of pig nestled into a suitcase above her head, there was really only one way to play this out. "Do you like it?" Nancy batted her eyelashes as she straightened her ski jacket.

"I do like it, very much. You are going to Marseille, no?"

When she nodded, he continued, "Do you live there?"

Cautious that he was trying to ferret information, Nancy nodded again.

He cleared his throat. "I don't suppose you'd like to meet again, perhaps for coffee? I know a place where you can still get decent stuff."

The only way to get good coffee from ingredients that didn't include grilled barley or chicory was off the black market. She was about to make an excuse when the train pulled into the Gare Saint-Charles. The platform was filled with police in uniform and other men trolling about in trench coats. *Oh no.* The excuse died on her tongue with the realization that she might need this man's help after all. "I would love to meet again."

She stood up and tried to pull down the pig suitcase, but it was far too heavy.

"Allow me," the man said. Nancy started to protest, but there was no way she could manage it by herself. Even the man, who had a burly, athletic build, was having trouble hefting it through the aisle. She took her smaller bag and followed him to the exit.

He was still wrestling with the suitcase as they entered the swarm on the platform and quickly attracted one of the policemen. "What's in there?" he asked, tapping at the suitcase with his baton.

"Just some old sweaters and things," Nancy answered. "It's mine."

He glanced at her dismissively before demanding her companion's papers.

"You don't need to see my papers." The man set the case down to whip out his wallet. The metallic badge he revealed was emblazoned with the eagle and swastika of the Third Reich, the words *'Geheime Staatspolizei'* glinting ominously beneath the emblem.

Nancy blinked. The man carrying her pig was a Gestapo officer. He clearly suspected that her suitcase was full of black market goods, but, she supposed, as a foreigner, he was probably also lonely and in need of companionship.

"Do you need a ride home?" the Gestapo officer asked after the policeman had strolled off.

She did, actually, but there was no way she'd let him know where she lived. She thought fast—Claude Ficetole's brother worked at the Hotel Terminus. It was usually a hotbed of Germans, but surely he could find her an empty room. "I'll be fine. I'll see you in a few days for our coffee."

"You can count on it."

Nancy let out an audible sigh of relief as he walked away, even though it meant she'd have to lug both the suitcase and her bag alone to the hotel.

The next morning, Henri's truck arrived at the Hotel Terminus, and Henri himself got out to help Nancy load her bags.

"What's in here?" he asked, lifting the suitcase.

"A pig. Trust me when I tell you it's a long story."

Claire, and sometimes Nancy, assembled tray upon tray of pork nibbles and pâté for their Christmas dinner. Most of the guests were, of course, downed airmen. Henri took this, and the pig story, in stride, though he did remark once again that he'd like to come home from work to not find a house full of men.

His gifts to Nancy, which he insisted on presenting in private, were a red embroidered pillow and two nightgowns made from silk fabric, one a pale blue and the other a vibrant pink. "I know it's not much, but since you've been having such trouble sleeping, I thought this might help."

They were indeed a bit economical compared to presents of Christmases past, but Nancy would cherish them as much as the rest, not the least because they came from Henri.

"Wait," he said with a grin. "There's one more." He dug into his back pocket and produced a crumpled piece of paper.

"What's this?" Nancy asked as she unfolded it. It appeared to be an ad stating, "Men Wanted."

"I saw it hanging outside the slaughterhouse and I couldn't help grabbing it down. I thought it was rather fitting, especially given the pig incident."

"Oh you." Nancy gave her husband a friendly swat.

The day after Christmas found Nancy back to work as pieces of cured *cochon* wrapped in cheesecloth were carried by PAO couriers to locations all over Southern France.

CHAPTER 13

AUGUST 1942

Throughout the spring and summer of 1942, as the Germans were making substantial gains in the Soviet Union and in North Africa, Nancy returned to Mauzac quite a few times to pass Garrow food parcels through the fence. She made a point of wearing her finest Chanel suit in order to showcase that she had the finances to bargain for Garrow's freedom, should the opportunity arise. Still, if this sympathetic guard existed, he wasn't making himself known.

The situation seemed to be deteriorating rapidly: rumors were flying that the Germans were going to invade the Free Zone, and that Garrow would soon be transferred to somewhere in Germany called Dachau to spend the next ten years doing forced labor, in which case she'd never be able to get him out.

Finally, one afternoon as she was returning to the village, a man on a bicycle passed her and she heard a clunk as a stone hit the ground near her feet. She looked down to see the stone was wrapped in paper. Feeling more optimistic than she had in a long time, she picked it up and placed it in her purse before nearly running back to her hotel room.

The paper contained instructions for her to meet someone at midnight on the railway bridge.

The optimism faded as quickly as it had come on. Midnight was long past curfew. *Was this a trap?*

Still, she had no choice but to try to find out if there was any way of negotiating Garrow's release.

At 11:30 p.m., Nancy managed to slip out of her hotel room. The village was enveloped in darkness, but she was somewhat familiar with the area due to all the trips she'd been making in the past few months. She knew the alleys that would keep her out of the sight of the local gendarmes, which was definitely an advantage since anyone caught outside during curfew hours could face arrest—or worse—especially if they were suspected of resistance activities. Or attempted bribery.

Nancy nestled herself in the shadow of a tree where she had a full view of the empty bridge and could hear the waves crashing below. She waited outside in the cold until 2:30 a.m., when she finally gave up. The person she was supposed to meet never materialized.

Having stayed up all night for nothing, Nancy was in a foul mood when she got on the train for Marseille the next morning. As usual, she was in the first-class compartment, but this time she had a man sitting on either side of her. To her left was a short, thin French soldier. To her right was a German officer dressed in that hateful grayish-green uniform.

Her foul mood now turned to downright rage. *What gives*

that man the right to sit in a first-class compartment, acting as if he didn't have a care in the world? She figured most people in her line of work wouldn't want to cause a scene and would go about their business or maybe even offer polite conversation. Not Nancy. Against her better judgment, she felt an irresistible urge to let the soldier know he was sitting next to an Anglophile.

She shrugged off her overcoat to reveal the kangaroo brooch she was wearing on her blouse: a token from a member of the Australian rugby team she'd helped through the PAO Line.

The officer paid no attention.

She then made a show of retrieving her book out of her bag, which was written in English, and put it on her lap, the title, *A Farewell to Arms*, on full display.

Still the German gave no reaction.

The ticket collector entered their cabin, and Nancy passed over her counterfeit papers. He examined hers and the German's without comment, but cleared his throat as he returned the French soldier's. "This cabin is for first-class passengers only. You have a third-class ticket."

"I'm sorry, monsieur," the little French soldier replied. "But you see, all of the third-class cars are full, and there are plenty of seats here."

The ticket collector was obviously about to tell the soldier to leave when Nancy spoke up. "How dare you command one of your own countrymen, and a soldier at that, to leave this car and go back to third-class while you allow this Boche to remain here undisturbed. Have you no heart? Have you no patriotism?"

"I have both a heart and patriotism." The ticket taker's gaze briefly flicked over to the German, who was pretending to not hear any of the conversation. "But I also have a job to do, and there are rules…"

"Fine," she snapped, grabbing her purse. "I shall pay the difference so the soldier can stay." She threw a handful of francs at him.

The ticket taker pocketed the money without counting it and moved on.

The French soldier smiled sheepishly at Nancy. "Thank you. I find these seats much more comfortable, anyway."

The German, mumbling something about cattle cars, climbed over them before strolling purposefully down the aisle.

Nancy moved her purse to his vacated seat as the French soldier chuckled.

As Henri always said, Nancy was 'not unlike a mule in her stubbornness' and so the next week found her returning to Mauzac. Her usual hotel room wasn't quite ready, so she decided to kill time in the local café. She was just digging into her sandwich when she felt someone come up behind her.

Her heart leaped into her throat when she realized the man was wearing the same uniform as the guards at the prison camp. Perhaps this was the 'friendly' guard at last. "Please sit down," she said through a mouthful of sandwich.

"Have I seen you here before?" the man asked as he waved a waiter over.

If this wasn't the right guard, she might be in deep trouble. She wiped her mouth before replying carefully, "Yes, I come here almost every weekend."

"To visit—"

"My cousin, Lieutenant Garrow." Deciding to take the chance, she looked down and shook her head. "I hate the fact that he is in prison." Now she looked up to meet the guard's eyes squarely. "And I would do anything to get him out."

"Ah." The guard leaned forward. "I might be able to arrange that."

Nancy sighed *finally* to herself. "For what price?"

"Five hundred thousand francs. And I need 50,000 of that as soon as possible."

"Is that all?" she asked, the sarcastic tone unmistakable. Fifty thousand francs was more than even Henri earned in a week. And, as she only had around 10,000 on her person, she'd have to get the money from her husband himself.

"Well, if that's the case…" The man rose to leave.

"Wait." To her relief, he sat back down. "If I were able to get you the money, how do you suppose we can get Lieutenant Garrow out of the camp?"

The guard gave her an oily grin. "Why, didn't I mention you'll also have to get a guard's uniform? In Garrow's size, of course," he declared as he stood. "You can find me at four o'clock at the edge of the railroad bridge. If you bring the money, we can make the arrangements."

As soon as the man had left, Nancy paid the bill and then headed to the post office to telegraph Henri.

Even in wartime conditions, the efficiency of the French Postal Service was unaffected and Nancy was able to pass off the 50,000 francs as planned.

The next day she set off for the prison camp to share the good news with Garrow. However, when she got to her usual spot next to the fence, a different guard, one she'd never seen before, told her to follow him through the gate and into the prison.

The inside of the building was almost as dilapidated as it looked outside, yet the office she ended up in was full of expensive furniture.

"Who are you?" she asked the man sitting behind the ornate maple desk.

"I am the prison commandant," the man replied in an accent that Nancy didn't recognize.

She was about to take a seat in an overstuffed armchair when the commandant cleared his throat and pointed to a hard wooden chair placed directly in front of his desk.

Feeling as if she were back in her school days, in trouble with the headmaster again, she sat. "Why am I here?"

The man lit a cigar. "I was told you received a considerable sum of money from Marseille yesterday. Forty thousand francs, to be exact."

Clearly someone at the post office was the informant—there was no way the guard could have known how much of the bribe Henri had given her.

She cast a haughty glance around the room. The sun shone in through a dusty window, revealing that the 'fine' furnishings were really just cheap knockoffs. "That amount may be what you would call 'considerable,' monsieur, but I assure you, it's a mere pittance for the Fioccas." She leaned forward. "I needed it to pay my bar bill at the inn."

"Bar bill?" He seemed momentarily stumped. "But..."

"Now," she gathered her Hermès purse before rising to her feet. "If you would show me to my cousin, Lieutenant Garrow."

"Of course, madame." The commandant lifted his phone and called for a guard.

CHAPTER 14

NOVEMBER 1942

Nancy was on the Agen train back to Marseille when a whole troop of *them* tromped down the aisle in their jackboots. Knowing something was desperately wrong, her heart thudded in time to their footfalls.

Eventually she came to the harrowing realization that the Nazis had invaded the Free Zone. The thought that the entire country was now under Nazi control sent a chill through her. A hush settled over the train, as, like Nancy, the rest of the passengers grappled with the weight of their new reality.

The ticket inspector, a different one than last time, stood at the front of the car, his eyes locked on the marching brigade. For lack of anything better to do, Nancy watched as the man's bottom lip began to tremble. A few moments later, as the train pulled into a station, the man's features tightened into a steely expression, as though he'd made some sort of inner decision.

Nancy echoed him and she sat straighter in her seat, steeling her spine and her spirit. Working with the Resistance was about to become even more dangerous, but if anything good could come out of the Germans invading the rest of France, it would be that more people rose in defiance, swelling the ranks of those who refused to bow to the invaders.

The next morning Henri was already at work when Claire entered the bedroom to tell her that there was a gendarme at the door. "Shall I tell him you are indisposed?" Claire asked worriedly.

"No." Nancy rose out of bed. "It probably has to do with Lieutenant Garrow's escape." She'd heard from Guérisse that the whole thing had gone off with barely a hitch. In a guard's uniform procured by Guérisse's men, Garrow had practically strolled out of the prison gates and into the awaiting car that Nancy had arranged.

She threw on a feathered robe and fluffed her hair before heading to the front door.

Claire had closed the door on the gendarme so Nancy opened it a crack. "Can I help you?"

"Are you Nancy Fiocca?"

"Yes."

The gendarme widened the door opening with his forearm. "Are you aware that a man named Garrow escaped from the Mauzac prison camp?"

It was clear from his intense stare that he was waiting for a reaction but Nancy refused to give him one. "Oh?"

"Do you know Lieutenant Garrow?"

"Of course I do," she snapped back. "He is my cousin." She decided to play friendly. "Would you like to come in for a drink?"

This obviously disconcerted the gendarme, but he accepted the invitation anyway.

"To tell you the truth, I'm quite pleased he escaped from prison," she announced as she opened a bottle of wine. It was early in the morning, but she figured the gendarme wouldn't mind a little drink while on duty.

She appeared to be right as he took a long gulp before asking, "Pleased?"

"Wouldn't you be if your cousin escaped a prison camp?"

He took another swig of wine. "I suppose I would." He held the glass up to the light. "Is this—"

"It's not black market, of course. It's from Monsieur Fiocca's private collection."

"I see." He drained his glass.

"Now, if you don't mind, I'm going to call my husband and tell him the good news."

The gendarme, who was obviously hoping for a refill, rose uncertainly. "The reason I'm here is to—"

"Tell me the good news about my cousin. I know, monsieur." She lifted the receiver and looked at him expectantly.

After a moment's hesitation, he tipped his cap at her. "*Au revoir*, madame."

As he walked toward the door, Nancy called Henri. "Hello darling, guess what?" Her voice was louder and more boisterous than necessary, mostly for the benefit of the gendarme, who was lingering at the door, but also because she heard a clicking sound in the receiver. "A very considerate gendarme just informed me that Cousin Ian has escaped from Mauzac."

Henri, like Nancy, must have assumed the clicking sound meant that the Gestapo were listening in. "Is that so?" he said, the surprise obvious in his voice.

Shaking his head, the gendarme finally left.

"Indeed," Nancy replied to Henri, her voice slightly quieter. "Can you believe it?"

"No."

"Well then, I'm sure you're busy at work, so I will talk to you later." After she hung up, she stared at the receiver for a while, wondering who had been listening in on the conversation.

Henri arrived home for lunch to find Nancy, a glass of wine in hand, attempting to ease her nerves by vigorously petting Picon.

Henri sat on the couch next to her and grabbed her hand. Picon, annoyed that the attention was off him, jumped down from Nancy's lap.

"What's wrong?" Henri asked, kissing her palm.

"The gendarmerie is obviously interested in what I've been up to. I can't help thinking that the next time I answer the door, it will be a Gestapo agent—they are swarming the south."

Henri sighed. "Now that Garrow is free, it might be time to let things settle a bit, and ease up on your activities."

She turned to face him. "I can't—now is the time to strike. The people of Marseille are finally realizing that the Nazis are their problem too, not just something for the north to deal with."

"That may be, but the Gestapo are getting closer to the PAO Line. I've heard talk about a woman they are calling the 'White Mouse'—they say she has a knack for disappearing just when they think they've got her in a corner."

"Who is the White Mouse? Not Andrée Borell—she fled to England a few months ago."

"It's not Andrée, Nancy. It's you. You are the White Mouse."

She grinned.

Henri started massaging the knots in her shoulders. "Now, don't let the fact that the Boches have given you a nickname go to your head. What it really means is that you are more in danger than ever."

She nestled into his embrace. "Don't you worry about me. I'll be fine."

"You're always fine." His hands kneaded her shoulders harder as he muttered under his breath, "until the day comes when you're not fine."

Nancy pretended not to hear him.

CHAPTER 15

JANUARY 1943

The arrival of the New Year brought little comfort to the people of Marseille, now that a grayish-green shadow in the form of the Wehrmacht had settled over what was once known as the Free Zone. Rumors were rife about local young men being sent to German work camps under the STO, or *Service du Travail Obligatoire*, a series of decrees further demonstrating the Vichy government's subservience to Hitler. Even worse was the founding of the Milice, a paramilitary organization founded to round up Jews and Resistance workers, the latter considering the Milice to be more dangerous than even the Gestapo because it was made up of native Frenchmen. These men not only had a thorough knowledge of the region, they were also well-acquainted with local residents, whom they encouraged to become collaborators and informants.

All of this gave the members of the PAO Line more reason to fear their neighbor than ever. Yet, as Nancy had predicted, the Line expanded considerably, probably beyond what was considered prudent, especially after what had happened with Paul Cole.

In late January, as Nancy made her rounds to her usual cafés, bars, and beauty salons—trying to keep up the façade of the flippant Madame Fiocca—she got the feeling she was being followed.

Indeed, as she stopped into Monsieur Brisbois's shop to pick up her latest messages, he leaned in close to her, his voice barely audible, "I would never want to scare you unnecessarily, but when you left yesterday, I saw a man in a black raincoat following you."

She felt a chill run down her spine. "Are you sure?"

He nodded. "Just be careful, Madame Fiocca."

Back on the street, Nancy became lost in her thoughts. The clicking sounds on the telephone were happening every time she made a call and Claire had told her yesterday that she had come upon an unfamiliar man standing just outside their apartment building who had asked for directions to the street adjacent to theirs. Clearly her phones were being tapped and the flat was probably being watched as well.

Nancy's journalist friends always used to tell her that she was born lucky. Had her luck finally run out? At any rate, it was evident that the situation was becoming dire, and she had to act soon to keep Henri, Claire, and herself out of danger.

When she broached the subject at dinner, Henri sighed heavily. "I'm glad you've finally come to the same conclusion."

"What conclusion is that?" she asked, swirling her wine glass.

"You have to leave Marseille."

Some of her wine spilled onto the table. "Leave Marseille?"

"Now."

She shook her head. "I won't leave you here to suffer whatever consequences I've racked up."

"And what is *your* plan?" Henri's tone became uncharacteristically angry. "Stay here and wait for the Milice or the Gestapo to come knocking at our door?"

She hung her head, once again feeling like a guilty schoolgirl. "No." This time when she met his gaze, there were tears in her eyes.

"Good." He sat back in his chair. "I want you to take the Line to Spain and then over the Pyrenees, and then, eventually to England."

He wanted her to escape by the same route she'd shown to so many others. "England? I thought you just wanted me to leave Marseille."

"England," he repeated firmly. "The Gestapo has a bigger network than the PAO Line and I don't think anywhere in France is safe for you right now."

"I'm not going without you."

Henri got up and came over to her. "You have to, at least for now. Consider it a strategic withdrawal—the kind any shrewd White Mouse would do. I have to wrap up a few things with my business before I join you." His lips turned up into the tiniest of smiles. "Someone has to earn the money to pay for all of your antics."

"But—"

"Just give me a few more weeks. I need to make sure the business is on a good footing and that my employees are looked after. The ones that are left, anyway," he added bitterly, for some of his employees had been Jews and had been forced to leave the factory.

Her heart felt as though it might tear in two, but Henri was right, as always. Even if he could leave with her, it would only put him in more danger.

He stroked her hair. "I want you to go tonight. Do you want me to contact Guérisse to help you get out?"

"No," she replied softly, knowing her fate had been sealed. "There's a safehouse in Toulouse. Guérisse moved his operations there after Garrow was transferred. I'll find him myself."

She laid out her clothes on her side of the bed as she packed. If only she could spend one more night safe in bed, Henri sleeping next to her. But reports of midnight arrests—where people had been dragged from their beds, never to return—had spread through the PAO Line, especially in those first weeks after Cole's betrayal had come to light.

As she piled some of her belongings into the trunk, she wondered if all her efforts had been worth it. But then she reminded herself of the hundreds of people she'd helped through the PAO Line and who were now safely in England or wherever their final destination had been. And even if she were indeed in hot water now, she felt that she wasn't quite done yet, that she hadn't yet accomplished enough for the cause. Especially since the Germans and the Milice had just yesterday begun rounding up Jews in the Vieux Port for deportation.

But for once I'll do what Henri has asked. Once all the dust had settled, she'd get right back to work.

As usual, Nancy overpacked. She had no idea what she needed or didn't need, so she filled a trunk full of her finest clothes and the two nightgowns Henri had given her. The plan was for Henri to bring the trunk with him to England. She used a much smaller bag for essentials, stuffing it with her best jewelry, including her gold bracelet, a jewel-encrusted watch, and a diamond brooch in the shape of a wire-haired terrier, which Henri, when he presented it, said looked just like Picon.

After careful thought, she slipped off her engagement and wedding rings and put them in the bag as well.

She gave the real Picon a final pat and hug before she met Henri in the hall. Grasping her hand as if he didn't want to let go, he walked her to the front door. "Remember Nannie, if you run into too much trouble, there is always the safety deposit box at the bank."

She dismissed that with a wave of her free hand—Henri's finances were the last thing on her mind. He sighed as he held up her ringless fingers.

"Just in case." She tried to smile as she patted her heavy purse. "The rings may be in here, but you'll always be in my heart."

He pulled on his own ring, but it was stuck fast on his finger. "I think it's safe for me to keep mine on."

"You better. You'll need it to keep the women away when I'm gone."

Picon, sensing that something was up, scratched at the bedroom door and yelped in a high pitch that Nancy had never heard before. "Make sure you find someplace safe for Picon to stay when you decide to join me."

"Nannie," Henri said in a soft voice. "I meant what I said when I told you I'll come to you soon."

"I know." Nancy couldn't stop the tears from falling. "You always mean what you say."

He wrapped his arms around her, and as he touched his wet cheek to hers, she knew that he was crying too. "Shall we meet in England then?"

She attempted to smile. "England for sure."

"All right then, my Nannie. Go now, and know that we will meet again someday."

"Someday," she echoed. "But please, Henri, make sure it is sooner rather than later."

Once on the street, she tried to walk away, but her feet felt leaden. She'd been putting on a brave face, pretending the threat had been one of her ruses, but now, confronted with the reality of being on the street alone, she was scared. As much danger as she'd put herself in all these months, their apartment on the Canebière had always been a safe haven, a place where she could be the old Nancy, basking in Henri's love. Now she was about to leave all of that.

She could have stayed there on the street for hours, just to be close to Henri, but a distant shout in German reminded her that she had to get out of Marseille as soon as possible. With that, she started off, clinging close to the shadows and refusing to look back.

CHAPTER 16

FEBRUARY 1943

*D*espite all her success in helping refugees reach England, it was becoming increasingly improbable that Nancy herself would be able to cross the Pyrenees. To get all the way through the PAO Line, one needed somewhat decent weather combined with good luck, but it appeared she'd run out of both. She attempted four times, and each time rain or the presence of German patrols—and, on one occasion, both—forced her to return to her decidedly shabby room at the Hôtel de Paris in Toulouse.

After the fourth failure, she was sitting on the train coming back from Perpignan, picturing how her journalist friends would laugh about Nancy's luck failing her for good, when the train came to an abrupt halt, jolting her and her fellow passengers forward. As she tried catching her breath, heavily armed policemen entered the train, their heavy boots thudding ominously on the floor of the train car. One of them shouted in broken French for everyone to get off the train and board the trucks stationed outside.

Run, a voice in Nancy's head screamed. But there was nothing she could do except join the line of passengers obeying orders.

A burly officer with a bright red scar running down his cheek herded Nancy's group toward an awaiting truck. As he turned his back to bark more orders, Nancy seized her chance. She leapt from the truck, her shoes hitting the gravel with a crunch, and dashed down a narrow side street.

Her lungs burning, she emerged onto the main road, only to find her path blocked by a throng of student protesters. Desperate, Nancy was trying to push through their nearly impassable barrier when a heavy hand clamped down on her shoulder.

A heavy dread settled in her still-burning chest. She turned slowly, coming face-to-face with the scarred officer, his expression that of a cat that had just snared a mouse. *A White Mouse.*

"You thought you could escape, mademoiselle?"

She almost snapped back, 'that's madame to you,' but then remembered she wasn't wearing her wedding rings.

As the officer tightened his grip, the world around Nancy spun and the voices of the protesters faded as the reality of her capture set in. He finally released the pressure on her shoulder only to shove the barrel of a pistol into her spine.

When she was back in the truck and sure no one was looking, she took a five pound British note out of her purse. It had been given to her as a souvenir by an Allied pilot who had signed it. Knowing its presence on her person would be hard to explain, she stuffed it into her mouth. The paper was rough and bitter, but she kept chewing until she was able to gulp it down her throat. The irony was that Henri always said she could eat money like no one else. She tried to console herself by imagining his laughter when she was finally able to tell him about this latest adventure.

The truck grumbled to a stop outside the bleak, imposing walls of the local jail. Scarface told Nancy to get out and follow him while the other train passengers queued up to have their papers examined.

This isn't good, she decided as she followed the officer into the jail and then down a gloomy corridor into a small room. Was she being singled out because they found out she was the White Mouse the Nazis had been searching for?

Scarface growled for her papers as another man entered the room. Meekly, she handed over her fake identity card, which gave her real name and address, although it stated she was born in Nice, not New Zealand.

The newcomer was massive, and, with his crooked nose and pocked face, exceedingly ugly. "Given that you reside in Marseille, why were you on a train traveling from Perpignan to Toulouse?" he barked in perfect French. Clearly this man was a native.

Why indeed? Not to escape France via the Pyrenees. "I was traveling with my husband on a business trip, but we got into a fight and he moved to another compartment."

The policeman cracked a knuckle on his giant hand. "You can't possibly expect me to believe that. You're not even wearing a ring. And we picked up everyone from the train."

Nancy grasped the arms of her chair. "Is he here, then? Have you seen my husband?"

"What's his name?"

This time she told the truth. "Henri Fiocca."

The policeman wrote a name down in his notebook before walking into the hallway, leaving only Scarface, who stood in the corner glaring at Nancy. She barely had time to steady her nerves before the policeman returned. "There's no one here with that name."

She faked a sigh of relief. "Well, maybe he escaped through the town. Some people did, you know, and got lost in the crowd of students. If you don't mind releasing me, I could meet up with him and he could take me back to Marseille."

"But you are in the middle of a domestic argument, don't you remember?"

She smiled at the policeman. "Getting arrested really does put things into perspective, doesn't it?"

"I don't know, I've never been arrested." The policeman snapped his notebook shut and stood. "I'm going to make some calls to Marseille and check out your story. In the meantime, you are going to spend the night here."

"But—"

"Good night, Madame Fiocca. If that is even your name."

She was taken to a small, dirty cell occupied by several other people. She had just claimed an upper bunk when Scarface told her to follow him back to the interrogation room.

Her initial interrogator had seated his burly body into a chair. "As I suspected, no one in Marseille has ever heard of anyone named Fiocca."

That comment almost made Nancy smile. Clearly this policeman had not called anyone in Henri's hometown. "Am I being accused of a crime here?"

"Someone blew up a cinema in Toulouse."

Nancy assumed it had been the Resistance, but not necessarily in the PAO Line. At any rate… "It wasn't me."

The policeman stood and folded his arms across his chest. "You are a prostitute, are you not?"

"Prostitute? Now wait a minute—"

Before she could finish, the policeman struck her across the face.

Shocked, Nancy held her hand to her stinging face as someone knocked on the door and another policeman, this one in a different uniform, stood in the doorway.

"Ah, Inspector Tremblay, come in." Her interrogator pointed at Nancy. "Do you recognize this woman?"

"Of course. We've picked her up from the streets in Lourdes several times."

Lourdes now? Nancy had never been to Lourdes. Clearly these men wanted to frame someone for the theater incident, and nothing she could say would convince them that she was not guilty.

So she decided not to say anything at all.

"Well?" the interrogator demanded. He slapped her again, but Nancy refused to cry out in pain.

"Forget it." Tremblay said. "She did this in Lourdes the last time we arrested her."

More than anything, she wanted to shout that he was a liar but knew it wouldn't do any good. She pressed her lips together tightly.

"Well." The interrogator came behind her and shoved her out of the chair. "Maybe after sleeping on it, you'll decide to talk."

Instead of taking her back to the cell, this time she was led to another small room, which she was told was the toilet room. The 'toilet' was really just a hole in the concrete floor and the whole area was covered with mold and smelled revolting. To make matters worse, a never-ending dripping sound echoed through the space.

Sick to her stomach, Nancy didn't want to even sit on the floor, let alone sleep there. She kicked some of the mold and other solid matter—she didn't stop to think what it could be—into the hole before finding the driest spot on the floor to sit on. The parts of her body that did not ache were numb and her cheek felt swollen and sore. She was too afraid of what invisible threats might be lurking around her to stretch her legs out, keeping her knees pulled into her chest. Today was a grueling day, but tomorrow would probably be even worse.

While Nancy had indeed been deceptive about her presence on the train, the police were trying to falsely implicate her in a crime she had not committed. If only they would actually call anyone in Marseille, they would know that at least she wasn't lying about her identity. And how dare that man from Lourdes mistake her for a prostitute? Her clothes may be wrinkled and dirty, but they were still finer than what most prostitutes could afford.

She was deep in thought when she heard keys jangle outside the toilet room. *Not again,* Nancy thought. She was too exhausted to endure another round of questioning.

The door opened and Nancy blinked against the light. A gendarme, much smaller than either Scarface or her interrogator, stood in the door. He pressed a finger to his lips before motioning for her to follow him.

He led her into a cramped office where he had laid out a tray of bread and tea. "It's just us two and the rest of the criminals in the building now. You can sleep here, in my office, with my coat as a blanket. I'll wake you in the morning to take you back."

"Thank you," Nancy said wholeheartedly, too tired to question why he was being so kind. She noted that he had lumped her in with the 'rest of the criminals,' but at least she had someplace warm and clean to sleep.

As morning dawned, the kindly gendarme awoke her just as he said and Nancy spent another hour in the toilet room before she was fetched for more interrogation.

This time, as an additional twist of cruelty, they withheld toilet breaks from her. Not that it made much difference given that they also refused to provide her with any food or water.

The interrogator was relentless in his conviction that she was both a common prostitute and the mastermind behind the theater bombing. Occasionally he would pepper his accusations with slaps or kicks.

At first, Nancy was able to ignore the pain, thinking only of Henri, but, as the hours dragged on, her resolve began to waver. Each blow became another reminder that Henri was far away and unable to rescue her this time.

In the early evening, after endless hours of being called a prostitute, and immediately following an especially hard kick to her shin, she imagined Henri's outrage at his wife being called *"une prostituée."* This brought back that familiar feeling of defiance and she finally spoke. "If you intend to falsely accuse me, then go ahead. Send me to one of your prison camps. But stop with these absurd inquiries and beatings. You call yourself a Frenchman, but you're worse than a Boche."

She expected this would anger the policeman even further, but his next question was delivered with more restraint. "Who else was on the train with you?"

"French people. I didn't know any of them."

"What class did you travel?"

"First, of course. I always travel first class."

She could have kicked herself for that answer, as it only invited him to ask where else she had traveled, but instead he declared, "French women don't travel first class without a hat. You don't wear a hat because you are a prostitute."

"Where have you been? French women don't wear hats anymore because the German officers' wives started wearing them, in an attempt to be considered *chic*." At this point, she'd gone the whole day without eating, and she could no longer contain her anger. "You clearly don't know anything about women's fashion—you must not have a woman in your life at all."

The interrogator slapped her one final time before calling for someone to take her back to the toilet room.

Thankfully, that night, around the same time, the kindly gendarme again came in and led her to his office.

Nancy miraculously managed to get a few hours of decent sleep. The next morning, after the gendarme had returned her to the toilet room, she gathered her wits for another grueling day. This time she decided she would just keep repeating "you're wrong," after every accusation.

As she was led out into the station lobby toward the little room, she was surprised to note the tall frame of Albert Guérisse standing next to her stone-faced interrogator.

Instead of being pleased to see a familiar face, she was crestfallen—his presence at the jail could only mean that the PAO Line had once again been compromised. Most likely even obliterated with Garrow now in England and Guérisse having obviously been arrested.

Since Nancy had vehemently denied having any part in the

Resistance, she pretended not to know the namesake of the PAO Line and tried to walk past him.

Guérisse clearly had no such qualms and pulled at her arm before giving her a wide grin. "It's good to see you, Nancy."

She tried to shrug him off, but, still holding her arm, he leaned in to whisper into her ear, "Give us a smile, you fool—I told them you were my mistress."

Her heart thumping, she tried to raise her lips into the semblance of a smile.

Less than an hour later, Nancy was free to go and found herself walking out of the station on Guérisse's arm.

"Okay," she said as soon as they got far enough away. "Tell me what is going on."

"We heard that you had been caught, but, after a day or so of expecting the axe to fall, we realized that you didn't betray anyone."

"Did you really think I would talk?"

His grin was back. "I didn't think so, but some people on the Line—who don't know you, of course—thought you might."

Nancy decided to ignore that statement. "But how did you—"

"I told them I was a member of the Milice, and a personal friend of Laval himself. I knew your papers had your real name, so I told them you were my mistress and that Henri was still in Marseille. I told them to call the station in Marseille to ask about Henri, and they did."

"They told me they did that days ago."

"They were obviously lying about that. We're lucky they were the type of policemen who appreciated a good mistress story… not to mention happy to meet friends of Laval's."

Laval was Marshal Pétain's vice-president and, in Nancy's eyes, another collaborator, like all members of the Vichy government. "Didn't they try to verify with Laval himself about your supposed friendship?"

"They did, but one of my contacts told me he's in Berlin and can't be reached."

Nancy shook her head. "I appreciate the effort, but still, you shouldn't have attempted it. What if they took you in too? The whole Line would have collapsed…"

"I know. But, I get to make the decisions." He clamped her on the shoulder. "We all know you would have done the same for me. Trust me when I say I think this was worth it."

CHAPTER 17

FEBRUARY 1943

While Nancy tried to figure out her next move, Guérisse arranged for her to stay with Françoise Dissard, a spinster in her sixties whose main hobbies were chain-smoking cigarettes and hating the Boches. As she declared as much to Nancy the first time they'd met, Nancy knew they were destined to be great friends, though she would never tell Françoise that her graying braids made her look like an old-fashioned German woman.

Thankfully for Nancy, another one of Françoise's hobbies was cooking. As she bustled around in the kitchen, Françoise explained that her nephew, who ate like a horse, used to live with her, but was now in a German work camp.

"Hence your hatred for the Boches," Nancy commented wryly.

Françoise stuck her head out of the kitchen, her chipped teeth grasping a bamboo cigarette holder. "Oh, I've hated them since before the Great War, but I suppose that explains why I go through three times the cigarettes I used to."

As wonderful smells—accompanied by the stench of tobacco, of course—filled the apartment, Nancy's gaze settled on Françoise's telephone sitting squatly on the table next to the couch. It had taken on a grimy, discolored appearance, the silver dialing mechanism marred by the cigarette tar that always coated her hostess's fingers. *One call couldn't hurt.* Just one call to Henri. She wouldn't tell him anything—in fact, she would hang up as soon as she heard his voice. She wondered if he'd gotten wind of her arrest or any of the prostitute accusations.

Nancy had to physically sit on her hands to prevent herself from dialing. One call might really hurt both of them. She would just have to wait for him to keep his promise to meet her in England. If she could only get to England herself.

Guérisse assured Nancy that they were going to make another attempt in a few days. Françoise, for her part, had other plans and asked Nancy if she could delay her Pyrenees bid because she was helping to assist the escape of ten Allied prisoners from Castres prison. "And…" she said, lighting yet another cigarette, "I was hoping you would help them get to England."

"You're talking about a prison breakout."

Françoise blew her smoke into a ring. "That's right."

Nancy just shook her head. She would have done the same thing, and had, in fact, half a dozen times before, though, from what she could tell, she had used infinitely more resources. "How can I help?"

"I think the escape itself is arranged—a guard, who has been paid off quite well, will give his companions a sleeping draught disguised in a good bottle of wine. The guard will take the keys, and *voilà,* the men can walk out."

To Nancy, it seemed so ridiculous that it might just work. After all, the plan to get Garrow out had been just as simple.

"They'll be coming here, of course," Françoise continued. "I'll cook, but I'll need you to ensure their clothes are clean for traveling." She blew out another ring of smoke. "Laundry was never my thing."

Nancy—knowing that the men could never travel about in soiled clothing, for the Gestapo kept an eye out for people who looked as though they had slept on the street—agreed.

The plan indeed went down without a hitch, and soon the men were in Françoise's apartment. Nancy was surprised to see a member of the PAO Line, Gaston—who had been arrested around the same time as Garrow—among the men.

"Was Cole the reason you got picked up?" Nancy asked, handing him a blanket.

"Cole?" Gaston asked, confused. "No. It was because the Germans were waiting for us during a parachute drop."

She explained the Cole situation, including what had happened with Garrow, as she distributed the rest of the blankets.

Gaston rubbed his forehead. "I did wonder how the Boches knew about the drop. Poor Lieutenant Garrow."

"What are these for?" one of the other men asked in an American accent, holding up the blanket.

It was Nancy's first experience with an American, though now that the United States had entered the war, it was inevitable that there would be more U.S. airmen appearing in France. She filled them in on the laundry situation—the blankets were for them to wrap their bodies in.

"How long will it take to clean the clothes?" Gaston asked, smoothing down his mud-covered trousers.

"A day or two, at least, to scrub them," Nancy replied. "But drying them will take the longest. I can't exactly hang ten sets of male clothing out on the line in broad daylight. In the meantime, be sure to talk in whispers, and, whatever you do, only flush the toilet when necessary."

In the end, it took Nancy three days of bending over a washbasin, scrubbing at the clothes with Françoise's boiled-down lye soap, before their clothes were finally ready to be hung up at night. The men occupied themselves with playing cards, naked except for their blankets. From their anxious looks every time someone knocked on the door, they also seemed to be waiting for the Gestapo to swoop in. Françoise was clearly not nearly as concerned and spent her time chain-smoking, occasionally moving her bamboo holder to sip on coffee from the side of her mouth.

Finally, they had everything ready to move out. As the Milice had started closely monitoring the 'leaky' Spanish border, Guérisse was to accompany them on the train to the Pyrenees to see if he could do anything to help Nancy get through this time.

It was best to travel in smaller groups, so Nancy paid for three first-class tickets for herself, Guérisse, and Gaston while the others scattered into different cars on the same train.

Wanting to ensure she looked the part, Nancy was dressed in a stylish navy-blue dress, her camel-hair coat, silk stockings, and, of course, no hat. Hoping that she was finally about to leave France, she also had the jewelry Henri had given her hidden in the lining of her purse. These items, along with the cash tucked into the cups of her bra, represented the last remnants of her former lavish life in Marseille.

They hadn't gone very far when the conductor, his face pale, burst into the compartment to announce in a tense voice that a German search party was about to board the train.

Not again. Nancy cast a bewildered look at Guérisse as the steady rhythm of the train faltered.

"We're going to have to jump," he told her, the calm of his tone contrasting the chaos erupting around them. He pointed out the window. "We'll meet at the top of that large hill to the south of us."

She nodded and stood as Gaston wrenched the window open. Though the train had put on its brakes, the moonlight revealed that the landscape was still moving past at a swift pace.

"Ladies first."

Nancy stood in front of the window as the wind whipped her face. Without another thought, she leapt from the train.

Her natural reaction was to put her hands out and execute a roll as soon as she hit the ground. Breathing heavily, she patted her limbs, making sure she was in one piece before she stood.

The rat-a-tat-tat of machine guns reminded her to start for the hill Guérisse had indicated. As the bullets whizzed past her, Nancy ran faster than she ever had in her life. She wanted to close her eyes and pretend she was somewhere else, but the ground was covered with vines and she had to focus to keep from tripping.

Finally she was out of range of the bullets, and could slow her pace. She made her way up the hill, her cut-up ankles dripping blood and her calves feeling as though they were on fire.

As she neared the summit and realized she was the first one there, she sank down into the cover of a tree.

Gaston arrived first. "Where is everyone?"

"I don't know," Nancy replied, still out of breath.

"How did you get here so quickly?"

She mustered a smile. "I suppose there's nothing more motivating than having machine guns firing at your arse."

He nodded. "You stay here, I'm going to double back and see if I can find any of the others."

Nancy was too tired to argue. She leaned back against the trees and closed her eyes. Subconsciously, she could hear footsteps and the sounds of people making their way through the vineyard, but she told herself it was simply Gaston searching for the rest of the group.

Her eyes flew open when she heard the unmistakable sound of someone approaching. "It's me, Nancy," Guérisse called out. He was still catching his breath when the American joined them, and soon the rest of the group was there. Except Gaston.

Nancy asked if anyone had seen the burly Resistance man. One by one, they all shook their heads.

"We'll find him," Guérisse said, though his tone sounded doubtful. "In the meantime, we have to find a better place to spend the night."

"Wait," Nancy said, panic rising in her chest. "My purse. I must have dropped it. We have to go look for it."

"Nancy." Guérisse put her hand on her shoulder. "You know that we can't."

"But my identity card and passport. My jewelry." *My wedding ring.*

"We can get you a new card. As for your jewelry," he dropped his hand. "You'll just have to ask Henri to buy you some more after the war."

. . .

Unfortunately, Gaston never returned, and the rest of them endured two bitterly cold nights in an abandoned barn, huddling close to each other in an attempt to stave off the chill. The overwhelming smell of pine brought Nancy back to the time she'd run away from home. She'd been a head-strong teenager, unable to live under her mother's strict rules any longer and her very understanding sister-in-law had let her stay with her. When the police had come looking for her and asked to search the house, Nancy had hidden under the wooden porch. It was after that she'd moved to Sydney to become a nurse.

After nearly three days without anything to eat or drink, the urgent need for sustenance and better shelter prompted Guérisse to lead them to a safehouse in Canet-Plage, just east of Perpignan. They were all filthy, so taking a train was out of the question and Nancy had to trek a dozen miles in her heels since her more suitable walking shoes had been in her bag.

They moved under the cloak of night, partly, of course, because it was dark, but also because the frigid evening temperatures made it unbearable to stop anywhere for long. It took them three nights to travel, and by the time they reached the safehouse, Nancy's feet were coated in blisters, and her body was covered in scabies from the necessity of having to sleep in pig pens during the day. Seeking medical help in the unfamiliar town was not an option, so she endured the humiliation of standing in a basin while the American scrubbed her with a wire brush soaked in disinfectant.

At this point, all of their clothing was in tatters, so Guérisse asked one of his contacts to get them more clothes, hopefully ones that were warm enough to make another run for the Pyrenees.

Unfortunately, with the rationing, any sort of clothing was in short supply. Nancy was given what resembled a shapeless sack with uneven holes cut out for the arm and leg openings. It was no Chanel, but at least it was free of dirt and didn't smell like pig manure.

Lacking suitable attire, and, quite frankly, the stamina to make another run for the Pyrenees, the group had no other option but to board a train back to Françoise's in Toulouse.

Nancy, by then, had convinced herself that there was another leak in the PAO Line—why else had they been stopped by Milice or German checks almost every time they tried to make their escape?

She confessed as much to Françoise, who was in complete agreement and encouraged her to inform Guérisse. As she knew Guérisse would take heavy convincing, Nancy drank a couple of glasses of brandy before approaching him.

"We were betrayed," Nancy told him bluntly.

"Not possible," he replied. "Our security protocols are too tight."

She glanced at Françoise, who motioned for her to keep going. "How else did the Germans know to check the train?" Nancy demanded. "And why were they shooting at us?"

"They would shoot at anyone if they knew they were running from a checkpoint."

"But you have to admit, it can't be a coincidence that almost every train I took was boarded by Germans."

"If there was a leak, I suppose that would make sense, but that's a big *if*."

"If, if, if," Nancy repeated disdainfully. "If my aunt had *un zizi*, she would be my uncle."

At that, Françoise burst into laughter, causing her bamboo cigarette holder to fall onto the carpet. She twisted her foot over the embers and the tiny hole in the rug before picking up the holder and replacing it in her mouth.

Although he'd known Nancy for over a year, Guérisse still seemed shocked at her foul language. "Even so…" He cleared his throat and started again. "At any rate, I suppose it'd be best to get you to England as soon as we can get you a new ID card. In the meantime, I have a meeting tomorrow morning with Roger le Neveu. He indicated his interest in meeting with you too, Nancy."

"Me? I'm not going dressed like this," she said, indicating the sack of a dress she was wearing.

"Don't worry, I have no intention of bringing you." He flashed her a lopsided grin. "For security reasons, of course."

"Right." Nancy rose. "Well, good luck then. Let me know how it goes."

CHAPTER 18

MARCH 1943

Guérisse never returned from his meeting with Roger le Neveu. A waiter at the café was a contact of Françoise's, and he told her and Nancy what had happened.

"Guérisse had just sat down and was asking le Neveu if he thought there was a mole in the PAO Line leaking information to the Gestapo. Le Neveu replied that he knew the man very well, and suddenly there was another man in a black raincoat pointing a gun into Guérisse's back," the source recounted.

After Nancy got over her initial outrage at Guérisse's arrest, she had to admit that it all fit into place now. Her suspicions had been confirmed, but that offered no solace to Guérisse, who was surely now languishing in a prison somewhere. She knew him well enough to know that he would rather undergo the worst torments the Gestapo had to offer than give up any names.

Of course she wanted to rescue him, partly to repay him for helping her, but even Nancy knew her time was running short.

Guérisse himself had said that this Roger le Neveu wanted to meet her. It was only a matter of time before he came for the rest of the PAO Line. Her only option was to make another play for England.

Françoise had taken Nancy's shoes in for repair and arranged for a new identity card, but was still in the process of drying the sack of a dress. As Françoise was much shorter and frailer than Nancy, she couldn't loan her any clothes other than a shabby overcoat, which hung awkwardly on Nancy, stopping mid-shin. Thankfully, the coat still had all its front buttons since the only thing that would fit underneath was her slip.

This time her escort was a former Air France pilot named Bernard Gohan. As they walked out onto the train platform, Nancy scanned the area as usual. To her alarm, she realized that the man standing adjacent to them had been her interrogator at the jail, the one who accused her of being a prostitute.

"Kiss me," she told Bernard.

Though he'd just recently joined the PAO Line, he understood the urgency in her tone and did as bid.

As they embraced, Nancy spun Bernard around so that he was blocking the interrogator's view of Nancy. Still, she didn't take any chances and her lips remained locked with Bernard's until the train arrived, thankfully on time for once.

Equally as fortunate for Nancy, the interrogator didn't board the train. She figured he might have been looking for someone, possibly her, though she was certain that Roger the Leak didn't have the slightest idea what she looked like.

. . .

Ironically, their first stop was Marseille. In addition to picking up a couple of airmen, Nancy had to inform the local branch of the PAO Line what had happened to Guérisse.

The route she chose to get to her second flat took her directly past her real home on the Canebière. As she passed by their building, she paused to look up. Even through the blackout shade, she could see that the lamp in the bedroom was on, indicating that Henri was home. She could go up there, just for a moment, to see him and tell him that she was all right. Not to mention grab some more of her own clothes and give Picon a cuddle.

But what if she'd been followed? The Line already had two traitors—what if Roger did indeed know what she looked like? Seeing Henri would only put him in more danger, but Nancy found it difficult to walk away. She put her hand on the marble façade of the building, as though through it, she could feel Henri. But the marble was cold and unfeeling, holding no trace of Henri's warmth. Still, it was the closest she'd been to him in months and she trudged away slower than she should have, marveling that, after three months on the run, she was further away from England than ever.

The network members at the second flat were already aware of Guérisse's arrest, but, like Nancy, no one thought for a minute that he would ever give any of them away. They also seemed sure that Roger was the informer and had probably been responsible for the train search on the trip to Perpignan and all the setbacks in reaching the Spanish border. It was the only explanation that made sense.

The next morning, still wearing the overcoat and slip, Nancy left Marseille, headed toward Madame Sainson's in Montpellier, along with two Allied pilots and Bernard. As the train pulled out of the station, Nancy had the feeling she was leaving Marseille for good—or at least until the end of the war. The thought of Henri sitting alone in the bedroom the night before, wondering where in the world his wife was while she was standing in the street below him, made her start to cry.

She wiped her tears as Bernard glanced at her. Knowing that he, and the pilots in the car behind them, were looking to her for leadership, she pulled herself as back together as she could.

Before knocking at Madame Sainson's door, Nancy checked the doormat. Satisfied it was as straight as it could be, she thumped once, hard, and then two more times slightly softer.

Madame Sainson opened the door a crack and then, after recognizing Nancy, the door was as wide as her grin. Thankfully the woman would have no need for her hidden grenade today.

"Come in, come in." After Madame Sainson shut the door behind them, she threw her arms around Nancy. "Are these the latest refugees?" she asked when she finally let go.

"Yes," Nancy answered. "Plus me."

Madame Sainson tilted her head. "You're leaving France?"

"Hopefully."

After showing the other men to their room, Madame Sainson sat Nancy down and poured her a sherry. The lines around her soft brown eyes had grown deeper, and Nancy imagined that even she hadn't been immune to the dangers that had been plaguing the Line as of late. "Now tell me, Nancy, what you've been up to these last few months. And what exactly are you wearing?"

. . .

Bernard left the next day for Toulouse, mainly to find out if Guérisse had given up any information. He hadn't, of course, and Bernard returned a few days later with a very lovely French woman, Marguerite, who also needed to leave France as soon as possible. She'd been working the PAO Line with her husband, but he had been rounded up in the Roger disaster.

After introducing her, Bernard pulled Nancy aside. "The good news is that it appears the Gestapo are currently concentrating their efforts on the PAO Line rather than pursuing escapees from France. This might be the best opportunity we have to make our way over the Pyrenees."

Nancy said a curse word under her breath followed by Roger's name, but Bernard was right: it might finally be time to leave France.

One of Madame Sainson's contacts was able to provide papers for them, and, as Madame Sainson was similar to Nancy's size, she loaned her some trousers and a few blouses. "The only problem is that I'm not sure who the next stop in the Line is in Perpignan. It's there they make arrangements for the guides to get you over the mountains," Madame Sainson informed them. "But I don't know how to contact them since I was only a safehouse. Guérisse always made the rest of the arrangements."

"It was probably better for you with the Roger situation," Nancy replied.

"What will you do when you get to Perpignan?"

Nancy shrugged. "I know approximately where the safehouse is—Guérisse once had me stand on the corner while he went in. I'm just going to go to the house I think it is and tell them I don't have a password but I work for the Line and I need their help."

Madame Sainson shook her head. "If it doesn't work, they could shoot you, you know."

Nancy didn't like to think about the consequences. "What other alternatives do I have?"

Of all the would-be escapees, only Bernard knew of Nancy's plan. She didn't think it prudent to tell Marguerite or the Allied pilots that she didn't really know how to make contact with the PAO Line in Perpignan. Bernard agreed that if Nancy didn't return from the safehouse after half an hour, he should take Marguerite and the pilots and leave as soon as possible.

As Nancy sauntered down Perpignan's main street, she checked the shop windows to make sure she wasn't being followed. She paused on the corner that Guérisse had left her on and counted the houses.

Here goes nothing, she thought as she crossed the street.

She knocked, and, as soon as the man opened the door, she told him in one breath: "I am Nancy Fiocca and I work for Pat O'Leary. I'm sure you've heard of his recent arrest. I need to get to Spain as soon as possible, along with four others, and I'm asking for your help. I don't have a password, but I don't need one, do I?"

His mouth open in amazement, the man studied her for a moment. Finally he invited her inside. "It sounds to me like you could use a drink."

CHAPTER 19

MAY 1943

Nancy's legs were as heavy as lead. *One more step.* It was the same mantra she'd been repeating for hours. Somehow one step had turned into hundreds, and those into thousands, until they were high up in the Pyrenees, the relentless wind whipping at her raw face. She quickly grew exhausted from tramping through the snow and found it exceedingly difficult not to fall asleep during their frequent breaks. She couldn't remember ever being so tired.

Finally the two hours were up and it was time for another ten-minute break. Per the guides' instructions, everyone removed their rope-soled shoes to peel off their wet socks and put on their extra pair.

Their guides had also warned them not to talk, but at this point, one of the pilots, an American named Frank, complained loudly about the process. "What's the point if you are just going to make us put our wet socks back on when our break is over?"

"It's to prevent frostbite," Bernard returned harshly. "And ours is not to question the guides' wisdom, it's just to obey."

KIT SERGEANT

The American muttered something under his breath. Jean, the lead guide, raised his eyebrows, but, as was his pattern, said nothing, nor did his companion, the exquisite Pilar, whose snow-covered lashes only added to her beauty.

Nancy had not worked with either of them before but knew Jean by reputation as one of the best guides the PAO Line had to offer. Before the war, his business had been smuggling contraband out of France, but now it was people. He was a wanted man in both in France and Spain—the rumor was that the Spanish police had accused him of murder—but he didn't seem to be bothered by the bounties on his head. He nodded at Pilar and she signaled for them to get back into their soaking wet socks. It was time to push onward.

Halfway through the next two hours, a ferocious snowstorm developed and churned the snow into a blinding frenzy. The ice shards piercing Nancy's already soaked clothes felt like machine gun shrapnel.

One more step.

The American ahead of her stopped suddenly and dropped into the snow, nearly causing Nancy to step on him.

"What are you doing?" she hissed.

"I'm done," he replied weakly. "Go on without me."

Nancy was surely tempted to do so, but she also knew that if the Germans found a dead body, they'd all be in danger. She kicked at the American's foot. "Get up and get moving."

This only caused him to plant himself more firmly in the snow.

She'd had enough. In the past few months, she'd had to leave her husband—not to mention her beloved dog—behind, had been arrested and tortured, was forced to jump off a moving train, developed scabies, and lost all of her precious jewelry and identity card. And here was this man, throwing a fit like a two-year-old because he was exhausted and nearly frozen. They were *all* exhausted and nearly frozen, but no one else was complaining.

Nancy reached out with gloved hands to grab the man's collar and tried to yank him to his feet. "Get up!"

"What are you doing?" The shocked man stood, towering over Nancy. "I'm going to report you to the American Consul."

"The only way you can do that is if you make it into Spain." She kicked some snow at him for good measure.

"Fine."

The blizzard prevented them from taking any more breaks. After what seemed like an eternity, they summited what proved to be the last mountain and Nancy took in the panoramic view of the Spanish countryside ahead of them. Behind them, France faded into the background.

Jean guided them to a secluded cabin nestled deep within the woods that someone had stocked with food, wine, and stacks of wood for the fireplace. Finally, Nancy was able to dry off and get some degree of warmth.

Jean stayed long enough to change into dry clothing before he left again to inform the British Consul in Barcelona of the new arrivals.

The next morning, Pilar took the party to a farmhouse in the valley. They spent the day lounging around, but when Jean returned, he told them that there was a heavy police presence in the area and that they'd be better off sleeping in the barn.

Nancy, confident that the next morning she'd be meeting with the consulate, slept better than she had in weeks, despite the prickly sensation of her haybed against her skin and the occasional sneeze emitted from her companions.

She was awoken in the morning by the sound of male voices speaking in a foreign language. Peering out from under her bed of hay, Nancy caught sight of men in uniform. She blinked as one of them picked up a pitchfork and stuck it in the stack where Pilar had been sleeping. Pilar emitted a guttural scream as she leapt up. With one hand on her buttocks—Nancy assumed that was where the pitchfork had made contact—Pilar leapt over a few more haystacks and then out the barn window.

The uniformed men, clearly startled, exchanged a few words in Spanish before creeping over toward Nancy's stack.

She put her hands in the air and got to her feet before the man with the pitchfork could take aim again. Nancy didn't speak Spanish, but thought she heard the words for black market. She figured it would be best to pretend she was from the all-powerful country that had just promised to export tons of wheat to a malnourished Spain. She raised her arms higher, to show that she was unarmed, before pointing at herself. "Americana."

One of the men spoke rapidly in return. Nancy flipped over her palms in a helpless gesture. "I don't understand." Just in case they had heard of the French White Mouse, she pointed again to herself and did her best imitation of an American accent. "Americano."

The man indicated she should follow him outside. The rest of them were quickly rounded up and assembled outside the barn. Though the men pointed guns at them, Nancy wasn't overly worried—surely Jean had made contact with the British Consul, and they would be coming for them soon. Perhaps they would even run into their car as they were marched down the road.

They were taken to the local police station and put into a tiny cell, which already held a dozen inhabitants. Nancy had just crammed herself into a spot on the floor when she was summoned by another policeman.

Not again.

They took her downstairs into a small room and then chained her legs together. "What are you doing?" she asked loudly.

"Miss—"

The correction was on her lips, but Madame Fiocca sounded too French. "I am *Mrs.* Nancy Farmer."

The man nodded before translating for the two policemen who sat staring at her, their arms crossed. One of them fired back an inquiry.

"Why were you in the barn?" the translator asked Nancy.

She wasn't going to give in that easily, not if that was the way they were going to treat her. Ignoring their inquiries seemed like her best bet. "I am Mrs. Nancy Farmer, and I am an American."

The translator again relayed her words to the policemen. The first one shook his head and spoke again.

"How do you know the other people in your cell?"

"I am Mrs. Nancy—"

"We know," the translator said. "But if you don't answer our questions, we could be here for days. And don't think they plan on giving you or your companions any food or water."

"Now wait a minute. I don't mind so much if you treat me poorly, but the others have done nothing wrong." *Not even that real American, the one who had laid down in the snow and threatened...* An idea suddenly occurred to Nancy. She put her hands on her hips. "If you don't manage to find us all something to eat, I shall be sure to report you to the American Ambassador."

The first policeman's eyebrows raised when the translator stated this threat. He exchanged a glance with his companion, who shrugged. The next thing Nancy knew, they were undoing the chains on her legs.

Less than twenty-four hours later, all of them had been released from the jail, and Nancy found herself in a rather luxurious hotel. The British Consul warned her that she would likely be charged with entering Spain illegally, which would incur a fine of a thousand pounds, but Nancy didn't mind as long as she was out of the jail cell.

After she revealed her real name to the consul, he told her that someone had delivered a trunk for her. Inside was some of her clothing from home with three words that had been cut out of a newspaper: *Love from Henri.*

She touched a finger to her lips before reaching out to trace over her husband's name. She had finally made it safely to Spain and, with the help of the consul, would soon be on her way to England.

And what about you, dear Henri? How far behind are you?

CHAPTER 20

JUNE 1943

Despite Nancy's success in finally boarding a boat to England, crossing the Bay of Biscay turned out to be a gloomy affair. The U-boats had begun withdrawing from the North Atlantic due to heavy Allied anti-submarine tactics, but, as the captain of the ship had relayed to Nancy, the bay provided a relatively safe transit area for submarines traveling to and from Germany. Although the ship's alarms frequently broke the rhythm of the voyage, Nancy refused to be frightened —she'd ventured too far into this journey to fall prey to the Germans now.

British Customs, however, presented yet another hurdle—as soon as the ship had docked, she was asked for her passport.

"I don't have one."

The official gave her a dark look, which she returned before stating, "Carrying British passports around Paris isn't much in vogue right now."

"Do you have any identification papers at all?"

The ID card she carried was in a different name. "Not with

me. The British Consul in Spain arranged for my passage on this ship. Why don't you follow up with them regarding my identity?" She tried to push past him, but he growled at her to get in the back of the customs line.

She had no intention of doing so, but stalked back toward the ship anyway. She spotted an officer she'd struck up a couple of conversations with and asked him to send a telegram to Lieutenant Ian Garrow at the War Office.

As she predicted, Garrow was ever efficient and she spent less than 24 hours waiting around the customs station before a train ticket to London was delivered straight into her hands.

Though it had been less than four years since she'd last been in London, it felt like a lifetime ago. Nancy recalled what the French Consulate had said to her when she'd left in September 1939: *if you go now, you'll probably never return to England.*

Well, he was right about one thing: Nancy wasn't returning to an England she recognized. The stately edifices of the Houses of Parliament, Palace of Westminster, and even the British Museum now bore the conspicuous scars of relentless bombings. The once-thriving roadways and bridges had been transformed, their surfaces marked by jagged scars and potholes bigger than she was.

Nancy took a room in the St James hotel in the West End, an area she had once known for its vibrant nightlife. Now, of course, blackout restrictions and wartime conditions had subdued its bustling scene. Still, Ian Garrow took her out to dinner at one of her favorite restaurants: Quaglino's, famous for its Art Deco-style interior.

Nancy was relieved to see that Garrow had regained the massive amount of weight he'd lost in prison, and though he'd also lost some of his hair, he was as tall as ever. Upon his return to London, he'd been installed in MI9 to continue to provide support for various underground escape organizations.

"How's Henri?" Garrow asked through a bite of rabbit pie.

Nancy hung her head. "I don't know. I haven't heard from him in nearly six months." She set down her fork to look at Garrow. "Have you heard anything?"

He shook his head. "Not about Henri, but I've been following the developments with the Line. After Guérisse's arrest, it became known as the Françoise Line."

Nancy couldn't help smiling at that. "Françoise Dissard is in charge now?"

"Indeed. I take it you knew her?"

"Yes. I stayed with her while my Pyrenees escape was being arranged."

"Same. Of course, I had to fatten up after my stint in prison."

"I'm sure with her cooking, Françoise was very helpful in that. If you could get past all the cigarette smoke, that is." Nancy stuck her fork in the crust of her pie before asking, "Were you aware of Roger le Neveu's infiltration of the Line?"

"Yes. After Guérisse's arrest, he apparently tried to contact Françoise, but she would have none of it. Luckily, the Gestapo don't seem to know much about her, but many of the rest of the network were arrested. It seems she's about the only one left of the Line." Garrow cleared his throat. "And Paul Cole has been released from prison."

"I didn't know he was in prison."

"He was arrested by the Vichy police, if you can believe it. They pride themselves on arresting any secret agent, Nazi or Allied. But we heard he was out, and in Paris, working for Hans Kieffer, once again providing the Germans with information about the Resistance."

"It's not a good time to be in France," Nancy said bitterly, thinking once again of her husband.

Garrow reached across the table and put a hand on hers. "Henri will be fine."

"I hope you're right."

∽

News of Nancy's appearance in London rapidly circulated among the numerous Allied servicemen and French refugees she had assisted in reaching England. Many of them insisted on introducing her to their wives and families, who thanked her profusely. While she refused to accept any money, she didn't often turn down invitations to restaurants or social gatherings, and soon her calendar was filled.

But at night, Nancy would lie awake, wondering when Henri would arrive.

After a few weeks in London, she no longer felt the need to keep looking over her shoulder. Using her real name, she rented an apartment in Piccadilly and occupied herself with hiring people to paint the walls and refinish the parquet floor.

After the flat was move-in ready, Nancy bought Henri a new wardrobe, including pajamas and slippers, since, knowing her husband, he wouldn't think to bring his own personal comforts with him. And of course she stocked the liquor cabinet full of French champagne and brandy.

One night soon after she moved in, she had a terrible nightmare that Henri was on a ship, heading toward England when it was blown up by a U-boat. She woke up shaking, her skin covered in sweat.

"He's dead," she said aloud.

She sat up and flicked on the lamp, which cast a narrow light about the small bedroom. His new pajamas were hanging over the closet door and she frowned when she thought about how optimistic she'd been when she bought them.

With the light still on, she laid back down in bed. Like Ebenezer Scrooge, she tried to convince herself that the nightmare had been caused by an upset stomach or because Henri was taking too long to come to England. But deep down she knew something was wrong.

She could barely drag herself out of bed the next morning. As much as she tried to shake the nightmare, the premonition that Henri would never arrive in London wouldn't leave her mind. The last thing she wanted to do was her usual routine of meeting friends for lunch and drinks.

I just want Henri.

It was still too dangerous for her to be with Henri in Marseille, but a longing to at least be in the same country as her husband suddenly bubbled up in her gut. If Henri would not come to her, she'd simply go back to France.

She still had the notion that she wanted to continue helping with the war effort, so maybe she'd just volunteer with an organization looking to send people into France. She'd heard about the Free French Movement, led by Charles de Gaulle, the exiled French general, from one of the downed airmen she'd helped rescue.

Joining them should be easy enough. She picked up the phone and instructed the operator to connect her to the Free French Headquarters.

"I don't know what you mean," the operator replied.

After Nancy repeated her request, the operator told her that she couldn't help her.

"Fine." Nancy slammed down the receiver. A moment later, she picked up the phone again. Luckily it was a different operator, and Nancy gave her the name of the downed airman. After briefly speaking to him, she finally rose from bed.

Dressed in the most French outfit she owned—a Chanel tweed skirt and matching jacket—she set out for the Free French Committee's offices at 4 Carlton Gardens, which was only a short walk from her Piccadilly flat.

After informing the secretary that she was already a member of the French Resistance, she was shown to a Colonel Passy's office.

The 'Colonel' was a young man in his 30s, with a clean-shaven face and kind eyes. He didn't particularly strike Nancy as someone who would be involved with the Resistance. When he didn't ask her to sit down, she cleared her throat. "I can only assume you've heard of me. I'm one of the Nazi's Most Wanted. They call me the 'White Mouse.'"

"You can't possibly be the White Mouse."

"I am indeed. Ask anyone who's been in France. Lieutenant Ian Garrow of MI9, for instance."

Colonel Passy waved his hand. "I don't know how much you know about the Free French, but we are the last vestiges of France's anti-collaborationist government and therefore view any British involvement as a violation of our sovereignty."

Nancy frowned. "What do you mean by sovereignty? You are a Frenchman in England, you cannot rule from here. And, anyway, aren't we all working to undermine Hitler?"

Passy set his pen down and cracked his knuckles. "In different ways, yes. But as I said, we like to maintain a high degree of autonomy."

"Okay, well, then, considering that I've lived in France for over a decade and my husband is French, I suppose yours is the organization for me."

"Listen, Nannie—"

"Nancy," she corrected pointedly.

"Nancy. I appreciate what you've done—especially if you really are the White Mouse, though I still have my doubts—but the truth is that we don't have any openings right now."

"No openings?" How could they not be desperate for anyone willing to go back to France and fight?

"Not at this time." He flashed her a rather insincere grin. "But if we do, we will call you."

Feeling deflated, Nancy let herself out. She had been so sure they would have been excited to welcome her on their team that she didn't know what to do with herself now. She decided to blow off her afternoon appointments and went back to her flat, where she flung herself onto the bed.

She didn't cry—not much could make her tear up these days—but she did lay in bed, staring up at the ceiling, for a few hours as she mulled over how she would get back to France.

In the late afternoon, the phone rang. Wondering if Passy had a change of heart, she picked it up on the second ring.

The man, who had a strong British accent, introduced himself as a friend of Ian Garrow before asking what she had been doing at General de Gaulle's office that morning.

"Pardon?" Nancy asked, stalling for time. "I wasn't—"

"You were wearing a pink tweed suit and left around ten-thirty."

Nancy rubbed her forehead, wondering what Colonel Passy would have thought about the British lurking outside his building. Talk about trampling on the Free French's supposed sovereignty. "I'm sorry, who am I speaking to again?"

"I'm with the SOE."

"The what?"

The caller sighed. "The Special Operations Executive. The SOE. We work with Resistance sectors in Occupied Europe. I'm with F Section, to be more exact, F standing for…"

"Let me guess. France."

"Right."

"And let me guess again: you want me to join your so-called F Section."

His voice took on a playful tone. "You are the White Mouse, aren't you?"

CHAPTER 21

JUNE 1943

A few days later, Nancy found herself bundled into a cab bound for the Surrey countryside. She tugged on the bottom of her FANY uniform jacket. With its narrow waist and slightly flared bottom, it was supposed to be a flattering cut, to emphasize an hourglass frame. FANY was short for the First Aid Nursing Yeomanry, though her recruitment officer had made it clear that she was a FANY in name only. Because the SOE operated outside of the military chain of command, it used agencies such as the FANY and Women's Auxiliary Air Force, or WAAF, as covers for their civilian female agents.

As the driver turned down a tree-lined pathway, Nancy rolled down the window to gaze open-mouthed at the enormous Victorian-style estate. "This can't be right," she mumbled as the driver turned off the car.

"Oh it is—you've arrived at Winterfold House, though I hear the other secret agents refer to it as 'The Mad House.'"

She blinked. "Did you say—"

"It's not really as secret as all that. After all, they train you in demolitions and how to shoot guns. You might be in the countryside, but people do have ears."

Wondering if this were a test, she merely asked the driver to retrieve her bag from the trunk.

As he drove off, his cab kicking up dust clouds, Nancy wondered what to do next. Surely this couldn't be the SOE's training school for its, as the driver put it, 'secret agents.' Should she just go to the door and knock?

While she was still standing there, a man opened the door and stepped out. He put a hand on his forehead to shield his eyes from the sun and then looked around. "Nancy?" he called as he caught sight of her.

She readjusted her bag before walking over to him. "I am indeed Nancy. Nancy Wake," she added, deciding to go with her maiden name just in case.

His blue eyes sparkling, he grabbed her hand and pumped it excitedly. "I'm Major Buckmaster, the head of F Section. I wanted to personally greet the White Mouse and welcome you aboard." He held her at arm's length to take in her khaki jacket and slacks. "I see you've got your uniform."

"Yes." She was brimming with questions, but it was evident that Buckmaster's thoughts were elsewhere as he ushered her into the parlor, where a lavish spread of bread, cheeses, and meats was laid out.

"Eat up," he told her. "You'll need the strength for the obstacle course."

"Obstacle course?"

"It's all part of the training," Buckmaster said as he munched on a cracker. "Now, I know you're coming from the field, but some of our newer recruits haven't been to France in ages, and, of course, they need to be as fit as possible. That's what Winterfold House is for—to test you, physically. We used to use Wanborough Manor, but..." he gulped down the cracker. "We conduct other tests here too, though."

Nancy's mind wandered back to the cab driver. Perhaps she'd already passed her first test.

"Aren't you hungry?"

She shook her head.

Buckmaster stuffed another couple of crackers and a piece of cheese in his mouth before wiping the crumbs on his pants. "Well, come on then. It's time for you to meet Denden."

Buckmaster led Nancy out the back door and beyond the sweeping patio as he chatted about the SOE, which had apparently been the brainchild of Winston Churchill himself.

Eventually they reached a muddy field filled with ropes, walls, and trenches. A short man in a military uniform was standing with his back toward them, shouting at another man who was attempting to scale one of the walls.

"Denden," Buckmaster called.

The man turned, revealing that his coat was cut more like Nancy's instead of the boxier type that the other men wore. In lieu of a tie, a bright orange scarf was knotted around his neck. He straightened the scarf when he caught Nancy looking at it. "Now, don't get any ideas, young lady. You're not my type. Not even the right gender."

Nancy's eyes shifted to Buckmaster, whose gaze was focused on the man running the course. She hadn't met someone so forward in a long time, especially not anyone British, with their normally stiff upper lips. "Don't worry—I wouldn't be interested in you anyway. I'm married."

"Married, eh?" The man's eyes widened. "Is your husband

here with you too?" He nudged Buckmaster with his elbow. "Don't you remember what happened with the Agazarians?"

Buckmaster brushed him off. "This is not like that. Her husband's not here. In fact, Nancy's just come to us from France."

"Ah." The man held his hand out to Nancy. "I'm Denis Rake, but everyone calls me Denden."

"And you're an expert in obstacle courses?" Nancy gestured nervously toward the climbing wall. "You can help me get over that?"

He shook his head. "Don't look at me. I'm not exactly sure why they put me here—I'm a wireless operator and I'm just back myself from the field because of my bum foot." He extended one leg out toward Nancy. "Injured it running from the Boches."

"And perhaps if you'd actually taken your own training seriously, you wouldn't have had that problem," Buckmaster cut in.

Denden grinned. "Say what you will, Buck, but you'll never convince me that I need a gun. They're too darn loud anyway." He looped his arm through Nancy's and led her closer to the course. "Which exercise do you want to try first?"

"None of them."

Denden giggled. "We're going to make a secret agent out of you yet, darling!"

"Make me a secret agent? What do you think I've been doing for the past two years?"

"You worked for the Resistance?"

"Yes. The PAO Line. And trust me when I tell you that I never needed to scale a wall or criss-cross my legs through tires."

"Don't I know it." He folded his arms over his chest. "But I take it you want to get back to France as soon as possible."

She nodded.

"Is that where your husband is?" he asked, his voice gentle.

"Yes."

"Then let me give you some advice." He nodded toward the field. "There's real training that goes on here, of course. You're going to have to get in good physical shape, and then they'll instruct you in map reading, helping land Lysanders, and most definitely in security—how to evade the Gestapo and the like. It's really not for your own safety, but for that of the rest of the people in your circuit. But most of all, this whole thing is like a prolonged psychiatric evaluation. They want to know that you can work in a group and that you're not just out for personal gain. And, that you won't crack if you're unlucky enough to get picked up and tortured."

"I've already been picked up and tortured. Twice, and I never gave anything away."

"I believe you," Denis replied. "But does Buck?" He gestured toward where Buckmaster stood checking his watch. He frowned in their direction as Denden gave him a little wave.

The obstacle course would soon come to be the biggest thorn in Nancy's side. Though he never actually navigated through it himself, Denden seemed to take a sadistic pleasure in working the would-be agents to the bone. For instance, the myriad ropes, tires, and trenches had been labeled with the letters A, B, and C and Denden instructed Nancy to climb over all the A's and then go under all the B's and then skirt the C's in a clockwise direction. She, of course, quickly forgot the directions, but when she tried to mimic the person ahead of her, Denden shouted, "Clockwise, not counterclockwise, Nancy," clearly having given everyone different directions just to confuse them further.

. . .

There were only a couple of other women in training besides Nancy, though she didn't really know them well since they had been cautioned not to tell each other any personal information. The other men seemed like carbon cut-outs of each other: clean-shaven, tall, and muscular.

And then there was Denden, who made sure he stood out from the others. Along with his exuberant charisma, he was resourceful and—as he was always telling her—the best wireless operator in the SOE. Nancy figured that was the reason they allowed a self-proclaimed homosexual who refused to shoot a gun into their elite ranks in the first place. And kept him, even despite his 'bum foot.'

As with most of the other rules at the Mad House, Denden ignored the one about giving away personal information. He told Nancy that spying was in his veins: his father had worked for Edith Cavell, the WWI British nurse who had run her own network to help hundreds of Allied men escape from German-occupied Belgium. Hers had also been infiltrated, and, according to Denden, his father had been put in front of the same firing squad as Edith.

After his father's death, Denden joined the circus as an acrobat, and, as a young man, traveled all over the continent, mastering both French and German. When England declared war on Germany, he traded in his gymnast slippers for combat boots, enlisting in the British Expeditionary Forces. After he was evacuated at Dunkirk, he returned to England and, eventually, became part of the SOE.

Luckily for her, Denden took it upon himself to help Nancy out, particularly with coding radio messages, which, for some reason, she really struggled with.

He took to calling her 'Ducks.' When Nancy asked if it was because she let things roll off her like water on a duck, Denden returned that it was more the way she waddled when she went through the tires on the obstacle course.

The last trial Nancy had to go through before she could move on from the Mad House was a session with the SOE's psychiatrist.

Having never been to a psychiatrist, Nancy asked Denden what she was in for.

"His method involves displaying blots and asking you what you see in them."

"Blots?"

"You know, ink blots."

"Won't they just look like ink blots?"

Denden grinned. "Naturally. But you'll want to indulge him. His brethren think that your responses can give them inside information into your psyche. I always say the blots look like frilly lace and tulle skirts, with a few knives and boxing gloves thrown in for good measure. That really confuses him."

When Nancy's turn finally came, the psychiatrist, whose name was Dr. Hughes, had her sit in a hard-backed chair across from him and then fired off a barrage of questions, which, in Nancy's opinion, bore no relevance to her role in the French Resistance. She decided that fabricating her answers would be far more entertaining than simply telling the truth.

"Are your mother and father happy together?"

As far as Nancy knew, her mother had never again heard from her father after he'd left them. "Of course."

"Did you consider yourself a happy child?"

Nancy had been the youngest of six, and the age difference between herself and her second youngest sibling, Ruby, was eight years. After Ruby had left home, their astutely religious mother had become even more overbearing, which was the main reason Nancy had run away from home. "The happiest."

"Have you ever lied about something important?"

Nancy cocked an eyebrow. "You mean like to the Germans? About something as important as my name and occupation?"

Dr. Hughes scribbled something on his pad of paper. "Right. Let's move on to the Rorschachs now." He put down the pad and picked up a square piece of paper with a large crease in the middle. It had clearly been folded while the ink was still wet, resulting in a mirror-like design on both sides. "What do you see?"

"Spilled ink."

"Yes, but do you see an image in the ink?"

She squinted her eyes. The splotchy blob almost looked like Hitler's mustache, but she decided not to follow Denden's advice. "No."

"Surely you can come up with something."

"I can tell you are very clumsy with ink."

Dr. Hughes sighed. "Let's try something else. I'm going to say a word and you will speak the first thing that comes to your mind. Are you ready?"

"Yes." She crossed her legs at the ankle. "Did we start yet?"

"No."

"No, as in we haven't started yet, or am I supposed to respond with what I think of when you say 'no?'"

"No, we haven't started yet. Are you ready now?"

"Now?"

He held up his hand and cleared his throat. Dropping his

hand, he said, "Roses. That's the first word. What do you think of when you hear roses?"

"Are red. And violets are blue…"

"Red." He wrote this on his pad. "Just one word. How about soda?"

"Whisky."

"Sugar."

Nancy licked her lips. "Wine."

"Brown."

"Brandy."

"Right." He put his pen down. "Perhaps you'd like to play with some blocks?"

That was definitely the last straw. "What exactly is your job, anyway? Don't you think you'd be more useful fighting the Boches like a real man instead of playing with blocks and spilling ink all over the place? Because if you don't, I do."

He gave her an indulging grin. "Who do you think is going to help all these 'real men' recover from their war neurosis, or what you might call 'shell shock' when they come home?" He waved his hand. "At any rate, I have all I need, thank you very much, Ms. Wake. Good day."

"Good day," she replied, suddenly disconcerted by his dismissal. Maybe she'd gone a tad too far this time. What if he'd decided she wasn't cut out to be an agent after all?

She was still stewing over her session with the psychiatrist when she went into the parlor after lunch. One of the only other women at the Mad House, Agathe, stood in front of the fireplace, her hands on her hips, shouting at Denden.

Nancy wanted to back out of the room, but Denden caught sight of her. "Ducks, can you believe this woman? She's trying to tell me it should never be made legal for a man to love other men."

"It's *illegal* for good reason," Agathe insisted.

"Well, it shouldn't be. It's perfectly natural."

"For some people," Nancy offered.

"Some people?" Denden's eyes held the twinkle they got when he was about to either make a gregarious insult or say something profound. "*Every* man should be homosexual, and if they aren't, it's just because they haven't had a chance to try it with me yet."

Even Nancy's jaw dropped open on that one. Agathe, with a gasp, put a hand over her own open mouth.

Denden, having delivered his final say in the matter, gave Nancy his customary little wave as he left the room.

Agathe dropped her hand. "You heard what he said to me. You'll back me up when I report him to Buckmaster."

"Buckmaster knows about Denden. Your report won't matter, and, at any rate, I'm not going to defend *you*. Denden is hands-down a way more valuable agent, not to mention he's my friend."

"Your so-called friend insulted me."

"Only after you insulted his entire way of living. Why do you care, anyway? A few good stiff drinks might help you forget all your misgivings."

Agathe narrowed her eyes. "And how many stiff drinks have you had?"

Drinking wasn't against the rules at Winterfold—in fact, it was somewhat encouraged as their instructors wanted to make sure they could handle their liquor without their tongues becoming too loose. Nancy had only indulged in one double whisky at lunch, but she couldn't resist adding a little fuel to the fire. "A few."

Agathe's hands went back to her hips. "Are you drunk?"

Nancy decided this didn't deserve a retort and stalked off. At the doorway, she turned back to Agathe and imitated Denden's wave.

"You'll pay for this, Nancy Wake," Agathe called after her.

CHAPTER 22

JULY 1943

The aftermath of the Agathe situation escalated quickly. Nancy's recruiting officer, Selwyn Jepson, arrived at Winterfold and ordered her to return to her London flat.

Nancy didn't see the point in arguing—the man was so ill-humored that she imagined he was severely constipated or else suffering from an ulcer.

Upon her return to London, she immediately called on Ian Garrow to let him know she'd been fired from the SOE. He seemed perplexed, but treated her to lunch to cheer her up anyway. They spent the evening making plans for her to try to join the Free French again.

She returned to her flat to find a telegram demanding she send back her FANY uniform. She rang up the SOE and told the secretary who'd answered that the only way they'd get their uniform back was if Jepson picked it up himself, along with offering an apology, of course.

A few hours later, the phone rang. "Miss Wake?" a tentative voice asked when she picked up.

"Yes?"

It was clearly the same secretary who had endured Nancy's earlier tirade. "Hold for Colonel Buckmaster, please."

"Nancy," Buck's exuberant voice cooed over the line. "Don't worry about sending back the uniform."

"Let me guess, Jepson's too chicken to come get it."

"No. You're not fired."

"What?"

"You still want to go to France, don't you?"

"Of course."

"Then we're sending you on to Scotland for combat training."

"But…" Nancy stumbled to find the right words.

"Your friend Ian Garrow convinced me that Agathe was confusing your natural enthusiasm with being intoxicated. He spent quite a few minutes waxing on about your bravery and commitment. I was never really worried anyway."

This time, Nancy was brought to Inverie Bay, a remote gem on the Scottish coastline that was accessible only by boat. The SOE training compound was a series of modest, white-washed buildings on the Knoydart Peninsula.

This time, she was the only female among thirty-six other recruits. Since Denden wasn't there, Nancy decided it would be best to limit her interactions and maintain a low profile, but this resolve lasted only a few days. For one, it was exceedingly hard to keep her mouth shut, not to mention the other men were quite friendly and, as a joke, nicknamed her 'Lil Führer.'

There were no ink blots or mad psychiatrists in Scotland, but the rain was incessant, making the overly complicated obstacle course even more difficult. After every trial, she'd return with her hair soaked, her clothes caked in mud.

Thankfully, there was never a shortage of hot water. After the morning run, the would-be agents, freshly showered and dressed in drier clothes, would head out to the barn to be instructed in not just firing the Sten and Bren guns, but also in how to clean and dismantle them for transport.

Although Nancy felt sure she knew more about working for the Resistance than 99% of the people at Winterfold, she'd never held a gun before. She found the Sten gun to be simple to use and much easier to handle than its bulkier cousin, the Bren.

As a whole, she felt that the new curriculum was far more practical than that of the Mad House, which led to an increased willingness to learn on her part. The instructors showed her exactly where on the railroad tracks to place pencil bombs for maximum impact, and how to render one of the German's Citroëns inoperable using a teaspoon of sugar.

Perhaps the least useful was what Buck had referred to as 'combat training.' Here the agents learned how to spar unarmed, block an incoming attack, and, the pièce de résistance, to find the spot on the back of the neck to hit in order to kill someone instantly.

Upon hearing the last bit of instruction, Nancy folded her arms across her chest. "You're telling little old me that really works? That a 10-stone woman can cause a giant Aryan to drop to his knees?"

"'Lil Führer, you know you can cause any man to drop to his knees," one of the men in the crowd called out unhelpfully.

The instructor flexed his arms. "It may seem unlikely, but if you can hit them in the right spot in the cervical spine, it will cause what they call a 'hangman's fracture.'"

Nancy couldn't fathom the idea of deliberately taking someone's life with her bare hands, but on the off chance she'd actually find herself in the right situation, she decided to give it a try and hit the practice dummy with all her might.

"Not bad. Let me see your hands." The instructor lifted her palms to the light as a few of the other men whistled. "Too soft," he declared. "You've led a pampered life."

"Once upon a time, they were stained with ink. I used to be a journalist." That was long before she'd met Henri, however. The thought of her husband caused her to yank her hands back.

"You can harden them with time and practice." To demonstrate his point, the instructor brought his hand down in a karate chop motion onto the nearby table.

During the evenings, provided there were no nighttime exercises scheduled, they were given a brief break from the incessant drilling and killing practice. After dinner, Nancy and a few select others would have a nightcap, or two, or three.

One night she stayed up just a tad too late to be fully functional for the sunrise run. She crawled out of bed, surveying the rainy, cold grayness of the pre-dawn morning before telling one of her trainers, "I'm not running today. I'm indisposed."

"Right," the trainer replied. "Maybe tomorrow then."

She placed a hand over her stomach. "My cramps usually last for several days."

The lie afforded her a few days' rest until the trainer asked when she expected to be over her 'little problem.'

"If you mean my period, it's well over. My issue now is that I hate running in the dark."

After that, the trainer changed the morning run to 8 am and Nancy, who was out of excuses, had no choice but to join them.

Nancy was clearly the weakest trainee but she didn't let that bother her. When she failed, again, at scaling the giant climbing wall, one of the men asked, "Lil Führer, what happens if you are confronted with a wall like this in France?"

"There are no walls like this in France," Nancy replied. "But if they somehow built one, I won't try to climb it, not even if the entire Wehrmacht was chasing me. I'd just stay on one side and try to negotiate with them." She checked her watch. "That's enough for today. It's about time to change for dinner."

Nancy always liked to be the first one at the dinner table, having learned from past incidents that being late allowed her friends an opportunity to carry out pranks. She'd had the salt and pepper shakers switched on her one too many times to dawdle over her hair or makeup.

Soon the table was filled, each man saluting their Lil Führer with an outstretched arm and she ate her food with relish. While she would never quite get used to the absence of communication from Henri, forming new friendships had helped to dull the pain a bit. And anyway, it was only a matter of time before she would be in France again.

The next morning, the would-be agents were informed that a few high-ranking F Section men would be arriving from London to monitor their progress and that their commanding officer would be making a report on each of them.

This filled Nancy with trepidation. It was possible that she hadn't been putting in her best effort on every task, especially in regard to the physical stuff, like the morning run and obstacle course. At any rate, she wanted to know exactly what was in her report.

She recruited her closest friend, Raymond Bachelor, who wasn't exactly keen on the idea. "You do know those reports are probably locked up in Sykes's filing cabinet."

She put a mocking finger to her cheek. "You're right. If only we knew how to break into offices and pick locks." She dropped her finger. "Oh wait, we do."

"You're worried about what that report might say about you, but what if you got caught breaking into Sykes's office? You'd be kicked out of the SOE, sure as Scotland's rain. And me too."

"I've already been kicked out once, and they knew enough to reinstate me. If you're that concerned, then just be my lookout. If you want, I'll read your report too."

Bachelor sighed. "I don't suppose you'd take no for an answer."

"No, I wouldn't."

That very day, Nancy wandered into the main reception room, where the keys to the offices were kept. She made some vague inquiry of the clerk, and while he was distracted digging through papers, she snatched the key to Sykes's office. She pressed it into the plasticine she'd brought from the training room before replacing the key and taking her leave.

"Let's see if this really works," Nancy muttered to herself as she meticulously filed down metal strips from a tin can to fit into the mold. She then poured glue over the strips to keep them in place.

The next day, the glue had set, turning the metal strips into what appeared to be a passable key, so she told Bachelor that the break-in was on for that night.

As Nancy and Bachelor crept through the shadows toward Sykes's office, their footsteps barely making a sound on the gravel path, Nancy mused that the white buildings looked a little like large ghosts in the moonlight.

"You have to do this fast," Bachelor reminded her, his eyes scanning the darkened windows of the building ahead of them. "If we're caught, it won't just be a slap on the wrist."

"I know, I know."

The outer door was unlocked, and, once inside, Nancy took out a small flashlight, its beam cutting through the darkness of the hallway leading toward Sykes's office. "Wait here," she told Bachelor. "Let me know if anyone comes."

She produced the makeshift key from her jacket pocket. The tin felt a bit rougher and far more flexible than a normal key and she held her breath as she inserted it into the lock. She had to wiggle it a few times, but finally she heard a soft click and the door opened.

Rows of filing cabinets lined the walls of the office. She'd never have time to go through all of them, but, figuring they probably kept the newest recruits' reports in the cabinets closest to the door, she headed there first. She opened the top drawer, her deft fingers moving quickly through the files. "Aha," she said aloud, pulling out a thick folder labeled "Wake, Nancy." Her hand holding the flashlight trembled a little, causing the light to scatter across the page.

To her relief, there was nothing horribly negative in her report. She beamed when she read the words, "Her positive morale and sense of humor are a source of encouragement for everyone."

As a favor to Bachelor for guarding the door, she took a peek at his file, and saw that his was full of even more praise. She memorized a few key phrases and then put everything back just the way she had found it.

"What did they say about me?" Bachelor hissed as she emerged from the office.

"You're reliable and do well under pressure." She grinned at him. "And I would add, good at listening to instructions."

They both froze as they heard a scraping noise. After a few moments of silence, Nancy took a deep breath. "It was probably just the wind. Let's get out of here before we give them something more to write about."

The 'high-ranking officers' included Maurice Buckmaster and his right-hand woman, Vera Atkins, who arrived together the next day. Buck was as exuberant as ever while Miss Atkins, in her sturdy gray dress with a high neckline, was much more reserved. They insisted on talking to the would-be agents one-on-one in the parlor, which they had converted into a temporary office.

Now that she knew the contents of her file, Nancy wasn't worried when they called her in. She entered the room to find Buckmaster behind a large wooden desk with Miss Atkins perched at the window behind him.

"Nancy, come in and have a seat," Buck commanded.

After they exchanged pleasantries, Buckmaster cleared his throat. "Nancy, I've looked at your report…" He paused before clearing his throat again.

If he was trying to make her nervous, it didn't work. She stared back at him without blinking.

"It was very good," Buckmaster said finally.

"I know." The words came out against Nancy's will.

"What do you mean, you know?" Miss Atkins demanded in her posh voice.

"I…" Now it was Nancy's turn to clear her throat. She supposed there was no use in lying to the head of F Section. "Well, I snuck into the office and read it for myself."

Miss Atkins' mouth dropped open as Buckmaster bumbled over the words, "What did you do?"

"You shouldn't be so surprised," Nancy returned. "After all, isn't this what we're supposed to be learning at your spy school?"

Buckmaster exchanged a startled glance with Miss Atkins before his lips turned up into a grin. "I suppose you're right."

From behind him, Miss Atkins crossed her arms impatiently.

"Anyway," Buckmaster shuffled some papers on his desk. "We are indeed going to get you back into France, but first you must complete your parachute training and then you'll be sent on to our finishing school at Beaulieu."

"Parachute training? Can't I be flown in, like Denis Rake was?"

"No," Miss Atkins replied. "Rake is one of our most skilled radio operators, and therefore, gets special treatment. Newcomers like you will be doing things by the book."

Nancy, knowing the answer, inquired anyway, "Is there actually a book?"

"No." Miss Atkins narrowed her eyes at Nancy. "I've heard about your exploits in France, but I wonder if you'll be able to keep them up without your rich husband to foot the bill."

The reference to Henri stung Nancy even more than Miss Atkins' harsh words, but she forced a smile anyway. "Well, I know the SOE has plenty of cash, so I don't think much will change."

Buckmaster straightened the pile of papers nearest to him. "Anyhow, we'll be in touch with more details once you've finished at Beaulieu."

CHAPTER 23

OCTOBER 1943

*P*arachute training took place at Ringway, an airfield near Manchester in the northwest of England. The training itself was intense and about as terrible as Nancy had predicted. The initial jump was made from a tower to simulate the experience, and, as trainees progressed, they were expected to practice their jumps from aircraft flying at low altitudes. Here the SOE actually had different requirements for women, who only had to complete four jumps during the daytime while men were to complete six jumps total, four during the day and two at nighttime. Considering that they were all going to be jumping from a plane into France eventually, Nancy didn't understand why women were afforded this so-called special treatment. Given that she was the only woman in her class, she didn't say anything about it, not even when the instructor told her, "Remember the advice your mother gave you: keep your legs together and lock them at the knees."

Unlike her fellow recruits in Scotland, some of the men at

Ringway went out of their way to make her feel inferior. One night at dinner, an American passed Nancy a small package. "This is in case you forget to follow the instructor's advice to keep your legs locked."

"Don't take that," Raymond Bachelor hissed in her ear.

But Nancy, thinking it was a packet of bandages, or possibly even chocolate, accepted it. When she opened the box, three small square bundles and a folded up piece of paper fell out. She held one of the squares up to the rest of the table. "What are these?"

Bachelor groaned as the American man asked, "Did you and your husband not find the need for condoms?"

Nancy could feel her face grow hot, but she kept her hand steady. "If we did, I paid no attention." She picked up the paper and unfolded it. "Oh look, there are instructions for how to use them." She traced her finger along the words as she read aloud, "Open the package and unfold the latex…"

At this, the red-faced American left the table.

After dinner was over, the commanding officer found Nancy in the parlor drinking a glass of wine. "I heard what happened at dinner, and I want to extend my sincerest apologies."

"Don't worry about it," she reassured him. "By now, I'm used to this type of behavior."

"Well, if that's the case…" The CO pulled at his collar. "I'll take your, uh, presents from you."

"Don't worry about that either." Nancy imagined she could find ways to incorporate them into her pranks. "I might find them useful after all."

. . .

The next morning found Nancy, clad in her standard-issue jumpsuit and helmet, standing with a group of fellow trainees near the airstrip. Butterflies swarmed in her stomach, and she nearly leapt out of her skin as the roar of an engine filled the air.

"Are you nervous, Nancy?" one of the men asked.

She shot him a determined look as she pulled the straps on her parachute pack tighter. "Never."

As the group boarded the plane, the atmosphere was charged with a mix of excitement and apprehension. They sat in two rows of five, their pale faces staring at each other while trying to avoid looking at the hatch that lay between them.

With a jolt, the plane started its taxi down the runway and then took off. As it climbed to the designated altitude, the butterflies in Nancy's stomach dropped in response.

After a few minutes in the air, the instructor began his final briefing, shouting to be heard over the engine noise. "Count to five after you jump, then pull the ripcord. Stay calm, and keep an eye on your landing zone. And, above all, keep your legs together, right Nancy?" He opened the hatch and a rush of cold air flooded the cabin.

He signaled for the first trainee to approach the door. Nancy watched as one by one her comrades leapt into the void without hesitation.

When her turn came, she crept toward the open hatch, her legs feeling as though they would give out on her. *It's okay—I won't need them in a few minutes anyway.*

"If you don't go now, you'll never get to France," the instructor bellowed.

"I'm going! Just give me one second." *If I don't get to France, I'll never see Henri again.* The simple thought was enough for her to let go and plunge into the vast emptiness.

The unfamiliar sensation of weightlessness made her momentarily forget where she was. But she was brought back to reality by the wind roaring past her ears. *One.*

She looked down to see the rolling green fields of Ringway spreading beneath her boots. *Two.* Were those tiny dots her fellow trainees?

Three. Legs together. *Four.*

She gritted her teeth. *Five.* She pulled the ripcord and suddenly she was swaying softly in the breeze instead of hurtling toward the Earth. She tried to convince herself that it wasn't that bad, that maybe she was going to survive another day after all.

She tugged on the parachute's lines to steer herself toward the landing zone, an orange X painted on the ground. She clenched her legs together even tighter as she bent her knees.

The landing came sooner than expected and when she heard the thud of her feet hitting the ground, she tucked in her head to roll into a somersault.

As she righted herself, she sighed, releasing a breath she hadn't realized she'd been holding.

"You alright there, Nancy?" Bachelor asked.

"I'm fine," she snapped. "I'm in one piece, aren't I?" *Aren't I?* Still slightly dizzy, she curled her toes on both feet and then rotated each ankle. It would appear that she was indeed in one piece.

The weather was poor for the rest of their time at Ringway, and their final exercise involved leaping from a hot-air balloon, an experience Nancy found even more loathsome than jumping from a moving plane. The inclement weather also meant that the men never got to complete their extra jumps, which felt like a bit of vindication to Nancy.

CHAPTER 24

NOVEMBER 1943

Having finished learning to parachute, Nancy next moved into the red-bricked Beaulieu Estate in New Forest to complete her training. She was delighted to find that she was not the only woman there—her new roommate was Violette Szabo, a Frenchwoman whose stunningly beautiful exterior contrasted with her own bawdy sense of humor.

The first night at dinner, Violette and Nancy sat together among the men. Nancy could tell by the way Violette tested the contents of the saltshaker in her hand before putting it on her food that she had endured a lot of the same teasing as herself.

As if on cue, one of the men, whom she recognized as a man named Tom from both the Mad House and Ringway, asked Nancy how many walls she'd failed to climb that day.

"Only one less than the bullets that you failed to shoot straight, Tom," she retorted.

"Hey, Violette," one of the other men called. "I heard you didn't make the cut at Ringway."

"I hurt my ankle," she replied, plunking the saltshaker down with an audible thump. "Running away from jerks like you."

That shut the man up, at least temporarily. "Does that mean they'll be flying you in?" Nancy asked Violette.

"No. Miss Atkins insisted I have to go back to parachute training after I'm finished here."

"Miss Atkins sure has a lot of opinions."

"Indeed. Kind of like these guys." Violette gestured down toward their hecklers.

"I hope they're not as bad as they were at Ringway."

"What is it with men? Are they threatened by us? Is that why they constantly feel the need to put us down?"

"They're not all bad," Nancy said in a conciliatory tone. "Just a few of them." She suddenly recalled the condoms she had stashed in her bag. "And hey, Violette, I just thought of a way we can get the bad ones back."

The next morning, Nancy, armed with one of the condoms from her drawer, found Tom's hat hanging in the hallway. She attached the condom to the side of it on the ribbon in such a way that he wouldn't notice it when he put it on. She and Violette made sure they pointed it out to the other trainees, who all had a hearty laugh behind Tom's back.

Tom seemed like the kind of man who would tattle to get back at her, so Nancy wasn't overly surprised when she was called into the lead instructor's barracks that afternoon.

"Where did you get the condom from, Miss Wake?" Captain Walker, a short, squat man in his fifties, asked.

Nancy at first tried to play innocent. "How did you know it was me?"

"Tom Fielding said he was at the table when you were given

them as a 'gift.' As he recalls, there were three of them in the package. If you hand over the other two, we can pretend this never happened."

"What never happened? That Violette and I, because we are women, have to put up with all this nonsense from the men?"

Captain Walker rubbed his face. "I suppose there are some people who don't think that women should be working for F Section."

"Oh, they don't mind women in F Section, so long as they are secretaries and not secret agents."

"You're not going to give up the other two, are you, Miss Wake?"

It wasn't really a question, but Nancy answered it anyway. "No. Rest assured I will be using them on anyone who I think deserves a little payback."

"That sounds a bit like a threat. Usually I ask that my trainees behave like gentlemen, but I don't suppose that applies to you."

"No, but I'll treat anyone who acts like a gentleman accordingly," Nancy offered.

When she returned to her room that night, Nancy immediately went to her top drawer, where she'd been keeping her underthings along with the other two condoms. "You didn't open this drawer, did you Violette?" she asked her roommate.

"Of course not. Why do you ask?"

Nancy frowned. "It looks like someone went through my things. It was probably Captain Walker, looking for these." She pulled out the remaining condoms that she had stuffed inside a stocking.

"Ah." Violette walked over to stand next to the dresser and

began to shred one of her own stockings. "Here, put these on top." She laid a few pieces of silk on top of the clothes in the drawer. "That way you'll be able to see if anyone went through it again. And maybe you need a better hiding spot."

In the end, they decided to hide the condoms in the space between the drawer and the dresser frame.

The next day when they returned from their run, the silk had indeed been disturbed, proving that someone had been rifling through Nancy's underthings.

Nancy thoroughly enjoyed certain parts of her training, such as learning how to make explosives from using everyday chemicals that were readily available at any British or French pharmacy. It helped that both Violette and Nancy had dabbled in cooking in wartime France and were used to carefully weighing out ingredients, not to mention they were more accustomed to shopping at pharmacies than the men were.

One of the men who grudgingly conceded to their expertise was a South American named René Dussaq. He'd been a stuntman in Hollywood before being recruited to the SOE as a weapons instructor.

"Have you been to France before?" Violette asked him as he took a cigarette break.

"Not yet. They think I'm more valuable here, training the likes of you."

"Why the French name, then?"

"I was born in French Guiana, but then moved to Argentina and then Cuba. My father is a diplomat."

"I can tell you spent a lot of time in America," Nancy told him.

"What do you mean?"

She pointed to his free hand, which was in his pockets. "Frenchmen don't jiggle their loose change like that."

"And your cigarette." Violette took it from him to demonstrate. "The French hold it like this." She grasped the cigarette near the burning end using her fingertip and thumb. "Not between their fingers." She took a drag before handing it back.

This time he was sure to hold it correctly. "Not even Miss Atkins remarked on that one. You two might have just saved my life."

"If you ever get to France, that is," Nancy reminded him.

The worst class was taught by Monsieur Lefevre, who had an annoying habit of saying *n'est ce pas* every other sentence, the French equivalent of "isn't that so?" His task was to teach them about the different German military ranks and their various insignia and uniforms. Nancy found it hard to concentrate on such mundane matters and focused instead on making tick marks every time Monsieur Lefevre said his catchphrase.

He soon caught on that she wasn't paying attention and made a habit of asking her questions she couldn't answer, such as the color of the collar tabs on an SS officer's uniform.

When Nancy stammered, "Uh, black?" he gave her a withering glance. "You must be referring to the Panzer division."

She threw down her pencil. "Panzer or SS—they're all Nazis. Does it really matter?"

"I would say it does, especially if you are flirting with someone you think is a German soldier when really they are the Gestapo, looking to arrest you."

The dryness of his sarcasm caused a few people behind Nancy to chuckle, which only infuriated her further.

"Let me guess," Violette called as she struggled to catch up with Nancy after class. "Monsieur Lefevre is next on your hit list."

"Without a doubt. I've got two condoms left, and one of them has his name on it."

Nancy and Violette arrived a few minutes early the next day. Violette was the one who inflated the condom and Nancy hung it behind the blackboard with a piece of string. The instructors often shared rooms, and it was the job of the incoming person to change out the main blackboard that hung on the wall.

Monsieur Lefevre was in an even more irritable mood than usual and didn't greet the class as usual, heading straight to the blackboard. As soon as he'd taken it off the wall, the condom bounced out.

"Not exactly a work of art *n'est ce pas?*" He turned toward the class. "Who is responsible for this vulgarity?"

No one said anything. Nancy could feel a dozen pairs of eyes on her. Surely the rest of the class must have known it was her, but no one said anything. Monsieur Lefevre probably knew it too, but he refused to give her the satisfaction and tossed the condom near the closed window as he replaced the blackboard and started his lecture.

Halfway through, Captain Walker stepped in. The draft from him opening the door awakened the condom, which bounced from the window to the floor and then near Monsieur Lefevre's feet.

Captain Walker's eyebrows rose, but he didn't say anything. He took a seat as Monsieur Lefevre waxed on about the Nazis' use of the swastika on uniforms and equipment.

Nancy snuck a glance at Violette, whose face was as red as her own. Nancy could tell she was struggling not to laugh.

That night, the silk was once again disturbed, and Nancy figured Captain Walker knew she only had one condom left.

CHAPTER 25

DECEMBER 1943

As frigid December set in, Nancy found that wintertime at Beaulieu, while beautiful, presented extra challenges. The obstacle course was covered in a layer of frost, making it even more slippery, and the running path was iced over in some parts and muddy in others.

Worse yet, Nancy was still struggling with coding so Captain Walker decided to bring in the SOE's expert, Leo Marks, to help. On the morning of his arrival, Nancy and Violette bundled up in their overcoats and heavy boots to make the trek over to the coding building. A picturesque layer of light snow covered the estate house, the bare oak and beech trees of the New Forest standing stark against the winter whiteness.

"This is the expert?" Nancy whispered to Violette as they entered the room. The man pointedly checking his watch couldn't have been more than twenty-five, with unruly black hair and a baby face.

He soon demonstrated his knowledge however, meaning that he nearly lost Nancy the moment he started talking about one-time pads and key distribution. Catching the look on her face, he slowed down. "Let's just use poem codes." He picked up a pencil and nodded at Nancy. "Give me a poem."

She started reciting the lewdest one she could think of:

> *She stood right there in the midnight air,*
> *With nothing on but her nightie.*
> *Her tits hung loose...*

"Okay, got it," Marks replied, cutting her off before she got to the worst of it. "I don't suppose even the Boches' best code-breaker could be able to crack that one." His voice softened as he turned to the gorgeous Violette. "What about you?"

She shook her head. "I can't think of anything."

"I have an idea." Marks picked up his suitcase and pulled out a piece of paper. "The best poems are original. I wrote this one myself. I was just waiting for the right person to use it."

Violette read it aloud:

> *The life that I have*
> *Is all that I have*
> *And the life that I have*
> *Is yours*
>
> *The love that I have*
> *Of the life that I have*
> *Is yours and yours and yours*
>
> *A sleep I shall have*
> *A rest I shall have*
> *Yet death will be but a pause*

For the peace of my years
In the long green grass
Will be yours and yours and yours

"It's beautiful," Violette put down the paper and wiped her eyes. For a moment, she seemed lost in her thoughts, but then she moved her head, as if shaking off some memory. "You said you wrote that yourself?"

"For my girlfriend. She died."

Nancy was starting to see Leo Marks in a whole new light as he took his pencil and sat down next to Violette. "Now, using the poem, assign a numerical value to each letter, ignoring spaces and punctuation. We'll start with the first letter T, which will equal 0, and then H is 1, E is 2 and so on. If a letter repeats, it doesn't get a new number."

Both Violette and Nancy went through their poems, writing the numbers under each letter until they had a ciphertext.

"Now," Marks continued, "Write down the message you want to encrypt. For example, let's just use 'HELP'. H is 1, E is 2, L is 3 and P is 15. So HELP would be 1-2-3-15. You can encrypt and decrypt messages by adding or subtracting the numerical values of the letters—T doesn't have to start at 0." He kept going until finally Nancy had an inkling of how to use her poem code.

"Thanks again for the poem," Violette told Marks when they'd finished. "You should think about being a writer."

His already ruddy face turned even darker. "Maybe someday, when this infernal war is over. For now, I've got my work cut out for me." He nodded at Nancy. "I just hope that whichever FANY is listening to your sked has a good sense of humor."

"Me too," Nancy replied.

. . .

That night, Nancy had a hard time getting to sleep. After she'd tossed and turned a few too many times, Violette's soft voice called out from the bunk below, "Nancy, I know you're still awake. What are you thinking about?"

Henri. It was always Henri at night, and most times during the day. When Nancy didn't reply, Violette spoke again. "I know we're not supposed to share details of our real lives, but what if we changed the names of the people we talk about? Are you married?"

Nancy's voice was barely a whisper. "Yes."

"Is he still in France?"

"I think so. In Marseille." Recalling Violette's reaction to Leo Marks's poem earlier that day, Nancy asked, "What about you? Are you married?"

"I was. But Étienne died in action last year. He never met his daughter."

At this Nancy climbed down the ladder to sit next to Violette. "I didn't know you had a daughter."

"Tania. She's just a little over a year old. I joined the SOE to get back at the bastards who took her father away from her."

Nancy took Violette's hand in hers. She'd always thought that Violette was especially daring, but she now understood her friend's bravery was on a much deeper level.

Violette smiled through her tears. "I forgot I was supposed to change their names."

"That's okay. I won't say anything." After a moment, Nancy added, "My husband's name is Henri."

Violette squeezed her hand. "We'll fight extra hard for Henri and Tania."

"And in memory of Étienne." Nancy stood up and made her way back to her own bunk. "Good night, Violette."

"Good night, Nancy. I hope you sleep better."

"Thank you—I think I'll be able to now."

As Christmas approached, Nancy's final condom felt as though it were burning a hole in her bureau. As their training went on, most of the men, including Tom Fielding and Monsieur Lefevre, had developed a grudging respect for Nancy and Violette, and Nancy didn't see the need to exact revenge on anyone.

The silk threads were disturbed every few days, meaning Captain Walker and his ilk were still trying to find the missing condom, giving Nancy an idea. She put a couple of pieces of candy in a box and then used the condom as wrapping. She then completed the package by tying one of her best silk ribbons around it.

As the SOE wanted to keep their methods as secretive as possible, the trainees weren't allowed Christmas leave. A few of the instructors had been granted holiday leave, but Captain Walker was installed in his quarters at Palace House. Nancy decided to give him the package at the small dinner celebration that was being held in the dining room.

A tiny smile played out on his normally stiff upper lip as he examined the gift. "This is how you chose to deploy your last one?"

"As an extra present to you—I didn't use it for a prank, though I had some good ones in mind."

"Such as?" Walker undid the ribbon and then fiddled with removing the condom.

Nancy shrugged. "As a water balloon or maybe even a fake grenade."

"Well," Walker held up misshapen latex before tossing it in a nearby trash can. "I guess I should say thank you."

"Thank *you*," Nancy returned sincerely. "As a participant in the Resistance for a long time, I didn't think there was anything you could teach me, but clearly I was wrong. I will be a better agent because of the SOE."

Walker nodded. "I think you will be a fine field operative. In fact, Buckmaster will be coming shortly after the New Year to finalize your assignment."

"Happy Christmas then."

"Happy Christmas," Walker returned.

That evening, Nancy and Violette exchanged their own gifts in the privacy of their room. Nancy had chosen a small bottle of perfume that reminded her of Paris and Violette had knitted her a scarf.

As Violette was to return to Ringway in a few days to repeat her parachute training, Nancy knew it would be a long time before she saw her friend again. Since Nancy's five siblings were all so much older than she, Violette had become the closest thing to a sister she'd ever had.

Nancy swung the scarf around her neck. "Maybe next year the war will be over, and you'll get to spend Christmas with Tania."

"I hope so," Violette replied, her voice breaking. "Although we'll never truly be a family, not without Étienne." She placed the bottle of perfume on top of her bureau. "Maybe you and Henri can then start a family of your own."

Nancy attempted a smile. "That will work itself out eventually. I just want to see him again."

"I hope you do." Violette crossed the room to give her a long hug. "Good luck, Nancy."

"Good luck, Violette. Give them hell at Ringway."

"And you give them hell in France."

∼

A few days after the New Year, Nancy was called to London to report to Buckmaster's office at 64 Baker Street. Luckily, Miss Atkins was noticeably absent.

Buck sat behind a cluttered desk, a detailed map of France marked with pins covering the wall behind him. Heavy blackout curtains blocked out the sun, and the only light in the room came from his desk lamp.

Nancy, suddenly feeling claustrophobic, dropped into the chair in front of his desk.

Buck set down his pipe as he nodded at her. "I take it you're ready to go back to France?"

"Of course."

He took the top folder off the stack to his right. "Your alias will be Madame Gertrude Andrée, a widow."

She swallowed hard, recalling that horrible dream she'd had of Henri dying from the U-boat.

Ignorant of Nancy's sorrow at the term, *widow*, Buckmaster continued, "You'll be parachuting into the Auvergne region. Your network's primary objective is to coordinate with the Maquis and provide them with arms, sabotage training, and intelligence."

The Maquis was a collective name for various groups of young men who had sought refuge in remote areas of France, mostly to avoid being conscripted to forced labor under the STO. Many of the SOE agents had established contact with various Maquis groups to train them in guerrilla warfare to help with the much-talked-about Allied Landing.

Nancy's eyes flicked over to the map. "Which Maquis group will I be working with?"

"A man named Gaspard is said to command around four thousand Maquisards around l'Auvergne."

Nancy gave a low whistle. "That many, huh?"

"Yes but…" Buckmaster refilled his pipe and soon the room was filled with smoke. "As with most of the local Maquis leaders, Gaspard doesn't seem the most welcoming to help from the SOE. Maurice Southgate, another one of our agents, will act as your liaison. He's already formed a relationship with the Maquisards in the area. Your network is named 'Freelance' and its leader will be Hubert. Your immediate responsibility is to distribute the weapons, explosives, and other supplies received through SOE airdrops, which you will also be organizing."

She didn't know much about Hubert, other than he was quiet but well respected among the other trainees at Beaulieu. "Right. And who will I be communicating this through?"

Buck flipped over another paper. "Your wireless operator will be Denis Rake. I believe you are familiar with the man."

"Denden?" After having just left Violette in a tearful goodbye, Nancy was ecstatic to have a friend in the field.

"Indeed. He's still refusing to parachute in, however, so we'll be bringing him in under the next full moon. The landing spot is a few hundred kilometers from l'Auvergne, so you'll be without a radio operator for a few days."

Typical Denden. "What about me? When do I leave?"

Buck closed the folder and met her gaze. "Tomorrow night.

You'll fly out from RAF Tangmere and drop just after midnight. Make sure all your preparations are complete by then."

Nancy stood. "I'll be ready. Thank you."

He held up a finger as he dug through his desk with his other hand. "Wait. I still have to give you your pills. Stimulants, relaxers, and, of course, the L-pill."

Buckmaster's pills were known throughout the SOE training camps. The purpose of the stimulants and relaxers was obvious, but the reason for the L-pill, a lethal pill of cyanide, was less straightforward. In the event an agent was picked up by the Gestapo and feared they would talk under torture, they were supposed to swallow it, thereby ending their own life and any possibility they'd give too much away. The agents had nicknamed it the 'Suicide Pill.'"

Nancy put the packet of pills in her purse. "Has anyone ever taken the L-pill?"

"Not yet." He reached into his drawer again and pulled out a small box. "On a lighter note, I always like to give my agents a good luck present." He handed it to her. "You could also sell this on the black market if the need arises."

She opened the box and pulled out a tiny gold bracelet. Her heart felt heavy as she remembered all the times Henri had given her jewelry. "Thank you, sir."

"Good luck, Nancy. Hopefully the next time I see you, the war will be over."

"Indeed, sir."

CHAPTER 26

FEBRUARY 1944

*A*s the plane rocked yet again, Nancy resorted to sitting on her hands, hoping the weight against them would help her forget the urge to vomit. Perhaps partying the night before in a club in Piccadilly hadn't been such a good idea after all, especially with René Dussaq urging her to 'drink like it was her last day on Earth,' after her final briefing with Buckmaster.

"It's not my last day on Earth," Nancy had replied after a gulp of brandy. "But it's definitely my last day in England, at least for a while. And there *will* be a tomorrow, but who knows what happens after that?"

They had stayed at the club until at least four o'clock in the morning, at which point they made their way back to Nancy's flat. Their unsteady walking was punctuated by the occasional parachute roll in the street, which had been initiated by Dussaq, the Hollywood stuntman.

After a particularly rough roll, Dussaq lay flat on his back, singing, "*Glory, glory what a helluva way to die.*"

Nancy grabbed his arm and got him back on his feet before he got run over. "It's also a helluva way to live."

Now, sitting in the massive Liberator B-24 bomber, trying to keep down the SPAM sandwich and coffee she'd been provided, Nancy had to admit that choking on her own vomit would be a helluva way to die.

Above all, Miss Atkins' harsh words echoed in her head. It was true, Nancy had done well in her exploits early in the war, but she'd had the name of Madame Fiocca going for her. Now the French would know her as Madame Andrée, and she would report back to London under the code name Hélène. Her life as Madame Fiocca was over for the foreseeable future. Most painful of all wasn't the loss of her name—it was that she wouldn't be Henri's wife to anyone she met in France.

She tugged at the prized camel-hair coat, one of several possessions that Miss Atkins had allotted. It was Miss Atkins' mission to make sure that everything about her agents screamed French, and she had even replaced some of the agents' English cigarettes with French ones. Nancy, however, stood firm on taking her favorite Elizabeth Arden face cream with her, and Miss Atkins had actually relented and provided her with a French cosmetics jar to keep it in.

Across from her, her circuit leader, Major John Farmer, code named Hubert, looked just as green as Nancy felt. She hoped that it wasn't an omen for how their mission would go. Buckmaster had assigned them the monumental task of assessing the military competence of the roughly four thousand members of the Maquis scattered around the Auvergne region in central France.

Nancy's stomach had gradually begun to settle, but then the pilot's voice came over the intercom, drawling in a Texas accent, "Dropping zone coming up."

She checked her parachute straps yet again, which dug uncomfortably into her shoulders. She supposed she hadn't needed all the layers she'd put on: beneath her coat, she wore army-issued coveralls on top of her tweed suit and silk stockings on her legs. Her plan was to shed the coveralls immediately after landing so she'd blend in with the natives. Of course, if any Germans were to come across her, they might wonder why she was wearing Chanel in the middle of a forest, but Nancy brushed that detail aside.

She peered through the open bomb-bay for her first look at France in almost a year. Even from 100 meters in the air, Nancy could clearly see the fiery glow of the bonfires and torches of the reception committee. "Every Boche between here and Russia will know we're arriving," she remarked to Hubert.

If Hubert had a reply, it was drowned out by a sudden jerk from the plane. The dispatcher clapped Hubert on the back. "It's time to jump."

Hubert gave a simple nod and then he was gone. Nancy watched him descend until he was just a speck, and then all of a sudden, a whiteness blocked her view. "His parachute opened," she said aloud.

"Did you think it wouldn't?" the dispatcher asked.

She shrugged.

His gaze swept over her camel coat and then down to her heeled shoes. "We've never dropped a woman before. Are you sure you want to do this?"

"Of course I'm sure," she snapped back. "Just let me know when it's time to jump."

After checking to make sure Hubert was clear, he told her, "You can go now."

Another urge to check her parachute came over her, but, not

wanting to display any more anxiety to the dispatcher, she dropped through the hatch.

Following a few heart-pounding seconds of an exhilarating freefall, Nancy's heart wrenched at the sudden tug from the static line deploying the parachute. As she drifted downward, the world below was bathed in a peaceful twilight, the would-be midnight blackness broken by the still-burning bonfires. Yet, as the ground drew nearer, another wave of apprehension washed over her. Surely the light and commotion would attract any Boche within a ten-kilometer radius. Denden would say she would be nothing but a sitting Ducks. Make that a very slow-flying duck, her open parachute presenting a sizable target, upon which a single, well-placed bullet could turn a leisurely descent into a fatal plunge.

Nancy was powerless to do anything but squeeze her eyes shut and lock her legs at the knees. She braced for the impact of the ground, but it never came.

When she opened her eyes, she realized she'd drifted away from the bonfires and toward darkness. The downward motion stopped as something scraped Nancy's face. She'd gotten trapped in a tree.

Her breath caught as she heard the sound of many boots stomping through the bush. Someone called out in French that they'd spotted her parachute.

The footsteps paused just below her. "Thanks be to England for at last sending us a gorgeous flower such as this one."

The accent was too perfect to be from a German, Nancy decided as her legs flailed out in the empty air. "Just get me out of this tree, would you?"

The man stepped back into her eyesight and motioned with his hand for her to grab the release mechanism of her parachute.

Right. Feeling even more foolish, she did and immediately dropped to the ground. As she straightened, she saw that the man standing before her was handsome, with dark eyes and a chiseled face.

"Are you Southgate?" she asked.

His eyebrows furrowed as he shook his head. "I'm Henri Tardivat. Most people call me 'Tardi,' though I'm hardly ever late."

The joke was lost on her as she dug sticks and leaves out of her hair.

"You must be Madame Andrée."

"Gertrude," she said pointedly. "You can call me Gertie." She lowered her hands before asking, "Where's Hubert?"

Tardi gestured toward the other field, where the bonfires were thankfully dying out. She pulled out her knife and reached toward her still dangling parachute.

"What are you doing?" Tardi demanded. "You're going to ruin it."

"What does it matter? We have to bury it anyway." The SOE had been perfectly clear on that account, but Tardi insisted that the silk would sell for a good price on the black market.

After Tardi retrieved the parachute and tucked it carefully under his arm, he informed Nancy that a car was waiting for them.

"A car?" Now she was sure everything she'd been taught regarding the Maquis' lack of security was correct. Not many people besides the Boches could afford petrol and she'd been advised to travel by foot, or, if absolutely necessary, by bicycle or train.

Tardi's car, it turned out, was a gazogène that ran on charcoal. With the headlights off, he drove Hubert and Nancy to a small farmhouse in the village of Cosne-d'Allier. Though the owners, a man named Jean and his wife, were not technically members of the Resistance, they were sympathetic to the cause and willing to put the newcomers up in their guest room for a few nights. There was only one problem—the guest room contained only one bed.

Nancy turned to Hubert. As he wasn't in any of her training classes, she'd only had a few conversations with her new circuit leader. Based on her observations, Hubert appeared to be both competent and committed, but they hadn't quite connected on a personal level.

"I can sleep in the corner of the room," he offered.

"Nonsense. We've both come a long way. You can lay in the bed as long as you stay on top of the bedclothes."

Clearly exhausted, he nodded his consent.

CHAPTER 27

MARCH 1944

Hubert and Nancy spent a few awkward nights in Jean and his wife's guestroom. To everyone's noticeable dismay, neither Southgate nor any of his associates showed themselves. Hubert began chafing at the bit. Nancy, who was starting to feel the same way, tried to be diplomatic. After all, even if they were able to make contact with Gaspard, the head of the local Maquis, they couldn't communicate with London as Denden hadn't arrived yet.

"Still, we can't just hang around this house all day," Hubert told her. "It's dangerous for all of us."

Since Jean wasn't a Resistance member, he wasn't sure how to directly contact Gaspard, but he offered to take them to a man called Laurent, who, Jean insisted, would know how to get in touch with Gaspard.

Once again, Nancy got into a car against her better judgment. But as Jean drove Hubert and her around the region, she realized quickly that walking or riding a bicycle through the mountains and craggy volcanic rock would have proven to be an arduous task. Gazing out the window of Jean's gazogène, she decided that the rough terrain could definitely be advantageous for the guerilla saboteurs collectively known as the Maquis.

They had to go through six or seven men before the last finally gave them directions to a house where he assured them they would find Laurent.

Laurent was tall, with a rugged jawline adorned with a hint of stubble. His speech lacked polish, but Nancy had a feeling that his keen eyes and mind didn't miss much. Though he raised his eyebrows when Hubert introduced Nancy as his courier, he didn't comment on the fact that she was a woman. "Gaspard isn't here."

Nancy heaved a sigh. Another dead end.

"But if you want to stay the night here, I can take you to him in the morning," Laurent continued.

After exchanging a quick glance with Hubert, Nancy ventured, "How many beds do you have available?"

After nearly a week of waiting and following up on multiple leads which turned out to be dead ends, Nancy and Hubert finally met Gaspard in the flesh, in an abandoned château in Mont Mouchet.

Gaspard strode into the room with the unmistakable air of someone who was aware that their arrival had been greatly anticipated. He was accompanied by several men whose appearance could only be described as weather-beaten, their gaunt faces and hollowed eyes bearing the evidence of having spent the last several months out in the elements. Clearly they were members of the Maquis.

Gaspard towered over Hubert. He held a dismissive expression, as if he'd already made up his mind that the two newcomers were of no importance even before he demanded who they were.

Hubert stepped forward, as if to extend his hand, but then thought better of it. "We are members of the Freelance Circuit, with the Special Operations Executive, from London—"

"London, eh? Do you even know what's happening with the war then, if you're from London?"

"I was in France when the Nazis arrived," Nancy offered. "I worked for the PAO Line with Ian Garrow and then Pat O'Leary."

"Never heard of any of that," Gaspard returned gruffly. "Why is it you needed to meet with me?"

"We're here to offer you assistance," Hubert answered. "Such as munitions—"

Again Gaspard cut him off. "We don't need any assistance."

His tone contained such finality that Hubert was at a loss for words. He glanced helplessly at Nancy, who held up her handbag. "I have several hundred francs in here, and there's plenty more to be had from the SOE."

"And how do you plan on asking for that? I don't suppose either one of you knows how to operate a transmitter."

Gaspard had them there—it was true they had no radio operator. Yet.

"Neither my men nor I need assistance at this time, but if we did, we would ask the Free French for it, not anyone in London, and especially not a couple of Britons who have just arrived," Gaspard continued.

Nancy wanted to point out that the Free French were also headquartered in London, but she could tell that arguing with this man would be pointless.

"I see." Hubert glanced at his watch. "If you don't mind,

we've come a long way and are hoping to rest a bit before taking our leave."

Gaspard waved his hand. "Take all the time you need." He nodded at his men. "Let's eat."

The men, who'd been lounging around the furniture, filed out to what Nancy presumed was the kitchen. All except for one of them who grudgingly showed her and Hubert to a back bedroom.

A fire had been lit, and, since the room felt exceedingly warm, Nancy opened the window. Leaning out, she heard a gruff voice ask in French, "Boss, are you sure you don't want to accept their offer? We could definitely use the money, not to mention the guns."

"And form an alliance with those moronic Londoners?" The voice was unmistakably Gaspard's.

Nancy hissed at Hubert that she could hear Gaspard and his crew. Hubert joined her at the window just in time to hear another man volunteer to seduce Nancy, steal her money, and then kill her.

Hubert gave her an incredulous glance, to which Nancy returned a grin. "I'd never let those shabby men within two meters of me, let alone try to seduce me."

Nonetheless, a few minutes later, there was a knock on the door. When Nancy answered it, one of the more unkempt men stood in the doorway. He offered her a nearly toothless grin and asked if she'd like to go for a walk outside.

"A walk? And then what, you expect to be invited into my bed?"

He had the grace to look taken aback and stuttered a denial.

Nancy moved to shut the door. "I have no desire to be seduced nor murdered. And I'll be holding on to my money, thank you very much, as your leader has made it clear he has no use for us."

The man bared another toothless grin. "I would never presume, madame." He glanced at Hubert, who stood behind Nancy with his arms crossed. "In fact, Gaspard would like to offer you both rooms for tonight. I'd show you to yours, Madame Andrée, but something tells me you'd like to find it yourself."

She grabbed her purse from the bedside table.

"It's just down the hall." The Maquisard pointed a dirty finger before strolling off in the other direction.

"I guess this means good night, then," Nancy said to Hubert.

"Gertie—"

"I'll be just fine," she insisted.

In the morning, Nancy's would-be seducer escorted them out of the château. At the front door, he hesitated. "Just so you know, there is another man that might take you up on your offer."

"Oh?" Nancy ventured.

"His name is Fournier. He and Gaspard don't get along, but Fournier is just as dedicated to the cause."

Hubert nodded. "Please tell us where to find him."

CHAPTER 28

APRIL 1944

Henry Fournier was the opposite of Gaspard in nearly every way that counted. Instead of exuding arrogance, Fournier listened to Hubert and Nancy's offer, his expression one of interest instead of completely detached. He too headed a band of Maquis, this one located in Chaudes-Aigues, a commune in the Cantal department famous for its natural hot springs. As a former hotel executive, Fournier used his own money to finance their exploits, though he seemed more than willing to accept financial assistance from the SOE.

Of course, there was still the matter of the missing radio operator. Despite his politeness, Fournier recognized that, without Denden, Nancy and Hubert would be unable to deliver on the promises of more supplies and money. Until the day they could be of more use to him, Fournier offered them accommodation in a hotel in Lieutadès, a tiny village situated high in the Massif Central mountains.

. . .

Nancy spent the next few days wandering the town, kicking at dirt and snow and wondering where in the hell Denden was. It was a gray, unpleasant spring, and while she and Hubert had separate rooms at the hotel, it wasn't the grandest place she'd ever been. Moreover, it was disheartening to finally be back in France but unable to really do anything to help the Resistance.

One morning, Nancy decided to take a break from her restless strolling to sit on the wall next to the cemetery. Suddenly, a car screeched to a halt only a few meters away and nearly knocked her from her perch.

The man who emerged from the vehicle was none other than Denden himself. "Picking out the most fitting grave, are we now, Ducks?"

She threw her arms around him before asking, "What took you so long?"

He pulled a bag and his transmitting suitcase out of the trunk before slamming the door shut. As the car drove off, Denden grinned. "Can you believe that one of the members of my reception committee was my former lover?"

Nancy's mouth dropped open. "Are you telling me that you've held us up here because you needed one last fling?"

"Of course." He put his arm around her as they started walking back to the hotel. "But now I'm really ready to get to work."

That afternoon, Fournier made a visit to the hotel. As he and Hubert sat hunched over a rough-hewn table, meticulously compiling a list of the supplies they needed, Nancy helped Denden set up his transmitting equipment, including the aerial—a spindly contraption of wires and metal that required careful handling.

Fournier and his men were still a little skeptical that all it took to get their ammunition and guns was a simple radio transmission, so Nancy invited them all to watch Denden's first communication. The Maquisards formed a loose circle around Denden's table, their expressions ranging from curiosity to doubt.

As Denden started tapping away on his Morse key, he whispered to Nancy that the audience was making him nervous.

"Don't mind them," she replied.

But after a few minutes, Denden again glanced at Nancy, his eyes wide, before he gestured for her to come closer. "Don't tell anyone," he said in English, his voice low. "But I got my times mixed up, and my sked isn't for another 24 hours."

Nancy knew he was referring to his scheduled time to contact the SOE. If he wasn't supposed to be transmitting at this time, it meant that no one in London would be listening. Her eyes wandered around the room, weaving through the anxious men shuffling their heavy boots on the wooden floor. "Don't forget to ask for further instructions," she commanded Denden loudly in French.

He nodded, understanding. After a few more taps on his Morse key, he told the room, "London is interested, but they want us to contact them again tomorrow."

The promise of a follow-up communication seemed to satisfy Fournier, and he nodded at his men. A low murmur of approval spread through the group as they filed out the door.

"That was close," Nancy stated when she and Denden were alone.

"You're telling me."

. . .

The next night, with much less of an audience this time, Denden was able to actually make contact. After what felt like an eternity, a series of rapid beeps indicated that London had received their message and had a reply. Denden's shoulders visibly relaxed as he decoded the message. Finally, he set down his pencil. "They confirm the drop at 0000 hours with the coordinates we provided. They will send a message via the BBC to verify the plane's departure tomorrow."

The following morning, Nancy perched in front of the radio, her fingers spinning the dial to find the BBC's broadcast. She had to listen to the *messages personnels* on five separate programs before she heard the key phrase to let them know the airdrop would be on: *the cow jumped over the moon.*

The plateaus atop the mountains that encircled Chaudes-Aigues proved an ideal location for airdrops. Remembering their own indiscreet reception, Nancy convinced Hubert to keep the fires small and shielded among the rocks and brush. As the flames burned, Nancy, Hubert, and Fournier and his men lay scattered among the field, their gazes focused on the western sky.

Shortly past midnight, the stillness of the plateau was broken by the faint hum of aircraft engines, a low, throbbing sound that steadily grew louder. Nancy, who'd just begun to doze off, sat up, her eyes straining against the darkness.

The plane circled overhead and the first parachute unfurled, its white silk illuminated by the faint glow of the full moon. Fournier and his team scurried across the field, chasing the parachutes with their arms outstretched, acting like children on Christmas Day. And indeed, it did seem like Christmas as the parachutes kept descending, bringing their much-needed supplies.

Fournier assured them that it would be safe enough to unpack the contents of the containers right there on the field. Hubert consented, though he insisted they at least move into a flat area shielded by low bushes and boulders.

It took them several more hours to empty the crates. The team worked quietly, the sound of wood splintering and the rustle of parachute silk the only noises breaking the pre-dawn stillness. Finally, as the first light crept over the horizon, the Maquisards returned to the shadows of the forest, their arms laden with weapons, ammunition, and other various supplies, including a manual written in French called *How to Use Explosives on the Ground*. Nancy silently congratulated herself—the operation had been a success, though the real work was just beginning.

The next six days fell into a relentless rhythm. Each morning and afternoon, Nancy, feeling a strange combination of exhaustion and exhilaration, would be positioned next to the radio, the static crackling through her weary ears. At night, she would again find herself in the field, catching up on her sleep under the stars. That is until the roar of a bomber plane jostled her awake.

For the last drop, Nancy had asked Denden for a special communication with London, and sure enough, a container landed that was marked 'Personal for Hélène.' Inside was the red embroidered pillow and two silk nightgowns that had been retrieved from her Piccadilly apartment. Someone, probably Miss Atkins herself, had also included more Elizabeth Arden face cream, packed into a French bottle, of course.

Predictably, Fournier was ecstatic at his own 'prizes,' which included hand grenades, Sten guns, rifles, pistols, and an array of different-sized bullets. Thanks to the members of the Freelance network, he and his men were now among the most well-equipped Maquis in France. Nancy, for her part, couldn't help taking satisfaction in knowing that Gaspard's Maquisards would be far less well outfitted.

CHAPTER 29

MAY 1944

Now that the dynamics had shifted, the Londoners found that they were in high demand. They moved out of the hotel and into the forest to be closer to the Maquis. For Nancy, as the lone woman living among thousands of rugged Maquis, it was an experience unlike any other. Every few days, they'd relocate to a different campsite, and she'd have to restart her search for the most comfortable patch of the forest. Usually she'd find a spot under a large pine tree and make a bed out of the needles. One of the men gave her a nearly threadbare blanket, and, as long as the night looked like it would remain clear, she'd put on one of the nightgowns Henri had given her and curl up with her red pillow. Though they were modest comforts compared to all the luxuries she'd once owned, they helped her forget her current, rugged existence for a bit. And of course, they reminded her of Henri.

Once she had settled into a suitable sleeping spot, her second mission was always to find what she called, *'Toilettes Pour Femmes.'* This was mostly due to the first night she spent with the Maquis, when she tried to relieve herself in what she thought were secluded bushes. However, as soon as she crouched down, her ears picked up a faint rustling sound and several pairs of boots peeking out from nearby shrubbery. Her shouted warning had been followed by the sound of stifled laughter. She knew that the Maquisards had gone months, maybe even years, without seeing a woman, but still... After a light scolding, all the men in the forest became well aware of Nancy's need to go to the bathroom in private and, as soon as they arrived in a new location, some of them would point out potential *Toilettes Pour Femmes* shielded by dense underbrush.

The Maquisards typically subsisted on foraged fare, including mushrooms, wild game like rabbits, and even dandelions when rations were low. Occasionally they would steal food from their fellow countrymen, a process Nancy put an immediate stop to, explaining that the Germans were the enemy, not the French. Unless of course, they were collaborators. Besides, London gave her plenty of money to distribute among the Maquisards, enabling them to buy bread, cheese, and occasionally horse meat from nearby farms.

Soon after Nancy had arrived, she noticed one young Maquisard, Théodore, grimacing as he tried to chew on a piece of stale bread. The smell of sweat and unwashed bodies was as ubiquitous in the camp as wine, but it hadn't occurred to Nancy that the lack of hygiene among the men could lead to health issues.

"Let me see your gums," she commanded Théodore.

He grinned at her, revealing a nearly empty mouth. What few teeth he had were nearly black.

"*Mon Dieu,*" she muttered, waving away his stale breath. "This can't go on."

. . .

When she told Denden about the request for as many toothbrushes as the SOE could provide, he laughed at her before asking, "Ducks, do you think the SOE is your personal delivery service?"

She gave him a patronizing smile. "Denden, we may be at war, but that doesn't mean we have to live like animals. Not to mention that teaching the men to have proper hygiene will make mealtimes more pleasant for everyone."

Denden, still chuckling under his breath, coded the message.

When the toothbrushes arrived in the latest drop, the reactions ranged from confusion to laughter.

"Are these really necessary?" Théodore held up a brush as if it were a relic from another world.

"Yes," Nancy answered. "And for you especially, young man." She handed him a tube of French toothpaste.

The next morning, as Nancy was getting ready to visit another camp, she couldn't help but smile at the sight of the Maquis brushing their teeth around the campfire. Though it might seem an insignificant achievement in the wider view of liberating France, Nancy still considered it a much-needed improvement.

~

The SOE's calculations indicated that no fewer than seventeen different bands of Maquis were scattered among the Chaudes-Aigues plateau, the leadership style of each commander as varied as the terrain itself.

As the *chef du parachutage*, Nancy had the task of coordinating supply drops for these myriad groups. Before she'd left London, Buckmaster had specifically requested that Nancy enlist Colonel Paishing's assistance. A veteran of the Spanish Civil War, he had formed a Maquis out of fellow Spaniards who had fled across the Pyrenees into France to avoid persecution under Franco's forces. According to Buckmaster, his expertise in guerrilla warfare and resistance tactics would make him a valuable asset to Freelance's efforts.

One humid afternoon, Nancy approached the camp of the Spanish Maquis leader. As she stepped into the clearing, her eyes took in a scene not unlike that of her own Maquis, although the murmured conversations among the men were all in Spanish. A man with a swarthy complexion and arms bulging with muscles stood in front of a table constructed out of tree trunks. By the way he was grunting to the men around him, Nancy could only assume she was looking at Colonel Paishing.

His eyes narrowed slightly as he saw Nancy approaching. "What do you want?" he demanded in French as a few of his men unshouldered their rifles.

Unfazed by the frosty reception, Nancy met Paishing's gaze. "I'm here as a request from the Special Operations Executive in London. They want to offer you guns and cash, and, as chef du parachutage, I can get you anything else you request."

Paishing waved a hand as if to brush her off. "We have no use for help from London, especially if it comes from a woman."

A couple of the men snickered and Nancy tried not to let her irritation show. This was going the same route as with Gaspard and the last thing she wanted to happen was for Denden to send a message to Buck that she'd failed again.

One of the men took a swig from a flask, some of the drink

escaping and running down his bushy beard.

Nancy was struck with inspiration and reached for the flask. "Can I have some of that?"

"*Esto no es vino, señora. Es aguardiente.*"

She'd had a few sips of the traditional Spanish spirit, known for its high alcohol content, before. "Whatever, just pass it over."

The man exchanged an amused glance with Paishing, who nodded.

Nancy took a hearty swig before wiping her mouth, the fiery liquid burning its way down her throat. She handed the flask back with a satisfied smile. "Very smooth."

The bearded man looked impressed. "Let's see if you can handle more."

Nancy, who still had an unusually high tolerance for alcohol, took another long drink. Colonel Paishing watched her, a curious look on his wide face.

When the flask was finally empty, one of the other men produced another one and the unspoken contest continued, Nancy matching the bearded man drink for drink.

The bearded man's flask-passing had become clumsy and he was now swaying. To Nancy's relief, he finally dropped the third flask on the ground, a look of defeat on his face. Colonel Paishing lifted Nancy's arm and she did a little victory two-step, her movements still fairly coordinated.

Releasing her arm, Paishing cleared his throat. "All right, Madame..."

"Gertrude Andrée," she said, supplying her code name. "But you can call me Gertie."

"Gertie. Maybe we could use some assistance after all." A reluctant smile formed. "You did say you would give us money, didn't you?"

"And guns. I think I can also arrange for a delivery of aguardiente—or at least some brandy—seeing as..." She nodded at the emptied flasks, "you'll be needing more."

"What about medical supplies?" one of the onlookers asked.

"Sure," Nancy replied.

Paishing's men, finally understanding what she could provide for them, began talking all at once while Nancy took mental notes in her slightly hazy brain.

As she prepared to leave, Colonel Paishing extended his hand. "Thank you in advance, Gertie."

"It's really the SOE you should thank," Nancy said. "And remember, we're all fighting the same enemy."

"Cheers to that." Paishing produced a flask from his own hip pocket, but Nancy waved him off. She'd had enough for one night.

CHAPTER 30

JUNE 1944

In the early days of June, the airdrops increased, bringing containers overflowing with not just the requested supplies and money, but copious quantities of khaki jackets and black boots for the Maquis. The men were thrilled with the more professional appearance the uniforms afforded them and Nancy was just as pleased since the fresh clothes got the men out of the foul-smelling, tattered attire they'd been wearing for months on end.

It was evident that London was preparing the Maquis for the so-called D-Day, the much-anticipated moment when the Allies would finally invade France and then from there, Germany. The latest deliveries also included a significant escalation in advanced weaponry—automatic rifles, compact machine guns, and specialized demolition charges. Of course, the men had had no instruction in the use of this new technology, so Nancy wasn't overly surprised when a message came through the wireless that a weapons instructor, code-named 'Anselme,' was being dispatched to their location.

When Denden passed on the message, he told Nancy, "They're sending this Anselme to a safehouse in Montluçon."

She shook her head. "We don't have a safehouse in Montluçon."

"According to London, we do. They said to confirm with Southgate."

"No one's heard from Southgate since before we arrived in France. He's most likely been arrested."

"Well," Denden held a match under the message. "I guess you're going to have to figure out the details—otherwise this Anselme won't be coming, and our men won't know how to use the new guns they've sent us."

Denden tended to be overly gloomy. She sighed before stating, "And I suppose the entire success of D-Day rests on whether or not I find this safehouse."

He gave her a wry smile. "You got it."

Fournier lent Nancy a car and driver, a young but seasoned Maquisard named Jean-Paul, and they set out for Montluçon, a journey which would normally take just a little over two hours. However, they'd been warned that there were patrols in the area so every few kilometers, Jean-Paul would slow the car to a crawl, the tires crunching on the gravel as they scanned the surroundings for signs of Germans.

Equally perilous as the German roadblocks was the threat of crossing paths with unfamiliar members of the Maquis—Gaspard's men, who were known to prefer to use their weapons over asking questions. Nancy kept a loaded Sten gun at her side just in case.

When they finally reached the cobblestoned streets of

Montluçon, Jean-Paul parked in a secluded alley. Nancy told him to stay in the car and wait for her.

Not having the first clue where to go, she headed toward the main square, which was lined with market stalls. She knew that the owner of the safehouse went by the name of Madame Renard, though the challenge was to locate her without arousing suspicion. Nancy chose her targets carefully, approaching older women who seemed less likely to be collaborating with the Germans. However, no one she talked to had heard of Madame Renard and Nancy was starting to think her hunt had been in vain.

Finally someone told her that a Madame Renard lived far off the square, but they weren't sure of the exact house. Recalling the time in Perpignan when she'd been in a similar situation, Nancy decided to just let her instincts guide her. Eventually she stumbled upon a cottage at the town's edge, partly concealed by vibrant bougainvillea vines. Figuring it was the most suitable-looking safehouse she'd come across, Nancy knocked on the door.

A woman cracked it open cautiously, revealing only her wrinkled face and a crop of white hair.

"Are you Madame Renard?"

"I suppose that depends on who is asking."

Once again, her instincts had been spot on. "I am Madame Andrée. We have many things in common, and though I won't be able to say the right words, I believe you have a package for me."

The woman's eyes narrowed. "What sort of things do we have in common?"

Nancy decided to go for broke. It was possible that the woman wasn't Madame Renard and was, in fact, a German collaborator, but there was also a chance that Anselme was at that moment listening to their conversation. "Our love for our country. My name, as I said, is Madame Andrée, but I also go by the name Nancy Wake."

At this, she heard another door open. "It's okay, madame," a voice said from inside the house. "I know her."

Madame Renard opened the door wider and Nancy stepped into the dark hallway.

Once her eyes had adjusted, she saw a familiar figure tucking a revolver back into his belt. Anselme was none other than René Dussaq, the SOE weapons instructor and former Hollywood stuntman whom Nancy and Violette had befriended at Beaulieu. The last time she had seen him, he'd been doing parachute rolls in Piccadilly Circus.

"Nancy, how the hell are you?"

She embraced her old friend before telling him, "It's Gertie now. Gertrude Andrée."

Over the lunch Madame Renard had prepared for them, Nancy informed Dussaq they would be traveling back to Chaudes-Aigues by car.

"Car?" Dussaq gulped down a mouthful of carrot soup. "But Nancy, you know what the SOE said about cars…"

"Trust me," she replied with a laugh. "You'll soon see why."

During the trip back, Nancy sat up front next to Jean-Paul with her loaded Sten gun. Dussaq sprawled across the backseat, his revolver trained on the door. However, the roads were noticeably empty, and in some places, the Germans had completely abandoned their roadblocks.

"It might be a little *too* quiet," Nancy remarked.

Jean-Paul nodded his agreement.

. . .

They made good time, and when they arrived back at Fournier's headquarters, they found that, in contrast to the deserted roads, the woods were abuzz with activity.

Nancy had barely climbed out of the car before Hubert approached, his eyes bright with excitement. His words, usually so calm and measured, tumbled out as one long stream, "TheAllieshavejustlandedonFrenchsoil!"

She locked the bolt of the Sten gun into the safety position and tucked it back into her shoulder sling. "What was that again?"

"The Allies have landed in Normandy. D-Day is here."

Dussaq, mindful of the gun, grabbed Nancy's arm before carefully twirling her into a wide arc. "Victory is coming. *Vive la France!*"

"*Vive la France!*" she shouted back, not caring if all the Germans in the forest heard her. The Allies were on their way.

CHAPTER 31

JUNE 1944

Nancy was slightly disappointed that she'd missed the beginnings of the D-Day celebrations due to her rendezvous with René Dussaq at Madame Renard's, but soon got over it as there were plenty of railways and bridges to be blown up. For the next week, the Maquisards made use of their recently acquired weapons and Dussaq's meticulous instructions on their proper deployment.

The Boches, of course, retaliated against these attacks with harsh reprisals. Unable to track down the Maquis, they took their anger out on the region's innocent Frenchmen and their families. Nearly every day, Nancy had to pass a farmhouse reduced to ashes, her stomach lurching at the sight of scorched human remains strewn in the grass or mangled bodies hanging from trees.

Still, the French citizens refused to stand down, and some houses began proudly displaying the French flag from their windows. New recruits appeared at all hours, having traveled hundreds of kilometers to join the Maquis. Though Nancy appreciated their determination—however delayed—Denden nicknamed them 'Moths' because, as he put it, they'd spent most of the war hiding in closets.

Despite what Denden might have thought of the Moths, they had abandoned their lives and families to fight the Germans. To Nancy, men like that represented the genuine spirit of the Resistance.

The Moths, of course, added to their ever-increasing need for more uniforms and supplies, so Nancy spent her days helping Denden code and transmit while her nights were occupied with picking up the subsequent airdrops and then unpacking and distributing the contents of the packages. Even though she'd probably overseen more than thirty airdrops, she didn't suppose she'd ever get over the excitement on the Maquisards' faces when they saw the contents of the containers and knew that someone across the Channel was backing their campaigns against the enemy.

Hubert, fearing the potential problems that the massive amount of men gathered on the plateau might bring, told her that he wanted to move further north. But Nancy, knowing that there were two airdrops coming up—including a bold one that would take place in daylight—managed to convince him to wait a few more days.

After one successful drop, an exhausted and filthy Nancy returned to Chaudes-Aigues with two things on her mind: a hot bath and a nap. The area was host to several hot springs, so Nancy, stripping down to her underwear, piled into one of them and had a blissful soak. Afterward, she donned one of her nightgowns and curled up in a hotel bed with her red pillow.

She had been subsisting on only a few hours of sleep and was ready to sleep the day away.

She'd dozed off for less than half an hour when the sound of heavy rifle fire snatched her from her dream. She leapt out of bed and threw on dirty clothes before grabbing her Sten gun. Rushing out of the hotel, she spotted Hubert and Fournier talking to a scout, who was waving frantically. As she ran closer, she overheard the scout gasp, "Boches in the thousands, coming up the mountain."

Thousands? "*Merde*," Nancy cursed aloud. Hubert had been right—they should have left this camp days ago.

"We must prepare to fight," Fournier declared. He turned to Hubert. "Find Gaspard and see what his plan of attack is."

"Gaspard?" Nancy repeated.

"Like him or not, he *is* the head of the Maquis around here," Fournier replied gruffly. "And I'm hoping he has a plan."

To Nancy, the only suitable strategy against such an enormous number of German troops was to withdraw from the area and regroup, preserving what men they could to fight another day. However, Gaspard's response, delivered with defiant resolve to Hubert's scout, was that they would battle to the death.

Nancy assumed he meant his own death and the potential sacrifice of his men, a decision she found both reckless and bewildering. The war, while finally turning in their favor, was far from over, and the loss of lives now could cripple their efforts in the long run.

Meanwhile, Denden had been working feverishly to get in touch with London. But the makeshift radio station, set up in a concealed dugout beneath a canopy of trees, hissed with static. Since it was hours before his sked, no one in London was listening and the lack of reply contributed to the SOE members' feeling of helplessness at the situation.

Finally, after what seemed like an eternity, a faint reply crackled through the radio, instructing Denden to transmit again in an hour.

Nancy ran her hands through her disheveled hair. "Denden, when you call back, make sure to reiterate that we are under attack. And tell them the order for Gaspard to evacuate his troops will need to come from London. We'll make it sound like it came from the Free French. Better yet, from de Gaulle himself."

Denden raised an eyebrow at this. After a moment, he gave her a slight nod. In the distance, they heard the dull thud of a bomb falling and then a resounding explosion. Denden's breath grew heavy, but he kept coding.

Unsure what to do herself, Nancy went back to the containers they'd picked up the night previously—which now felt like a hundred years ago—and began unpacking them. She then loaded them into Fournier's car, the vehicle's frame groaning under the weight.

The drive to the plateau was a blur. She had come a long way since her ambulance days, but still, every bump on the uneven road sent a jolt through the car, rattling both the crates and her nerves. Nancy tightened her grip on the steering wheel, expecting a hundred Germans to emerge from the woods at every turn.

When she finally reached the plateau, the sight of the Maquisards brought a brief surge of relief. Many of them were unfamiliar, and she could only guess that they were Gaspard's men. When Gaspard himself emerged from the woods, she gave him a little wave and then pointed to the crates in the back of the car. This time he didn't refuse help, and gave the order for his men to unload the supplies.

When the car was finally empty, she drove back to Denden. She was so drained that even climbing out of the driver's seat felt like an impossible task. As Denden was still waiting on the reply from London, Nancy told him she was going to lie down for a few minutes.

"Now?" Denden demanded, gesturing with his arm toward a bank of trees, beyond which came the sounds of heavy artillery.

"I'm so tired I could sleep anywhere."

"There's a farmhouse a few meters away…" Denden hadn't even finished his sentence before Nancy was off.

She crawled into one of the beds and pulled her red pillow from her purse. Even without her nightgown, she managed to fall into a blissful sleep.

She awoke with a start when someone shook her. "Gertie, you can't sleep here, it's much too dangerous." It was Fournier.

"It's fine," Nancy mumbled, but Fournier pulled her out of bed, telling her that the house had already been hit once.

Reluctantly, she put her boots back on and followed him outside. As soon as she stepped into the street, a shell exploded a few meters away.

"It's much worse out here," she declared. Fournier, having done his duty, strolled off while Nancy curled up in the shade of a pine tree. "Don't wake me up unless the Germans are actually beside me," she muttered to no one before once again falling asleep.

A few hours later, feeling somewhat revived, Nancy returned to Denden. The message had come through from London, complete with an evacuation order that supposedly came from de Gaulle. Nancy drove off again to hand-deliver it to Gaspard, who grunted, but, after hours of defending an onslaught of German bombs, appeared ready to comply.

"I'll see you at the rendezvous," she called before getting back into the car. They were supposed to make their way to a small village close to Saint-Santin, which was a little over a hundred kilometers to the northwest.

She was on her way back to Fournier's group when she heard an ear-splitting howl coming from above her. Without taking her foot off the gas, she looked out the open window to see a plane hurtling toward her.

A staccato burst of machine gun fire scattered the dirt of the road in front of her, sending a wave of fear down Nancy's spine. As the plane dipped lower, she could make out the pilot's form inside the cockpit. It was enough to bring her back to reality and she slowed the car without coming to a complete stop.

The renewed burst of bullets ended a meter ahead of the car as the plane climbed up, probably readying for another pass. A glance in her rearview mirror confirmed the plane was going to come in from behind this time.

Knowing she'd never be able to outrun it, she slammed on the brakes. With no time to spare, she abandoned the car and ran toward a ditch, belatedly noticing that someone else was inside of it, waving a flag. Hoping it wasn't a German, she leaped into the ditch just as the plane dipped again. She shut her eyes as more bullets flew, this time landing just in front of the ditch.

As the plane gained altitude, Nancy was able to breathe again. The disheveled man, clearly a Maquisard and not a German, pointed toward the forest behind them. "Hurry, before he comes round again."

Nancy half-stood, as if to make a run for it, but then realized she'd left her bag in the passenger seat. "I'll be right back," she told the Maquisard before scampering back to the car.

Bullets had torn through the upholstery of the seat, showing its metal frame in some places, but she had no time to assess the damage. Grabbing her purse, she flew back into the ditch right before a well-placed bullet caused the entire car to burst into flames.

The pilot, probably assuming he'd finally scored, circled back to join his formation, which was flying toward Gaspard's camp.

The Maquisard tentatively took his hands away from his head. "What's in that bag anyway?"

Sheepishly, she undid the metal clasp to show him. It was stuffed to the gills with chocolates, tea bags, a couple of bottles of face cream, and, of course, her nightgowns and red pillow.

He shook his head at her, muttering something about women always being difficult. She tossed him one of the chocolates before clambering out of the ditch.

There were still a couple of planes overhead, which half-heartedly shot bullets toward them as Nancy and the Maquisard ran toward the camp. It was much less densely-populated than before, as many groups had already started their retreat. Fournier had instructed his men to go in bands of fifty to a hundred men, each taking a slightly different route through the rugged wilderness. Denden and Hubert had already left, but Nancy found René Dussaq waiting for her.

Darkness was already falling, so Dussaq and Nancy decided to leave with the next group. Nancy was, for once, grateful for her long pants, which, during the heat of the day, she usually rolled up to her knees. Now she unrolled them to protect herself against the thorny vines and brambles of the forest. "How are we going to get across the river?" she whispered to Dussaq. "They must have Germans stationed at every bridge."

"Luckily for us, Fournier and his men planned ahead for a scenario like this," Dussaq informed her with the hint of a grin.

Sure enough, at some point, the Maquisards had submerged large stone blocks that sat below the surface of a deeper portion of the river. They were far enough under the surface to be undetectable from the air but were still functional as stepping stones. Her pants once again rolled up, Nancy was able to make her way across the swift-moving river without so much as getting her knees wet.

The leader of their little group was a former officer in the French army who was also an experienced tracker. He was void of most of his teeth and offered little conversation, but appeared confident in his abilities to get them safely to the rendezvous.

Nancy's group first went south and then gradually made their way north in a circuitous route that twisted through the dense wilderness. Occasionally they heard the wails of planes, but they were mostly concentrated near the top of the plateau, far away from them. The Boches probably figured, wrongly, that the Maquisards would be unable to cross the river.

Assuming that they were out of danger, at least for the time being, the group paused at a well-kept, expansive farmhouse to ask for water and whatever food could be spared. The man with the neat beard who answered the door cast his eyes over the disheveled Maquisards and offered to let only Nancy inside the farmhouse for a glass of milk.

"No thank you," she told him firmly. "If you can't spare water for men who have just been in a battle for your country, then I have no need of your milk."

The next farmhouse was far more dilapidated, but here they were provided with the much-needed water and some coffee, and the farmer also directed them to his garden and told them they could take whatever they needed. Nancy was starting to realize that out here, it was the individuals with fewer possessions—not those who had plenty of money to spare—who were more willing to provide assistance. This, of course, made her think of Henri, who was always willing to help those in need.

After three days and nights of walking, Nancy's group encountered Gaspard and his crew a few kilometers outside of Saint-Santin. To her astonishment, Gaspard looped his arm through hers. *"Bonjour,* Madame Andrée," he said cheerfully as he matched her stride.

"Bonjour, Gaspard. How goes it?"

"Just fine, I think. We managed to destroy at least a thousand of their troops in all, while losing only a hundred of our men. Not to mention successfully evacuate the area."

She breathed a sigh of relief. Maybe now the Germans would think twice before attacking them again. "And here you are to live another day and fight another fight."

"Yes." He didn't say anything about the orders, but, even with the words left unspoken, she could sense that he was conceding that it had been the right decision to evacuate. And maybe, just maybe, he was finally appreciating Nancy's importance to the Maquis as well.

As the summer rays began to dwindle, they came upon an abandoned house on the edge of town. "This is it," Gaspard announced. "Our new headquarters." He turned to Nancy. "There's a small bedroom at the top of the stairs that I thought you could have."

"*Merci*, Gaspard."

"Ducks!" Nancy turned to see Denden, who held up a small bottle. "I found your perfume. I hope you don't mind, I used some of it."

"Not at all," she said, accepting the bottle, the contents of which were far more diminished than she'd expected. "Did you put it on your feet?" He'd always been complaining about how bad his sore feet smelled and told Nancy he often dreamt of bubble baths and foot powder.

"No. I drank it."

Her mouth dropped open as another man stepped forward. "And his burps smell like flowers!"

She giggled loudly, but stopped when she saw the serious look on Denden's face. He pulled her aside as the other men continued to greet each other and exchange their escape stories. "Ducks," he said before taking a deep breath. "I thought the Germans were coming through the forest right at me, and… I had no choice."

At first she thought he was talking about the perfume, but then the true meaning of his words washed over her. "Your transmitter," she gasped out loud.

"I buried it. And burned my codes."

"Denden," she groaned. "That puts us back at square one, with no way to contact London."

"I know, but it would have been much worse if the Boches had gotten their hands on either my radio or my codes."

"True." She patted his shoulder.

"You're not mad at me, are you, Ducks?"

She'd never seen Denden so vulnerable. "Of course not. I don't blame you at all."

But that didn't solve the problem of how they were going to get another radio.

CHAPTER 32

JUNE 1944

There was no way they would be able to operate without communication from London for long, so Nancy racked her brain for what to do. Even if she could somehow manage to get her hands on a transmitter, Denden still had no codes. She'd have to find another wireless operator to pass on the message that the SOE needed to drop in another radio and codes as soon as possible.

Upon hearing that there was a Free French operator in a nearby town, she borrowed a bicycle. The trek was nearly all uphill, and she was forced to half-push, half-carry the bicycle up the mountain and fell several times. A bruised and overheated Nancy arrived at the operator's safehouse to find that he had fled the area only hours before her arrival.

When she returned and told Denden the news, he began pacing the floor, declaring, "This is all my fault."

"I already told you that no one blames you."

"No. I always end up disappointing you. Remember when it took me so long to actually get to Auvergne? It was because I met someone and stayed in Châteauroux to be with him. Wait a minute." Denden stopped walking. "Someone told me there was another SOE operator there too."

At this her ears perked up. "An SOE operator in Châteauroux? What's the address?"

"You know I have no head for addresses." He grabbed a piece of paper and started sketching. "The house looked like this though. I can't remember his name, but he had a slight hunchback. Stayed with the bartender at a bistro in the town square." Abruptly, Denden stopped drawing. "But Ducks, Châteauroux is over two hundred kilometers from here. How are you going to get there? The Germans have surely blown up any train tracks in the area, and we left all the cars on the plateau."

"I guess I'll have to go by bicycle."

Denden looked pointedly at her scraped, bruised legs, but didn't say anything.

The rest of the leaders had much more to discuss regarding the possible bike trip. They called a meeting and spoke about her as though she wasn't there. Hubert thought that Nancy wouldn't have the stamina to make the trip out through the mountains, let alone return. Fournier was of the mind that it was unwise to travel without the proper papers, especially since any German in the area would be hell-bent on revenge for what had happened at the plateau.

"I agree with all of that," Laurent put in. "I actually drove down from the plateau in my car, and they have roadblocks everywhere. It took a bit of skill and a lot of luck to get through." At this, he actually looked at Nancy, his eyebrow raised. "While Madame Andrée may be skilled, she probably won't be as lucky."

Nancy rolled her eyes. Laurent had been one of their first contacts when she and Hubert had arrived in France. As one of Gaspard's lieutenants, he was a minor leader of a few dozen Maquisards. What did he know?

The man who finally convinced the others that Nancy would be fine was the one she'd least expected to be on her side. "Fournier," Gaspard said in his commanding voice, "You're right about the risk of traveling the main roads without papers. But a bike trip through the less obvious routes might be the best shot of avoiding their checkpoints."

Seeing her chance, Nancy added, "As a woman, I'd be the least suspicious out on the roads. Plus, we all know how important it is to reestablish communication with London."

The men exchanged glances. "All right," Hubert, her immediate boss, finally said. "We don't seem to have any other choice."

"What will you be wearing?" Denden finally piped up.

"This," Nancy said, gesturing toward the blouse and trousers she'd been wearing since they'd left the plateau.

Denden narrowed his eyes, taking in the stains and ragged holes dotting her clothes. "What if you get stopped by a German? You'd never be able to flirt your way out in that getup."

Rude as Denden's comment was, Nancy had to admit he was right.

The next day, Nancy, still in bedraggled but at least cleaner clothes, set off for a tailor in Aurillac, about a ten-kilometer bicycle ride from Saint-Santin. The tailor was one of Laurent's contacts, and Laurent had promised that he would be able to make Nancy a more suitable outfit for her journey.

Though Laurent had been one of the main detractors when Nancy had proposed the mission, after realizing she was determined to go, he decided to assist in her preparations in any way he could. Besides offering up the tailor, he also got word to every Maquisard from Saint-Santin to Châteauroux that Nancy would be cycling through the area in the next few days.

Upon reaching Aurillac, she parked her bicycle next to a wall in the alley and walked into the tailor's shop.

Even with the tight timeline, the tailor, a Monsieur Roux, was more than willing to help. "Come back in an hour for a fitting. In the meantime, I know a cobbler who can get you shoes without a rationing coupon."

As Nancy walked back outside to retrieve her bike, she noted a man exiting the building across the street. She cursed inwardly, knowing without having to look that the armband on his dark blue jacket would bear the Milice emblem, the symbol of the collaborationist police force.

The cobbler's shop was a bit off the beaten path, and Nancy took a couple of wrong turns. When she finally located the right place, she was greeted by a man waving his arms at her as soon as she walked in the door. "*Non, non.* You must leave town now."

She sighed audibly. "The Milice?"

"Yes. Monsieur Roux has sent a message saying that they wanted to know about the woman in wrinkled trousers walking around town."

She held her hand up in acknowledgment as she left the store. She rode as quickly as she could back to Saint-Santin, cutting through fields instead of using roads, all the while frustrated that the whole visit had been a failure. There was no way she could return to the tailor's now. *At least not in slacks.*

She braked her bicycle as she passed by a farmhouse whose owners she knew to be friendly to the Resistance.

After a young man answered the door, she asked if they had any women's clothes. He scratched his head. "My grandmère's old trunk is in the attic. There might be something in there."

The best Nancy could find was a lace Victorian dress with a high collar. It was far from her style, and hadn't been fashionable for at least a generation, but it would have to do.

There was no way she wanted Denden or any of the other men to see her dressed like that, so she made arrangements with the young man's father to bring her to town the next morning in his vegetable cart.

The next morning, she rose early and put on the dress, cursing at the tiny pearl buttons which were nearly impossible to fasten. Wearing no makeup and with her hair pulled back severely, she met the farmer out front.

Of course, Denden chose that moment to do his morning ritual of relieving himself in the field.

"Is that you, Ducks?" He put his hands in his mouth and gave a loud whistle. "Come quick, boys, and get a look at our Madame Andrée!"

Laurent came clambering out of the house, followed by a sleepy-looking Hubert. They both started laughing when they caught sight of Nancy in her getup.

"Hey, Gertie, I didn't know you had a date this morning," Fournier called from a window.

"You can go now," Nancy murmured to the farmer, her face hot.

. . .

Laurent had been right about the roadblocks—they were stopped at least a half dozen times on their way to Aurillac. Each time, the Germans questioned the farmer regarding his destination and then searched through his cart. Thankfully, they paid no attention to the farmer's supposed daughter with her plain face and ugly dress.

The tailor didn't appear to recognize her, but after Nancy reminded him about the suit and fitting, he got right to work taking her measurements. He promised to sew all night and send it over to Saint-Santin first thing in the morning.

CHAPTER 33

JUNE 1944

It was a fine morning in late June when Nancy finally set off on her mission. Deciding that her old bike would never make the trip, Laurent had graciously stolen for her another, much sturdier one. Hubert, Laurent, Denden, Fournier, and even Gaspard had come out to see her off, calling out various last-minute instructions and reminders to stick to the roads. Denden tried to slip her a small pistol, but the other men had objected to her carrying a weapon.

She had no papers at all, since the Germans had issued an order that all persons in the area needed a new identity card, and Nancy had no intention of applying for one. Denden's anxiety was slightly eased by the presence of the brawny giant Maquisard who'd volunteered to accompany Nancy to Montluçon so that he could visit his ailing wife.

The route Laurent had mapped to Montluçon was a difficult one, weaving through the less traveled roads and hidden trails of the French countryside. It also, luckily, contained numerous Resistance scouts on the lookout for Germans.

Nancy tried not to think of the hundreds of kilometers she'd be covering and focused only on pushing the pedals up and down. Right when they were about to start climbing an enormous hill, her heart caught as someone jumped out from behind a tree.

No older than twenty, his face smudged with dirt, the boy raised his hand in a subtle wave. It was a scout, signaling that the way was clear. Nancy nodded in response, her heart rate returning to its former, still-quickened pace.

Gradually, she got used to the men appearing suddenly from the woods and went back to concentrating on her pedaling. But, a few hours into their journey, a scout signaled for them to stop, causing Nancy to nearly fall off the bike.

Her body tense, she got off to steer her bike further into the woods. Together with the Maquisard, she buried herself in the underbrush, the thorns cutting up her bare legs. The scout positioned himself behind a hedge and peered through the foliage, monitoring the road for any sign of the enemy.

The usually pleasant rustling of leaves and distant chirping of birds somehow added to the tension instead of lessening it. After several minutes, with Nancy's muscles aching both from the ride and the strain of holding still, the scout gave a low whistle, indicating that it was safe to get back on the road.

Nancy mounted her bike again, ignoring her growing exhaustion to focus solely on the rhythm of her legs.

About halfway to Montluçon, a downed tree forced them to turn back and take the main road. The Maquisard motioned for her to get off the bike. "Just push it," he said in a gruff voice. "That way if we see any cars, we can jump into the culvert."

Too tired to reply, she merely nodded. Walking with the bicycle proved even more arduous than riding and Nancy was only too glad to get back on once they returned to the dirt path through the woods.

They arrived at Montluçon an hour before dusk, and Nancy reluctantly said goodbye to the Maquisard. Even though most of the time they'd been too out of breath to make conversation, she'd miss his company.

The terrain between Montluçon and Saint-Amand was marked by challenging hills and each push of the pedals sent sharp pangs of pain through her already-throbbing calves, which began to downright burn. To top it all off, night was beginning to fall, so Nancy stopped at a bistro several kilometers outside of Saint-Amand and bought a sandwich and a glass of wine. She listened out for any mention of Germans in the area, but from what she gathered, they'd been fairly dormant lately.

Satisfied that there were no immediate threats, Nancy drained the last of her wine and left the bistro to step back into the cool night. She was too tired now to keep going, so she headed toward a nearby barn, her footsteps muffled by the soft ground.

The interior of the barn was dimly lit, with enough moonlight streaming through holes in the wooden planks for her to see that it was empty of any human presence. The hay smelled unpleasantly of animal musk, but it was dry and would have to do.

She decided to sleep in her underwear—reasoning that it was better than appearing as if she'd spent the night rolling around in hay—and carefully folded her newly made jacket and skirt before laying them in a relatively clean corner. It wasn't the first time she'd had to sleep in a barn, and it probably wouldn't be the last. Hopefully she could avoid the scabies this time, though.

As she lay down with nothing between her and the prickly hay, Nancy felt the day's exhaustion settle over her. She wanted to stay alert for at least a little bit, just in case, but the buzzing of the insects was like a lullaby and lured her to sleep right away.

Near dawn, she was awakened by an air-raid siren. She stiffened, blinking at the faint light filtering through the barn. She hoped the siren meant that Allied planes were in the vicinity on reconnaissance. If it was an attack, she'd have to conquer that later, she decided as she got dressed, carefully picking the stray pieces of hay off her suit.

She wheeled her bike out of the barn. Her sore muscles screamed at her not to get back on, but she had no choice. Groaning against the pain, she mounted the bike and began pedaling. *Up, down. Down, up.*

She took a coffee break at Saint-Amand and overheard that there had been a German raid in Bourges the afternoon prior. She casually strolled over to the map on the wall and found Bourges. Her path would take her right through the village, but she reasoned that if the raid was yesterday, there was no reason for the Germans to linger in the area.

Bourges was eerily quiet, with no one in the streets and all the shutters shut tight. She'd been wrong about the presence of Germans—several of them were patrolling the streets and she braced herself for a confrontation. They must have been looking for something—or someone—in particular, because they didn't pay much attention to Nancy and didn't even stop to ask for her nonexistent papers.

In the afternoon, she stopped at a black-market restaurant in Issoudun that Laurent had told her about. Ever conscious of her appearance, she went first to the bathroom and tried to brush as much dirt as she could off her skirt before combing the stray leaves and dust out of her hair.

She took a seat at the bar and ordered a bottle of brandy and two glasses in a surprisingly steady voice.

"Who is the other glass for?" the bartender asked.

"You," she said, pushing it toward him. Laurent had told her that the proprietor acted as his own bartender and also had a rather loose tongue, especially when alcohol was involved.

By the time they'd downed a couple of glasses each, Nancy had learned that the Germans had shot some suspected spies in Bourges just that morning.

"No wonder it was so quiet," she said aloud.

She then asked where the markets were, and, in a whisper, which of them would sell her goods without any rationing coupons. "After all, I'm just a housewife trying to keep my family fed," she declared.

The bartender leaned in conspiratorially. "Try the stall by the old church. They won't ask questions as long as you have the right amount of money."

Before leaving Issoudun, Nancy stopped at the market. The old man vendor was too occupied counting up the coins she gave him to ask for her rationing book. She filled her little string bag with rotting vegetables before climbing back on her bike. She figured if she were stopped by a patrol, she could just claim that she'd been out picking vegetables to feed her family.

By her estimation, she only had about fifty kilometers to go, though the afternoon sun was relentless and, of course, every muscle in her body was aching. Especially sore was the area in her nether regions, and the mere act of sitting on the bike made her want to cry out in pain. She gritted her teeth as she resumed the mental chorus that had by now become second nature. *Up, down. Down, up. Up, down.*

The last portion of the trek seemed to be the most hazardous, as several German trucks passed by her. Every now and then, the soldiers in the open-topped trucks would holler and wave at her and she had no option but to return their wave, even though deep down she harbored an overwhelming desire to break their necks.

At that point she was so tired she could barely fathom taking a longer route to Châteauroux but after running into a few roadblocks—thankfully her flirting prevented anyone from asking for her papers—she decided to enter the town from the southwest road.

When the outline of Châteauroux finally came into view, she was so relieved she felt like crying. However, her relief was short-lived—a German patrol was posted on the opposite side of the road.

As the soldiers watched her approach, Nancy fought the urge to pick the leaves out of her hair. Instead, she gave them the most casual wave she could muster. The soldiers raked their gaze over her before waving back, motioning for her to continue on her way.

Thank goodness. The whole expedition—biking two hundred kilometers through German Occupied territory in under thirty-six hours—really had been all too easy, Nancy thought, except for the toll it had taken on her poor body.

But now it was time to put Denden's vague directions to use. Since he didn't have much information about the house where the hunchbacked radio operator lived, she decided to start with the bartender. She cycled down the main street but couldn't find the bistro Denden had described. Hoping she wasn't drawing too much attention to herself, she turned around when she got to the end in order to go back up the street.

A man of about forty was walking up the sidewalk and she could feel his eyes on her. She in turn focused on the buildings to her right as she passed him.

"Madame Andrée?"

She was so intent on locating the bistro that she almost didn't recognize her own code name. When he repeated the name, she braked and glanced backward. "Bernard?"

The man's weather-worn face broke out into a wide smile. "What are you doing here?"

Bernard was a courier for the one of the neighboring Maquis she sometimes outfitted. "I could ask you the same thing."

He shook his head, meaning, *not here on the street*. With a wave over his shoulder, he walked a few meters and then paused. Nancy hardly noticed the expectant look on his face—she was too busy staring at the building he was standing next to. It was the bistro, and it was exactly as Denden had described. She had missed it twice, probably due to her exhaustion.

Bernard waved again and then went inside. She dismounted, her legs trembling and threatening to fold underneath her. She wanted to throw the bicycle into the nearest ditch, but instead carefully set it against the side of the building. She tried to walk as normally as she could as she entered the bistro, though the friction of her skirt rubbing against her chafed thighs made her want to scream.

"We're in desperate need of a radio," Bernard told her under his breath. "Our operator was killed by Boches and his transmitter was destroyed."

She nodded. "We're in a similar situation. I heard there was an SOE operator in the area."

"SOE? I was told the one I'm looking for is with the Free French."

"Hmm. Maybe there are two operators. The one I was told about has a connection to the bartender here."

"Let's check it out," Bernard said, leading her over to the bar.

After hours spent on the bicycle by herself, Nancy was glad to have friendly company. She signaled the bartender and ordered two sandwiches and two pints of beer. When the bartender dropped off the beer, Nancy leaned in to ask him if he had a roommate.

"Why do you want to know?" the bartender asked gruffly.

"I have a friend of a friend of your roommate. My friend's name is Justin," she replied, using Denden's code name.

"Never heard of him."

"But he knows of your roommate." She sat back in her stool. "Does he have a …?" She tried to think of a polite way to say 'hunchback' but ended up gesturing it by bending over and waving her arm over her back, the simple act sending shooting pains up and down her spine.

The man sighed before whispering an address.

Since the hunchbacked radio operator was SOE, Bernard and Nancy decided that she should be the one to contact him first. Bernard waited down the hall while she knocked on the door to the apartment.

The young man who answered the door had a scowl on his face that made him appear years older. His hunchback, however, was much less prominent than she'd expected, and it was probably caused by hours spent bent over his radio set and code pads, rather than anything medical. "What?" he demanded.

Once again, in lieu of the right instructions Nancy relied on her bluntness. "We don't have a passcode but I work for the SOE and know that you do too."

"I don't."

"You do and I need you to send a message to Maurice Buckmaster."

His left eyebrow rose involuntarily. Clearly the name meant something to the young man. "If you don't have a passcode, then I can't help you. How do I know you're not Gestapo?" He made to shut the door in her face.

She stuck her leg out to block him. "Your aerial is still attached to the roof." She had no idea if that were true, but by the terrified look in his eyes, she knew she'd hit home. "If I were Gestapo, you'd already be arrested. Now please help me."

"No." He kicked her foot away and then promptly slammed the door.

"Well, that didn't work out in our favor," she said as she walked toward Bernard.

"I guess not. Time to try mine?"

She nodded.

Bernard's contact lived a few blocks off the main street. They walked the several blocks together, Nancy grateful that she didn't have to get back on the bike for at least a few hours.

There were many more German soldiers roaming around that part of town, and, in contrast to the ones she'd seen on her way in, these men seemed more suspicious of everyone on the street. Nancy began to sense that something wasn't right.

When they finally reached the contact's flat, a modest apartment above a quiet shop, Bernard knocked in a distinctive pattern, and the door was opened by a wiry man in his late thirties. His eyes darted nervously over their shoulders before he ushered them inside.

"You shouldn't be out on the streets," he said after he'd shut the door. "The Germans are conducting raids."

The knot in Nancy's stomach grew as Bernard inquired about the wireless operator.

"He skipped town a few hours ago." The man shook his head. "You know how radio men are when it gets too hot."

The prospect of returning to Saint-Santin empty-handed was unthinkable for Nancy. "Did he take his transmitter with him?"

"No. It's in his apartment, along with about a dozen Germans."

She was so desperate she contemplated breaking in and stealing the transmitter out from under them.

The contact must have seen the look on her face. "They're Gestapo, madame. Don't mess with them. They're waiting for any Resistance member to go looking for a radio operator." He nodded toward the window. "And so are those men on the street."

Bernard turned to Nancy. "We have to leave town, now."

"But I need to find an operator and a radio. I came all this way." She gestured toward her calves, which were covered in scratches and bruises.

The contact crossed his arms in thought. "There's a Maquis in the le Creuse department who might have a radio."

Nancy grabbed his arm. "How far is that on a bicycle?"

The contact squinted his eyes. "Probably about two hours."

She sighed and then looked at Bernard, who shrugged. "I don't have a bike."

"Give me your message, and I'll take care of it."

Once again alone, she made her way out to the le Creuse Maquis. As she neared the encampment, the usual sounds of the forest gave way to the murmur of human activity and the smell of cooking food.

Nancy's presence did not go unnoticed—the men guarding the perimeter leered at her and she thought she even heard a wolf whistle but she had been around enough half-dressed, unkempt Maquisards to not be intimidated. She met their gazes with an unflinching stare. "I'm with Gaspard. We need to get a message to London."

One of them waved for her to follow him. He led her toward a makeshift office where a small, balding man sat scribbling a note. "She knows Gaspard," the man said by way of introduction.

The seated man stood and offered an ink-streaked hand. "I'm Claude Gautier, the leader of this group."

After she explained the situation, Gautier regarded her thoughtfully. "Buckmaster is SOE, no?" he asked finally. "We are aligned with the Free French."

"Listen, I'm well aware of the animosity between the two groups, but we are all fighting the same enemy and I need your help."

He waved his hand. "Of course, of course. My wireless operator is getting some much-needed sleep. I wouldn't want to disturb him, but I will tell him the situation when he wakes up in the morning. If he agrees to help you, then I don't have a problem with that."

Nancy wondered what kind of Maquis he was running, with men being able to doze through essential operations. Though she agreed with the necessity of getting a good sleep, it was a luxury out of reach for her at the moment. As exhausted as she was, she needed to get back to Saint-Santin as soon as possible and couldn't wait around until morning. She dictated both Bernard's and her message to the Maquis leader, emphasizing the recipient: "Colonel Maurice Buckmaster of F Section."

"Buckmaster." Gautier folded the paper and put it in his pocket. "We'll send it out first thing."

She decided to ride straight through, hoping there would be fewer German roadblocks at night, especially because she was taking the most direct route possible. With each pedal stroke, an excruciating pain pulsed through her nerves. As the night grew darker and darker, Nancy started to question if pedaling through a pitch-black forest had been a good idea after all.

When she approached Montluçon, someone suddenly jumped into the road, startling her to the point where she almost lost her balance.

"It's a boy!" the figure exclaimed.

Like a developing photograph, the recognition slowly materialized in Nancy's clouded mind. Finally she realized that the man standing at the side of the road with his bicycle was the Maquisard who'd started the journey with her. It had only been three days, but it felt like forever ago. She braked gently but didn't stop, afraid that if she got off the bicycle, she'd never get back on again.

"My wife wasn't sick, Madame Andrée, just pregnant." He mounted his bicycle. "She didn't want to say anything until I was there."

"Congratulations on your baby boy." Nancy gave him the

largest smile she could manage and gestured with a sore arm for him to follow her.

When she finally arrived back at the house early in the morning, Laurent was sitting on the porch and watched as she came to an unsteady stop. "Madame Andrée, are you okay?"

Though her brain knew that she was on solid ground, it still seemed to swirl beneath her legs. She threw the bicycle down in the dirt before collapsing.

"Hubert, come quick," she heard Laurent call. "Gertie's back and she needs our help."

Together the two men carried Nancy into the house, each small movement causing her to groan in pain. Her thighs were so chafed that she couldn't bear to stand or sit, so they laid her gently on the couch. Even through her watering eyes, she could read the question on their faces.

"The Free French… Maquisards… le Creuse…" She was so exhausted, she thought she might fall asleep mid-sentence. "Are going to send a message. Buckmaster," she managed to get out before her eyes closed.

She felt a warm hand on her head. "Good job, Gertie. And thank you."

CHAPTER 34

JULY 1944

It was several days before Nancy began to feel a semblance of her old self. Hubert had called for a doctor, but besides wrapping her inner thighs with bandages, there wasn't much else he could do medically.

Nancy was moved to a back bedroom so she could sleep. On the third night, she dreamt of taking a hot bath, the fragrant steam rising around her while Henri refilled her champagne flute, smiling that familiar smile that crinkled the corners of his eyes.

Her own eyes flew open when she recognized that the faint humming noise in the background was a plane. *If that's a bomber, I'm toast.* There was no way she could get out of the bath. As understanding dawned, she realized she wasn't in the bath in her Marseille apartment, but lying in a bed with scratchy sheets in a rural part of Saint-Santin.

A minute later, Denden burst into her room.

"Is there a plane outside?"

"Plane?" Denden looked confused. "Nothing to be frightened of. I came to tell you that we're back in business, thanks to you." He gestured to someone standing behind him and motioned for him to enter. The newcomer was thin, with sandy hair and didn't look a day over 20. "This is Roger. He's just arrived from England and doesn't speak much French, but that doesn't really matter for a wireless operator." Denden held up a suitcase. "And guess what this is?"

Nancy painfully sat up. "It worked? Buckmaster got the message?"

"Indeed. We now have new codes, a transmitter, and Roger."

"Thank god for that," Nancy said before she fell asleep again.

When Nancy was finally ready to move about, she dressed and went downstairs to find lunch. She was startled to see a small man with a mustache sitting in her usual chair, which was, of course, the best one at the table. "Who are you?" Nancy asked unceremoniously as she perched in the rickety stool across from him.

"I am Colonel Aubert."

Hubert walked into the kitchen. When he saw the Colonel there, he looked slightly guilty.

Colonel Aubert set his beady eyes on Hubert. "I don't suppose you told her my purpose for being here?"

"Not yet."

The colonel cleared his throat. "I am with the French Army and have been told to take over the outfit here and make it, shall we say, more military-like." Now his gaze turned to Nancy. "I thank you for the radio, but I don't think we will be needing your services anymore."

Nancy, trying not to reveal how shaky her legs were, stood up. "Who exactly are you to be dismissing *me*?"

"I told you, I am Colonel—"

Nancy cut him off. "I don't really care what your name is." She doubted he was who he said he was, but it wasn't as if she could ask to see his papers—everyone around her used an alias and false papers. He was clearly a power-grabber and possibly even one of Denden's Moths, finally emerging from his hiding place to claim victory as the war was coming to a close. "You might think you've taken command, but I'm not sure how you think you'll get arms and money without permission from the *chef du parachutage* for this Maquis."

His pompous mustache seemed to lose its grandeur as he looked at Hubert for help.

Hubert shrugged. "She is the *chef*."

The colonel frowned. "I will somehow manage." He waved his hand at Nancy. "As I said, you're dismissed."

Hubert folded his arms across his chest. "If she leaves, then I do too. That means my men will be gone as well."

The colonel picked up his sandwich. "Well, if that's the case, *au revoir*."

Hubert and Nancy promptly gathered the rest of the house for a meeting outside in the yard.

"How long has that horrible man been here?" Nancy demanded.

"He came unannounced while you were in recovery," Hubert answered. "I didn't have the heart to tell you about him—I knew you'd hate him instantly."

So that explained the earlier guilty look on his face.

"Would you like Denden and me to shoot him?" Dussaq asked.

"You know I can only shoot people when I'm drunk,"

Denden cut in. "And Ducks is out of perfume." He shot Nancy a sheepish look. "I drank the rest of it the other night."

"What about Tardivat?" Hubert asked.

Denden nodded. "He'll probably have some alcohol."

"No," Hubert said. "I mean, his camp up north. We could relocate there."

Tardivat was the man who'd greeted Nancy when she'd landed—or rather, became entangled in the tree. She knew his Maquis was somewhere in the Allier. She rose from her spot on the ground and dusted off her hands. "Anywhere is better than here."

Laurent tugged at his ear before exchanging a glance with Gaspard, who nodded at him. "This seems as good as any time to tell you that we've been planning to split for a while," Laurent said. "We're going to round up our Maquis and head back toward our old camp. The Germans have obviously come south and the plateau's been the best vantage point so far."

Gaspard put a hand on Nancy's shoulder. "If the *chef du parachutage* doesn't mind throwing us some supplies once in a while, we should be okay."

"You can count on it."

"I'm taking my men too," Fournier added. "That way we can attack the Germans from all angles."

Dussaq reached out to give Nancy a hug. "I've been ordered to help out with Fournier's Maquis." He took a step back. "I hope you won't miss me too much."

Nancy offered her friend a grin. "Maybe we'll meet again in Piccadilly Circus."

"Only if we can do cartwheels."

"When the war is over, I'll definitely take you up on that offer."

Hubert cleared his throat. "If these awkward goodbyes are

finished, we should get going. We've got a long road ahead of us."

Denden grabbed Nancy's hand. "Luckily for us, no one has to ride a bicycle down it."

Despite Nancy's awkward first encounter with Tardivat, after their second meeting, she developed a grudging respect for the man. It was immediately obvious that the members of his Maquis were well-oiled and disciplined, a testament to Tardi's effective command.

Hubert decided to set up camp in the same area as Tardi's, near a field that they had occasionally used for airdrops.

Most of the men set up canvas tents in the clearing while Denden and Roger requisitioned an old farmhouse for transmitting, Denden loudly claiming the only room that had a bed. Usually Nancy could plead with the Maquisards to get whatever she wanted, but that never worked with Denden. She decided that sleeping on the dilapidated couch had to be better than lying her still-sore body down on pine needles, but, as she discovered the first night, it was only by a narrow margin.

The next morning, Tardi requested a meeting with Nancy. They met in the living room/Nancy's bedroom. "I'm told you're the woman who gets things," Tardi said as he sat down, immediately sinking into the couch cushions.

"I am. What is it that you need?"

"Guns and ammunition. Bren guns preferably." He ran a hand through his dark hair. "We ambush the Wehrmacht convoys heading for Normandy. This area is well-suited for that sort of thing since the main roads run through thick forests perfect for hiding bombs and men."

"Ambush, huh? I'd like to accompany you sometime."

"So you'll be able to get me the guns?"

"Yes, but..." Nancy trailed off as an idea occurred to her. "I'll help you if you can help me." She bounced on the couch, the springs creaking and the woodwork groaning. "I'd like a better place to sleep."

His eyebrows furrowed. "You want a new couch?"

"A mattress preferably, and some place with privacy."

Tardi glanced out the window, deep in thought. "The mattress shouldn't be a problem, but as for privacy among the Maquis, that might be more difficult to come by." He sat forward. "What about a bus?"

"A bus?"

He nodded enthusiastically. "I was thinking of requisitioning one for when we move—I don't like to stay in the same place too long. What if the bus doubles as your new room?"

Nancy knew she couldn't be too picky, but a bus didn't strike her as the most comfortable sleeping arrangement. "Make sure it's one where the backseats face each other, that way I can set my mattress on top of them."

"You got it."

Although Nancy had every intention of getting him the Bren guns anyway, Tardi kept his end of the bargain and was excited to show off her new accommodations. He'd had his men clean the bus from top to bottom. As Nancy made her way to the back, she saw he'd laid the mattress over the seats just as she'd envisioned, and draped the silk from a couple of parachutes on top of it.

"Just as I told you when we met, parachute fabric can really come in handy."

"Indeed." Nancy tested the mattress, which held her weight much better than the couch.

That night, dressed in one of her nightgowns, and with her customary red pillow, she had one of the best nights of sleep she'd had in a long time.

The next day, once again true to his word, Tardi invited Nancy on one of his ambushes. As the sun heated up the late morning, Tardi and his men buried their homemade tin-can explosives in the lush foliage on the side of the main road and then dragged the long string mechanism uphill to where they would have a clear view of the ensuing destruction.

Breathing heavily with exhilaration, Nancy felt the ground start to vibrate, and soon the scout flashed his mirror, indicating that the convoy was indeed approaching. A few seconds later, the lead escort vehicle came into view.

She had just counted ten trucks when the first bomb went off, the explosion making the ground tremble even more. Her fingers tightened on her own Sten gun as the men surrounding her sprang into action, shooting their Bren guns from their high vantage point.

Dozens of Germans poured out of their wrecked vehicles, attempting to retaliate with their superior armory, but Tardi was right: the forest was a great concealer of both men and bombs.

Spying the perfect target—a truck already on fire—Nancy put her gun down and pulled a grenade out of her belt. She pulled the pin out just as she'd been taught and threw it downward with all her might. It exploded a meter before the truck, but still managed to toss a few Boches into the air.

Some of the Maquisards took advantage of the confusion

and began to rush the convoy, getting close enough to toss their incendiary devices—which were nothing more than glass bottles filled with petrol—directly at the Germans. The bottles ignited on impact, and soon the screams of men filled the air as they flailed about, trying to extinguish the fires engulfing their grayish-green uniforms.

Even through air thick with smoke, Tardi's whistle blew loud and clear. "Pull back, men!" He put a hand on Nancy's shoulder. "It's time to go now, Madame Andrée."

A part of her wanted to stay and watch the damage they had inflicted, but she recognized the need to quit while they were ahead.

Half a dozen Maquisards continued to provide cover fire, their bullets creating a deadly barrier between the disoriented Germans and their comrades retreating deeper into the forest. Once Tardi and Nancy's group were high enough, it was their turn to provide cover while the ones lower on the hill began to pull back. The whole withdrawal was a well-rehearsed maneuver that allowed Tardi's men to disengage without leaving anyone behind.

The blow they had struck against the Germans might have been small, but it still counted for something, and Nancy's respect for Tardi had grown into downright admiration.

She told Denden as much later that evening when she recounted the ambush.

Denden, who had chosen to stay back at camp, was more impressed with the image of Nancy shooting guns and throwing grenades. "Don't you at least feel a bit guilty for taking a human life?"

Nancy, never having considered it that way, shrugged. "I'm

not sure if I killed anyone, and anyway, I hate them, Denden. Don't you?"

"I do, of course. The only good German in my opinion is a dead one."

Nancy nodded. "War is war. And I had to show these Maquisards that I'm just as game for shooting Germans as they are. Especially around a man like Tardi."

"He's definitely a man," Denden agreed. "I'd have him in an instant if he was of the right persuasion."

"I think he's married."

"That hasn't stopped people before."

"It's certainly stopped me," she said, feeling a sting of pain in her chest. She blinked back a tear as she realized the pain wasn't necessarily at the memory of Henri, it was more that it had been a while since she'd thought of him at all.

Denden picked up her change in mood. "Are you okay, Ducks?"

She shot him a small smile. "I'm just tired is all. Shooting Germans will do that to you."

The same lookout who'd flashed the mirror came running into their camp early the next day, his dirty face flushed and his eyes wide. "The Germans are coming," he panted, his breath creating a faint mist in the gray morning air. "I think they want retribution for the ambush."

Tardi, whistle at the ready, blew several short bursts and dozens of men came running out of their tents. The Maquisards snapped into action with a practiced efficiency. In no time, they had the camp packed up and the fire pit covered, leaving no trace of their presence. Denden and Roger came out of the farmhouse, their arms full, and then loaded their equipment onto the bus next to Nancy's bicycle.

Tardi had previously mapped out both an escape route and a new spot to set up camp, and Hubert and the Maquisards set off in different directions. Left behind, Roger, Denden, and Nancy exchanged bewildered glances.

"Does this thing actually work?" Denden asked, gesturing toward the bus.

"I think so," Nancy said. "I'll drive."

"No, I will," Denden told her. "I heard all about your ambulance fiasco."

As the bus lurched forward, rumbling down the narrow road that led away from the camp, Nancy felt the knot of tension in her stomach ease slightly.

They had evaded capture by mere minutes. Later, when they had a chance to catch their breath and regroup, news trickled in from locals that around a thousand Germans had descended upon the abandoned field and farmhouse, their fury evident in the way they scoured the area for any sign of the Maquisards, without success.

CHAPTER 35

JULY 1944

This time Hubert elected to set up camp a kilometer away from Tardi's new base. The newest Freelance site was luckily close to another field suitable for drops as they'd been informed that London was sending in two new weapons instructors to replace Dussaq.

Nancy was part of the reception committee and as she sat in the wet grass, it occurred to her that the Resistance forces themselves were a lot like dew—ever present in the evenings, but ready to disappear as soon as the sun came up.

The dull roar of the plane snapped her out of her revelry. She looked up to watch the parachutes descend, their canopies glowing in the light cast by the signal fires. Unlike previous drops, which had delivered containers laden with supplies, tonight's cargo was men.

The first one hit the ground near Nancy hard and cursed loudly.

The unexpected burst of profanity broke the tension, and

Nancy's lip twitched. "Was that in English?" she asked Hubert, who was crouched nearby.

"Yes—in an American accent," he answered, a note of surprise in his voice.

She held up a bottle of champagne as she approached the newcomer. "Welcome to France."

Captains Reeve Schley and John Alsop could only speak a few words in French. Hubert didn't think it very wise of the SOE to be sending so many non-natives into Occupied France, but Nancy appreciated their determination. Plus they were in uniform and Schley, the taller of the two, had beautiful leather boots to go with his wool trousers and jacket. Nancy knew it would lift the Maquisards' somewhat waning spirits to see an Allied officer proudly wearing full military attire instead of prowling around in mufti like the rest of them.

Nancy also noted that the new loot contained several awkward-looking long steel tubes with nozzles at the end, like thin trumpet bells.

"Bazookas," Captain Alsop said when he caught her looking at them.

"Ahh." Dussaq had always been going on about how superior the rocket launchers were, to the point where some of the Maquisards had started calling him Bazooka. Too bad Dussaq was off with Fournier's Maquis, although maybe she could arrange for the delivery of one of the new weapons to their group. "Do you know how to use them?"

"Of course. I can show you, if you'd like."

"I'll learn along with the men." She gave him a grin. "After all, someone will have to act as your interpreter."

"There should be one more case here," Schley looked around, his eyes wide and unfocused. "My personal effects."

"I think we unpacked all of the crates," Hubert told him. "I didn't see a suitcase."

Alsop glanced over at Schley. "Were your glasses in there?"

Schley nodded, and Nancy understood why his gaze seemed so off. "Let me guess, you are blind without them."

He nodded again.

Hubert muttered something to himself about the SOE sending in a blind weapons instructor who didn't speak French.

"I'm sure your case will turn up." Nancy took the two Americans' arms in hers. "Come meet Denden, our wireless operator."

Though the suitcase never appeared, among the miscellaneous items that Schley and Alsop brought from London were a couple bottles, ironically, of French champagne. Schley claimed they were reserving them for V-Day, but Denden convinced them to open them and have a few glasses on the bus while they "got to know each other."

"Are either of you married?" Nancy asked them, hoping the answer was yes. Both men were in their early 30s and had that fit, muscular, military look that she knew Denden was partial to.

"No," Schley replied.

"But we both have girls back home," Alsop added.

Denden shrugged as he topped off Nancy's glass.

She took a long swig. "What was the reaction in London regarding D-Day?"

Alsop leaned back in the seat. "What you would have predicted. Morale is high, even despite the Doodlebug attacks."

The Doodlebugs were the Germans' V-1 flying bombs, which, Nancy was aware, were currently wreaking havoc in Britain.

"I wish we could say the same for the morale in Southern France," Denden said. "We're doing what we can until the Allies get down here, but the reprisals have been brutal."

Nancy reached out to pat her friend's hand. "The Allies will be here soon." She held up her glass. "And then we will truly be drinking to victory."

Schley drained the rest of his glass. "Has your group ever been attacked by Germans?"

Nancy and Denden exchanged a knowing glance. "A few times," Nancy replied. "Actually, just this morning they tried to raid our camp, but luckily we'd already left."

Schley tried to set his cup down on the small stump Nancy used for a table, but, without his glasses, he misjudged the distance and the cup tumbled to the floor. It didn't break and, equally as lucky, was already empty.

Nancy checked her watch and gasped as she realized it was already four in the morning. "On that note, you guys better get going. I've got to get what little beauty sleep I can."

"I'll say," Denden muttered as he got up.

"Oh, and Captain Schley?" Nancy called at his departing figure. "I wouldn't worry so much about the Germans coming back. They're not like lightning—they usually don't strike twice. At least not in 24 hours' time."

"Yeah right," Denden replied, louder this time. "Haven't you ever heard of the *Blitzkrieg*?"

When Nancy woke up a few hours later, she assumed the pounding she heard was in her head and a direct result of all

KIT SERGEANT

the champagne from the night before. But that didn't explain the scattering of birds and the billowing dust outside the bus window.

She sat up in bed. *Boches.* Denden had been right—they had struck twice. She threw some clothes over her nightgown and dashed out of the bus and toward the shed Denden had requisitioned for his quarters.

"Denden." She shook his shoulder hard. "Get out of bed."

"What is it, Ducks?" he asked sleepily, trying to shrug her off.

"It's the Germans. Yes, you were right," she acknowledged. "Now go tell those Americans we've got to get a move on. I'm going to find Hubert."

A minute later, Denden came running out of the shed, followed by Schley and Alsop, the latter with his shiny boots covering his otherwise nearly bare legs.

"What happened to your pants?" Nancy called.

Schley ducked his head sheepishly. "I put my boots on first and then couldn't get my pants up, so I just cut them off."

He still didn't have his glasses, so the cuts were completely uneven. *So much for showing off his brilliant uniform.*

"Did you find Hubert?" Denden demanded.

"No. Which means I'm in charge, at least for now." Nancy glanced down and noticed with horror that the pink satin of her nightgown was visible under her half-buttoned shirt. She pulled up her collar as she started barking commands. "Find Roger and pack his radio and codes in the bus. We have to make sure his equipment is intact so he can send a message to London. You go with him."

"No," Denden insisted. "That will only take one operator— Roger can handle it. I'm going to stay here with you."

She nodded. "Then get packing."

One of their scouts rushed up to Nancy. "How many?" she asked.

He was doubled over, panting, but managed to choke out, "Over six thousand."

She took a deep breath and then glanced over at the Americans. From their blank looks, Nancy surmised they clearly didn't know their numbers in French.

"Have you seen Hubert?"

The scout shook his head.

They were ridiculously outnumbered—besides her, Denden, Roger, and the Americans, there were around two hundred seasoned Maquisards plus about 30 Moths who'd just joined them a few days ago. She wasn't sure how many men Tardi had, but it definitely wasn't six thousand.

"Go to Tardi's camp and make sure he knows about the ambush," she instructed the scout, who gave her a salute before running off.

Schley, calling out to Alsop and the other men who were still milling about, rushed to the back of the barn, where they'd stored the containers from last night's drop. He and the other men soon emerged carrying the bazookas on their shoulders.

Denden, who'd been about to hoist Nancy's bike on top of the bus, paused to stare at Schley in his makeshift shorts. Denden's wolf whistle soon turned into a high-pitched scream.

"Denden?" Nancy started to rush over to him. "Are you shot?"

Denden, still holding the bicycle, was convulsing. Alsop grabbed Nancy and held her back. "Let go of the bike, Denden," Alsop commanded.

As soon as he did, his body grew still and he flopped to the ground.

"Denden?" She shook him, and luckily his eyes flew open.

"Wait," Nancy noticed the electrical cables hanging off the bus. "Did you just electrocute yourself?"

"It's not funny," Denden stammered, his teeth still chattering.

The scene was starting to resemble a dark comedy and Nancy didn't know whether to laugh or cry. Her decision was practically made for her when some of their men entered the perimeter, their faces etched with pain. Any lingering thoughts of laughter disappeared as Nancy took in their blood-stained clothes.

"Denden, will you help them?" She nodded at the bleeding, bruised men.

"Why me? I almost died myself."

"You seem fine now, and you know I don't like the sight of blood. It's either that or grab a bazooka and fight."

Denden grimaced. "I'll stay with the wounded then."

"Here," Alsop dug bandages and a small bottle of alcohol out of his bag and handed it to Denden.

When Roger appeared carrying his equipment, the Americans, carefully avoiding the electrical wires, finished securing the bike to the top of the bus and then Roger drove off.

Another scout arrived and Nancy asked about the Germans' position.

He exhaled sharply before replying, "They've dug in at the crossroads of the two main roads. They've even deployed panzers there."

"Well," Alsop hoisted his bazooka. "These can help with that."

Nancy, unsure if she'd be able to handle the weight of the rocket launcher, grabbed her Sten gun and as many grenades as her trouser pockets would hold. "Let's go."

Her intent was to launch a surprise attack on the Germans

from the woods, but a few of the Moths decided to use the main road, despite Nancy's warnings to the contrary.

A few minutes later, the unmistakable harsh staccato of machine-guns firing resounded in the distance. It was soon accompanied by the shouts of many agonized men. The screams had to have been from the Moths falling victim to the German's artillery, but there was nothing Nancy could do about it. *If only they had listened to her.*

Upon hearing the screams, Schley hesitated, but Nancy motioned for them to keep moving. When they at last spied the Germans' position, Nancy, taking a cue from Tardi's ambush method, instructed a line of men to stay back and cover them while the Americans and a few other men hoisted their bazookas on their shoulders. As he demonstrated what to do, Alsop shouted instructions in English, and Nancy translated them to the Maquisards.

It seemed simple enough: Load the rocket. Use your optical to aim. Pull the trigger.

As Schley readied a bazooka, Nancy asked if he was able to see.

"Does it matter? The Germans are that way." He fired the bazooka, and to Nancy's amazement, the rocket struck its target—or what she presumed to be Schley's intended target anyway—a distant panzer. The panzer caught fire, and another one, hit by Alsop, exploded. The next round took out the machine gun posts and, for a moment, it was blissfully silent. Even the Boches had ceased their shouting.

Nancy held her gun up, ready to shoot if they pursued their attackers, but the Germans seemed reluctant to do so.

"We only have a few more rockets. We didn't have time to unpack them all," Alsop told her, the regret obvious in his voice.

Once again, it was up to Nancy to take charge. "We'll fire

these last few and then send a message to Tardivat to launch an offensive from his vantage point. I think we've confused the Boches enough that we'll be able to pack up the rest of the camp and move on to the next rendezvous point."

The Americans gave her a full salute, which she returned with an enthusiastic grin.

When they returned to camp, Nancy found Denden armed with a carbine on his shoulder, a line of grenades secured to his belt, and a Colt pistol holstered at his side.

"Don't you hate guns?" Nancy asked.

"Not at the moment," he returned with a slur. He bent over one of the men lying on the ground and poured some of the alcohol over a wound before taking a swig.

Denden was clearly drunk. Nancy, noticing that the safety was off on his Colt, asked him to hand over the gun and grenades. He did so, but insisted on keeping the carbine. She could only hope that the chamber was empty—she had enough to deal with already without having Denden literally shoot himself in the foot.

The next task was to figure out how to get a message to Tardi about the rendezvous. There wasn't much choice but to go herself to his station on the hill. One of the other Maquisards—an experienced one—volunteered to accompany her, and together they set off on foot. When they got close enough to hear the Germans' renewed gunfire, they crawled the remaining distance on their bellies until they found one of Tardi's scouts, who agreed to send the message on.

This time she found Denden asleep on the ground next to the wounded men he'd been tending to. Nancy packed up what little was left of the camp—they'd only been there for a couple of days and got most of the radio equipment out that morning, so it didn't take long. When she'd finished, she found Schley and Alsop sitting on tree stumps nearby, smoking cigars and trading sips from Denden's alcohol bottle.

"Want one?" Schley held up a cigar. "They're Cuban. I didn't want the Germans to get them."

"Might as well." She accepted the proffered cigar. "We're going to hold up here until Tardi makes his move."

They were all puffing away when they heard boots crashing through the forest. All three of them reached for their guns, but the men who came through were Maquisards from a nearby camp, their progress slowed by the bodies they were carrying.

"I believe these men were from your unit," one of them told Nancy.

The seven corpses were the Moths who'd tried to take the main road. Nancy examined their bodies, which were riddled with bullets from machine gun fire. Many of them also had a bullet through the skull, their faces disfigured. Most likely the Germans shot them point blank in the forehead to make sure they were dead and then hit them in the face with their rifle butts.

"Put them in the shed for now," Nancy said, her voice choked. "We'll come back to bury them when it's safe."

Schley handed her his handkerchief.

"Speaking of which, where the hell is Tardi?" she demanded, her voice less shaky now.

As if to answer her question, a volley of gunshots rang through the forest. Nancy mustered a smile. "That'll be him. Let's get out of here."

. . .

Roger was waiting for them at the rendezvous. He'd already strung up his aerial and had his codebook ready to send notice of the attack to London. *Good ole' Roger.* He was a bit wet behind the ears and—like the Americans—didn't speak a lick of French, but nothing seemed to faze him.

A few hours later, Tardi and his men also joined them. "Aren't you glad that you delivered us all those Bren guns?" Tardi asked, his brown eyes still merry despite having spent hours shooting at Germans.

"That, and I'm glad you got the message," Nancy replied.

"We had just sat down to eat breakfast, actually, when the scout arrived."

She couldn't resist returning his grin. "Are you telling me that Frenchmen actually left their food uneaten?"

"We made an exception since it was you asking for help. Not to mention…" Tardi shrugged, "It wasn't that great of a breakfast anyway."

By morning, Hubert had resurfaced. It turned out that, having woken up very early, he decided to go look for Schley's missing suitcase but got caught up in the crossfire as the Boches began their ambush. He'd spent the day hiding in a barn and waited until nightfall, when the Germans had left the area, before attempting to leave.

"I feel completely useless, like I let everyone down," Hubert declared as they sat for a breakfast of carrots.

"You missed all the fun," Schley said. "And the cigars."

"Not to worry," Alsop reassured Hubert. "Gertie had everything under control."

"Well, maybe everything except for Denden," Nancy returned modestly. "Where is he, anyway?"

"Probably sleeping off his hangover. Or his electrocution," Alsop added.

"Probably both," Schley commented, and the three of them laughed, to Hubert's bewildered look.

"We'll explain later," Nancy told him. She stood up. "In the meantime, now that the Germans are gone, we have to clean up their mess. Finish your breakfast," she told the other men. "We've got bodies to bury."

In the past few days, Nancy had done a lot of strange things, from engaging in combat and possibly having killed men, to teaching Frenchmen the art of wielding bazookas, and, of course, enjoying cigars with American soldiers. But entering the dark, fetid barn where her fallen comrades lay mutilated was one of the most difficult tasks she had to perform in a long time, probably since leaving Henri.

Though she knew she wasn't to blame for their deaths, she couldn't help feeling somewhat guilty. The only way to alleviate that guilt was to give them a proper burial. She carefully bathed their bodies and did her best to make them presentable, even though the bodies ended up being wrapped in Tardi's unlimited supply of parachute silk.

"Shall we dig here?" Schley asked, looking around their abandoned camp.

"No," Nancy replied. "We have the time—we are going to put them in the cemetery on the hill. They died for France. It's the least we can do."

CHAPTER 36

JULY 1944

*A*fter the German attack, Hubert decided they would move deeper into the forest, making it that much more difficult for the Boches to locate them. There were no sheds or farmhouses in the area, so most of the men slept under flimsy tents made from parachute silk while Nancy made herself comfortable in her bus.

She found the site quite agreeable, for not only were they surrounded by Tardi's men and other small groups of Maquis, but it was close to a large, clear pond that was perfect for washing up. Denden—who for some reason preferred to bathe in private—set up a small lean-to with a corrugated roof to serve as the men's showerhouse.

They were not overly isolated, for each day brought new Moths willing to join the fight. Captains Schley and Alsop were kept busy training the new men, instructing them how to load, aim, and clean every piece of artillery they had. There were over 7,000 Maquisards in the area, and anyone in need of weapons instruction would pay the Americans a visit.

Nancy resumed her role of *chef du parachutage,* arranging and overseeing the airdrops from London to replace the spent ammunition and lost artillery, and, during one particularly necessary drop, a new pair of glasses for Schley.

When Schley and Alsop weren't busy instructing their new recruits in proper weapon use, they indulged in their more perilous pastime—getting as close as they could to German convoys to take pictures. When Nancy said she'd prefer them to be throwing grenades, Alsop reminded her that they couldn't afford to draw too much attention to the area, lest they needed to move yet again.

Nancy opened her mouth to retort but Alsop cut her off. "Every time we toss a grenade, we risk German reprisals. We've seen what they do to villages, to civilians."

Even Nancy couldn't argue with that logic, especially not after what had happened with Monsieur Beaumont.

The elderly man owned a nearby farm and had been instrumental in providing the Maquis with food at great risk to himself. Not long after they had relocated, Nancy was walking through the woods toward his property when she heard a commotion.

Staying hidden in the brush, she managed to get a view of the stone farmhouse. German soldiers in their grayish-green uniforms had surrounded it, and, as Nancy watched, more exited the house, dragging Monsieur Beaumont with them.

"Where are the Maquisards?" one of the soldiers barked as they threw the man on the ground.

Monsieur Beaumont spat at the soldier's feet but did not answer.

The first soldier motioned to another, who raised his rifle.

Nancy closed her eyes, her stomach churning as she realized what was about to happen.

Several gunshots rang out. When she opened her eyes, Monsieur Beaumont's body lay crumpled on the ground, lifeless.

She stayed hidden, watching as they rifled through the dead man's belongings. They searched the house, but for some reason ignored the barn, which was in the back of the property.

As soon as she heard their jackboots crunch down the gravel path, she rushed toward the barn. Inside, she found Monsieur Beaumont's horse, a beautiful bay, tied to a post, its eyes wide. As Nancy approached him, the horse shifted nervously and pawed at the ground.

"Easy, boy," she whispered, rubbing his sweaty neck. She dried her hands on her trousers before moving to untie the reins. "Let's get you out of here before someone turns you into horsemeat."

His ears flicked back, as if he understood what she'd said.

There was nothing she could do for its owner, who had died protecting his fellow Frenchmen, but at least she could save this horse's life. She decided to bring him back to the camp with her, knowing Schley, who'd begun his career in the States as a cavalryman—hence his spectacular boots—would be especially pleased.

In keeping with the theme of naming pets after alcoholic drinks, Nancy decided to call her new friend Aguardiente.

Both Schley and Alsop were thrilled when she returned to camp holding a horse's reins. That evening, the three of them took turns riding Aguardiente, Nancy trying to forget what she'd witnessed earlier that day and the grim realities of war altogether.

. . .

But those grim realities had a way of rearing their ugly heads when one least expected it. The next morning, Nancy was just about to bathe in the lake when one of the scouts rushed over to her.

"What is it now? More reprisals?" Nancy asked, her thoughts shifting back to Monsieur Beaumont.

"No," the scout replied. "It's not the Boches this time; it's another Maquis."

"What about them?"

"They've been holding women hostage," the scout said, glancing around nervously. "They are using them... for their own pleasure."

It had been months since Nancy had laid eyes on someone who was the same gender as herself. "Who are these women?"

"The men said they were spies."

"Spies?" Nancy frowned. "Even if they were German spies, that's no reason for them to be abused." She threw on her boots. "Will you take me to them?"

The scout shook his head. "I don't think you should be among these men, Madame Andrée. They're not with Fournier—or even Gaspard—and they're what you might call 'rough around the edges.'"

"Then tell Hubert to demand that these women be turned over to him. I want them brought before me, and I'll be the one to decide if they are indeed spies."

"Yes, Madame Andrée."

That afternoon, the three women were brought into camp. Nancy had set up a makeshift interrogation station on the bus and decided to see one woman at a time while the others were given food and water, under the watchful eyes of multiple guards, of course.

The first one, clad in a tattered flowered dress, couldn't have been more than seventeen. Beneath her dirt-covered face, her eyes held an anguished look, reflecting the trauma she'd clearly been through.

But then again, they all had been through trauma. After all, this was war.

Nancy led the girl to the back of the bus where she'd laid the mattress on its side so they could sit facing each other. She decided to get straight to the point. "Are you a spy for the Germans?"

The girl's eyes widened even more. "A spy? Against France? I would never do anything of the sort."

The girl seemed so sincere that Nancy had no reason to suspect that she was lying. Peering closer, Nancy could see that, under all that grime, she was pretty, with a trim figure. Nancy hoped to hell that the Maquisards hadn't accused her of a crime she didn't commit because they wanted to rape her. "What's your name?"

"Anouk," the girl replied. "What's yours?"

"Madame Andrée. But you can call me Gertie," Nancy said, her voice softening. "Anouk, you are free to go. Make sure to eat something, and, after I am done with the other women, I can show you where you can bathe and get you some clean clothes."

"Thank you, madame. You are very kind."

Nancy patted Anouk on the shoulder before leading her out of the bus. "We're going to have to talk about disciplinary action for that Maquis group when we're done here," she told one of the men outside.

The next woman was several years older, though her

appearance was just as disheveled. She confessed right away that she had fallen in love with a member of the Milice.

"Oh," Nancy replied, unsure at first what else to say. Though she had always felt that mingling with Nazi collaborators, especially ones as awful as the Milice, was reprehensible, that didn't mean the woman deserved to be mistreated by her own countrymen. Nancy told her they were finished with the interrogation. "You may go. But maybe next time you can fall in love with someone loyal to France."

The woman nodded.

Her anger at the Maquis growing, Nancy called for the next woman. This one was middle-aged, with an obstinate air about her. "Are you a spy for the Germans?" Nancy asked, expecting another denial.

"Yes," the woman declared. "I am from the Alsace region and consider myself German. I hate both the British and the French." She focused her beady eyes on Nancy. "I've seen you traipsing around these woods. I know where your old campsite was."

"You didn't—" the thought was almost too horrible to complete. "Did you tell the Germans about the location of our camp?"

"I would have, but they already knew."

A part of Nancy wanted to send her back to the Maquis and let them treat her as horribly as they pleased, but this woman posed a significant threat to all of the Resistance. As there were no jails anywhere in the vicinity, there was only one solution.

"I'm very sorry, but this is war," Nancy told her in a firm voice. "You must know the punishment for someone caught spying for the enemy."

The woman lifted her chin. "As do you."

"I do indeed, and I have no doubt I'd be subject to worse if caught by your comrades."

"You do not plan on torturing me?" The woman's voice was casual, as if she were asking what Nancy wanted for dinner.

"No. We are just going to shoot you."

The woman conceded her fate with a mere nod of her head. If she had any fear, she refused to let it show.

"Let's go." For a moment, Nancy wondered if the woman would try to flee, but she stood and defiantly strode to the front of the bus.

"She needs to be kept in custody," Nancy told the closest guard. "And, in fact, we need to arrange a firing squad."

"A firing squad?" the other guard echoed. "For a woman?"

"Yes. A German spy." She turned to him. "If you won't shoot her, then I will."

"Yes, Madame Andrée."

"And give her your jacket." At the very least, she wouldn't have to die wearing only rags.

The woman spat at Nancy's feet. "I don't need anything from you."

"Have it your way." Nancy nodded at the Maquisard and he led her off into the forest.

A couple of minutes later, several men carrying rifles on their shoulders marched past her. Another minute went by, giving Nancy time to think about the repercussions of her order. Unlike the Germans on the hill that may or may not have died at her hand, this was a woman she'd looked in the eyes as they exchanged conversation. In a way, she would be dying at Nancy's hand. *But,* Nancy reminded herself, she was a spy for the enemy, and by ordering the killing of this woman, she was saving countless lives—possibly even those of her friends.

A gunshot echoed through the forest, followed by several more.

The deed was done.

After Nancy had helped Anouk bathe and get changed, the girl declared she wanted to stay at camp.

"Don't you have a home?"

Anouk didn't answer, but her tears told Nancy everything she needed to know. The Germans had probably killed her parents, maybe even her whole family. "I can become your personal maid," the girl said as Nancy handed her a handkerchief. "I'll do whatever you need."

"It's okay, you can stay here. You can even sleep with me on the bus."

Though Nancy missed Claire desperately, she didn't think she was in need of a maid. But Anouk was so grateful for Nancy saving her from the Maquis that she went out of her way to please her—even washing and drying her nightgowns. Unfortunately, when she hung them up on the makeshift clothesline, Schley caught sight of the silk dancing in the breeze and burst out laughing. "Are those yours?"

"Hush," Nancy said as she yanked them down, a part of her wishing Schley was still nearly blind. "Sometimes a woman just needs to feel like a woman."

"You mean when you're not shooting Sten guns?"

"Exactly."

. . .

The next morning, Nancy was walking near the lake when she saw that Schley was bathing, his clothes and camera underneath a nearby tree. Unable to help herself, Nancy grabbed his things and sat by the edge of the lake.

"Looking for these?" she asked, waving his boxer shorts at him.

"Gert, what do you think you're doing?"

"Waiting for you." She held up the camera as if she would take a picture.

It was a chilly morning and Schley's teeth were chattering as he told her, "Don't worry, I've got all day to spend in the lake."

She set down the camera. "We can make a deal. Don't tell anyone else about my nightgowns, and I'll leave the camera here and walk away so you can get out of the lake."

He seemed to be considering her offer as a plane flew overhead. They both caught sight of the swastika painted on the side, and suddenly things weren't so funny anymore.

"Deal," Schley called, and Nancy walked off to find Anouk.

Anouk was literally cooking up a storm, or at least a wonderfully fragrant soup, over the campfire. Since the moon was mid-cycle, there probably wouldn't be an airdrop that night and it had been Denden's idea to host a banquet to honor the Maquisards for all the work they'd been doing lately.

Roger and Denden spent the day asking for donations from the locals and came back with ample loaves of freshly baked bread and quite a few bottles of wine. The Maquisards tried to make themselves look as presentable as they could, Nancy refraining from going down to the lake while they bathed.

The evening air was still, and they lit as many candles as they dared. Denden sat at the head of the table and led them in toasts to everyone he could think of, all of them taking a healthy sip of wine after each toast. There was one to France, naturally, and Britain and the US, then Winston Churchill and Franklin Roosevelt. His last one was to both the Allies and the Wehrmacht.

"You are thanking the German army?" Hubert demanded. "What for?"

"Why, for not interrupting our dinner, of course."

Most of the table booed at this, but they drank anyway.

Just as soon as Nancy had dug into Anouk's soup, one of the men on guard approached her. He pointed to a Maquisard behind him. "He says he has a message from Fournier, but that it's not urgent."

The new man stepped forward, his eyes widening as he took in the candles, bowls of soup, and bottles of wine strewn about. "Do you eat like this every night?"

"Yes, always," Denden replied drunkenly from the head of the table. "Don't you?"

"Stop," Nancy told him. "We don't want him going back to Fournier and thinking we're spending the Maquis' money." She turned to the man. "This was all donated by locals."

The man didn't seem to care as he took a seat at the table. "Is there any more wine?"

The celebration continued into the early hours of the morning, until a blast of lightning forced everyone back to their tents. Anouk and Nancy, their feet slipping in the mud, ran to the bus, laughing. Though the lightning was fierce, Nancy was ready to continue the party in the bus, but Anouk fell asleep right away.

Nancy was attempting to scrub the dirt off her legs and dress when she heard Aguardiente neighing from his makeshift stall in Denden's showerhouse. Not wanting to be alone, Nancy grabbed some carrots and made her way through the rain.

Aguardiente, clearly not used to hearing the rain pound the galvanized roof, was agitated and it took Nancy a few minutes of rubbing his flank and feeding him carrots before he calmed down.

She spent the next few hours conversing with Aguardiente. No one was around, so Nancy was free to talk about her old life with Henri and, of course, Picon, who she knew would love Aguardiente. When the lightning finally let up, she went back to the bus, figuring that Aguardiente was plenty calm now. Besides, she was exhausted.

She awoke to Anouk shaking her. "Madame Andrée, come look." It was a gray, rainy morning, but even through the mist, Nancy could see the showerhouse. Or what was left of it, anyway. The lean-to had fallen over and the roof was missing, the men's toiletries strewn on the ground in a jumbled pile. Nancy's stomach heaved as she took in the piles of manure dotted in among the razors and toothbrushes, many of which had been crushed by horse hoofs.

Denden walked over to take in the mess. "I would have thought you'd be the last person to take it out on the toothbrushes."

"This wasn't me, dummy. Aguardiente must have gotten spooked by the storm and ran off after he did this." She decided to leave out the part of her talking to the horse all night.

Denden brushed rainwater from his hair. "I guess no one ever taught horses to leave a bathroom as they found it."

"I guess not."

She didn't relish breaking the news to Schley and Alsop, but they were better off hearing it from her. She passed the dented galvanized roof as she headed over to the American's tents. Alsop's tent was easy to find, as it was bright yellow. Despite the rain, he had fallen asleep with his head against the right flap, causing it to bulge.

"Alsop," she called, and then kicked the left side of the tent when he didn't answer.

He finally emerged, his face looking jaundiced from the yellow dye.

"Aguardiente has run off."

"Wha—" He shook his head, trying to wake himself up.

"Guess I'm going to be sending another message asking for toothbrushes," Denden called as he approached. He stared at Alsop for a few seconds before turning to Nancy. "Now I know I'm hungover—I'm seeing yellow." With that, he strolled off to his tent.

Nancy explained to Alsop what had happened, and that, since the shower house was destroyed, he'd better hope the rain would wash the yellow off his face.

After she told Schley, he went off into the forest to see if he could find Aguardiente but came back empty-handed. Nancy hoped against hope that the horse would be okay, but knew exactly what would happen if any other Maquisard—or German, for that matter—came upon him.

She spent most of the day in a funk until Denden, as usual, cheered her up. She laughed heartily when he told her his idea for the next BBC message: *Ducks' horse destroyed the bathroom.*

CHAPTER 37

JULY 1944

By mid-1944, the landscape of the French Resistance had become a complex mosaic of different ideologies and Nancy found it hard to keep them all straight. There were Maquis for staunch nationalists, socialists, communists, civil servants, former Milice, and dozens more, not to mention all the new Moths joining every which one.

Consequently, London was continuously sending drops. While Nancy reveled in being able to supply most of the groups with whatever they needed, she also held back in equipping the Maquis she didn't think worthy, including the ones who had raped Anouk and the other women.

Nancy usually drove herself around the area to distribute the goods and meet with the area leaders, but there were a few times when she ran into German roadblocks. On one occasion, finding herself in a particularly hairy situation, she had to shoot her way out with her Sten gun.

One afternoon in late July, she arranged a meeting with one of the local leaders at a black market restaurant and decided to treat herself to a decent meal. She sat at a table near the window and scanned the room. There was a band of unruly Maquisards causing a commotion in the corner. Suspecting that they were of the same group that had mistreated Anouk, a part of her wanted to confront them, but she knew it would be safer to just ignore them.

One of the more obnoxious men eventually approached her table, the scent of alcohol spewing from his pores. "Spending Maquis money, are we now?"

She pushed her empty plate away. "Of course not." Like Hubert and Denden, she was allotted her own personal allowance from the SOE, but the Maquisard didn't need to know that.

"You are," the man replied, spittle flying out of his mouth. "And you should be stopped."

Nancy fingered the trigger of her Sten gun, but luckily the man stumbled back to his own table. Though she couldn't hear what he was saying, he was shouting furiously and pointing at her.

The leader she was supposed to meet had not appeared, and it was clear that waiting any longer might invite more trouble. She tossed several francs on the table and left the restaurant, feeling eyes boring into her back.

Stepping out into the sunshine, she fumbled through her enormous purse to find her keys. She hadn't realized how tense she'd been until the wave of relief washed over her when she reached her car. Just as she unlocked the door, a drunken shout from behind made her turn around.

To her horror, she saw the same Maquisard exiting the restaurant, a maniacal grin on his face and a grenade clutched in his hand. "As I said, you need to be stopped."

She jumped into the car and tried to drive away, but her shaking hands couldn't fit the key into the ignition.

In slow motion, as if in a nightmare, her eyes steadied on the man. He pulled the pin and then made to throw the grenade at her, but, in his drunken stupor, he took too long in his aim. The grenade exploded in his hand with a deafening roar and flash of light that momentarily blinded Nancy.

Once her senses returned, she saw that the Maquisard lay motionless on the cobblestones, his chest blackened and his arm missing. Smoke filled the air, and the front of the restaurant was a shattered mess. She grimaced when she saw the shards of bone and fragments of flesh that had landed on the windshield.

A few men came running outside, but there was nothing left of the would-be assassin. Nancy was too much in shock to get out of the car. With shaking legs, she drove straight back to camp.

By evening, word of the encounter had gotten out through what Nancy liked to call the 'forest wireless' and Tardi insisted that she needed a bodyguard to accompany her at all times. Colonel Paishing, the leader of the Spanish Maquis whom Nancy had impressed with her alcohol tolerance, had been conferencing with Hubert at their camp and immediately volunteered himself and two of his men. "They'd be more than happy to help out the *chef du parachutage*, especially after all you've given us."

It was settled then, and soon Nancy had an entourage of three cars and drivers. At first she rode in the middle car with Colonel Paishing. The plan was, if they got into trouble, the front and rear cars would stop to fight and the middle car would keep traveling. As the cars were all open-topped, she usually emerged covered in the fine red dust. After a few days of this, she insisted on riding in the front car. The Spaniards called her very brave, but her reasoning was simply to avoid the dust train that followed the front car.

Her Spanish bodyguards always showed her the utmost deference and insisted on calling her *Jefa,* which she understood to mean "boss" in Spanish. Occasionally their trips would take all day and they would stop to eat at a café in some village. They'd been warned that it was a place like that where Nancy had almost had to eat a grenade, and two of the Spaniards insisted on entering the café first, their Sten guns at the ready. Once they made certain that everything was secure, they would return to the car and escort Nancy and Colonel Paishing, who refused to leave Nancy's side, into the café. They'd have her sit at a table in the middle of the room and stand over her as she ate. In the beginning, she tried to order them a round of aguardiente, but they all refused, stating they never drank on the job.

By the end of July 1944, the tides had definitely turned and the liberation of France seemed to be more imminent with every passing day. Nancy figured now it was only a matter of *when,* not *if* the Allies would come to the region.

Not everyone shared her optimism, however. Tardi, in particular, was determined to retaliate against the Germans with the goal of forcing them to withdraw. One evening, while sitting around the campfire, he proposed an attack on the German headquarters in Montluçon. "We can get them just as they're sitting down to lunch. Instead of dining on schnitzel and schnapps, they'll be eating our bullets."

Of all the men Nancy had worked with since the beginning of the war, it was Tardi, with his supreme organization and relentless determination, whom she respected the most. But this plan was too spiteful even for her. "This isn't a defense move—you're talking about deliberately attacking them. What about repercussions?"

Tardi, clearly not understanding her reluctance, shook his head. "We've just about got them on the run. What if we could finally eliminate them from the region for good? Then we'd never have to be on the defense again."

Even Nancy couldn't help managing a smile as she pictured an Allier department free of Nazis, where the residents could come and go as they pleased without worrying about roadblocks or being murdered in their sleep.

"Gertie," Tardi leaned forward. "What if I told you these men were the same ones who killed those Moths that you buried?"

"Are they?"

He gave a noncommittal shrug. "Maybe. I can't say for certain. But will you join us and pretend that they are?"

With their usual precision, Tardi and his men meticulously planned the raid from start to finish. For days, they watched the garrison to determine how many guards were on duty and when their shifts changed. They then hid a cache of arms and explosives inside a house in close proximity to the Germans' headquarters, ready to be retrieved just after midday, when the Nazis would be enjoying their pre-lunch drinks.

When the day of the attack came, Nancy, clad in blue overalls to imitate a worker's attire, rode with her Spanish bodyguards into town. As the cars pulled to a stop, she glanced up at the imposing building. With its large windows and stucco exterior, it had clearly been some sort of office or administrative building before the Nazis requisitioned it.

After Tardi's men had neutralized the guards, Nancy entered the headquarters through the back door and, choosing speed over stealth, clomped up the stairs. The door to the conference room was to the left, just as Tardi had indicated in his plans. Nancy took the grenade from the pocket of her overalls and threw her weight against the door. She barely registered the shocked faces of a dozen Germans as she pulled the pin out of the grenade and threw it before slamming the door and running as fast as she could down the stairs.

Several other Maquisards, having also hurled their grenades through different doors, were also racing to get out of the building. They regrouped on the clearing outside of the building.

Soon a series of sharp blasts could be heard, and the ground shivered under Nancy's feet. She was too elated to feel any guilt over the deaths of possibly hundreds of Boches.

A few townspeople emerged from their homes. "Have the Allies arrived?" someone shouted at Nancy.

Her ears were still buzzing, and she could scarcely make out the sound of her own voice. "No, not yet. Go back inside." It appeared as though the building's foundation was secure, but Nancy wanted to make sure no civilians would be hurt if it were indeed to collapse.

Maybe the townspeople's ears were also ringing, or maybe they were choosing to ignore Nancy. At any rate, their gaze fell on Schley and Alsop's somewhat disheveled uniforms. "The Allies *are* here!" Several men and women descended on them, some of them pumping the Americans' hands.

"They think they've been liberated," Schley called.

Nancy glanced back at the Nazi headquarters. No one was

running after them—there was probably no one left alive in the building to pursue them—but they still needed to leave town as soon as possible.

She climbed into the nearest car. Colonel Paishing was behind the wheel, and, after Schley and Alsop jumped in, she instructed Paishing to drive away. The two Americans were slapping each other on the back. This time, Paishing didn't refuse her offer of a shot of aguardiente and, once they were back at camp, toasted to their success.

CHAPTER 38

AUGUST 1944

In the middle of August, they received word that the Germans had finally begun evacuating the Allier department. London assured Denden that the Allies would be landing on France's southern shores 'any day now,' but in the meantime, they had liberated Toulon and Marseille.

Nancy clapped her hands when she heard the news, tears of relief forming in her eyes. At last, Henri would be safe.

The next parachutage that came held a special surprise for Nancy: her FANY uniform. Schley whistled with approval when she walked out in it. "It's not quite a silk nightgown, but at least you're finally getting the recognition you deserve, eh, Gertie?"

To Nancy, it wasn't so much about getting recognition as that she was tired of hiding who she really was. "That's Nancy to you, Reeve Schley. Nancy Fiocca." It felt good to say Henri's last name and even better was the thought that it should only be a few weeks at the most before she could get back to Marseille and see Henri again.

That is, if he was still in Marseille—she hadn't heard anything from him in over a year and a half.

Nancy pushed that last niggling thought out of her mind, knowing that, before anything, she had to finish her job, which had become somewhat easier lately now that the Wehrmacht in the region seemed to be suffering from a lack of organization. Some checkpoints were still heavily guarded, while others were completely abandoned, and the Maquisards would often come across deserted supply trucks, their engines still warm and their contents hastily strewn about. Of course, the Maquisards, who had been acting as saboteurs for years, seemed to welcome the transition to an offensive role, and often used the Germans' own supplies against them. The balance of power had shifted and now it was the occupying Nazis who were fearing for their own survival.

Ironically, the Maquis' primary task had now become to hinder the Germans' withdrawal from France, each ambush and every piece of destroyed equipment eroding the Boches' defensive capabilities that much more.

When the group arrived in Cosne d'Allier to blow up a railroad bridge, Nancy found that Hubert was also dressed in his uniform. Normally, they would have opted for a late-night operation, but they were under a time constraint—destroying the bridge meant stranding thousands of Germans on the wrong side of the Belfort Gap. The townspeople, probably thinking they were the Allied army, came out in droves to watch.

"This must be the most people I've ever seen at a demolition," Alsop remarked dryly.

But Nancy paid little attention to the spectators. Her focus was on positioning the explosives at the bridge's weakest point to maximize the damage. Based on a quick survey, it was clear that the base of the bridge would be the best spot, but that also meant she would have to climb down to reach it.

With a sigh, she took some of the TNT, which had been molded into a block, in one hand and a time-delay fuse in the other. Hubert followed her down while Tardi and Colonel Paishing took the other side of the bridge.

Once the TNT had been secured, Nancy set a timer for five minutes and then headed back up.

The view at the top took her by surprise: the bridge was teeming with dozens of townsfolk. Nancy cupped her hands around her mouth and shouted, "Get off now! This bridge is going to blow!"

A few people stopped to stare at her, but most made no move to get off. Her eyes landed on a toddler a meter in front of her. Nancy made a big show of picking the toddler up and running him back to the grass, and then went back for another child, calling to the rest of them, "You only have a minute!"

More people started to move off. In the last dozen or so seconds, Tardi and Colonel Paishing ran from the other side, pushing the last wanderers off the bridge.

Thankfully, the bridge was empty as the initial explosion boomed out. There were a couple more thundering blasts, which were soon accompanied by the groaning of metal as the bridge began to collapse. Only a few seconds later, the entire structure plummeted into the river with a giant splash.

The townspeople stomped and clapped, a few of them embracing Nancy in giant bear hugs. It either hadn't occurred to them that, due to the collapsed bridge, they would be stranded on one side of the river for quite some time, or else they just didn't care.

. . .

The Germans, or what was left of them, regrouped in their garrison in Montluçon, and Tardi decided to attack them once again. Armed with bazookas, his men, accompanied by Schley, Alsop, and Hubert, set off while Nancy and Denden stayed behind to inform London of their plans.

The next day, a scout arrived with a message from Tardi declaring that they'd captured half of the barracks and, if Nancy wanted to add some excitement to her day, she should join him in tackling the other half. The message ended with a request to bring plenty of extra bazooka rockets.

Nancy picked up a carbine from the bench beside her. "What is Tardi's location?"

The scout pointed at Denden's map. "Near this bridge."

She grabbed the requested ammunition and then several grenades for good measure before locating Colonel Paishing. "Are you up for giving me a ride?"

There was a roadblock on the bridge. Nancy, reassuring Paishing that it was Tardi's men, got out of the car and approached.

As a bullet whizzed past her head, she shouted, "Stop—it's me!"

More bullets rang out.

Shielding her eyes from the sun with her hand, Nancy realized that the men were wearing uniforms—somewhat stained and threadbare, but uniforms just the same—in grayish-green.

Cursing loudly, she sprinted toward the car, which Paishing had already turned around. The moment she leapt inside, Paishing sped off, the machine guns behind them now firing full throttle.

"That was close," she said when she could finally breathe again.

A few minutes later, they passed another bridge. "Maybe this is it," she told Paishing, who was clearly reluctant to slow down. Upon spying Tardi himself, Paishing finally braked.

"Well that was a pretty stupid thing to do," Tardi said when Nancy got out of the car.

"You saw?"

"The whole thing."

"Such is war," Nancy stated in a nonchalant tone, refusing to be embarrassed. "Here's your extra rockets."

Tardi loaded his bazooka and then helped Nancy take cover behind one of the barracks they'd captured. All the while, occasional rifle shots rang out, some too close for comfort. Tardi pointed upward at a distant building. "There are snipers up there, and, since we've run out of missiles, we haven't been able to return fire."

Tardi positioned his bazooka and took aim. After he squeezed the trigger, a plume of fire erupted from the muzzle, followed by a deafening roar. Soon the entire building was engulfed in flames, the snipers burning with it.

"I guess that's the end of that." Nancy stood up. "Is there anything else I can help you with?"

Tardi, his face covered in dirt and sweat, shook his head. "I think we're good now."

Tardi and his men were able to control the full fort for a few days, but then, when more German reinforcements arrived, they withdrew and returned to camp. It had been raining for several days and Tardi's lip curled as he took in the mud-soaked tents. "Since when did our camp become a swampland?"

"I suppose you and your men slept soundly with roofs over your heads in that dry barracks. Meanwhile," Nancy gestured toward the bus, which had sunk several centimeters into the mud. "We've been dealing with this."

Tardi rubbed the beard stubble on his chin. "Well, the Germans are on the run, for the most part anyway. What do you say we move to a more permanent headquarters? One that will keep us dry?"

Hubert provided the perfect solution: a château a few kilometers outside of Montluçon. As it didn't have running water or electricity, the Germans never deigned to claim it, and the owner told Hubert they could occupy it until the war was finally over.

It took them one whole wet, mud-soaked night to pull the bus out, but they finally got it working in the morning. As the relentless rain continued to pour outside, Nancy and several dozen men dragged mattresses into the château.

It was clear that it had been several years since anyone had lived there, and Nancy took charge of the cleaning by ordering the men to sweep and scrub the floors and dust off the thick cobwebs covering most of the interior. Compared to the swampy terrain of their old camp, the decrepit château soon proved to be a veritable oasis.

Rather than return to her previous landing fields, which were several kilometers away and probably also bogged down by mud, Nancy informed London that the drops would now be taking place on the château's grounds. Instead of relying on bonfires, she decided to incorporate battery-powered floodlights. "Denden, since you are so good with electricity, I'm going to put you in charge of setting them up."

Denden, recalling the time he'd nearly been electrocuted, waved her off as everyone else in the room laughed. "I'm a wireless operator, not an electrician."

Tardi, of course, took charge of the new plan, and soon the château's outer walls were decorated with wires and switches that would light up the grounds like Christmas whenever there was an approaching plane. And once again, it felt just like Christmas when the parachuted containers descended from the sky, a spectacle Nancy had the pleasure of witnessing from the dry interior of her bedroom.

CHAPTER 39

AUGUST 1944

A few days after they'd moved into the château, they received word that Paris had been liberated. It was hard to put into words the excitement that swept over Nancy upon hearing that news. But amid the rejoicing, a sobering update came from London: Hitler had ordered his armies to renew construction on the Siegfried Line along Germany's western border, opposite what remained of the Maginot Line.

This, of course, incensed the whole of the Maquis. Gaspard soon sent word that there was a factory still producing ammunition in his area. He wanted help in destroying it, and when Tardi asked for volunteers, Nancy was among the first to step forward. She'd do anything to stop the Germans from producing a single bullet more.

Gaspard's team had been surveilling the factory for several days and knew all the details of the guards' shifts and what time would be ideal for attacking it. When Tardi's band arrived at Gaspard's camp, the latter immediately took out a hastily drawn blueprint of the grounds.

Gaspard stabbed at the blueprint with his rough hands. "There are four gatehouses, one on each corner of the factory, with two sentries each." He marked lines near one of the corners. "Each of them parades in front of the gatehouse in opposite directions. You'll see that the surrounding area is covered by scrub, but the Germans cleared a ten-meter perimeter around the factory in order to patrol it. We'll want to get the guards the moment they pass each other."

Tardi nodded. "The first objective would be to take out all eight sentries."

"Right. We'll need four teams, one per guardhouse." He pointed his pencil at three of his men and then, to Nancy's surprise, at her. "Gertie will be in charge of the group taking the west side."

She barely had time to sputter, "Yes, sir," before Gaspard continued, "Then together, we'll all move into the factory, set the charges, and then run like hell."

This time they all shouted in unison, "Yes, sir!"

At midnight, Nancy found herself lying belly down on the wet ground a few hundred meters away from the factory, a Maquisard from Gaspard's group on either side of her. The Germans had kept the factory lights off, probably to avoid becoming a bomb target, and the night felt as dark as one of Dr. Hughes' ink blots.

Nancy counted the minutes until the time when the two sentries, discernible only as slightly less black shadows against the black night, passed each other. As the shadows crept closer to each other, she gave a low whistle and she and the Maquisards sprang into action.

The plan was for her and one of the men to each knock a

guard unconscious while the other Maquisard stood by in case anyone needed backup. As Nancy ran toward her target, he seemed unaware of her, even as she got close enough to see his grayish-green uniform and the outline of his face under his helmet.

Suddenly the guard turned in her direction, the gleam of his bayonet unmistakable even in the dim light.

Realizing that he was about to turn his gun on her, Nancy formed her hand into a block the way she'd been taught during combat training in Scotland and brought it down on the spot at the base of his spine. To her shock, he fell at her feet, the gun clattering onto the concrete.

For a second, she was stunned. *Had it really worked?* One of the Maquisards picked up the guard's limp wrist. "No pulse," he said, grinning through the dark at Nancy.

"I killed him." Now there was no question about it—Nancy had really killed a man. *A Boche*, she reminded herself. It was either him or her.

"Madame Andrée, you're bleeding." The other Maquisard took a handkerchief and tied it around her arm.

His bayonet must have made contact with her arm. *Maybe it's him AND me*, was her last thought before she passed out.

She woke up a couple of minutes later in the brush outside the factory. One of her men stood over her. "Are you all right, Madame Andrée?"

She sat up, the sudden movement causing another wave of dizziness. "The factory?"

The man checked his watch. "If my timing's right, it's about to blow."

"Perfect," Nancy said before blacking out again.

. . .

It took Nancy another day in her bed at the château to recover from her wound, which a local doctor had decided was a deep, but treatable flesh wound. Gaspard and Tardi's team had indeed succeeded in blowing up the factory, thanks in part to Nancy's effort in taking out the sentry.

She was still feeling a little squeamish about having killed a man with her bare hands, but Denden, with his typical bluntness, managed to comfort her with a reminder that the only good German was a dead one.

"And besides…" Denden patted her good arm. "They'll have fewer guns at the Siegfried Line because of us."

"Us?" Nancy repeated. Denden, naturally, had refused to be part of the attack, but had wasted no time in relaying the good news to London.

"Of course, us," Denden said, rolling his eyes. "Who do you think keeps London entertained with stories of your heroics? Without my dazzling reports, you'd just be another Maquisard with a death wish. And someone's got to ensure that your name makes it into the history books."

Now it was Nancy's turn to pat him on the shoulder, though she did it with a little more force than he had. "And you're doing a great job of it. I'm sure the Germans are downright shaking in their boots over your Morse coding abilities."

He winked. "You bet they are. Now go blow something else up so I can write another thrilling report."

Denden decided that the destruction of the factory, combined with the liberation of Paris and Nancy surviving her latest brush with death, was cause for yet another celebration.

Nancy, her legs still a bit shaky, raided the cellars in search of wine, but didn't find more than a couple of dusty bottles. Denden and the rest of the men seemed to throw themselves into the party-planning and told Nancy to relax while they took care of the details.

Relax? She wouldn't relax until the war was officially over and she was back in Marseille, in Henri's arms. So she busied herself unpacking the latest packages from London. One of them contained a box of chocolates and a card, signed by Buckmaster himself. With a start, Nancy realized that it was her thirty-second birthday.

Another year had passed, but what would this one bring? *Hopefully peace.* And the long-awaited reunion with Henri.

Her uniform was in a much worse state than it had been when it arrived from London, but Nancy decided to wear it anyway. As she trudged down the back steps of the château, Tardi met her there, holding an enormous bouquet of wildflowers that someone had probably picked from the gardens that morning.

"What is this for?" she asked.

"We have much to celebrate. Didn't you know it was your birthday?" He shoved the bouquet at her. "Hold these in your left arm."

"Why left if I'm right-handed?" The reason soon became clear as dozens of sharply dressed Maquisards emerged from the bushes on the lawn. Led by Schley and Alsop, they paraded by her with great pomp, their salutes razor-sharp.

Laughing, Nancy returned the salutes with her right hand. The procession seemed never-ending, and, indeed, after a few minutes, she finally caught on that the men were looping back to march past her multiple times.

"All right, all right," Tardi finally called. "Let's go eat."

A fine spread of cheese, ham, and bread—accompanied by many, many bottles of wine—was laid out in the parlor. Denden, who was drinking straight out of a champagne bottle, greeted her with a kiss on the cheek before shoving a full bottle of perfume at her, complete with a red bow. "You don't have to worry about me taking sips from your cologne anymore. Happy birthday, Ducks."

There were other presents too: Alsop gave her an etching of a parachute flying through the air, which he had drawn himself; the dozen silver spoons were from Schley; and, from Colonel Paishing, a silver flask engraved with the words, 'For aguardiente only.' One of her other bodyguards, declaring he had no money, had written her a poem.

A row of tables with wildflower centerpieces had been set up in the hall. After the sumptuous meal came the speeches, Tardi, Hubert, and countless others ending every one of them with *Vive la France, Vive les Allies,* and *Vive Madame Andrée.*

Even after all the food and wine had been consumed, the party raged on. It was as if everyone wanted to delay the cleanup for as long as possible.

Kind of like what's happening with the war, Nancy thought. Now that the Germans presented less of a threat, it was time to confront the wreckage that had been left behind and give the dead a proper burial. For those who survived the war, she supposed there would be celebrations and, someday, reckoning for the collaborators. *But not yet.*

When Nancy finally awoke the next morning—she'd taken the suggestion to relax to heart—there were still wine glasses and plates with scraps of food scattered among the tables. She had just started to clear them when Alsop shouted, "Madame

Andrée, come quick—the entire Wehrmacht is marching up our driveway!"

She dropped a glass on the floor, cursing loudly before telling Alsop to close all the windows. Had the enemy caught wind of last night's party and, knowing there were dozens of Maquisards under one roof, decided to catch them in one fell swoop? "Tell everyone to stay inside," she hissed at Alsop.

She crept upstairs to a bedroom overlooking the front yard. The road running parallel to the château's front gate and beyond the garden was the main road from Montluçon. From behind a curtain, Nancy observed the convoy that, like last night's line of saluting soldiers, seemed to go on forever. This time there were no repeats, though all the German soldiers' slumping postures did seem to mirror each other.

"What's going on?" Denden asked in a drowsy tone. He'd clearly been awoken by the lumbering of the trucks.

Nancy pointed out the window and Denden's eyes, no longer sleepy, widened. "But I don't think they're stopping."

Denden took position on the other side of the window. Both of them were holding their breath, as the soldiers continued to march past the gate.

"Must be what was left of the Montluçon garrison," Denden finally declared. "Should we tell Tardi in case he wants to finish them off?"

Nancy waved her hand. "Let them go with their tails between their legs. We have to clean up from last night."

"Do we have to?" Denden grinned at the departing convoy. "Something tells me there are going to be a lot more parties in our future."

CHAPTER 40

SEPTEMBER 1944

*I*n September, Denden received word that the Germans were finally evacuating the ultimate nest of collaborators, Vichy. Hubert and Gaspard had previously arranged to reclaim the former capital together with their respective Maquis, but Tardi reported that Gaspard, predictably, had gone ahead to take most of the credit. Still, Vichy, where Marshal Pétain's puppet government had once been housed, epitomized everything Nancy had been fighting against for the past four years and she was ready to play a role in its liberation.

They found the road to Vichy to be filled with townspeople waving French flags and singing "La Marseillaise." If there were collaborators left, Nancy couldn't identify them among the people cheering and tossing flowers into their open cars. Everyone was in a celebratory mood and extended their thanks to anyone in uniform, including Nancy.

. . .

The next day they headed to Vichy's Great War memorial, where another impromptu celebration had been organized. Nancy was asked to lay wreaths in honor of those who had given their lives in both World Wars.

She made her way toward the center of the crowd, where the mayor was giving a speech of thanksgiving. Numerous townspeople were dressed in their best outfits, evidently retrieved from storage in anticipation of the long-awaited liberation. She could feel someone sizing her up and tugged on her wrinkled khaki suit.

"Nancy? Nancy Fiocca?"

It had been so long since she'd heard someone call her by her real name that Nancy was doubly startled. She immediately recognized Madame Richard, a receptionist who'd worked at the Hôtel de Louvre at Paix in Marseille and had helped plan her wedding. The older woman hugged Nancy and thanked her for her service. Her next words were drowned out, however, by a loud cheer that went through the crowd.

"What?" Nancy shouted. She leaned closer to Madame Richard.

"I said, I was sorry to hear about Henri."

Despite the warm September day, Nancy suddenly felt a cold shock, as if she had jumped into ice water. "Henri?"

A wave of startled realization washed over Madame Richard's face. "You didn't know. Oh, Nancy, I'm so sorry."

Once again the woman tried to embrace her, but Nancy pushed her away and shoved through the crowd. She felt as though she would keel over, but someone caught her. "Ducks, what is it?"

"Denden…" She burst into tears, unable to finish her sentence.

"Come on," Denden took hold of her arm and practically dragged her over to the side of the square.

She was now babbling. "She said he was dead, but he can't be dead." Nancy looked up. "Is he dead, Denden?"

"Henri?" His voice was uncharacteristically soft.

She nodded.

"I don't know." Denden took her hand in his. "Let's go to Marseille and find out."

A few hours later, Nancy found herself sitting numbly in the backseat of a car with Hubert and Denden, Colonel Paishing in the driver's seat. No one questioned the sanity of driving south through a war-ravaged country, with its pock-marked roads and missing bridges, nor spoke of the possibility of an ambush by rogue enemy units.

The drive was slow-going, and many times they came to a blown-out bridge and had to turn around.

Nancy paid no attention to anything but the *what-ifs* running through her head. What if Henri really were dead? What if she had to live the rest of her life without him? And the worst question of all: *What if his death was my fault?*

When they finally arrived in Marseille, Nancy, her voice hoarse, gave Colonel Paishing directions. She wasn't prepared to go to their old apartment on the Canebière. If what Madame Richard had said was true, there wouldn't be anybody there anyway. In the end, she decided to go see Monsieur Brisbois at his butcher's shop.

Colonel Paishing waited in the car while Hubert and Denden stood a respectful distance behind her as she peered through a dusty window. Though a closed sign was placed over the door, the shop was intact. After spotting Monsieur Brisbois, she knocked on the glass.

He opened the door slowly. "Madame Fiocca."

The sympathetic look in his eyes nearly brought her to tears again. "Do you know what happened to Henri?"

"Come inside." He squeezed her shoulder before settling his gaze on Hubert and Denden.

"They're with me."

Monsieur Brisbois led them into a back room with a table and chairs. He bustled around the kitchen, as if to delay telling Nancy what he knew.

Finally he walked over to the table holding a tea set. "I don't have much anymore—no one in Marseilles does."

"Thank you." Nancy's hand was trembling as she picked up her cup.

Monsieur Brisbois watched her for a moment before his gaze moved to Hubert and Denden.

"Henri," she finally prompted.

Monsieur Brisbois gave a deep sigh. "It was the spring of 1943, after Guérisse was arrested."

"March," Nancy supplied dully.

"Yes," he nodded. "It was cold and gray. Guérisse was in prison and apparently needed to pass on some information. Everyone here was laying low, and I only know what I've heard from others…" he trailed off.

"Tell me," Nancy insisted.

He scratched the back of his neck. "There was another prisoner with Guérisse, and they were about to let him go, so Guérisse gave him a message to take to Henri. He told him the password so Henri knew he was trustworthy."

Nancy shut her eyes. The message was probably about the

dangers Roger the Leak presented to the line. "But the 'trustworthy' prisoner was really a German agent."

Monsieur Brisbois's one-word reply was nearly inaudible. "Yes." He cleared his throat. "I saw the Gestapo take Henri away in a van."

Oh, Guérisse, for all your safeguards, you still let the bad men in. First Paul Cole, then Roger le Neveu, and now the man who'd betrayed Henri. "Did the Gestapo know that I was the White Mouse?"

"I think they probably worked that out—it was obvious that a woman had once lived at the flat. But of course, Henri refused to tell them where you were."

"They would have tortured him."

Once again, Monsieur Brisbois repeated, "Yes."

"And his death? Do you know when he died?"

Monsieur Brisbois squeezed his eyes shut. "June 1943." A tear slipped down his craggy face.

Nancy didn't press him for the date—she didn't have to. It would have been June 16, the night she dreamt that Henri had been killed by a German U-boat.

She'd once thought that when she married the love of her life, all her dreams had come true. But this time it was a nightmare that had come to pass. "They killed him because I was the White Mouse. They killed him because of me."

Denden reached for her hand. "You can't blame yourself, Ducks."

"No," Hubert agreed. "Think of all you've done for the war since then." He tried to smile. "How would any Maquisard ever have survived without our Madame Andrée?"

Monsieur Brisbois cleared his throat again. "Madame Fiocca, there's one last thing you should know. It's about your father-in-law."

Nancy's lip curled in distaste. "Of all the men to survive the war…"

"He was a customer here as well, and knew that I was familiar with Henri." Monsieur Brisbois rubbed his forehead. "He came around shortly after Henri was arrested, and—well, there is no other way to say this—your father-in-law is not your friend."

"I've known that for a while."

Monsieur Brisbois nodded. "He visited Henri a few times in jail and tried to convince him to tell them your whereabouts. He wanted Henri to save his own life…"

"And, as always, Monsieur Fiocca didn't give a lick about mine," Nancy filled in.

"But Henri would have never said anything."

She rose from the table. "And that's why I'm still here, and he's not." Her voice wobbled as the tears that she'd been holding back finally started their course. Henri had always been so full of life that it was impossible to believe he was gone. He would never again come home for lunch, ready to indulge in her latest scheme, never complain about all the men in their apartment, never reach down to pet Picon…

"Picon," she said aloud. She turned her tear-streaked face once more to Monsieur Brisbois. "Do you know what happened to my dog?"

His eyebrows rose, as if pleased to finally deliver good news. "Last I heard he was with the Ficetoles."

Once again Denden and Hubert were willing to accompany Nancy, no questions asked. But the building where the Ficetoles had once lived had been flattened by a bomb. The whole street was a blackened, abandoned mess.

"What now?" Denden asked, resignation in his voice. It was clear he didn't have high hopes for the fate of Nancy's dog.

But Picon was all that Nancy had left. She turned down another street and asked someone on the corner, "Do you know where the Ficetoles live?"

The man shook his head. In the distance, they could hear rifle shots ring out. "There must still be some German holdouts," Hubert decided, coming up behind her. Nancy knew he was going to say that they'd better get inside, but she suddenly remembered that the Ficetoles' niece lived a few blocks away.

As she approached the apartment building, she suddenly heard a frenzied barking. "It can't possibly..." she said aloud, but then her eyes lighted on the first-floor as a small ball of fur launched itself at the closed window. "Picon!"

"I think he remembers you," Denden declared as the little dog pawed and scratched at the glass.

"Who's there?" A woman's head peered down from an open window above them. "Quiet, Picon!"

"It's me," Nancy called up. "Nancy Fiocca."

"Nancy?" The woman leaned out as far as she dared. "You're back! I'll be right down."

As she opened the front door, Picon hurled himself into Nancy's arms. She scratched him behind the ears in the spot he always loved as the woman came out.

Nancy barely recognized her old friend, Nicole Ficetole. She'd lost a lot of weight and her hair was completely gray. Feeling her gaze, Nicole, in turn, searched her friend's face.

"Don't worry," Nancy said, turning her eyes away. "I know about Henri."

"I'm sorry."

"It's okay. If you don't mind, I'd like to take this little guy..." she raised Picon. "Home now."

"Of course." Nicole reached out to pet the dog. "He was a good friend to me. Will you let me come see him once in a while?"

As Nancy nodded, Nicole's face clouded over. "About your flat. If you haven't been home, you should know that after Henri... well, while he was in prison, the Gestapo moved into your apartment."

Nancy blinked back a fresh round of tears. All she wanted to do was crawl into bed and weep over her lost husband, and now she didn't have a home to go to.

"Do you think they're gone now?" Denden asked Nicole.

She shrugged. "It's possible—a lot of the Nazis fled as soon as the Allies entered the city."

Denden once again took Nancy's arm. "Let's go see."

They found the apartment to be not only vacant of humans, but also eerily void of almost every trace of the Fioccas' former possessions. How the Gestapo planned on getting her velvet couch or four-poster bed back to Germany, Nancy had no idea, nor did she care.

She set Picon down on the parquet floor. He ran from empty room to empty room, sniffing, evidently trying to figure out if indeed this was his former home.

Or maybe he was searching for Henri. The thought was so depressing that Nancy sank to the floor.

"Ducks?" Denden sat down beside her and took her hand in his. "What are you going to do now?"

"I don't know. I waited for so long for the war to be over and now... now this." What *would* she do? The life she had known as Madame Fiocca disappeared when Henri died. Not to mention neither the SOE nor the Maquis needed her now.

Picon trotted back to the living room, having located a ball from who knows where. He dropped the ball next to Nancy's leg and then wagged his tail expectantly.

As she picked it up to toss it, she remarked dryly, "I guess there are some things that don't change."

"Your life isn't over, you know. The war isn't either yet, but hopefully it will be soon." Denden rubbed her palm with his thumb. "You have to promise me that you yourself will never change, that you'll stay the same old Ducks forever."

She managed to turn her lips into a semblance of a smile. "I'll try."

"I know it will take a bit of time, but when you're ready, Ducks, will you…"

"Yes?" she prompted him.

He turned to her, his eyes sparkling. "Will you introduce me to some rich Marseille men?"

It did take Nancy some time to recover from the loss of Henri, but not as long as she'd feared. The truth was, she'd known in her heart for a while that Henri was gone and had been unconsciously learning to live without him, even while fighting the war.

There was practically nothing left in Henri's bank account—Nancy assumed that her father-in-law had somehow gotten his dirty hands on it—but she used what was left to install herself and Picon at a hotel, and then buy a dress in the latest style and new shoes.

It felt good to be in feminine clothes again after all this time. So good that she decided to meet Denden, Hubert, and Colonel Paishing at the Hôtel du Louvre for a drink, but only after she'd gotten her hair done.

Although the entrance off the Canebière was no longer crowded with Germans, by habit Nancy went through the back door and immediately spotted the men at the opposite end of the bar. Colonel Paishing was talking to a couple of ladies while Hubert nursed his beer. Denden, looking exceedingly bored, glanced up as she waved at him. He nodded politely as though she were a stranger and then took a swig of his drink.

Antoine, the head waiter, passed by her carrying a tray of drinks and nearly dropped them at her feet. "Madame Fiocca, is that you?"

"It's me, Antoine," she said laughingly, keeping her eyes on her friends in the corner.

Denden peered at her sharply and then recognition finally dawned. "Ducks?"

"Good god, it *is* Gert!" Hubert called.

"Who knew you could clean up so well?" Denden added. "That dress really suits you, even more than your stained uniform."

Colonel Paishing sidled up to her and took her arm. "Mind if I escort you to dinner, Madame Andrée?"

"Colonel Paishing, you can call me Nancy now."

"Nancy…"

"Fiocca."

"Nancy Fiocca," he repeated, slurring his words. Colonel Paishing was obviously already a few beers in. Or maybe he'd had one too many sips of aguardiente. "*Excusez moi,*" he said in a terrible French accent. He waved his arms, commanding everyone in the room's attention. "I want to introduce you to Madame Fiocca. She's the bravest woman the world has ever seen, and you should thank her personally for helping defeat the Nazis."

"Hear, hear!" someone called, tapping on their wineglass with a knife. *"Vive la Allies. Vive Nancy Fiocca!"*

As the rest of the room erupted into cheers, Nancy's heart felt heavy. The restaurant was ripe with memories of Henri. They'd held their wedding reception there and that fateful meeting with Captain Wilson—at the same bar where Denden and Hubert were currently installed—was what had caused her to dive into the Resistance so readily in the first place. The world, it seemed, had come full circle.

As one table near them loudly toasted the Fioccas again, Nancy figured many of them had probably once known her, Henri, or her father-in-law. Maybe even all three.

She looped her free arm through Colonel Paishing's. "Never mind them. What are we having for dinner?"

EPILOGUE

With the war over and having met her goal of helping to rid the world of Nazis, **Nancy Wake** was left wondering what to do next. One thing was for sure—she never wanted to ride a bike again. She moved to Paris, embarking on a series of office jobs as well as dabbling in politics.

Upon receiving the UK's George Medal, the US Medal of Freedom, the Medaille de la Resistance from France, three Croix de Guerre medals, and the Badge in Gold from New Zealand, she became one of the most decorated women of WWII. In addition, in 1970 she was named a *Chevalier* of the Legion of Honour by France and promoted to *Officier* in 1988. In 2004, Australia finally recognized her heroism with the Companion of the Order of Australia.

In 1957, at the age of 45, Nancy remarried. Her new husband was an RAF officer named John Forward who had been shot down during the war and was a POW until he was released after the Germans surrendered. Nancy and John moved to Australia a few years later. In 1985, Nancy shared her story with an entirely new generation via her autobiography, *Nancy Wake: The White Mouse.*

In 1994, the Returned and Services League of Australia acquired her medals via a Sotheby's auction, and they are now on display at the Australian War Memorial. Her response to why she'd auctioned them off was, "I can't take them with me, I don't have children, and they might melt in the place that I am going, so why wouldn't I sell them?"

She died on 7 August 2011, just a few weeks before her 99th birthday, declaring that she wanted her "ashes scattered over the hills where I fought with brave men." Accordingly her remains were returned to the woods surrounding the Château de Fragne near Montluçon.

Denis Rake was awarded the UK's Military Cross and France's Croix de Guerre. He was also named a *Chevalier* of the Legion of Honour. After the war, Rake became a steward on cruise liners before taking a valet position with Douglas Fairbanks Jr, who encouraged him to write an autobiography. Published in 1968, it was called *Rake's Progress: The Gay and Dramatic Adventures of Major Denis Rake MC, The Reluctant British Wartime Agent.* Not much of his life after that is known, though at some point, he'd written to F Section leader, Maurice Buckmaster, stating, 'I know I'm crazy. I started life like that long ago and must end the same.' Rake died in September 1976 at the age of 74.

Reeve Schley, who was awarded the US Bronze Star Medal and the Croix de Guerre, actually wrote the recommendation for

Nancy Wake to receive the American Medal of Freedom. He eventually moved back to the States and began breeding horses. He died in 1993 at the age of 85.

John Alsop, having served in the Connecticut House of Representatives became known as "one of Connecticut's most influential and colorful Republicans." He ran, unsuccessfully, for governor of Connecticut in 1958. Like his fellow American, Schley, he also received the US Bronze Star Medal. He died in 2000 at the age of 84.

Henri Tardivat joined the French Army during the final stages of the war and lost his leg because of an injury he sustained during the battle in the Belfort Gap. Tardi then transitioned to civilian life, moving to Paris to embark on a business career. He and his wife had a daughter they named Nancy in honor of her godmother. He passed away in 1985 at the age of 65.

Violette Szabo, Nancy's friend from Beaulieu, was sent on two missions to Occupied France by the SOE. During the second one, in June 1944, Violette was captured by Germans and then sent to Ravensbrück concentration camp. She and fellow SOE members Lilian Rolfe and Denise Bloch were executed in February 1945. Along with Odette Sansom and Noor Inayat Khan,* Violette was awarded the George Cross, Britain's highest award for civilians for 'acts of the greatest heroism or of the most conspicuous courage in circumstances of extreme danger.' Since it was bestowed posthumously, Violette's four year old daughter, Tania, accepted it on her behalf. A 1958 movie about Violette's life, *Carve Her Name with Pride,* brought renewed attention to Leo Marks's poem, "The Life That I Have," which Violette had used for coding.

Ian Garrow was promoted to the rank of major in early 1949 and retired from military service in 1958 as an honorary Lieutenant-Colonel. He passed away in 1976 at the age of 72.

After **Albert Guérisse**, aka Pat O'Leary, was arrested, he was sent to a series of concentration camps, including Natzweiler. There he encountered another woman who'd once worked on the PAO Line, Andrée Borrell.* She was accompanied by fellow SOE agents Sonia Olschanezky, Vera Leigh, and Diana Rowden, shortly before they were executed.

Guérisse received 37 decorations, including the UK's George Cross and France's Croix de Guerre and the Légion d'honneur. The British Empire also conferred an honorary knighthood (KBE) for his leadership of the PAO Line. Guérisse died in March 1989, at the age of 77.

*Read about Odette Sansom, Noor Inayat Khan, Andrée Borrell, Sonia Olschanezky, Violette Szabo and many more SOE women in Kit Sergeant's other World War II series, starting with *The Spark of Resistance: Women Spies in WWII-* a sample follows!

For more information on the fates of the characters in this

book, be sure to visit https://www.kitsergeant.com/?page_id=1101

A note to the reader: Thanks so much for reading this book! If you have time to spare, please consider leaving a short review for Nancy Wake on Amazon. Reviews are very important to authors like me and I would greatly appreciate it!

Be sure to check out my other books, including *The Women Spies of WWII Series,* starting with *The Spark of Resistance* and/or join my mailing list at www.kitsergeant.com to be the first to know when my newest Women Spies book is available!

Read on for samples of *The Spark of Resistance: Women Spies in WWII* and *L'Agent Double: Spies and Martyrs in the Great War!*

THE SPARK OF RESISTANCE
PROLOGUE

MAY 1945

*V*era Atkins barely recognized the woman standing alone on a platform at Euston railway station. She was clad in a bedraggled coat, unusually thick for this time of year, that hung too loosely on her frail figure. "Yvonne?"

The woman turned. At only eighteen, she had been one of the youngest hired, and still bore the look of a child, though now a starved one with dark circles around her eyes and matted blonde hair.

Miss Atkins had the mind to hug her, but was afraid she'd either break the girl's bones or Yvonne would collapse under the weight of her former boss's arms.

"I'm sorry to keep you waiting," Miss Atkins said instead. "Was your journey all right?"

Yvonne attempted a smile. "As good as could be expected."

Pleased as Miss Atkins was to see Yvonne, her thoughts were eclipsed by one, niggling inquiry. She voiced it after they had settled into the car, Miss Atkins sitting as straight as always, Yvonne's head leaning against the seat. "What do you know of the other girls?"

Yvonne's eyes flew open. "The other girls?"

"Yes. Who else was with you?"

Yvonne closed her eyes again, scrunching her face in recollection. "I saw Alice at Ravensbrück, and they said there was another British woman there, Lise, but she was in solitary confinement and I never got a good look at her face. And I encountered Louise, Nadine, and Ambroise at Saarbrücken when I was taken there, temporarily. I remember going into a prison hut and seeing them, and thinking, 'The whole women's branch of F Section is here.'"

Miss Atkins mentally matched the code names with the real identities of her girls: *Didi Nearne, Odette Sansom, Violette Szabo, Lilian Rolfe, and Denise Bloch.* Nearly forty women had gone into the line of fire, and most of them, except Yvonne, were still missing in action. "I've been looking into it, but I was notified that there had been no British females held at any concentration camp."

Yvonne turned to her. "I never told them I was a British agent. I thought I would have a lighter punishment if they believed I was French. But I knew that Louise, Nadine, and Ambroise felt differently." She shook her head sadly. "They were moved out of Torgau the night before I was."

"And what do you think became of them?"

"I don't know," was Yvonne's terse reply. "I'd heard they were brought back to Ravensbrück, same as me, but I never saw them again."

They arrived at Yvonne's father's house. Miss Atkins reached out, as though to touch her former employee's tangled curls, but thought better of it. She folded her hands across her lap. "Don't worry," she told Yvonne as the driver helped her out of the car. "I will find them."

THE SPARK OF RESISTANCE
CHAPTER 1

~~~

MATHILDE

*H*e moved through the crowded restaurant with the lithe limbs of a Gypsy. Indeed, his eyes were as black as a Roma, though his hair was styled like a Frenchman's.

Those dark eyes now focused on Mathilde. "Do you mind if I sit here?" He did a good imitation of a Parisian accent, but she could detect a hint of something else.

"Not at all." Jeanne leaned forward, the décolletage of her velvet top dipping low. She patted her impeccably coiffed hair. "And you are?"

"Armand Borni." He glanced over at Mathilde, as if to weigh whether or not his perfectly French name fooled her.

Mathilde stretched her lips into a thin smile. It was one of those dull evenings at La Frégate, the kind when she questioned just what she was doing there. Jeanne had requested their usual seat near the entrance, the better to watch the comings and goings of wealthy Parisians attempting to escape the gloom of their lives under the Occupation.

The undoubtedly fictitious Armand arranged his napkin on his lap. He met Mathilde's eyes for a split second before hers dropped, focusing on his teeth, which, like his accent, were obviously fake. She tucked a strand of her own unruly dark hair back behind her ear as she caught sight of a pair of German officers entering the restaurant.

The crowd immediately fell into a palpable hush, the way Mathilde's classmates used to at boarding school whenever the subject of their gossip came into earshot.

"Feldwebel Müller," Monsieur Durand, the owner, rushed over to the newcomers. "How good of you to come." He reached out to pump the German officer's hand a few times before turning to his companion and repeating the gesture.

Armand's face showed the tiniest frown before it returned to its carefully staged neutral expression.

Jeanne looked up. "It's Feldwebel Müller and Leutnant Fischer again. They come here every Friday night."

Mathilde, still unversed in the Wehrmacht ranking system, glowered as Monsieur Durand led the men to his best table, where an older couple was already seated. The restaurant owner gestured for a passing waiter to assist in moving the couple. "Those Nazis must be pretty important for Durand to oust the Bergers from their table."

"Of course they're important," Jeanne responded pointedly. "Even though they are low-ranking officers, if La Frégate becomes part of the *Gaststätten für Reichsdeutsche*, Monsieur Durand will probably get a pay raise."

"What is the *Gaststätten für Reichsdeutsche*?" Mathilde's tongue stumbled over the unfamiliar German words.

"It means 'restaurants for the German Reich.' My husband's printing house was told to make pamphlets for the visiting German soldiers. They have lists of all the vendors promising accommodations for them, even..." Jeanne leaned forward to whisper, "brothels." She sat back and took a sip of wine. "Any business in the pamphlet gets special treatment and won't be subject to rationing." Her voice dropped once more. "Not to mention Durand's mother-in-law is half-Jewish. He probably hopes to work his connections so she doesn't get deported."

Mathilde, never the type to conceal her emotions, shuddered. It wasn't enough to see the grayish-green suited soldiers marching around her beloved city. The notion of watching them ravage a meal in her favorite restaurant made her sick to her stomach. "I don't understand how we let them into Paris so easily in the first place, and now here we are, catering to their every whim."

"What do you mean?" Jeanne asked. "You are not wishing that we were still fighting them, are you?"

Mathilde sighed. "No. What was to be done was done. But I still hate that they are here. I cannot stand to see the swastika flying over the Eiffel Tower."

Throughout the women's conversation, their new guest had remained silent, but chose that moment to speak up. "You cannot just hate the Germans."

"What do you mean?" Mathilde asked, turning toward him.

He laughed. "I've only known you for a few minutes, but even I can see that you deal in absolutes. You cannot simply hate them, you must despise them with every thread of your veins."

She put a manicured finger to her lips as she glanced at the oblivious Germans across the room, indulging in a steak meal even though today had been declared a meatless day. "Why leave anything half-finished? If one is to hate, one must do it fully."

Armand's expression deepened for a brief moment before

he dug into his salad, stabbing at a piece of lettuce with more force than necessary.

"There are ways, you know," Armand's statement as they left the restaurant was carefully casual.

"Ways to what?" Mathilde asked, her eyes on Jeanne, who was several steps away, trying to wave down a rickshaw cab.

"Defeat the Nazis."

"I'm not sure if you know this, but our soldiers refused to fight them here." Mathilde spoke deliberately slow, as though Armand were half-deaf, not concealing the fact she recognized he was a foreigner. "We signed a peace treaty that resulted in our soldiers being captured as prisoners of war. And now they've taken over our city and shame us every way they can." She nodded toward a nearby placard that had been printed in German above the old street sign. Because of the blackout, the streetlights remained unlit and the French sign was barely visible, but the black-lettered words on the German one were quite legible, though unpronounceable. *As bulky and awkward as a swastika*, Mathilde thought. *As unwelcome as the Germans themselves.*

"I am well aware of Paris's plight," Armand replied. He leaned in closer, his voice low. "What would you think if I told you we could establish communication with London to pass on our own propaganda? To encourage our compatriots to challenge the Germans any way they can?"

Mathilde's mouth dropped open.

Armand glanced at Jeanne's back. "I cannot say anything else here. There are spies everywhere. But not the right kind."

Jeanne finally succeeded in her task and turned to Mathilde as the rickshaw driver paused in front of them.

"Aren't you coming?" Jeanne demanded. "Curfew is in half an hour." They all looked at their watches. Mathilde had once thought time was beyond being owned, but the Germans had even taken control of the city's clocks and turned them all to Berlin time, two hours ahead of Paris. As a result it seemed even the sun was reluctant to confront Hitler; with winter looming, it set earlier and earlier in the evening, shrouding the already-dispirited city in even more darkness.

Armand shut his pocket watch with an audible click as Mathilde waved her friend along.

"Come to my apartment," Mathilde said once Jeanne's cab had pulled away. She wrapped her thin fingers around Armand's and led him down the street.

"I know nothing of espionage," she told him when he was comfortably seated on her couch.

"But you know France... much more than an exiled Pole."

Mathilde nodded to herself as she fixed them chicory coffee. "You're Polish. What happened to make you hate the Germans so much?"

He laughed. "Besides being from Poland?" His tone dropped as Mathilde sat beside him. "I was a fighter pilot before I was taken prisoner by the Nazis. They sent me to a POW camp."

Mathilde's eyes widened. "Did they torture you?"

"I managed to escape before they could do their worst. A widow hid me in her house and then gave me her husband's papers." His voice grew hoarse. "But my brother is somewhere in one of those camps. And my parents are still in Poland." He put his hand over hers. "You have to help me. I will not accept that Poland is defeated."

She squeezed his hand. "I think the same of France. And

now that the occupiers refuse to hire me as a nurse, I have more time on my hands."

His face hardened. "I should warn you that this work will be extremely dangerous—"

"I don't mind the risk," Mathilde interrupted. "As you said, I do know people in most parts of the country, especially in the Free Zone." This included her husband, but she of course made no mention of him.

He took on a dreamy look. "Can you imagine you and me plotting against the Germans? You'd become the Mata Hari of the Second World War."

"Mata Hari? Didn't she betray her own country?"

He laughed and Mathilde couldn't help but smile. She paused to mull over what Armand was proposing. In what he would probably claim was her characteristic, all-in way, she decided to be the best spy the Allies had. "If we are to be working together, I suppose I should know your real name." She said it both out of curiosity and as a test, to see if he trusted her fully.

He did not hesitate. "Roman Czerniawski."

It was her turn to laugh. "That's quite a mouthful. I shall call you 'Toto.'"

"Toto? As in the dog in the *Wizard of Oz*?"

"Yes." She touched his arm. "As in my dependable sidekick."

"Oh, so now I'm your sidekick? It was my idea in the first place."

She shrugged. "You're cute, with big brown eyes just like Toto."

"What's your full name?"

"Mathilde Lily Carré."

He put his hand on her knee. "I think Lily suits you better than Mathilde. I'm going to call you Lily from now on."

She bestowed her most seductive smile on him, thinking he wouldn't be the first man to refer to her by that particular name.

THE SPARK OF RESISTANCE
CHAPTER 2

ODETTE

The gray-haired gentleman took a sip from his teacup before asking, "Tell me, Mrs. Sansom, how did you come to have those pictures of Calais's beaches?"

"Were they helpful? I've been wanting so badly to do something for the war effort, so when I heard that the Royal Navy was requesting pictures of the French coast, I sent them in right away." Odette frowned. "I know they were just panoramics of my brother and me when we were growing up, but—"

"Oh, they will work quite well. I take it you were born in France?"

"Yes. I moved to England when I got married, but I grew up in Amiens, and my mother is still there, suffering under German rule. My father was a banker, but he died at Verdun in the Great War."

Major Guthrie cleared his throat. "As did many. At that time, we thought it would be the war to end all wars, but now, with the Nazis…" He trailed off, appearing at a loss for words, the way Englishmen often were when the subject of Hitler was brought up.

"If it would help, I could draw you a picture of the Amiens village square."

He seemed relieved at the digression. "I think we probably have one in our files." He set his teacup down before clearing his throat again. "Mrs. Sansom, I believe that your French background might be quite useful to the War Office."

She sat back. "The War Office? What would the War Office want with me?"

"We need people who are familiar with France, and who speak the language, of course."

After a moment's thought, she replied, "I do want to help as much as I can, but I have three young girls, and my husband, Roy, is fighting on the continent." Major Guthrie's face fell, so she continued, "Perhaps I could do some translating for you? Or house soldiers?"

"Yes." He attempted a wan smile. "Raising three children on your own is quite a large undertaking. But I would like to pass your name on. As you said, we might have some part-time work for you."

"Of course."

It wasn't until she got back to Somerset that she realized Major Guthrie had neglected to return her photographs.

A few weeks later, Odette was sitting in a lounge chair, taking in the pleasant country sun when her youngest daughter, Marianne, dumped a packet on her lap. "Here's the mail, Mummy." Marianne waved an opened envelope in the air.

As it fluttered, Odette caught sight of a red cross printed at the top. "What's that?" she asked, her heart beginning to race.

What if Roy was hurt? The prospect of losing her husband didn't fill her with as much fear as one might expect. Their relationship had been strained long before he went off to war, and she had more than proven herself capable of being the sole provider of care for her children. Still, she'd hate to have to tell her daughters that their father had been wounded... or, worse yet, killed.

"It's Uncle Louis," Françoise, her oldest daughter said sadly, sounding much older than ten. She sat at her mother's feet. "He's in a hospital in Paris."

Odette snatched the letter from Marianne and scanned it, but there was not much more information about her brother than what Françoise had already stated.

"But you can't go and visit him, can you?" Marianne's voice had taken on the little girl's whine it often did when she was upset.

"Even if you could go, you can't stop Grandma's house from getting overrun by Nazis." At eight, Lily, the middle child, was ever the realist.

"No," Odette refolded the note. "No, I cannot go to France. I wish I could."

"What's this?" Françoise's deft fingers lifted another official-looking envelope. "Who is Captain Selwyn Jepson?"

"I don't know," Odette answered wearily, longing for a moment of peace, away from prying young girls.

"He's asking you to visit him in Whitehall next week."

Odette gathered up the rest of the letters, the one from Jepson falling to the bottom of the pile. "It probably has something to do with that part-time job Major Guthrie mentioned."

"Are you going to work for the war?" Françoise demanded.

"If I can fit it in, I'd like to do some little thing," Odette replied.

"But you aren't going to leave us, are you, Mummy?" Marianne's voice grew even higher as her eyes reddened. They'd already been forced to evacuate their London home for the safety of the Somerset countryside, away from the Luftwaffe bombers that had been terrorizing the city for the past year. It had been enough uprooting for the six-year-old. For all three girls, and Odette herself, for that matter.

Odette reached out to pat Marianne's hand. "Of course not, *chérie*."

THE SPARK OF RESISTANCE
CHAPTER 3

DIDI

*D*idi tossed yet another rejection letter onto the floor. "The Women's Royal Naval Services only wanted drivers."

Her sister Jackie, older by four years, nodded at the paper on the ground. "I must have gotten twice as many as you. The WRNS sent me that exact same letter. I probably shouldn't have told them I can't drive in complete darkness with all of these black-outs."

"Do you think…" Didi cleared her throat. "Did it ever occur to you that we shouldn't have come here?" It hadn't been easy getting out of Occupied France, even though they were British citizens, but they'd eventually managed to escape via Spain. The entire journey had taken nearly six months, and now that they were finally free, relatively speaking, they were having difficulty securing jobs.

Jackie raised a thin eyebrow. "What would you have done, stayed in France? You know the Germans regarded us as nothing but foreigners."

"We lived in France almost our whole lives. Britain feels more foreign to me."

"Well," Jackie bent down and picked up the letter. "If you want to go back and be subject to the will of the Nazis, then do it. I'm going to stay here and do what I can to fight the Germans." She crumpled the paper. "If only they would let me."

A few days later, Jackie received a note from a Captain Selwyn Jepson of the War Office asking for an interview.

"I told you my time would come," Jackie told Didi.

Didi snatched the notice from her sister. "He says you 'possess qualifications which may be of value in the war effort.' What does that even mean?"

"Why, I suppose it could mean nothing at all," Jackie replied loftily, clearly not believing her own proclamation.

Everything had always come easy to her beautiful older sister and Didi felt the need to take Jackie down a peg. "Especially if they find out you can't drive during the blackout."

The words hit their mark and Jackie's smile drooped into a frown.

The pangs of guilt were too much for Didi. "On the other hand, maybe this Selwyn Jepson is an important man and needs you for a task no one else can do," she added. "The return address is the War Office, after all."

Jackie nodded. "I'm sure you'll get a similar letter soon."

But she didn't, and, as the date for Jackie's interview came closer, Didi grew even more anxious.

"Be sure to tell them about me," Didi called after Jackie as she left for the War Office wearing her nicest dress, a smart blue one sprinkled with white polka-dots.

Jackie turned back and waved a gloved-hand. "I will."

"And good luck!"

Jackie straightened her straw hat before continuing down the street.

Didi spent a few tense hours waiting for Jackie to return. She meant to clean the small room they shared in the boarding house, but found it hard to concentrate on any one task.

"Well?" Didi asked by way of greeting once her sister came home.

"Well what?"

"What did Captain Jepson want?"

"It was a job as a driver for FANY—the First Aid Nursing Yeomanry."

"A driver? Did you tell him you can speak fluent French?"

"Yes."

Something about Jackie's behavior wasn't sitting right with Didi. "And the driving at night thing? He didn't mind about that?"

"No."

Now Didi knew Jackie was hiding something—it wasn't like her sister to give one-word answers. "Why would they hire you for a job any English girl could do?"

Jackie cast her eyes around the empty room. "Okay, as it turns out, I'll be working with a brand-new organization. The SOE."

"What does that stand for?"

"Special Operations Executive." The pride was obvious in Jackie's voice. "The French section. They wanted me because I grew up in France and can speak the language fluently. The FANY driver thing is just a cover."

"A cover for what? What work will you be doing?" Her eyes widened as a thought occurred to her. "Are they sending you back to France to be a spy?"

"Listen," Jackie put a hand on Didi's arm. "I've already told you too much. I promised Captain Jepson I wouldn't say anything about this to anyone."

"What about me?" Didi asked. "Did you tell them you had a sister who also speaks French?"

"Of course," Jackie replied distractedly. "Now I have to figure out what I'm going to wear to my first training session."

~

Finally, a month after Jackie's interview, Didi received her own meeting request from Captain Jepson. She too put on her best dress and, after placing her gas mask in her purse, set off for the address given in the letter, which turned out to be a sparse room in the Victoria Hotel.

With his beautifully-cut gray suit and groomed salt-and-pepper hair, Captain Jepson looked nothing like a military recruiter. After asking Didi to sit in the lone chair opposite his desk, he started by telling her his task was to recruit women for the SOE.

"Why women?" Didi asked.

"In my opinion, women are much more suited for this type of position than men. Women have a far greater capacity for a cool and lonely courage."

It didn't take Didi long to realize her suspicions about her sister working for an espionage unit had been correct. "I would like to be considered for the same sort of thing that Jackie is doing."

His gaze traveled from her jaunty hat to her sensible-heeled shoes. "I think you might be a bit young to be an agent."

"I'm nearly twenty-two, and only four years younger than Jackie."

He nodded before picking up a paper. "Your full name is Eileen Mary. Where did Didi come from?"

She shrugged. "The family legend is that Jackie had a hard time saying 'Eileen.' Didi rolled off the tongue easier, so Didi I became."

"And are there other Nearne children?"

"I have two brothers. My middle brother, Frederick, is in the Royal Air Force."

"You are the baby of the family." Jepson made a mark on the paper in front of him. "Your father is a doctor, so the family is obviously well-off, and you were educated in a Catholic school."

The finality in his voice, as if he'd already rejected her, made Didi's heart beat faster. "When the Nazis came, we were forced from our home. They told us we were 'enemies of the state,' even my mother, who was born in France, because she married an Englishman. They confiscated most of our possessions, so we are no longer considered, as you put it, 'well-off.' Jackie and I had to learn to chop firewood, cook, and clean."

"Why do you want to go back to France now so soon after leaving?"

"Both Jackie and I want to do something to fight Germany. That's why we came here to England in the first place." Didi could tell she was losing the battle. She spread her arms out. "Look, I can keep my own company. Should the need arise, I can work all alone. I can do anything you ask. I just want to be able to do something for the war. Even a little thing."

"Some little thing." Jepson made another mark on the paper with his pen before settling his gaze back to her. "You seem to be a bright young woman, though you've also led a sheltered life. I'm not sure you are ready to be a field agent, but perhaps we can start you as a wireless operator or a decoder."

She folded her arms across her chest. While she was disappointed that she wouldn't be heading back to France as an SOE operative any time soon, Jepson hadn't completely refused her. "I'd prefer to learn how to work a wireless." She figured the training for that line of work would be the most beneficial when she finally convinced Jepson to put her in the field.

Enjoyed the sample? Pick up your copy of *The Spark of Resistance* on Amazon today or read for free with Kindle Unlimited!

Read on for a sample of *L'Agent Double: Spies and Martyrs in the Great War*

Be sure to join my mailing list at www.kitsergeant.com to be the first to know when my newest Women Spies book is available!

L'AGENT DOUBLE PROLOGUE

OCTOBER 1917

The nun on duty woke her just before dawn. She blinked the sleep out of her eyes to see a crowd of men, including her accusers and her lawyer, standing just outside the iron bars of her cell. The only one who spoke was the chief of the Military Police, to inform her the time of her execution had come. The men then turned and walked away, leaving only the nun and the prison doctor, who kept his eyes on the dirty, straw-strewn floor as she dressed.

She chose the best outfit she had left, a bulky dove-gray skirt and jacket and scuffed ankle boots. She wound her unwashed hair in a bun and then tied the worn silk ribbons of her hat under her chin before asking the doctor, "Do I have time to write good-byes to my loved ones?"

He nodded and she hastily penned three farewell letters. She handed them to the doctor with shaking hands before lifting a dust-covered velvet cloak from a nail on the wall. "I am ready."

Seemingly out of nowhere, her lawyer reappeared. "This way," he told her as he grasped her arm.

Prison rats scurried out their way as he led her down the hall. She breathed in a heavy breath when they were outside. It had been months since she'd seen the light of day, however faint it was now.

Four black cars were waiting in the prison courtyard. A few men scattered about the lawn lifted their freezing hands to bring their cameras to life, the bulbs brightening the dim morning as her lawyer bundled her into the first car.

They drove in silence. It was unseasonably cold and the chill sent icy fingers down her spine. She stopped herself from shivering, wishing that she could experience one more warm summer day. But there would be no more warmth, no more appeals, nothing left after these last few hours.

She knew that her fate awaited her at Caponniére, the old fort just outside of Vincennes where the cavalry trained. Upon arrival, her lawyer helped her out of the car, his gnarled hands digging into her arm.

It's harder for him than it is for me. She brushed the thought away, wanting to focus on nothing but the fresh air and the way the autumn leaves of the trees next to the parade ground changed color as the sun rose. Her lawyer removed his arm from her shoulders as two Zouave escorts appeared on either side of her. Her self-imposed blinders finally dropped as she took in the twelve soldiers with guns and, several meters away, the wooden stake placed in front of a brick wall. *So that the misaimed bullets don't hit anything else.*

A priest approached and offered her a blindfold.

"No thank you." Her voice, which had not been used on a daily basis for months, was barely a whisper.

The priest glanced over at her lawyer, who nodded. The blindfold disappeared under his robes.

She spoke the same words to one of the escorts as he held up a rope, this time also shaking her head. She refused to be bound to the stake. He acquiesced, and walked away.

She stood as straight as she could, free of any ties, while the military chief read the following words aloud:

By decree of the Third Council of War, the woman who appears before us now has been condemned to death for espionage.

He then gave an order, and the soldiers came to attention. At the command, *"En joue!"* they hoisted their guns to rest on their shoulders. The chief raised his sword.

She took a deep breath and then lifted her chin, willing herself to die just like that: head held high, showing no fear. She watched as the chief lowered his sword and shouted *"Feu!"*

And then everything went black.

∼

A Zouave private approached the body. He'd only been enlisted for a few weeks and had been invited to the firing squad by his commander, who told him that men of all ranks should know the pleasure of shooting a German spy.

"By blue, that lady knew how to die," another Zouave commented.

"Who was she?" the private asked. He'd been taught that everything in war was black and white: the Germans were evil, the Allies pure. But he was surprised at how gray everything was that morning: from the misty fog, to the woman's cloak and dress, and even the ashen shade of her lifeless face.

The other Zouave shrugged. "All I know is what they told me. They say she acted as a double agent and provided Germany with intelligence about our troops." He drew his revolver and bent down to place the muzzle against the woman's left temple.

"But is it necessary to kill her—a helpless woman?" the private asked.

The Zouave cocked his gun for the *coup de grâce*. "If women act as men would in war and commit heinous crimes, they should be prepared to be punished as men." And he pulled the trigger, sending a final bullet into the woman's brain

L'AGENT DOUBLE CHAPTER 1

M'GREET

JULY 1914

"*H*ave you heard the latest?" M'greet's maid, Anna, asked as she secured a custom-made headpiece to her mistress's temple.

"What now?" M'greet readjusted the gold headdress to better reflect her olive skin tone.

"They are saying that your mysterious Mr. K from the newspaper article is none other than the Crown Prince himself."

M'greet smiled at herself in the mirror. "Is that so? I rather think they're referring to Lieutenant Kiepert. Just the other day he and I ran into the editor of the *Berliner Tageblatt* during our walk in the Tiergarten." Her smile faded. "But let them wonder." For the last few weeks, the papers had been filled with speculation about why the famed Mata Hari had returned to Germany, sometimes bordering on derision about her running out of money.

She leaned forward and ran her fingers over the dark circles under her eyes. "Astruc says that he might be able to negotiate a longer engagement in the fall if tonight's performance goes well."

"It will," Anna assured her as she fastened the heavy gold necklace around M'greet's neck.

The metal felt cold against her sweaty skin. She hadn't performed in months, and guessed the perspiration derived from her nervousness. Tonight was to be the largest performance she'd booked in years: Berlin's Metropol could seat 1108 people, and the tickets had sold out days ago. The building was less than a decade old, and even the dressing room's geometric wallpaper and curved furniture reflected the Art Nouveau style the theater was famous for.

"I had to have this costume refitted." M'greet pulled at the sheer yellow fabric covering her midsection. When she first began dancing, she had worn jeweled bralettes and long, sheer skirts that sat low on the hips. But her body had become much more matronly in middle age and even M'greet knew that she could no longer get away with the scandalous outfits of her youth. She added a cumbersome earring to each ear and an arm band before someone knocked on the door.

A man's voice called urgently in German, "Fräulein Mata Hari, are you ready?"

Anna shot her mistress an encouraging smile. "Your devoted admirers are waiting."

M'greet stretched out her arms and rotated her wrists, glancing with appreciation in the mirror. She still had it. She grabbed a handful of translucent scarves and draped them over her arms and head before opening the door. "All set," she said to the awaiting attendant.

· · ·

M'greet waited behind a filmy curtain while the music began: low, mournful drumming accompanied by a woman's shrill tone singing in a foreign language. As the curtain rose, she hoisted her arms above her head and stuck her hips out in the manner she had seen the women do when she lived in Java.

She had no formal dance training, but it didn't matter. People came to see Mata Hari for the spectacle, not because she was an exceptionally wonderful dancer. M'greet pulled the scarf off her head and undulated her hips in time with the music. She pinched her fingers together and moved her arms as if she were a graceful bird about to take flight. The drums heightened in intensity and her gyrations became even more exaggerated. As the music came to a dramatic stop, she released the scarves covering her body to reveal her yellow dress in full.

She was accustomed to hearing astonished murmurs from the audience following her final act—she'd once proclaimed that her success rose with every veil she threw off. Tonight, however, the Berlin audience seemed to be buzzing with protest.

As the curtain fell and M'greet began to pick up the pieces of her discarded costume, she assured herself that the Berliners' vocalizations were in response to being disappointed at seeing her more covered. Or maybe she was just being paranoid and had imagined all the ruckus.

"Fabulous!" her agent, Gabriel Astruc, exclaimed when he burst into her dressing room a few minutes later.

M'greet held a powder puff to her cheek. "Did you finalize a contract for the fall?"

"I did," Astruc sat in the only other chair, which appeared

too tiny to support his large frame. "They are giving us 48,000 marks."

She nodded approvingly.

"That should tide you over for a while, no?" he asked.

She placed the puff in the gold-lined powder case. "For now. But the creditors are relentless. Thankfully Lieutenant Kieper has gifted me a few hundred francs."

"As a loan?" Astruc winked. "It is said you have become mistress to the *Kronprinz*."

She rolled her eyes. "You of all people must know to never mind such rumors. I may be well familiar with men in high positions, but have not yet made the acquaintance of the Kaiser's son."

Astruc rose. "Someday you two will meet, and even the heir of the German Empire will be unable to resist the charms of the exotic Mata Hari."

M'greet unsnapped the cap of her lipstick. "We shall see, won't we?"

Now that the fall performances had been secured, M'greet decided to upgrade her lodgings to the lavish Hotel Adlon. As she entered the lobby, with its sparkling chandeliers dangling from intricately carved ceilings and exotic potted palms scattered among velvet-cushioned chairs, she nodded to herself. *This was the type of hotel a world-renowned dancer should be found in.* She booked an apartment complete with electric Tiffany lamps and a private bathroom featuring running water.

The Adlon was known not only for its famous patrons, but for the privacy it provided them. M'greet was therefore startled the next morning when someone banged on the door to her suite.

"Yes?" Anna asked as she opened it.

"Are you Mata Hari?" a gruff voice inquired.

M'greet threw on a silky robe over her nightgown before she went to the door. "You must be looking for me."

The man in the doorway appeared to be about forty, with a receding hairline and a bushy mustache that curled upward from both sides of his mouth. "I am Herr Griebel of the Berlin police."

M'greet ignored Anna's stricken expression as she motioned for her to move aside. "Please come in." She gestured toward a chair at the little serving table. "Shall I order up some tea?"

"That won't be necessary," Griebel replied as he sat. "I am here to inform you that a spectator of your performance last night has lodged a complaint."

"A complaint? Against me?" M'greet repeated as she took a seat in the chair across from him. She mouthed, "tea," at Anna, who was still standing near the door. Anna nodded and then left the room.

"Indeed," Griebel touched his mustache. "A complaint of indecency."

"I see." She leaned forward. "You are part of the *Sittenpolizei*, then." They were a department charged with enforcing the Kaiser's so-called laws of morality. M'greet had been visited a few times in the past by such men, but nothing had ever come of it. She flashed Griebel a seductive smile. "Surely your department has no issue with sacred dances?"

"Ah," Griebel fidgeted with the collar of his uniform, clearly uncomfortable.

Mirroring his movements, M'greet fingered the neckline of her low-cut gown. "After all, there are more important issues going on in the world than my little dance."

"Such as?" Griebel asked.

The door opened and Anna discreetly placed a tea set on the crisp white tablecloth. She gave her mistress a worried look but M'greet waved her off before pouring Griebel a cup of tea. "Well, I'm sure you heard about that poor man that was shot in the Balkans in June."

"Of course—it's been in all of the papers. The 'poor man,' as you call him, was Archduke Franz Ferdinand. Austria should not stand down when the heir to their throne was shot by militant Serbs."

M'greet took a sip of tea. "Are you saying they should go to war?"

"They should. And Germany, as Austria's ally, ought to accompany them."

"Over one man? You cannot be serious."

"Those Serbs need to be taught a lesson, once and for all." Upon seeing the pout on M'greet's face, Griebel waved his hand. "But you shouldn't worry your pretty little head over talk of politics."

She pursed her lips. "You're right. It's not something that a woman like me should be discussing."

"No." He set down his tea cup and pulled something out of his pocket. "As I was saying when I first came in, about the complaint—"

"As *I* was saying..." she faked a yawn, stretching her arms out while sticking out her bosom. The stocky, balding Griebel was not nearly as handsome as some of the men she'd met over the years, but M'greet knew that she needed to become better acquainted with him in order to get the charges dropped. Besides, she'd always had a weakness for men in uniform. "My routine is adopted from Hindu religious dances and should not be misconstrued as immoral." She placed a hand over Griebel's thick fingers, causing the paper to fall to the floor. "I think, if the two of us put our heads together, we can definitely find a mutual agreement."

He pulled his hand away to wipe his forehead with a handkerchief. "I don't know if that's possible."

M'greet got up from her chair to spread herself on the bed, displaying her body to its advantage as a chef would his best dish.

"Perhaps we could work out an arrangement that would benefit us both," Griebel agreed as he walked over to her.

Griebel's mustache tickled her face, but she forced herself to think about other things as he kissed her. Her thoughts at such moments often traveled to her daughter, Non, but today she focused on the other night's performance. M'greet always did what it took to survive, and right now she needed the money that her contract with the Berlin Metropol would provide, and nothing could get in the way of that.

M'greet was glad to count Herr Griebel as her new lover as the tensions between the advocates of the Kaiser—who wanted to "finish with the Serbs quickly"—and the pacifists determined to keep Germany out of war heightened throughout Berlin at the end of July. Although Griebel was on the side of the war-mongers, M'greet felt secure traveling on his arm every night on their way to Berlin's most popular venues.

It was in the back room at one such establishment, the Borchardt, that she met some of Griebel's cronies. They had gathered to talk about the recent developments—Austria-Hungary had officially declared war on Serbia. M'greet knew her place was to look pretty and say nothing, but at the same time she couldn't help but listen to what they were discussing.

"I've heard that Russia has mobilized her troops," a heavyset, balding man stated. M'greet recalled that his name was Müller.

"Ah," Griebel sat back in the plush leather booth. "That's the rub, now isn't it?"

Herr Vogel, Griebel's closest compatriot, shook his head. "I'd hoped Russia would stay out of it." He flicked ash from his cigar into a nearby tray. "After all, the Kaiser and the Tsar are cousins."

"No," Müller replied. "Those Serbs went crying to Mother Russia, and she responded." He nodded to himself. "Now it's only a matter of time before we jump in to protect Austria."

As if on cue, the sound of breaking glass was heard.

M'greet ended her silence. "What was that?"

Griebel put a protective hand on her arm. "I'm not sure." He used his other arm to flag down a passing waiter. "What is going on?"

The young man looked panic-stricken. "There is a demonstration on the streets. Someone threw a brick through the front window and our owner is asking all of the patrons to leave."

"Has war broken out?" M'greet inquired of Griebel as she pulled her arm away. His grip had left white marks.

"I'm not sure." He picked up her fur shawl and headed to the main room of the restaurant. Pandemonium reigned as Berlin's elite rushed toward the doors. Discarded feathers from fashionable ladies' hats and boas floated through the air and littered the ground before stamping feet stirred them up again. M'greet wished she hadn't shaken off Griebel's arm as now she was being shoved this way and that. Someone trampled over her dress and she heard the sound of ripping lace.

She nearly tripped before a strong hand landed on her elbow. "This way," the young waiter told her. He led her through the kitchen and out the back door, where Griebel's Benz was waiting. Griebel appeared a few minutes later and the driver told him there was a massive protest outside the Kaiser's palace.

"Let's go there," Griebel instructed.

"No." M'greet wrapped the fur shawl around her shoulders. "Take me home first."

"Don't you want to find out what's happening?" Griebel demanded, waving his hand as a crowd of people thronged the streets. "This could be the beginning of a war the likes of which no one has ever seen."

"No," she repeated. It seemed to her that the Great Powers of Europe: Germany, Russia, France, and possibly England, were entering into a scrap they had no business getting involved with. "I don't care about any war and I've had enough tonight. I want to go home."

Griebel gave her a strange look but motioned for the driver to do as she said.

They were forced to drive slowly, as the streets had become jammed with motor cars, horse carts, and people rushing about on foot. M'greet caught what they were chanting as the crowd marched past. She repeated the words aloud: *"Deutschland über alles."*

"Germany over all," Griebel supplied.

The war came quickly. Germany first officially declared war on Russia to the east and two days later did the same to France in the west. In Berlin, so-called bank riots occurred as people rushed to their financial institutions and emptied their savings accounts, trading paper money for gold and silver coins. Prices for food and other necessities soared as people stocked up on goods while they could still afford them.

Worried about her own fate, M'greet placed several calls to her agent, Astruc, wanting to know if the war meant her fall performances would be canceled. After leaving many messages, she eventually got word that Astruc had fled town, presumably with the money the Metropol had paid her in advance.

She decided to brave the confusion at the bank in order to withdraw what little funds she had left.

"I'm sorry," the teller informed M'greet when she finally made it to the counter. "It looks as though your account has been blocked."

"How can you say that?" she demanded. "There should be plenty of money in my account." The plenty part might not have been strictly true, but there was no way it was empty.

"The address you gave when you opened the account was in Paris. We cannot give funds to any foreigner at this time."

M'greet put both fists on the counter. "I wish to speak with your manager."

The teller gestured behind her. M'greet glanced back to see a long line of people, their exhausted, bewildered faces beginning to glower. "I'm sorry, fräulein, I can do nothing more."

She opened her mouth to let him have the worst of her fury, but a man in a police uniform appeared beside her. "A foreigner you say?" He pulled M'greet out of the bank line, and roughly turned her to face him. "What are you, a Russian?"

M'greet knew her dark hair and coloring was not typical of someone with Dutch heritage, but this was a new accusation. "I am no such thing."

"Russian, for sure," a man standing in line agreed.

"Her address was in France," the teller called before accepting a bank card from the next person.

"Well, Miss Russian Francophile, you are coming with me." For the second time in a week, a strange man put his hand on M'greet's elbow and led her away.

M'greet fumed all the way to the police station. She'd had enough of Berlin: due to this infernal war, she was now void of funds and it looked as though her engagements were to be canceled. She figured her best course of action would be to return to Paris and use her connections to try to get some work there.

When they arrived at the police station, M'greet immediately asked for Herr Griebel. He appeared a few minutes later, a wry smile on his face. "You've been arrested under suspicion of being a troublesome alien."

M'greet waved off that comment with a brush of her hand. "We both know that's ridiculous. Can you secure my release as soon as possible? I must get back to Paris before my possessions there are seized."

Griebel's amused smile faded as his lip curled into a sneer. "You cannot travel to an enemy country in the middle of a war."

"Why not?"

The sneer deepened. "Because..." His narrowed eyes suddenly softened. "Come with me. There is someone I want you to meet." He led her to an office that occupied the end of a narrow hallway and knocked on the closed door labeled, *Traugott von Jagow, Berliner Polizei*.

"Come in," a voice growled.

Griebel entered and then saluted.

The man behind the desk had a thin face and heavy mustache which drooped downward. "What is it, Herr Griebel?

You must know I am extremely busy." He dipped a pen in ink and began writing.

Griebel lowered his arm. "Indeed, sir, but I wanted you to meet the acclaimed Mata Hari."

Von Jagow paused his scribbling and looked up. His eyes traveled down from the feather atop M'greet's hat and stopped at her chest. "Wasn't there a morality complaint filed against you?"

M'greet stepped forward, but before she could protest, Griebel cleared his throat. "We are here because she wants to return to Paris."

Von Jagow gave a loud "harrumph," and then continued his writing. "You are not the first person to ask such a question, but we can't let anyone cross the border into enemy territory at this time. People would think you were a spy." He abruptly stopped writing and set his pen down. "A courtesan with a flair for seducing powerful men..." He shot a meaningful look at Griebel, who stared at the floor. "And a long-term resident of Paris with admittedly low morals." He finally met M'greet's eyes. "We could use a woman like you. I'm forming a network of agents who can provide us information about the goings-on in France."

M'greet tried to keep the horror from showing on her face. Was this man asking her to be a spy for Germany? "No thank you," she replied. "As I told Herr Griebel, I have no interest in the war. I just want to get back to Paris."

Von Jagow crossed his arms and sat back. "And I can help you with that, provided that you agree to work for me."

She shook her head and spoke in a soft voice. "Thank you, sir, but it seems I'll have to find a way back on my own."

"Very well, then." Von Jagow picked up his pen again. "Good luck." His voice implied that he wished her just the opposite.

L'AGENT DOUBLE CHAPTER 2

MARTHE

AUGUST 1914

Marthe Cnockaert didn't think anything could spoil this year's Kermis. People had been arriving in Westrozebeke for days from all over Belgium. She herself had just returned home from her medical studies at Ghent University on holiday and had nearly been overcome by the tediousness of living in her small village again. She gazed around the garland-bedecked Grand Place lined with colorful vendor booths in satisfaction. The rest of Europe may have plunged into war, but Belgium had vowed to remain neutral, and the mayor declared that the annual Kermis would be celebrated just as it had been since the middle ages.

The smell of pie wafted from a booth as Marthe passed by and the bright notes of a hurdy-gurdy were audible over the noise of the crowd. She had just entered the queue for the carousel when she heard someone call, "Marthe!"

She turned at the sound of her name to see Valerie, a girl she had known since primary school. "Marthe, how are you? How is Max?" As usual, Valerie was breathless, as though she had recently run a marathon, but it appeared she'd only just gotten off the carousel.

Marthe refrained from rolling her eyes. "Max is still in Ghent, finishing up his studies." Valerie had never hidden the fact she'd always had a crush on Marthe's older brother, even after she'd become betrothed to Nicholas Hoot.

Valerie sighed as she looked around. "There's nobody here but women, children, and old men. All the boys our age have gone off to war and now there's no one left to flirt with."

"Where is Nicholas?"

"He was called to Liége. I suppose you've heard that Germany is demanding safe passage through Belgium in order to get to Paris."

"No."

Valerie shrugged. "They are saying we might have to join the war if Germany decides to invade. But the good news is some treaty states that England would have to enter on our side if that happened."

"Join the war?" Marthe was shocked at both the information and the fact that Valerie seemed so nonchalant about it. There were a few beats of silence, broken only by the endless tune from the carousel's music box, as Marthe pondered this.

"Ah, Marthe, I see you have returned from university." Meneer Hoot, an old friend of her father's, and Valerie's future father-in-law, was nearly shouting, both because he was hard of hearing and because the carousel had started spinning.

"Yes, indeed. I am home for a few weeks before I finish my last year of nursing school," Marthe answered loudly. "Glad to see you are doing well. How is your wife?"

"Oh, you know. Terrified at the prospect of a German invasion, but aren't we all?"

Marthe gave him and Valerie a tentative smile as the church bell rang the hour. "I must be getting home to help Mother with dinner."

Marthe knew something was wrong as soon as she entered the kitchen. "What is it?" she asked, glancing at her father's somber face.

"It's the Germans. They have invaded Belgium."

Marthe fell into her chair. Mother stood in the corner of the room, ironing a cap.

"Belgium has ordered our troops to Liége." Father sank his head into his hands. "But we could never defend ourselves against those bloody Boches."

Mother set her iron down and then took a seat at the kitchen table. "What about Max? Will he come home from Ghent?"

Father took his hands away from his face. "I don't know. I don't know anything now."

"I suppose we should send for him," Marthe said.

Mother cast a worried glance at Father before nodding at her daughter.

For the first time Marthe could remember, Kermis ended before the typical eight days. That didn't stop the endless train of people coming into Westrozebeke, however. The newcomers were refugees from villages near Liége and were headed to Ypres, 15 kilometers southwest, where they had been told they could find food and shelter.

Max sent word that he would be traveling in the opposite direction. He was going to Liége, a town on the Belgian/German border that was protected by a series of concrete fortifications. The Germans were supposedly en route there as well. Both Father and Mother were saddened by Max's decision to enlist in the army, but Marthe understood the circumstances: Belgium must be defended at all costs. She wrote her brother a letter stating the same and urged him to be careful.

As Westrozebeke became a temporary camp, Marthe's family's house and barn, like many of the other houses in the village, were quickly packed with the unfortunate evacuees. Soon the news that Liége had fallen came, and not long after, the first of the soldiers who had been cut off from the main Belgian army arrived.

Marthe stood on the porch and watched a few of them struggle through town. Their frayed uniforms were covered in dark splotches, some of it dirt, some of it blood. Their faces were unshaven, their skin filthy, but the worst part was that none of them were Max.

Upon spotting Nicholas Hoot's downtrodden form, Marthe rushed into the street. "Have you heard from Max?" she asked.

Nicholas met her eyes. His were wide and terrified, holding a record of past horrors, as though he had seen the devil himself. "No."

"C'mon," Marthe put his heavy arm over her shoulders. "Let's get you home."

. . .

Mevrouw Hoot greeted them at the door. "Nicholas, my son." She hugged his gaunt body before leading him inside.

After his second cup of tea, Nicholas could croak out a few sentences. After a third cup and some biscuits, he was able to relay the horrific conditions the Belgian soldiers had experienced at Liége, especially the burning inferno of Fort de Loncin, which had been hit by a shell from one of the German's enormous guns, known as Big Bertha. De Loncin had been the last of the twelve forts around Liége to yield to the Boches.

"Do you know what happened to Max?" Marthe asked.

Nicholas shook his head. "I never saw him. But it was a very confusing time." His cracked lips formed into something that resembled his old smile. "The Germans are terrified of *francs-tireurs* and think every Belgian civilian is a secret sniper out to get them." The smile quickly faded. "The Fritzes dragged old men and teenagers into the square, accusing them of shooting at their troops. It was mostly their own men mistakenly firing upon each other, but no matter. They killed the innocent villagers anyway." He set his tea cup down. "The Huns are blood-thirsty and vicious, and they are headed this way. We should flee further west as soon as possible."

Mevrouw Hoot met Marthe's eyes. "I'll tell Father," Marthe stated before taking her leave.

Mother was ready to depart, but Father was reluctant, stating that if Max did come home, he would find his family gone. Marthe agreed and disagreed with both sides. On the one hand, she wanted to wait for her brother, and judge for herself if the Germans were as terrible as Nicholas had said. On the other hand, if he was indeed correct, they should go as far west as possible.

The argument became moot when Marthe was awakened the next morning by an unearthly piercing noise overhead. The shrieks grew louder until the entire house shook with the crescendo, and then there was an even more disturbing silence.

Marthe tossed on her robe and then rushed downstairs. No one was in the kitchen, so she pulled Max's old boots over her bare feet and ran the few blocks to the Grand Place. She could see the mushroom cloud of black smoke was just beginning to clear.

She nearly tripped in her oversized boots when she saw someone lying in the roadway. It was Mevrouw Visser, one of her elderly neighbors. She bent over the bloodied body, but the woman had already passed.

The sound of horse hooves caused Marthe to look up. She froze as she saw the men atop were soldiers in unfamiliar khaki uniforms.

"Hallo," called a man with a thin mustache and a flat red cap. He stopped his horse short of Mevrouw Visser. "Met her maker, has she?" The way he ended the sentence with a question that didn't expect an answer made Marthe realize the British had arrived. The men paused at similarly lying bodies, giving food and water to those who still clung to life, but after an hour or so, they rode off.

Marthe went home, her robe now tattered and soiled, her feet sweaty in her boots. "What now?" she asked her father, who was seated at the kitchen table, also covered in perspiration, dirt, and blood.

"Now we wait for Max."

A knock sounded on the front door and Marthe went to answer it, fearing that she would greet a Hun in a spiked helmet. But the soldier outside was in a blue uniform. "The bloody Boches are on their way," he stated in a French accent. "You must flee the village, mademoiselle."

She glanced at Father, who was still sitting at the kitchen table. "I cannot."

The French soldier took a few steps backward to peer at the second floor before returning his gaze back to her. "Our guns will arrive soon, but we are only a small portion of our squadron, and cannot possibly hope to hold them for long. We are asking the villagers to allow us access to their homes in order to take aim."

She nodded and opened the door. He marched into the kitchen and spoke to her father.

Marthe went outside, and looked up and down the street, which was now dotted with soldiers in the blue uniforms of the French. The sound of hammering permeated the air. The soldier she had spoken to went upstairs to pound small viewing holes into the wood of the rooms facing the street. She helped Father barricade the windows and front door with furniture.

Marthe and her parents sequestered themselves in her bedroom, which faced the back of the house. Although half of her was frightened, the other was intensely curious as to what would happen. She used her father's telescope to peer through a loophole in the wood-barricaded window.

"I see them!" she shouted as a gray mass came into view.

"Marthe, get down!" her father returned.

She reluctantly retired the telescope, but not before she peered outside again. The masses had become individual men topped by repulsive-looking spiked helmets. There were hundreds of them and they were headed straight for the Grand Place.

The windows rattled as the hooves of an army of horses

came closer. Marthe knew that many of those carts were filled with the Boches' giant guns.

The French machine guns, known as *mitrailleuse,* began an incessant rattling. *Rat-a-tat-tat:* ad infinitum. Marthe couldn't help herself and peeped through the hole again, watching as the gray mob started running, men falling from the fire of the *mitrailleuse.*

Mother's face was stricken as a bullet tore through the wood inches above her daughter's head. Wordlessly Father grabbed both of their hands to bring them downstairs. At the foot of the stairs was a French soldier rocking back and forth, clutching his stomach. Father tried to pull Marthe toward the cellar, but she paused when she saw the blood spurting from the soldier's stomach. All of her university training thus far had not prepared her for this horrific sight, his entrails beginning to spill out of the wound, but she reached out with trembling fingers to prop him against the wall. "You must keep still."

His distraught eyes met hers as he managed to croak out one word. "Water."

Marthe knew that water would only add to his suffering. The sound of gunfire grew closer, and Father yanked her away.

They had just reached the cellar when a shell sounded and a piece of plaster from the wall landed near Father. He struck a match and lit his pipe. "Courage," he said. "The French will beat them back," but the defeated tone of his voice told Marthe that he did not believe it to be so. Nothing could stay that rushing deluge of gray regiments she had spotted from the window.

When the *mitrailleuse* finally ceased its firing, Marthe crept upstairs to retrieve water. The man at the stairs had succumbed to death, and there seemed no sign of any live blue-clad soldiers anywhere in the house. The hallway glistened with blood and there were a few spots where bullets had broken through the exterior wall. An occasional shot could still be heard outside, but it sounded much more distant now. Marthe glanced at her watch. It was only two o'clock in the afternoon.

The front door burst open and she turned to see a bedraggled young man standing in the doorway with his eyes narrowed. Something in the distance caught the sunlight and she glimpsed many men on the lawn, their bayonets gleaming. Marthe marveled that the sun had the audacity to shine on such a day.

The soldier before her holstered his revolver and spoke in broken French. *"Qui d'autre est dans cette maison avec vous?"* He marched into the room, a band of his comrades behind him. Marthe assumed he was the captain, or *hauptmann*. The men outside sat down and lit cigarettes.

She felt no fear at the arrival of the disheveled German and his troops, only an unfamiliar numbness. She replied in German that her parents were downstairs.

"There are loopholes in the walls of this house," the captain stated. "Your father is a *franc-tireur*."

Marthe recalled what Nicholas had said about the Hun's irrational fear of civilian sharpshooters. "My father is an old man and has never fired a shot at anyone, and especially not today. The French soldiers who were here were the ones shooting but they have gone."

"I have heard that story many times before. Yours is not the first village we have entered."

You mean demolished, Marthe corrected him silently.

"Fourteen of my men were shot, and the gunfire from this house was responsible. If those men who were with him have run, then your father alone will suffer."

"No, please, Hauptmann." But the captain was already on his way to the cellar. Two other burly men stalked after him.

Marthe was about to pursue them when the first man appeared on the steps, dragging her mother. The other soldier, a sergeant judging by the gold braid on his uniform, followed with her father, who held his still smoldering pipe.

The soldiers shoved her parents against the wall of the hallway. Marthe bit her lip to keep herself from crying out in indignation, knowing that it couldn't possibly help the situation they were in. She cursed herself for her earlier curiosity and then cursed fate for the circumstances of having these enemy men standing in her kitchen, wishing to do harm to her family. If only they had left when Nicholas gave her that warning!

"Take that damned pipe out of your mouth," the sergeant commanded Father.

The soldier who had manhandled Mother grabbed it from him, knocking the ash out on Father's boot before he pocketed the pipe with a chuckle.

"Old man, you are a *franc-tireur*," the captain declared.

Father shook his head while Mother sobbed quietly.

"Be merciful," Marthe begged the captain. "You have no proof."

"You dare to argue with me, fräulein? This place has been a hornet's nest of sharpshooters." He turned to one of the men. "Feldwebel, see that this house is burned down immediately."

The sergeant left out the door, motioning to some of the smoking men to follow him to the storage shelter in the back of the house, where the household oil was kept.

"Hauptmann—" Father began, but the captain silenced him by holding up his hand. "As for you, old man, you can bake in your own oven!" He dropped his arm. "Gefreiter, lock him in the cellar."

The corporal seized Father and kicked him down the steps, sending a load of spit after him.

"Filthy *franc-tireur*, he will get what he deserves," the corporal stated as he slammed the door to the cellar.

Mother collapsed and Marthe rushed to her. "You infernal butchers," she hissed at the men.

"Quiet, fräulein," the captain responded, taking out a packet of cigarettes. "Our job is to end this war quickly, and rid the countryside of any threats to our army, especially from civilians who take it upon themselves to shoot our soldiers."

The feldwebel and two other men entered the house carrying drums of oil. Mother gave a strangled cry as they marched into the living room and began to pour oil over the fine furniture.

The captain nodded approvingly before casting his eyes back to Marthe and her mother. "You women are free to go. I will grant you five minutes to collect any personal belongings, but you are not permitted to enter the cellar. Do not leave the village or there will be trouble." He lit his cigarette before dropping the match on the dry kitchen floor. It went out, but Marthe knew it was only a matter of time before he did the same in the living room where the oil had been spilled.

Marthe ran upstairs, casting her eyes helplessly around when she reached the landing. *What should she take?* She threw together a bundle of clothes for her and Mother, and, at the last second, took her father's best suit off the hanger. She shouldered the bundle and then went back downstairs, grabbing Mother's hand. They went outside to the street to gaze dazedly at their home where Father lay prisoner in the cellar.

The German soldiers walked quickly out of the house, carrying some of the Cnockaert's food. Gray smoke started coming from the living room. Soon reddish-orange flames rose up, the tongues easily destroying the barricaded windows.

Marthe put her hands on the collar of her jacket and began to shed it.

"What are you doing?" Mother asked, her voice unnaturally shrill.

"Father's in there. I have to try to save him."

Mother tugged Marthe's jacket back over her shoulders. "No," was all she said. Marthe lowered her shoulders in defeat. As she stared at the conflagration, trying not to picture her poor father's body burning alive, she made a vow to herself that she wouldn't let the Germans get the best of her, no matter what other horrors they tried to commit.

Eventually Mother led Marthe away from the sight of their burning home and down the street to the Grand Place. The café adjacent to the square was filled with gray-uniformed men who sang obscene songs in coarse voices. A hiccupping private staggered in the direction of Marthe and Mother as the men in the café jeered at him. Marthe pulled her mother into the square to avoid the drunken soldier.

The abandoned Kermis booths had now become makeshift hospital beds for wounded Germans. The paving stones were soaked in blood and perspiring doctors rushed around, pausing to bend over men writhing in pain. In the corner was a crowd of soldiers in bloodied French uniforms. Marthe headed over, noticing another, smaller group of women and children she recognized as fellow villagers. She had just put her hand on a girl's forehead when a German barked at her to move on.

"Where should we go?" Mother asked in a small voice.

Marthe shook her head helplessly, catching her eye on Meneer Hoot's large home on the other side of the square. They walked quickly toward it, noting the absence of smoke in the vicinity. Marthe reached her fist out to knock when the door was swung open.

Marthe's heart rose at seeing the man behind the door. "Father!"

"Shh," he said, ushering them into the house.

"How on earth—" Marthe began when they were safely ensconced in the entryway of the Hoot home.

"I took apart the bricks from the air vent. Luckily the hauptmann and his men were watching the inferno on the other side of the house."

Mother hugged him tightly, looking for all the world like she would never let him go. Father brought them into the kitchen, where Meneer and Mevrouw Hoot greeted them. Several other neighbors, including Valerie, were also gathered in the kitchen, and they waited in a bewildered silence until darkness fell.

Meneer Hoot finally rose out of his chair. Taking the pipe from his mouth, he stated, "We have had no food this morning, and I'm sure it is the same for you all. Unfortunately," he swung his arms around, "the bloody Boches ransacked our house and there is nothing to eat here." He put the pipe in his mouth and gave it a puff before continuing, "I am going to get food somehow."

Mevrouw Hoot clutched his arm. "No, David, you cannot go out there."

Father also rose. "I will join you."

Meneer Hoot shook his head. "No, it is safer for me to go alone."

Mother gave a sigh of relief while Mevrouw Hoot appeared as though she would burst into tears. Meneer Hoot slipped a dark overcoat on and left through the back door.

An eternity seemed to pass as they sat in the dark kitchen,

illuminated only by the sliver of moon that had replaced the sun. The silence was occasionally broken by Mevrouw Hoot's sobbing.

Marthe was nodding off when she heard the back door slam. Someone lit a candle, and Marthe saw the normally composed Meneer Hoot hold up a bulky object wrapped in blood-stained newspaper. His rumpled trousers were covered in burrs and his eyes were wild-eyed. He tossed the bulk and it landed on the kitchen table with a thud.

Mevrouw Hoot unwrapped the package to reveal a grayish sort of meat from an unfamiliar animal.

"I cut it from one of the Boches' dead horses," Meneer Hoot told them in a triumphant whisper. He lit a fire and put the horsemeat on a spit. Marthe wasn't sure if she could eat a dead horse but soon changed her mind as the room filled with the smell of cooking meat. Her stomach grumbled in anticipation.

Just then the kitchen window shattered. Marthe looked up to see a rifle butt nudging the curtain aside. The spikes of German helmets shone in the moonlight beyond the window. The Hoots' entire backyard teemed with them.

"We must get downstairs, now!" Meneer Hoot shouted. He grabbed his wife and rushed her into the hallway. Father did the same with Mother, and Marthe followed, stumbling down the steps to the Hoots' cellar.

To Marthe's amazement, she saw the large room was already nearly filled with other refugees—men, women, and children of all ages—with dirty, tear-stained faces.

The sound of many boots thundered overhead and it wasn't long before the Germans once again stood among them. One of them pointed his rifle at the opposite wall and shot off a clip, the bullets ricocheting around the room, followed by wild screaming. Somebody had been hit, a child Marthe guessed sorrowfully by the tone of its wail.

She wanted to go aid the poor creature, but she felt the sharp point of a bayonet at her chest. "Get upstairs," the bayonet wielder sneered.

The soldiers lined up the cellar's occupants outside, and separated out the men. Without allowing a word of parting, the Germans led the men of the village down the hill, and Marthe watched Father's lank form until she could no longer see him. The remaining soldiers shepherded the women and children back down into the Hoot's now blood-covered cellar.

L'AGENT DOUBLE CHAPTER 3

ALOUETTE

AUGUST 1914

The smell of gasoline and the wind in Alouette's hair was as intoxicating as ever. She eased back on the stick of her Caudron, enjoying the adrenaline rush that always ensued when the plane rose higher. The French countryside below appeared just like the maps in her husband's office: the rivers, railroads, even the villages seemingly unchanged from her vantage point. The world beneath her might soon be engaged in combat, but, a few thousand meters above the ground, she was alone in the sky, the universe at her beck and call. She flew along the Somme Bay at the edge of the English Channel, marveling at the beautiful beaches and marshes that must be thronging with wildlife.

After half an hour, she began heading back to the Le Crotoy aerodrome to land, using the coastline as a navigation guide. She held the tail of the Caudron low and glided downward.

. . .

Alouette found the aerodrome in a state of commotion, with men running all about on the ground. As she turned the engine off, Gaston Caudron, the inventor of the plane, climbed up the ladder to stare into the cockpit.

"What's going on?" Alouette shouted over the noise. It sounded as though every plane in the aerodrome was running.

"We're taking the planes to the war zone."

"Okay." Alouette refastened her seatbelt and tilted her head, indicating she was ready for Caudron to spin the prop to start the plane up again.

His eyes, already jaundiced, bugged out even more. "You can't possibly think you can go to war."

"This is my plane."

He held up a hand to his mouth and coughed. "As I recall, I designed it for your husband."

"You know that Henri lets me fly it any time I want to." She tapped the ignition switch with impatience.

"Still, civilians can't fly planes during wartime." His voice softened. "You wouldn't want to hurt the war effort, would you Madame Richer?"

Alouette's hand dropped to her side. "No. No I would not."

Caudron stepped as close as he could to the edge of the ladder as she climbed out of the plane. "I guess I'll see about my motor-car in the garage at Rue," she said, navigating down the ladder as Caudron arranged himself in the cockpit.

"You'll find it a challenge to get back to Paris—all the petrol supplies have been requisitioned for the army."

"I'll be able to get as far as Amiens," she said, jumping down to the ground. "After that I shall find a way to manage, somehow."

"Good luck," Caudron replied ominously as he started the engine.

She saluted as he pulled her plane out of the aerodrome.

Alouette estimated that her car had enough petrol to carry her 30 miles, figuring she could stop at the aerodrome in Amiens, or at least a garage somewhere along the route to Paris. But near Picquigny, the car began to sputter and soon stopped completely. Alouette walked a few miles and was relieved to find a garage, albeit looking abandoned. She knocked on the closed shutters of the attached house.

A woman's hand opened the window a sliver. "Yes?"

"Can you please tell me, madame, where the mechanic is?"

The woman opened the window enough to eye Alouette up and down, from the lace neckline of her fashionable dress to the flower-trimmed hat she had donned after changing out of her flight gear. "He's gone to war," the woman finally replied.

Alouette got a similar response from the next garage she tried. One elderly woman seated on her porch did not appear as hostile and Alouette called out to her. "Do you have any vehicle I could use to take me to Amiens? My car has stalled and I need to find a mechanic."

The woman appeared likely to flee back into the house, so Alouette pulled her wallet out of her purse. "I can pay you."

Alouette soon found herself in the back of a hay cart pulled by reluctant horses, and being jolted from side to side at every rut in the road. They had to pull into the ditch almost every mile, at least it seemed to Alouette, as regiment after regiment of soldiers passed them, heading north. They drove by several villages in turmoil, the residents packing every belonging they owned onto motor-cars, rickety carts similar to the one Alouette found herself in, or even on the backs of donkeys.

"Why are you leaving?" Alouette called to one man as he balanced his rocking chair on a small wagon.

"The Germans are advancing toward the Marne," the man replied, the terror obvious in his voice.

Alouette tipped her flowered hat and focused her eyes on the road ahead of them. She had to get back to Paris as soon as possible.

The farm woman pulled back on the reins when they reached the aerodrome, about half a mile outside of Amiens. "You sure this is where you want to be?" she asked, eyeing the aerodrome. The doors had been left open, revealing its nearly empty chambers inside.

"Yes, madame." Alouette placed a few extra bills into the farm woman's hand. "If you could just wait a minute."

The farm woman gave a deep sigh before nodding her acquiescence.

When Alouette entered the practically deserted cavern, she heard someone call, "Madame Richer! Whatever are you doing here?"

As she turned, she caught sight of the well-built Captain Jeanneros. "Oh, Captain, is it possible for you to send a mechanic to help me with my car? It has stalled on the road."

The captain threw his head back and laughed. "Only such things could happen to you, Madame Richer. The Germans are pushing toward here and I only have a few litres of petrol left. Of course, you can have some if you need it. But as for the mechanic, I cannot spare one. I'm very sorry, but I'm the last of the squadron now. All the others have gone."

Alouette sighed. "I'm not sure the petrol will do me much good if I cannot get my motor-car fixed."

Captain Jeanneros scratched his head. "I can give you one tip, madame. Do not stay long in this district, or soon you may find it impossible to leave at all."

They had passed the first houses in Picquigny on the return journey when Alouette heard the farm woman suck in her breath. Alouette sat straighter in the cart, catching sight of a crowd assembled in the spot where she'd left the car. To her horror, she noted two armed gendarmes approaching.

"Now you've really done it," the farm woman muttered.

The gendarmes paused near the back of the cart. "Hand over your papers," the shorter one commanded.

Alouette did as she was bid, her heart racing. She garnered that her presence in the back of the farm cart, combined with her Parisian attire, not to mention her presence in the war zone, must have looked suspicious to the rural population of Picquigny.

The short gendarme folded Alouette's papers and tucked them into the pocket of his uniform.

"Sir," the farm woman spoke up. She hesitated for a brief second before resignedly pointing a gnarled finger to the cans of fuel in the rear of the cart.

Alouette's heart sank at her escort's sudden betrayal.

"Where did you get that petrol?" the other officer demanded. "Why are you harboring fuel when the Allies are in desperate need of it?"

"Monsieur—" Alouette attempted an explanation, but the short gendarme cut her off. "You must come with us." He gave a sharp whistle and the farm woman set the horse in motion, both officers keeping pace on either side of the cart.

"Death to the spy!" an old man shouted as the crowd of villagers also started moving forward.

Alouette felt terror rise in her chest. The mob swirled around the cart like an ocean tide. The villagers had already deemed her a traitor and any attempt she made to contradict them would be futile.

She was under arrest.

The mob of villagers followed the gendarme-escorted farm cart to the police station.

One of the gendarmes pulled Alouette out of the cart. "Lynch the spy!" someone shouted as a spray of gravel landed at her feet. She looked up to meet the angry glare of a white-haired man. The tears that gathered in her eyes did not soften him—if anything, they seemed to be an admission of guilt—and he drew back his arm to launch the next cluster of rocks. "Die, double-crosser!" This time a sharp stone connected with Alouette's jaw and the tears coursed their way down her face.

Although the villagers were not permitted into the police station, the window in the room where Alouette was taken for questioning stood open and the crowd gathered outside of it.

The evidence of Alouette's supposed damnation was spread out on the table. Her revolver was placed prominently in the center, surrounded by the cans of petrol and the documentation she had presented to the gendarme.

An older officer sat himself at the table across from the still-standing Alouette. "Name?" he demanded.

"Alouette Richer," she replied, a hint of pride in her voice.

She briefly crossed her fingers behind her back, hoping he would recognize her name from the newspapers.

The village gendarme gave no sign of appreciation as he copied it down. "Sit."

She fell into a chair with a sigh. She had recently flown from Crotoy to Zürich, to great fanfare, and the Parisian papers followed her triumphs, publishing several articles and photographs of her in aviator gear standing beside her plane. But now that war had come, a curtain had dropped over everything that had occurred before its outbreak.

"You have no right to a revolver," the officer commented, a growl in his voice. "How did you come by it?"

"My husband, Henri Richer, gave it to me. He knew I'd be traveling alone and wanted to ensure my safety."

Once again, the gendarme showed no recognition of the name. "Let me see your handbag."

Reluctantly, she passed it across the table.

He dug out her wallet and pulled out a wad of bills. "Who gave you all this money?"

Alouette bit back another sigh. She supposed the 300 francs in her wallet was a small fortune to the country inspector, who probably earned less than half that in a month.

"I am not a spy," she insisted. "My husband is a wealthy man…"

"I know, I know," the gendarme held up his hand. "He must have given you all that money to ensure your safety." He rose heavily to his feet. "What he didn't understand was how incriminating carrying that amount of cash would be in a warzone. I have no choice but to detain you."

"But monsieur—"

"Pending further inquiries, of course," the inspector remarked as he shut the door behind him.

. . .

Alouette was left in the room for over half an hour. She used that time to compose herself. The last thing she wanted was to show fear to the men at the station. Indeed, when a younger officer at last unlocked the door, she kept the expression on her face neutral. He escorted her to an empty cell.

Alouette patted the pillow and then spread her skirts prettily before she sat on the bed.

The young gendarme watched, an amused expression on his face. "This is not the first time you've spent the night in jail," he stated.

"Oh, it is, monsieur," Alouette said, taking her hat off and running a hand through her golden hair. "But it's better than sleeping in my broken-down motor-car by the side of the road."

"Indeed, it probably is." He returned shortly with a packet of biscuits and stale coffee. Alouette could sense that she'd at least made a friend of one of the aloof gendarmes.

That same young man came in early the next morning to announce that Alouette had been released. He waved a telegram with the word PARIS stamped on the front. "It seems you have friends in high places."

Alouette picked her hat off of the chipped nightstand and tucked her hair beneath it. "It would seem so, wouldn't it?"

"Where will you go now?"

She pursed her lips. "My petrol?"

He shook his head. "Seized for the army."

"Then I shall walk to Amiens."

The young man's face spread into a smile. "Good luck, Madame Richer."

"And to you, monsieur."

Alouette passed many villagers going the opposite way as she. They were obviously refugees, judging from their weary, and in some cases, panic-stricken expressions. The pronounced silence was only broken by the occasional droning of an airplane. As soon as one became audible, the bewildered townspeople would duck their heads, as if heeding an unheard call, the call of terror that an enemy warcraft was about to drop a bomb upon them.

Alouette found Amiens in utter chaos. Every door stood open as the townspeople rushed to and from their houses, packing up all of their belongings. Children, dogs, and a few roosters ran wildly through the streets. All roads that led to the town seemed to be filled with refugees repeating the same desperate phrases: "The Germans are coming. What shall we do?"

She headed through the hordes of anxious people gathered outside the railway station. She found a man in a conductor's uniform to ask about the next train to Paris.

"Trains?" he asked in an incredulous voice. "My lady, this station is closed, and the rest of the staff has been cleared out. Gone to war," he continued proudly, but Alouette was only half-listening.

For a moment, she thought she would give in to the same useless panic that had overcome the people surrounding her. She allowed herself a few seconds of despair before returning to reality. She needed to find some other way to get to Paris if she desired to not be in a region that was about to be infested with the enemy.

She spotted an open garage across the street and walked

over to it. A young woman in a tattered dress sat on the steps leading toward the door. She glanced up as Alouette approached. "They say that the Germans murder any children they see." She sniffed. "And I have two little boys." She buried her head in her handkerchief.

Alouette climbed up the steps and put a tentative hand on the woman's shoulder. "Nobody can be so cruel as to hurt young innocents," she stated. "Not even the Germans."

She handed the woman a soiled but dry handkerchief. The woman blew into it noisily before stating, "If you are looking for a vehicle, I have nothing left."

"Not even a cart?" Alouette asked, the hopelessness threatening to surface again.

The young woman looked doubtfully at Alouette's dress. "I do have a man's bicycle. Do you know how to ride?"

Alouette took a deep breath. Her brother had had one when they were growing up, but she was never allowed to ride since it couldn't be ridden sidesaddle. "Not exactly, but if I can fly planes, surely I can ride a bicycle." She dug into her purse to find the gendarme had left her a few francs, which she extended to the young woman. The woman pulled herself up, using the banister to steady herself, and led Alouette into the garage.

Alouette walked the bicycle along the road until she was well out of the way of the crowds. The threat of falling on her face paled in comparison to the possibility of being taken as a German prisoner if she stayed here. Mounting the bicycle proved a difficult feat given her dress and handbag. As she pushed down on a pedal, the bicycle wobbled sideways instead of going forward and she hopped off, the bicycle plunging into the dust of the roadway.

She heard a low noise and turned her head with her eyes closed, hoping that it was not the stomping of German boots. A young soldier in a blue coat and bright red trousers was sitting on a nearby bench, laughing.

Alouette put her hands on her hips. "Well, don't just sit there. Give me a lesson, would you?"

He pointed at the bandage covering one of his eyes. "Even I can see that is a man's bicycle."

"Oh, do you have a woman's available?"

The soldier shook his head.

"Then do you know of another reason why I should not ride this bike straight to Paris?"

"Yes," he said, recovering from his earlier mirth. "The road to Paris has been captured by the Germans."

Alouette wiped her sweaty palms on her skirts and gazed at the dust blowing across the road. A German invasion in the carefree French capital seemed as far-flung a threat as someone predicting a thunderstorm on a sunny day. "My husband is in Paris."

"Oh?" The soldier's voice dropped an octave. Alouette smiled to herself. There was something so naively amusing about young men thinking that every woman was ready to fawn over them.

"At least I think so," Alouette replied. "He enlisted as an ambulance driver, but hasn't gotten orders yet. I had to detour to Crotoy to check on our plane."

The young man raised his eyebrows.

"Confiscated," Alouette said in answer to his unasked question.

"Yes, the military will do that. When I was at Charleroi—"

"You were in the Battle of the Sambre?"

"Yes, why?"

Alouette looked down. "No reason." They said that war had a way of turning boys into men, but the young man's affable manner hadn't struck her as though he'd seen many hard battles. Even despite that bandaged eye.

"Anyway, both sides are using airplanes for reconnaissance now." He shrugged his shoulders. "What war innovations will they think of next?"

Alouette was lost for a second, dreaming of being in the sky, finding the enemy among the trees. When she returned to reality, all she could focus on were the man's bright red pants. "Those uniforms… are they new?"

"They are, but the style dates back to Napoleon."

"Perhaps General Joffre might want to reconsider the color of your trousers. A line of soldiers all wearing those would be quite easy to spot from the air."

"Perhaps," he agreed with a smile. "I think that trains are still running to Paris from Abbeville."

Alouette picked up the bicycle. "Well, what are you waiting for, then?"

The soldier taught her how to keep her balance. In only half an hour's time, Alouette was able to ride steadily, although she was only able to mount the bicycle from the curb and could not stop except by jumping off. "I think I'll be able to manage myself, now. Thank you for your kindness."

The young soldier tipped his hat toward her, revealing a bruised and bloody forehead. "Good luck, mademoiselle."

Alouette had no idea riding a bicycle could be such taxing work. She passed numerous refugees on her way to Abbeville. So preoccupied were they in their own misery that they did not pay much heed to the girl wobbling along, trying both to balance and keep her dress out of the bicycle's chain at the same time. She kept her berth wide, lest she fell again, and called out to a man pushing a wheelbarrow, who heeded her by moving closer toward the side of the road. As Alouette overtook them, she realized the wheelbarrow was not filled with food or worldly possessions, but an invalid woman.

Alouette saw she was approaching a hill and leapt off the bicycle. She tossed her hat into a ditch before picking the two-wheeler back up and walking up the summit. She could feel her stamina fading fast, but would not allow herself to rest, fearful that if she sat down, she might not be able to get back up again.

Catching a train proved just as difficult in Abbeville as Amiens. The watchman there told Alouette that there was no way to know when the next train to Paris would leave.

Alouette was about to turn around in anguish when the man told her there was a branch line in Sergueux. Knowing that was her last chance, Alouette managed to get her aching limbs mounted once again on the bicycle and pedaled off.

She was relieved to see a train sitting in the station, although it seemed to consist mostly of open cattle wagons. "Will that be leaving shortly?" Alouette inquired of an official standing near a car.

The man shrugged. "We are waiting for information on the movement of the troops."

Still, Alouette bought a ticket and boarded a cattle wagon.

Enjoyed the sample? Pick up your copy of *L'Agent Double: Spies and Martyrs in the Great War* today or read for free with Kindle Unlimited! Thanks for reading!

Be sure to join my mailing list at www.kitsergeant.com to be the first to know when my newest Women Spies book is available!

SELECTED BIBLIOGRAPHY

Braddon, Russell. *Nancy Wake*. Little A, 2019.

FitzSimons, Peter. *Nancy Wake*. 2001.

Long, Helen. *Safe Houses Are Dangerous*. 1989.

Ottis, Sherri Greene. *Silent Heroes*. 2021.

Wake, Nancy. *White Mouse*. 2011.

ACKNOWLEDGMENTS

Thank you to my Advanced Review team for their eagle eyes, including Alison Steadman, Angie McCain, Cathy Allen, Helen Finch and Jan Stockton, as well as Matthew Baylis for his excellent editing skills and Hannah Linder for yet another beautiful cover.

And as always, thanks to my loving family, especially Tommy, Belle, and Thompson, for their unconditional love and support.

Printed in Great Britain
by Amazon